Seron

Get ready to meet some completely different people!

Seon

Search for the Emerald Tablet

AN ADVENTURE ROMANCE BY

Sean Broadchest

Published 2017 by
Raw Sienna Press,
Moose Jaw, SK Canada
rawsiennapress.com
publish@rawsiennapress.com
ISBN: 978-0-9737480-5-5

Persons and events in this novel are fictitious. Any similarity to real persons or events are purely circumstantial.

Information about the Emerald Tablet can be found on Wikipedia (http://en.wikipedia.org/wiki/Emerald_Tab- let). It has been adapted and fictionalized for this book. Any text and/or images taken from the Wikipedia article and used here under the Creative Commons License (http://en.wikipedia.org/wiki/Wikipedia:Text_of_Creative_Commons_A ttribution-ShareAlike_3.0_Un- ported_License).

Table of Contents

Chapter 1 - Christine

Robert Jackson stood at the large patio doors, looking out over the beautifully manicured lawn and garden beyond the terrace and swimming pool. His eyes were focused on nothing in particular. They just swept across the hectares of land that are the back portion of his country property. Little did he know, that within the hour, his entire life was would be turned upside-down.

He was deep in thought, reminiscing about his late wife, Christine, whom he loved dearly. She passed away some five years earlier, and he still missed her terribly. He often wondered why she died so suddenly, and violently, while she was still a beautiful young woman of forty-five. He always felt it was patently unfair of Christine to be taken away from him. Being so much older than her, he thought he was safe from ever being left without her. *He* was supposed to die first! Now, he was alone, very alone.

Robert, commonly known as RJ, withdrew from social life after Christine's death. She was his life, his love, his everything. They were very close, and immensely happy together. Robert would never forget the telephone call from the police, informing him of his wife's death in a bizarre traffic accident. If his heart was broken to know his beloved Christine was gone, it completely shattered when he saw her at the morgue, when asked to identify her remains. Something deep inside Robert died that day; he wasn't the same again. He only vaguely remembered them saying she turned off the highway, and was driving down the dirt road leading to their estate. She was following a truck carrying construction materials, when a long, flat plate of steel flew off the back of the truck directly through her windshield. She was decapitated! Death was instantaneous! It was all a haze now.

At sixty-three, Robert didn't feel he was anything special. He never considered himself to be a handsome man—not ugly, of course, but not overly good looking; average at best. He was in reasonably good health and kept himself fit. He was modestly prosperous, thanks to a successful career in real estate, and some good, solid investments. The home he and Christine shared for twenty-one years was a large, beautiful, two-storey country house situated on about thirty hectares of land.

As he looked out, he could picture her standing by the pool looking absolutely stunning in the brown and tan tiger print string bikini she knew drove him to distraction. And she loved to drive him to distraction! Chris was a fit and trim 5'5" with stylish, short, dirty-blond hair that framed a classic oval face with incredible big blue eyes, cute nose, and wide mouth with full, sensuous lips. A man could get lost in those eyes, and Robert often did. Chris kept herself in shape; she exercised almost every day; it showed in her fine muscular definition. She wasn't bulky in any way, but you could tell she was in great shape. That was just one reason she looked so delicious in that bikini—and pretty much anything she wore. Even just before she died, there wasn't a bit of cellulite to be found anywhere on her body. She had an ideal figure—at least, as far as Robert was concerned. Her bust, a little less than a C-cup, was high on her chest, which then narrowed to lovely waist, and perfect hips.

Chris was a beauty, and she knew it. Oh, she didn't flaunt it about, but neither was she afraid of wearing clothes that accentuated her figure, and showed some skin. The short shorts, and short skirts, she wore served to stretch out her beautifully toned legs. Robert always found it interesting, and pleasantly surprising, that Chris dressed to please him. She didn't seem to care a whit if anyone else noticed; the only thing important to her was whether she pleased her husband. She loved him as much as he loved her, and maybe more. Robert never understood why such a beauty, who could have melted any man's heart, chose to fall in love with him.

Whether Chris dressed up, or dressed down, Robert found his eyes roving longingly over her. A sly grin appeared as he thought of the many times he wanted to peel off her clothes, and enjoy her wonderful body—a body she never refused him. In fact, Chris seemed to have one main purpose in life—to seduce her husband at every possible opportunity. He often wished staff and guests could simply vanish at the snap of his fingers so he could indulge his fantasy. To his surprise, he found himself having a powerful manhood reaction. *Gone for five years and she can still turn me on!* He thought he should be embarrassed, but he wasn't. After all, Chris was his wife. He closed his eyes, and breathed deeply. After a few minutes, he was back to normal.

Robert turned slowly to look around the house. Christine was everywhere. There wasn't a wall with artwork she hadn't chosen. The Inuit sculptures she so loved and collected, were displayed proudly in three curio cabinets. Throw pillows, area rugs, figurines on the dining table, dinner service, cutlery, linen designs, even the monogrammed bath towels—all Christine. He could swear he still smelled the scent of her favourite perfume lingering around the house.

Robert mourned his beloved deeply. First, the absolute shock, then the rage, then the searing pain. Finally, he began to accept that Christine was gone—but not forgotten. He was bitterly disappointed, and empty inside. Thankfully, the pain was beginning to ease. He could now remember all the great times, the great accomplishments, the great love they shared together. Tears still filled his eyes, but gone were the bouts of uncontrollable weeping that accompanied the excruciating pain he felt through his whole being.

Although Robert withdrew from society, their good friends had not withdrawn from him. He was still getting regular phone calls checking to see how he was doing. He could probably eat out every night of the week, if he accepted all the dinner invitations he received from friends, and former colleagues.

Robert decided to retire only a year before losing Christine. He felt he made enough money to keep them both comfortable for the rest of their lives. As they had no children, they didn't have to worry about leaving a large estate. He wanted to spend more time with the woman he loved so much. He remembered how excited Chris was when he told her he'd be staying at home with her. He could focus on their investments to give him something to do. Now, alone, and with way too much time on his hands, Robert truly needed, and appreciated, the support of their friends. He could have easily returned to real estate, which would keep him busy, but he just didn't have the heart to do much anymore.

Robert heaved a heavy sigh. He knew he had to go into Airdrie to get much needed groceries. Carmen gave him a list several days ago. He procrastinated because it meant putting on a brave face, and trying to appear normal. There was nothing for it. He had to go.

Carmen Lopez had been with them almost from the time they moved into the main house. She ruled the kitchen with an iron hand. She was a fabulous cook. They always wondered how she could make a healthy, nutritious meal taste so good. Her desserts were to die for! And, not a calorie in any of them! Or at least that's what she always said. She cooked not only for Robert, but for the staff as well—Andrea, the gardener, and Jake, the handyman.

After another heavy sigh, Robert retrieved the list sitting on the table by the front door. He made his way into the kitchen to check with Carmen if there was anything else to add since she made up the list.

"Carmen!"

"*Sí, señor.*"

"I'm going to the market to get the groceries. Are there any more things you want to add to the list?"

Carmen's response was quick and imperious, "It is about time, señor, or we will all be losing much weight." Robert tried very hard not to laugh. "Let me see the list, *por favor*." She perused the list carefully. Suddenly, she turned, walked over to a drawer, and pulled out a pen. Back at the list, she changed the quantities on a few items, and added a couple more. "There, señor. The list is good now."

"Thank you, Carmen. Is there anything you need for yourself?"

After a moment of thought, "No, señor, there is nothing. *Gracias*."

With the revised list in hand, Robert made his way slowly out the door and towards the garage. He knew this would be a very large grocery order, because he waited so long. He wondered if he should ask Jake to come along to give him a hand. But Jake was a chatty guy, and Robert just didn't want to be chatting the whole time. He was content in his solitude. He'd go alone.

He walked in the garage side door, grabbed a stack of plastic grocery boxes, and tossed them into the back of his Toyota Land Cruiser. He turned, and pressed the button that opened the garage door. He climbed into the SUV, and sat there a few minutes, contemplating the ordeal he'd be facing—interacting with people.

Okay, RJ. You know you've got to do it. So, buck up, put on your happy face, and let's go!

He started the Land Cruiser, pulled out of the garage, and headed down the lane towards the road.

Chapter 2 - Twilight Zone

Robert reached the end of the drive and stopped. He took a deep breath, and blew it out slowly. He hated going into town for any reason. It meant driving down the road where his beloved Chris was taken from him. He'd driven here hundreds of times since Chris died. There was never any "Twilight Zone" moment where he saw her ghost wandering down the road. It was always very ordinary—like nothing really happened there at all.

His signal light was clicking away, reminding him to make his turn, once again, down the dirt road towards the highway. Another deep sigh. After checking for oncoming traffic, he pressed the accelerator, easing his big SUV onto the road. Now, he accelerated hard, as though to get through this leg of his short journey as quickly as possible. It was about six kilometres to the highway, and another eight to town.

The dirt road was very dry; it hadn't rained for a couple of weeks. An oncoming vehicle was kicking up quite a dust storm. Robert slowed, concentrating hard on the road ahead. Suddenly, he saw her! It was Chris! Now, he knew he was losing it for sure!

Yet there she was, stumbling, more than walking, down the road towards him. Robert came to a full stop. His heart was pounding like a bass drum in his ears. It couldn't be! He was seeing things. Surely, it was an optical illusion caused by the thick dust cloud left by the vehicle that just passed. And yet, the form of a slender woman was clearly visible ahead. Long, windblown, dirty-blond hair half covered her face, and yet, the features he could make out were plainly Christine. Everything about her was Christine. He shook his head. He looked again through the tears forming in his eyes. She was still there, still moving slowly towards him—in some sort of daze.

This couldn't be happening! He thought he'd been making

progress at dealing with his great loss. Now, he was hallucinating! Nothing like this happened in the five years since her death. Not even as he went through his most difficult time. He looked up again. The dust was settling now. And...she was still there. He wiped his eyes, and looked hard at the woman who was now only twenty metres away. Her figure, her hair colour, even the blouse and short skirt she was wearing—Christine! As he concentrated more on her face, he realized that, even though she very much resembled his sweet love, there were some differences. This woman's hair was much longer, but the same colour.

He sat there in a kind of trance as he took it all in. Then, as she stumbled, he snapped out of his reverie. He opened the door, and jumped out. He ran towards her, prompted by a sense of urgency. When he reached her, she collapsed into his arms. She looked up at him, her eyes pleading; there was fear there, too. Robert swept her up, and carried her, with arms dangling, to the SUV. She felt light as a feather in his arms, yet her body was obviously firm and toned. As he walked, he wondered what kind of ordeal this woman had gone through to reduce her to this state.

He opened the front passenger door and gently placed this mystery woman on the seat, which he reclined, so she wouldn't swing forward, and hit the dashboard. He fastened the seat belt snugly. He stood there for a few moments looking at her. As dusty and windblown as she was, she was a stunningly beautiful woman.

"What do I do with you now?" he wondered out loud. He took her right hand to place it on her lap. Her eyes opened. She turned her head and looked fearfully at Robert. All he could think of saying was, "It's alright. You're safe now. My name's Robert Jackson—RJ."

"Where am I?" It was more of a croak from her parched throat.

"You're on a dirt road just off Highway 567, and about four kilometres from my home, and ten kilometres west of Airdrie." He felt silly at his accuracy; the shock of the moment was obviously affecting his usual common sense.

She looked as though she would pass out again. Robert excused himself as he reached across her to the cooler built into the centre console. He pulled out a fresh bottle of water, opened it, and offered it to her. She seemed reluctant to drink. She looked hard again at Robert, as if analyzing his face. She made her decision. Bringing the bottle to her lips, she took several long pulls of the cool water. A very slight smile crossed her face, and her eyes softened.

"What day is it?"

"It's Wednesday, June 12th and it's just after 11 a.m." Again, with the accuracy. *Calm down, RJ! Calm down!* he told himself.

"Two days. It's been two days!" more to herself than to Robert. "Could you please take me back to my motel?"

"You need some attention. We're just a few minutes from my place. Carmen, my cook, can see to any needs you have."

She was insistent. "No! You must take me to my motel right away."

"Seriously, your clothes are a mess, and you're pretty weak. Let me at least make sure you're okay, and maybe give you another set of clothes. My late wife was pretty much the same size as you, and I still have some of her things packed away."

"It could be very dangerous for you, if you're seen with me." She spoke now in a half whisper, as though someone might be listening.

With a strength and firmness in his voice, "I don't care about that! I'll take you to your motel once I know you're okay."

She sighed. *Men! Why do they insist on getting involved when they should be running the other way?*

He looked at her curiously as she took a couple of long drinks of water. He wondered what on earth she could be talking about; what happened to her; what sort of trouble she could be in. He was rudely shaken from his thoughts when she spoke again. "If you insist on being a good Samaritan, I strongly suggest we get moving—in one direction or the other. We can't just sit here in the middle of the road. It's too dangerous."

He quickly closed the door. With a speed that even surprised him, he moved around his vehicle, and jumped in the driver's seat. He threw the transmission into gear, then pressed the accelerator to the floor, as he turned the steering wheel hard to the left. With dirt and stones kicking up everywhere, he managed to take his big SUV through a tight 180-degree turn.

Robert was now in full possession of his faculties. He'd awakened from what had become a five-year dream—or was it more of a nightmare? He felt his muscles tense as he bent himself to the task of protecting this strange woman, who appeared out of nowhere. His mind, which had been in a state of stupor for so long, was racing. His focus was total.

Within minutes, he was back at the lane to the house. With complete control of his vehicle, Robert turned sharply, and continued to drive at speed towards the main house. He skidded to a stop at the front door. He turned to look at his unknown passenger. Unknown! Of course! He suddenly realized he didn't even know her name.

"I don't even know what to call you."

She smiled warmly at him. "Jenna. Just call me Jenna."

Chapter 3 - Rest in Peace

Jenna allowed her body to relax in the comfortable leather seat of Robert's SUV. She was very tired, and worn out. The drugs had sapped the energy out of her. It seemed like ages since she felt relatively safe, and with Robert, she felt safe. Strange to be this way about a man she didn't know at all. Except that they had now exchanged names, the only thing she knew about him was that he appeared out of nowhere, and swept her up into his strong arms, as she was about to collapse. *Great way to meet a guy*, she thought.

"Did many cars pass by while we were out on the road?"

Robert opened the passenger door, and was by her side again. Jenna's eyes were closed, and he thought she had slipped into unconsciousness again. The sudden question caught him by surprise.

Jenna opened her eyes and turned to face him. She repeated her question. "Did many cars pass by while we were out on the road?"

Robert thought about it for a moment. "No, I don't think anyone drove by at all. Otherwise, we would probably have been run down because of the dust cloud."

"Was there any oncoming traffic, or cars following us as we drove here?"

Again, Robert had to think about it. It was such a furious rush to get to the house, he wasn't paying much attention. "Nothing oncoming for sure, but I wasn't looking in the mirrors. Nothing caught my eye, though."

"That's good." Her voice was barely a whisper. "Then no one knows I'm with you."

Robert helped her out of the SUV. Jenna was weaker than she expected. Her legs buckled beneath her. Robert picked her up again, carrying her to the door.

"Dang! The door's locked." With his house keys deep in his pocket, and Jenna in his arms, he couldn't very well get at them. Jenna reached out with her left hand and rang the door bell. "Now, why didn't I think of that?"

Carmen answered the door, and looked aghast at the sight confronting her. There was her boss with a woman in his arms whose clothes were torn and dusty. Her first thought was maybe Robert accidentally ran her down. Before she could speak, or move out of the way, Robert pushed past her, quickly slamming the door behind him. Jenna passed out again and hung limp in his arms.

"Carmen, quickly, go open the door to the blue bedroom."

Something in his tone made it obvious this was not a time for questions, but a time for action. She ran up the stairs to the blue bedroom, opened the door, and threw the bed covers out of the way. Robert was only a few steps behind her. She moved aside quickly as Robert gently lay Jenna on the bed.

"She's been drugged, and she's very weak. I think she's dehydrated too. I don't know yet if she's injured anywhere. There are some obvious scrapes and bruises, but that's all I can see."

"Her clothing are very dirty and teared, señor. She must to be clean-up." Carmen was taking command again. "Go away, señor Robert, so I can clean her. Go make tea of camomile."

Robert turned to leave. He knew Jenna was in good hands with Carmen. At the bedroom door, he turned and asked, "Do you think she's about the same size as señora Christine?"

Carmen gave the woman a quick appraising look. "Sí, I think the exact same size. *¿Por que, señor?*"

"I still have some of Christine's clothes packed in boxes in the closet. I'll dig something out for her. The clothes she's wearing are ruined."

As he headed downstairs, he heard Carmen shout. "*¿Cuál es su nombre, señor?*"

"Jenna!"

Carmen moved quickly now, with the same efficiency as when in the kitchen. Within minutes, she had Jenna stripped naked. She checked Jenna over, looking for any signs of broken bones, or puncture wounds. Gently she turned her on her side to check her back. There were many bruises on her body, arms, and legs, as though from being punched, and superficial scrapes on her arms and legs caused, no doubt, from stumbling and falling. She let Jenna gently down on her back again.

Carmen understood now why Robert chose the blue bedroom. It had a large en-suite bathroom. She ran warm water in the basin, and threw a bath towel over her shoulder. With a wet face cloth and some body wash, she began to wash the dirt from Jenna's body. It took many trips back and forth to the basin. After a few minutes, Robert returned with the tea to find the door closed.

Carmen heard him. "Do not come in, señor. La señora has no clothes on. Leave tea and clothes at the door. Go downstairs to wait, *por favor*."

Robert placed the tea tray on the floor. He walked briskly to his bedroom. He stared at the door to what was once Christine's closet. After they packed her clothing, he didn't have the heart to give them away; the boxes sat stacked in the closet; he hadn't even looked inside since. He shook himself back to reality. With determination, he opened the door, walked in, and scanned the boxes.

Each box had a list attached to it. *Good old Carmen*, he thought. She insisted that a written list of the contents be attached to each box. At the time, it seemed like way too much effort, and he was loath to do it. He was thankful now, that she insisted. He quickly scanned the lists. He pulled out boxes that contained jeans, blouses, and skirts. It struck him that she might need some underwear, so he pulled out a box with bras and panties.

He opened the underwear box first. He selected some nice white bras and black bras, and an assortment of coloured panties. It felt strange picking out some of Christine's unmentionables for a strange woman to wear. Although everything had been washed or dry-cleaned, he could swear her scent was still there. He placed the selected items on a chair by the bed. Next, he chose several different pairs of jeans, a selection of blouses, and a couple of nice skirts. He took his little pile of clothing to the door of the bedroom, and noticed the tea tray was gone.

He knocked at the door. "Sí."

"I have some clothes now. I'll just put them down by the door. How is the señora?"

"*Gracias, señor*. La señora is awake, but weak. She drinks her tea. When she is dressed, you may come in."

"Wait a moment. I'll get her some pyjamas."

Robert rushed back to Christine's closet, and looked for a box with some nightwear. It was up on a shelf. He pulled it down, opened it, and extracted some black silk pyjamas from the top of the box.

"I've put some pyjamas here too. So, you can take the clothes now."

"You must go away now, señor, so you do not see la señora with no clothes."

Robert didn't know where he should go. He thought of Christine's clothes strewn all over his bed, and decided to go tidy that up. He closed his bedroom door behind him. He looked at the mess, and chuckled to himself. He began to toss clothes back into boxes. He stopped suddenly. *I'd better put this stuff in the right boxes, or Carmen will have my hide*, he thought. He unpacked the items he'd already thrown in, and put them back into their appropriate boxes, and returned the boxes to the closet.

At the closet door, he turned, and looked in again. *Hope you don't mind, sweetheart. I'm sure you'd do the same. You were always so very generous.* A tear trickled down his cheek. He wiped it away and closed the door.

From the hallway, he heard Carmen. "You may come in now, señor."

Robert made his way to the other bedroom. "I will make some soup *por la señora*, for nourishing. You may go in, but do not make her tired with your questions!"

He moved quietly into the room. Jenna was sitting up in bed. He was taken aback at just how much she looked like his Christine, especially wearing those black silk pyjamas. Jenna looked at him curiously. Then she remembered vaguely he'd mentioned having some of his late wife's things.

"Does it upset you that I'm wearing your late wife's clothes? You're looking at me very strangely."

"No, I don't mind at all. It's just that you look so much like her."

"Could it just be your imagination?"

"I'll be back in a minute."

He hurried to his bedroom, where he picked up a framed photo of Christine wearing a sexy, form-fitting gown. He returned, and handed the picture to Jenna. She looked at it closely. It was uncanny how Christine resembled her in many ways. The overall shape and size, and hair colour. The face was a bit different—big blue eyes compared to her own green eyes, nose a bit smaller than hers, basically the same mouth. Anyone looking at them side-by-side might easily think they were sisters.

Jenna handed the photo back to Robert. "I can see why you've been staring at me so much."

"You can't imagine the shock I had when I saw you there on the road. It was very near the place where Chris was killed in an accident. I thought I was hallucinating, you see. That's why I just sat there."

"You must have loved her very much."

"Yes, I did."

"How long has it been?"

"Five years, now."

"She looks very young."

"She was thirteen years younger than me. She was only forty-five when she died."

"Do you have any children?"

"No, Chris couldn't have children. Something to do with the eggs not getting out of the ovaries properly. The medical term is Unruptured Follicle Syndrome. Doctors don't know why it happens, so they don't know how to fix it."

"I'm so very sorry, Robert."

"Please, call me RJ. Only Carmen calls me Robert."

"Okay, RJ. You must think I'm completely out of my mind with all my wild questions, and fears."

"I don't think you're out of your mind. I think you're in some serious trouble. I want to help in whatever way I can."

"Oh, RJ, you don't know what you're saying. If you get mixed up with me, you'll be in just as much trouble as I am."

"I've spent the last five years in some sort of fog. Today, I woke up, thanks to you. Maybe I need to be in some sort of trouble. Maybe I need an adventure. And you sure look like you can provide both!"

Jenna laughed quietly. She looked at Robert very softly. Here was a real man—a good man. She could trust this man, and trust was a scarce commodity for her these days. Should she drag him into her adventure? She felt desperately alone. Could she deal with her tormentors on her own? At first, she thought she could. After the last two days, she wondered seriously if she would survive at all.

"RJ, if I tell you about my little adventure, you could be risking your life. I'm not kidding. It's very serious. If you try to help me more than you already have, if you're seen with me, you'll be in danger. I feel I can trust you. And goodness knows I would love someone close to me I can trust. I don't know if I can get through this on my own."

"Then, I'm your man!"

"Please don't do this because I remind you of your late wife. I'm not her. I'm me. And I'm a pack of trouble."

"I know you're not Christine. Call me chivalrous if you like. I'm from the old school, where it's a man's honour and duty to help a lady in distress. And goodness knows I haven't done *that* in a while. I'm here for you along with whatever I've got."

"How can you just make that offer without knowing anything about me?"

"I've worked with people all my life, Jenna. I know a good person when I meet one. And you strike me as being a good person. If you're in some sort of trouble, it's because others are causing it. Somehow, I just can't see you as a troublemaker."

"You're not going to back down, no matter what, are you?"

"Nope!"

"Then I'll tell you all about it after I get some rest. I don't feel so drugged now, but I'm really weak and tired. I need to get some proper sleep."

As if on cue, Carmen appeared at the door with a bowl of soup, and some toasted buns. "You must go now, señor. I will give la señora some food, and then she must rest."

"Yes, of course, Carmen. You're the boss!"

"You will find some dinner for you on the table, señor."

"*Gracias*, Carmen."

Robert made his way down to the dining room. He felt alive again. He was surprised at how hungry he was too. He sat down at the table, and quickly demolished his dinner. It was, as usual, excellent.

After eating his meal, and a nice piece of apple pie, he headed for the living room. He wandered over to the music system, where he turned on some nice quiet music. A few steps away, he plopped himself down in his favourite chair. He closed his eyes, and for the first time in years, he thought of nothing. His mind was completely at peace. Thoughts of Christine were never far away, yet at this moment, his mind was completely devoid of thought. He relaxed his muscles. The stress of the day slipped away. There was only music and peace.

In the blue bedroom, Jenna had slowly sipped her soup, and ate the wonderful homemade buns under Carmen's watchful eye.

When she finished, Carmen commanded her to get some rest. Jenna didn't argue. She wriggled down under the sheets, nice and cozy in the comfortable bed. She closed her eyes, and slipped into the most peaceful sleep she'd had in what seemed forever.

Chapter 4 - The Emerald Tablet

It was six o'clock when Robert woke up in his bed. He only had a vague recollection of moving from the living room to his bedroom the night before. He felt surprisingly well rested and full of energy. As he lay there, he cast his mind over the incredible events, and emotional roller coaster, that was yesterday. He smiled to himself thinking, *What kind of adventure have I gotten myself into?* It would be a while yet before he'd find out. Carmen wouldn't appear in the kitchen until seven, and he was sure Jenna wouldn't be greeting the sunrise, after all she'd been through.

There was no way he would get any more sleep. He felt restless and anxious to do something—anything! He jumped out of bed, pulled on a t-shirt and shorts, and laced up some sneakers. He quietly walked down the hall, stopping for a moment outside Jenna's room. There wasn't a sound. He gently opened the door, and peeked in the room. Jenna was dead asleep. He knew he should close the door again, but stood there looking at her face. It seemed very peaceful compared to yesterday. He forced himself to close the door. He hadn't made a sound so far, and wanted to keep it that way.

He made his way quickly to the exercise room. Christine insisted they have a room where they could have exercise equipment, and a view to the outside. As he entered in the room, it was filled with light coming in through the floor-to-ceiling windows that made up one entire wall. He slid back two of the glass panels to open the room up to the terrace. He set the treadmill to one of his favourite programs, and connected the heart monitor. For Christine, he bought only the best. Of course, he got a lot of use of the equipment too. He wanted to keep fit not only for himself, but for Chris as well. Every time he ran this particular program, he was amazed the treadmill had a decline capability that let him run downhill. He started the program. For the next thirty minutes, he'd be running uphill, downhill, on the flats, and at different speeds. It was a gruelling workout, but he felt he needed it.

When the treadmill finally stopped, Robert was bathed in sweat. He placed his hands over his head, and breathed deeply to get the most oxygen possible. He kept an eye on his heart rate as it began to slowly decrease to normal. After five or six minutes, he walked over to the Bowflex where he began a thirty-minute cycle of resistance training exercises. He wasn't so much interested in building bulk, as he was to tone his muscles, and develop stamina.

When he finished, Robert stripped, and threw his clothes into the hamper. He walked to the far end of the room, took a towel and swim trunks from cupboard, and placed them on a shelf next to the small shower. He turned on the shower adjusting the temperature to lukewarm, then stepped in, letting the water pour over him. It felt good! He felt alive! He turned off the water, and gave himself a quick towel down before putting on the swim trunks. He walked out onto the terrace with the towel over his shoulder. When he reached the end of the pool, he tossed the towel onto a chair, and jumped in. For the next thirty minutes, he swam dozens of laps.

When he finally climbed out of the pool, he saw Carmen standing at one of the tables on the terrace. She had an unusual grin on her face, which had Robert wondering what she was up to. He grabbed the towel and dried himself as he walked towards her.

"*Buenos días, señor Robert.*"

"*Buenos días, Carmen. Como estas?*"

"*Muy bien, señor.*"

"How is señora Jenna this morning? I'm sure you've been to check on her."

"Sí, señor. I have been up to the bedroom. She still sleeps. We must not disturb her until she wakes of herself."

"I agree. She needs a lot of rest."

"She has been through much, la señora. You said she was given drugs?"

"Yes. When I found her, she was stumbling down the road, and her eyes were swimming around in her head. She collapsed in my arms just as I reached her. I don't know what drugs were used, but they obviously caused her to be unconscious. You saw how she looked when we arrived yesterday."

"Señor Robert, la señora looks like she was beaten. She has many marks on her body—marks made by hands and fists, señor. The scratches, they come from falling on the ground. Who could do such things?"

"I don't know, Carmen. I don't know. But I think señora Jenna will be telling me the story today. She's in a lot of trouble, and very afraid of someone." For a few moments, they stood there lost in thought. Suddenly, Robert remembered he never made it to town to get the groceries. "Carmen, I obviously never got the groceries yesterday. The list is in the pocket of my shirt. I may have thrown it in the laundry last night. You'll need to give the list to Jake, and send him for the groceries. He can use the household debit card to pay for them."

"Sí, señor Robert. But, I do not like to send him for anything because it takes so long, and he sometimes forgets things."

"Maybe if you send Andrea with him. There will be lots of boxes, and she can make sure he gets everything."

"Sí. Andrea will keep him straight. What you would like for breakfast, señor?"

He thought for a moment. "A good solid meal, Carmen. Something tells me I'll need one today. Yes, I think this will be quite the day."

"*Bien, señor*. It will be ready in about 20 minutes. Do you want to eat out on the terrace?"

"Sí, Carmen. It's a beautiful day."

"*Bien, señor*."

Robert moved quickly back into the house, up the stairs, into his room, and directly into the master bathroom. He removed his trunks and hung them on a towel bar. After a vigorous shower, he dressed casually, and made his way back to the table on the terrace, just as Carmen was laying out breakfast. Like the previous evening, he was famished, and ate his breakfast with gusto.

Jenna awoke from a wonderful, relaxing sleep. She stretched and yawned with a smile on her face. When was the last time she felt so safe and comfortable, she thought? She looked at the clock on the bedside table. It was 9 a.m. She must have slept for at least 14 hours! But then, she needed it after the ordeal of the past few days.

She swung her legs over the bed, and carefully stood up,

testing her strength. She walked into the bathroom, and looked at herself in the mirror. *Nice outfit*, she thought. *This lady had good taste.* She returned to the bed where she slipped off her pyjamas, and laid them out carefully. When she returned to the bathroom, she looked again in the mirror. She was rather shocked at what she saw. They had obviously done a good job beating her. There were nasty bruises across her front, and her back. At least they didn't smack her face around too much. "Girl, what have you got yourself into?" she said out loud.

She scanned the counter top and couldn't help laughing at what she saw. Obviously, RJ wanted to please. She felt she was in her own little Noah's ark—there seemed to be two of everything. Two different toothbrushes, two different toothpastes, two different body washes, two different shampoos, two different conditioners, two different body lotions, two hair brushes and two combs. She was sure she'd find two towels by the shower, and she wasn't disappointed.

She chose a toothbrush and toothpaste, and brushed her teeth. She made a selection from the body wash, shampoo, and conditioner then headed to the shower. She was tempted to take a nice long bath using one of the assortment of bubble baths lined up on a shelf near the big tub, but opted for the shower instead.

After adjusting the water temperature, she stood there for a good 15 minutes, letting the hot water run all over her body. Finally, she took the body wash and a luffa sponge, and scrubbed herself vigorously. She wanted to feel clean—clean from those who assaulted her. It hurt as she scrubbed bruises and scratches, but she didn't care. She just wanted to feel clean again. When she was finally satisfied, she turned off the water, and dried herself with the luxurious Egyptian-cotton bath sheets she found hanging next to the shower.

Back in the bedroom, she walked over to the closet, and slid back the door. She didn't know what to think. This RJ was some guy, and his late wife had some great taste in clothes. She selected a pair of jeans, and a nice powder blue blouse. She remembered that Carmen put some things in a dresser drawer. When she looked, she found bras and panties. She didn't know whether to laugh or cry. She picked a white bra and blue panties. When she was dressed, she looked approvingly at herself in the mirror.

Jenna knew that, by now, the others would be up and waiting

for her. She made her way down the stairs. She looked around, but no one was to be seen. The house was quiet too. All for her benefit, no doubt. She wandered about, managing to find her way to the kitchen.

"*Ah, buenos días, señora.* You slept well?"

"Yes, thank you, Carmen."

"The clothing of señora Christina fit you very nice, señora."

"Thank you. She does have lovely things."

"Señor Robert is on the terrace. I will bring your breakfast there."

"Thank you, Carmen. How do I get to the terrace?"

"Ah, I show you." Carmen, with Jenna in tow, made her way to the terrace where she left Jenna at the door.

Robert turned around, smiled, and greeted her. "Well, good morning Jenna. I trust you rested well."

When Jenna saw Robert, she couldn't help but smile. She wasn't sure why, but she had this big, stupid grin on her face—like a school girl meeting the boy she has a crush on, for the first time. She thought, *Oh, for goodness sake, stop it girl. You just met the man.* To Robert, she said, "Yes, thank you, I had a very nice long sleep. You were right in bringing me here. I did need some looking after."

"Yes, you did." Then he stammered, "You look great, by the way."

"Your late wife had great taste in clothes, so you can blame her for that. And you picked out some very lovely things for me to wear. I appreciate that."

"Please stop referring to Christine as my 'late wife'. Use Christine or Chris instead. 'Late wife' seems so impersonal."

"Okay, RJ, I'll do that. Thanks for telling me."

"Please, sit down. I'm sure your breakfast will be here any minute now, courtesy of the ever-efficient Carmen Lopez."

"She's a real sweetie, and you know it."

"Carmen has been with me for more than twenty years now. She's a jewel—in the rough, mind you. She can be a real tyrant when she wants to be. I learned long ago not to argue with her. Being her boss doesn't mean I'll get my way." With that, he chuckled loudly and Jenna joined in.

Within a few minutes, Carmen brought out a nice hearty breakfast for Jenna, and retreated back to her kitchen.

Jenna looked at the massive breakfast of eggs, hash browns, bacon, toast with preserves, fruit cup, coffee, and juice wondering where she'd put it all. Then again, she felt ravenously hungry. She looked up at Robert.

"Go ahead and dig in. Looks like Carmen gave you a bit of everything."

With that comment, Jenna remembered her Noah's ark of bath products, and burst out laughing.

"Did I say something funny?"

"No. No, it's not that. I was thinking about all the choices you left me on the bathroom counter. Two of everything, so I could choose something I liked. A little bit of everything—just like Carmen."

Robert was surprised to find that he was blushing deeply. He could see how it was a bit of overkill.

"I'm sorry, RJ, I didn't mean to embarrass you."

"Oh, don't mind me. I'm just having a silly schoolboy moment. That's all."

Robert was silent while Jenna plunged into her breakfast—moaning and groaning with appreciation.

"That was absolutely delicious!"

"Carmen has to be the best cook in the world. She can make anything taste great. Actually, I don't know what I'd do without her. I can always count on her to keep this place running in tip-top order—especially since Chris died."

"I'm sure it's been very difficult for you. And now, you want to make your life even more difficult by throwing in with me?"

"It's time I stopped moping around. If Chris was here to see how I've been behaving, she'd be the first to give me a hard time. Her philosophy was always to celebrate all the great times spent with someone, rather than to dwell on the fact they're gone. And I've been doing far too much dwelling. No, it's time for me to take my place in the world. You're obviously in some sort of trouble, not of your making, and I think finding you wandering in a daze down the road was no accident. You need someone not only to protect you, but to provide the kinds of resources that I have at my disposal. Sounds strange, but there it is."

Jenna gave Robert an appraising look. She saw a man in good shape who had an appearance of determination on his face—especially his eyes. She had already decided that Robert was a good man. Now, he was repeating what he said to her last night—that he was intent to watch over her, and help her whether she liked it or not. Something stirred deep down inside her, that hadn't stirred for a long time. She couldn't allow feelings to get in the way of the quest. Besides, she thought, he's still way too much in love with Christine.

"Then I'd better tell you what you're getting into."

She turned her chair to face Robert. He did the same. They were now directly facing one another. Robert said nothing, choosing to wait for Jenna to tell her story.

"Have you ever heard of the Emerald Tablet?"

"Can't say as I have."

Jenna took a deep breath and began her story:

"The Emerald Tablet is said to be an explanation of the secrets of the universe, and in particular, the concepts of alchemy. Whenever alchemy is mentioned, it's usually in terms of changing base metals, like lead for instance, into gold. But, alchemy goes way beyond that, even to the ability to prepare substances that can give you a form of immortality. Even today, many alchemists consider the Emerald Tablet to be their holy grail.

"Legend has it the Emerald Tablet was prepared as far back as the time of Adam, from the teachings received from the angels, after Adam and Eve were thrown out of the Garden of Eden. Apparently, *that* Emerald Tablet even made it onto Noah's ark, so these secrets would not be lost.

"Of course, as with most legends, there are many sources of 'truth' about an object's origins. In this case, the Emerald Tablet is also known as the *Tabula Smaragdina*, and is thought to have been written by the Egyptian god Thoth, or his counterpart in the Greek pantheon, Hermes.

"It was called the Emerald Tablet because it's thought to have been written on a large piece of pure emerald—not inscribed, but written in relief, as though it was proof that you could actually do these things. Any jeweller will tell you that working with any gemstone, including emerald, is very difficult. One false move and the gemstone breaks into pieces. If you consider that the Emerald Tablet is said to be about 25 centimetres by 30 centimetres and 2 centimetres thick, you're talking about a massive piece of emerald that weighs about 4 kg!

"Now, getting back to the story...

"It's also said that a fellow named Hermes Trismegistus was supposedly named in the text as the original author. No one knows for sure who wrote it, and when it was written, or whether it was, in fact, written on a priceless piece of emerald, or on a piece of greenish coloured stone.

"The first known version of the Emerald Tablet was written in Arabic dating to between the sixth and eighth centuries A.D. I have a fanciful depiction of this back at my motel, and you can even buy a supposed replica of the stone version online. It was translated into Latin in the twelfth century. Since then, it's been translated into many languages. Newton translated it, and there's even a Google translation. Of course, no one knows for sure if the Arabic tablet is the real thing. Legend has it the skeleton of our friend Hermes Trismegistus was found holding the tablet. Of course, all these things have disappeared.

"A legend is a legend, right? And, only really crazy people go chasing after legends, right?

"Well, this is where it gets interesting. About three months ago, an archaeologist named Ambrose Scott reported finding a piece of solid emerald, about the size of the Emerald Tablet, at a site in Jordan, where he was digging. He described it as being covered with raised characters of unknown origin or language. There was no way to date the tablet, as it seemed to predate the site in which it was found. Dr. Scott apparently never took a photo of the tablet, which is unusual. Almost immediately after reporting the find, he went on a mysterious three-week trip, telling no one where he was going. He simply informed his research assistants he expected to be meeting with the Jordanian Antiquities Department. The day of his return, he vanished altogether! No one has seen, nor heard from him, since. You can well imagine the tablet went missing too.

"After Dr. Scott's report, there was a real buzz in many communities: alchemists, museums, private collectors, and crazies, who saw in the tablet a chance for immortality, wealth, and power. It was heralded as the true Emerald Tablet of ancient origin, although no one else has seen the real item. Before long, many started looking for the illusive Emerald Tablet.

"So, you're probably wondering what I have to do with all this. Well, I'm one of those people who's looking for the Emerald Tablet. You see, Dr. Scott was a professor of archaeology at the University of Alberta, and I work in the U of A Department of History and Classics' Archaeology Section. My name is Carpenter, by the way, Jenna Carpenter, and I live in Edmonton, not far from the university.

"A couple of months after Dr. Scott went missing, all his personal belongings, and papers were sent to us for processing. I was given the task of sorting through Dr. Scott's research notes.

While I was looking through one of his notebooks, I noticed something sticking out of the thick hard cover. With a little effort, I managed to pull it out. It was in a language I don't understand, and I believe it is a description of where Dr. Scott hid the Emerald Tablet. He must have known that every treasure hunter would want to have the tablet for the price of the emerald itself, let alone the content. I respect Dr. Scott and his integrity. So, I decided the Emerald Tablet needed to be safeguarded, and took it upon myself to find it. I tried to keep this note secret, but news of it must have leaked out somehow. I've been running ever since.

"There are some really nasty people who will stop at nothing to get their hands on the tablet. One, in particular, is Randolph Carver. As far as I'm concerned, he's a total psychopath. It was his henchmen that drugged me, and beat me up. I'm alive only because I didn't have Dr. Scott's note on me when they caught up with me, and they must've figured they'd wait for another chance, since I was the only one who knew where it was. Obviously, they didn't find it in my motel room either."

Jenna stopped here. She knew that Robert would have a lot to digest. She looked into his face again, and could plainly see he was tossing all this round in his mind. He was looking intently at her now. His piercing eyes were locked with hers, and it seemed to her he was searching into the very depths of her soul. In a way, it frightened her, and yet, it was strangely a source of comfort too. She tried to read his face, but it was set in stone. Not a muscle moved. No emotion betrayed. Only his eyes piercing into hers.

After several minutes passed in silence, Robert smiled broadly at Jenna. "Well, I'd better get my fedora and whip, if I'm going to play the part of Indiana Jones!"

At first, Jenna didn't know what to make of this trivial comment. Her brows knit and she looked rather impatiently at him. Robert cut her off before she had a chance to respond, with an earnest comment of his own.

"Jenna, I'm not making fun of you. Remember how you laughed about me putting out so many bath products? Well, I couldn't help but think that your story was right out of the pages of an Indiana Jones adventure. I listened very carefully to every word you said. I watched your body language too. Yesterday, I told you I worked with people for many years, and can tell if I'm being snowed or not. Well, I believe everything you've told me. I also believe that if we're going to recover the good Dr. Scott's

Emerald Tablet, we'll need to think a lot like my alter ego, Indiana Jones. I have no doubt you put yourself in harms way when you decided to find it. I have no doubt you're in danger for your life, and that I'm placing my life on the line by helping you. Like Indiana Jones, I'm not going to back down. We're in this together now—for better or for worse. The only thing I ask of you is that you trust me completely; that you don't hold anything back, nor hide anything from me. I'll do the same with you. It's the only way we'll see this through in one piece."

Jenna was totally floored by what Robert just said. If there was an Indiana Jones in her life, this would be him. Robert now had a look of calm resolve about him. She instinctively knew she could place her full trust in this man. What a difference twenty-four hours could make! Whatever tension there was in Jenna's body now vanished. She tried hard to suppress the tears welling up in her eyes, but it was too much. She was overcome with emotion. She leaned forward towards Robert, put her arms around his neck, and kissed him hard on the lips. When she pulled back, she saw Robert blushing deeply. Jenna thought she should be ashamed of herself, but it didn't happen. Instead, she felt badly that she had probably embarrassed Robert.

Robert sat there in shock. He wasn't sure what the shock was, exactly. He just knew he was in shock. He tried to analyze it. He always tried to analyze things. Although Jenna looked a lot like Christine, she certainly was different. No, he definitely didn't think he was being kissed by Christine. This was definitely a Jenna kiss. He felt a bit guilty that he didn't feel guilty in the slightest at having been kissed by Jenna. In fact, it felt kind of good. To his surprise, he wanted to lean forward and return the kiss with one of his own. This was probably not good. But, it wasn't bad either, was it?

His brain turned into mush at this point and all he could think of saying was, "Wow! Felt that one right down to my toes!" He then closed his eyes, and thought, *What an inane thing to say!*

Jenna looked pityingly at Robert. She didn't know if she should say something, or just kiss him again. She decided, in this case, silence and inaction were the better part of valour.

Robert finally came to, and smiled at Jenna. "Sorry, it's been a while since I've been kissed at all—let alone like that."

Jenna was about to say something, but bit her tongue, and kept quiet.

Robert looked resolutely at Jenna. "What we need now is a plan of action."

Chapter 5 - Interrogation

Jenna didn't want to break Robert's concentration, so she stayed very quiet, as she scrutinized his face. Almost imperceptibly at first, she began to notice a strange, quirky smile appear on Robert's face. She didn't know what to make of it. Yet, she knew she could trust Robert with all the knowledge she possessed, and even with her very life. Ah, now she had it—it was what writers might call a wry smile. His eyes narrowed as he looked more intently at her. If it was anyone but Robert, she would have felt extremely uncomfortable.

Finally, Robert spoke. "I'm trying to put my head around everything you've told me. There are plenty of gaps I'd like you to fill in for me. It's important that we both be on the same page here. Do you mind if we play a game of forty questions? I ask and you answer?"

Jenna could now understand what Robert was up to. She smiled back at him sweetly. "Yes, of course, RJ. Ask away, and I'll answer as best I can."

"I hope you'll forgive me if it feels more like an interrogation. The questions might be disjointed, and all over the map, as they pop up in my head."

"Will you be taking notes, RJ?"

"No, I can remember things quite well. It comes from many years of working in real estate, where I had to keep track of all the details for lots of properties at once. Clients felt confident when they could ask about this property or that one, and I could quickly rhyme off the details without looking at the spec sheet. It's a little talent that has served me well over time."

"Okay, I'm ready to go."

"Before we start, Jenna, would you like another coffee or some tea or juice? This could take a while."

"Maybe I'll have another coffee, then."

Robert rose from his chair. He gathered up some of the dirty dishes on the table before making his way to the kitchen. Jenna followed his lead, cleared up the remaining dishes, and followed him. Carmen was a bit surprised to see them both with their hands full of dirty dishes. She quickly retrieved them—from Jenna first, and then from Robert. Robert asked Carmen to make a pot of coffee, and bring it out with a warmer to keep it hot. Carmen quickly acknowledged his request. The pair made their way back to the terrace.

Robert and Jenna were engaged in some idle chit chat when Carmen arrived with the coffee, and a couple of fresh cups, about ten minutes later. After placing the tray down and plugging the warmer into a long extension cord, Carmen turned to leave.

"Carmen, please be sure that señora Jenna and I are not disturbed for any reason other than a serious emergency. No phone calls. No visitors. You don't need to come out to check on the coffee, or if we need anything. We need time to discuss some very important matters."

"Sí, señor Robert. I will close the doors behind me when I go in."

"Gracias, Carmen."

When Carmen had left, Robert poured them both some coffee. Then began Jenna's interrogation.

"I guess the first thing I want to know is just how much you believe that Dr. Scott actually found a mystic tablet made of solid emerald. On a scale of 0 to 10, what's your belief level?"

Jenna considered carefully. She hadn't really thought about it in that way before. She simply assumed that Dr. Scott was honest about his find, and launched forward on her quest on that assumption.

"Let me answer like this: that Dr. Scott actually found something, I'd have to give that a 10; that he found a mystic tablet, being the legendary Emerald Tablet, in particular, I really couldn't say. He gave no indication of knowing what the content of the writing might be. That he found a tablet made of solid emerald, I'd have to go with a 5 on that one. He mentioned in his report that it could be either emerald, or some form of clear green quartz. He was very specific about it not being stone."

"You said you found some kind of note inside the hard cover of a notebook. Just how did that work?"

"Dr. Scott used small notebooks with thick cardboard front and back covers. When I examined the notebook, I noticed there was a small corner of something sticking out of the back cover. It looked like he used a sharp knife to split the cardboard in two from the top to make a cavity. The note was in the cavity. It looked like he used some glue to seal it closed again, but for some reason, the glue didn't hold well, and a corner of the note stuck out. I had to use a razor knife to slice it open again."

"So, you feel he concealed this note in a secret place only he could find again."

"Yes. I don't think he meant for anyone else to find it. He had no way of knowing, of course, that he would disappear, and his notebooks, and other personal effects, would make their way back to the university for examination."

"It seems strange that he didn't keep this particular notebook on his person, or very close by, if it had information that would lead to the tablet. Do you know if this notebook was found with all the others, or separately?"

"I have no idea, RJ. I simply received several boxes of his stuff from the Jordan dig site. The notebooks were all packed together in a box, with some file folders containing general information about the dig."

"Hmm." Robert tossed in his mind what Jenna had just said. There was something odd about the whole thing, but he couldn't put his finger on it. "Jenna, what were the contents of the notebooks? Were they generally the same type of stuff, or were they quite different?"

"I think I know what you're looking for, RJ. You're wondering if this particular notebook was somehow special. Am I right?"

"Yes and no. I hate to be the interrogator again, but please answer the question I asked, and don't try to second-guess me, because even I'm not sure where this will lead next."

"Okay, RJ." Her face broke into a mischievous smile. "Shouldn't we have a big bright light pointed at my face, or something?"

They both laughed. The tension that was building up evaporated.

"Maybe I should have you looking directly into the sun, then. And it's too bad I don't have a polygraph machine kicking around to check your answers on."

Again, they both laughed. Jenna could see that, even in this serious situation, Robert could ease off, and have a bit of fun. She liked his quirky sense of humour.

"Okay, please answer the question lady. Investigators might

say you're trying to put off a tough question." Robert's tone was mock officious.

Jenna considered what Robert had asked. She cast her mind back to the notebooks, and what they contained. She took a deep breath, and answered.

"RJ, as far as I can remember, all the notebooks contained Dr. Scott's personal notes about the dig, some reminders, some questions he felt needed answering about various artifacts or fragments that had been dug up. They were a kind of working diary. The notebook with the secret compartment was no different from the rest, except maybe that it looked like it was the last one he used. The others were all full and this one only about a third full."

"Jenna, if these notebooks, or diaries, contained information about the dig and artifacts, why would they not have stayed at the dig site?"

"I don't know, RJ. I could only speculate."

"Then speculate."

"There are two possible reasons. First, work at the site continued for about a month after Dr. Scott disappeared. Because there was no one available immediately to take over the site, the university decided to stop work temporarily. When they did that, the university received several crates of artifacts that needed further study, along with Dr. Scott's things. Second, it could be that these notebooks were considered more personal to Dr. Scott than they were part of dig documentation. I was tasked to go through all Dr. Scott's things, and extract anything I felt was germane to the dig site, and forward the rest to Dr. Scott's lawyer.

"Is it normal for archaeologists to hide significant artifacts they find at dig sites?"

"There's really no such thing as normal when it comes to archaeology, RJ. The archaeologist who heads up each dig decides how to handle various artifacts. If an artifact is considered significant, it is usually recorded, photographed, described in great detail, and either packaged and sent to the university's archaeological department for further study, or sent to a specific museum, depending on the license provided by the host country's antiquities department. Sometimes, if an artifact is considered highly valuable, the head of the dig might keep it under wraps, until it can be safely conveyed to the specified destination. This is done to try to eliminate the possibility of theft by so-called tomb robbers and artifact smugglers."

"Do you think Dr. Scott thought he might be in danger?"

"Given the fact he concealed the location of the Emerald Tablet, I think he suspected that the news would get to Carver, and others like him, and they would come looking for it. I think he put himself in danger when he concealed the tablet. Guys like Carver will stop at nothing to find such an artifact."

"This brings us to your friend Carver. Nice name! How does he fit into all this?"

"In the world of antiquities, Randolph Carver is considered to be the biggest of the private collectors, and the most ruthless. Although he's never been caught doing anything illegal himself, he has a group of men and women, who do all the dirty work. If there's something he wants, he gets it at any cost. He's immensely wealthy. He'll stop at nothing to get his prize—even torturing and killing people along the way. Many law enforcement agencies have tried to bring him down, but he's always been found squeaky clean."

"Sounds like a nice guy! Do you think it was his gang that roughed you up?"

"I'm pretty sure it was."

"Do you remember anything from that ordeal? You said something about it being two days."

"The last I remember, I was in my motel room at the Super 8 in Airdrie on Monday afternoon. There was a knock on the door. When I looked through the peep hole, I saw what looked like a housekeeper. When I asked who it was, she replied she was from housekeeping. When I unlocked the door, she pushed in against me, and put a cloth over my face. After that, I vaguely remember being asked questions, and being punched, and smacked around. I have the impression this was done somewhere other than my motel room, but I have no idea where. The next thing I knew, I was wandering down a dirt road, and being swept up in the arms of a very nice man."

"And you think it was this guy, Carver?"

"I can't think of anyone else it could be. Like I said, he's ruthless when it comes to getting his prize. Although I was pretty messed-up, I didn't get the impression there was a boss in the group interrogating me. No one the others deferred to. No one sitting back and watching the action."

"So, how did Carver get wind of the note you found in Dr. Scott's notebook?"

"Carver seems to know everything. Artifacts that have been cloaked in secrecy have gone missing within weeks, or even days, of being found. Only a very few people knew about these artifacts, and they were kept very hush hush. Of course, it could be the diggers. But it could also be university employees, like me, or museum curators, who are on Carver's payroll. No one knows."

"Who did you tell about the note?"

Again, Jenna had to stop and think carefully about what happened from the time she found the note and when she ended up in Airdrie. "Let's see: I found the note, and examined it; I decided that this was a kind of map to the location of the tablet; I needed to take some time off to go look for it; I went to Dr. Bart to ask for the time off; he asked why the short notice; I thought I could trust him, and told him what I wanted to do. Come to think of it, he didn't seem too concerned about my quest, nor did he suggest the quest should be a university affair. He just told me to take as much time as I wanted, and to contact him if I needed anything. As you can imagine, I was quite excited. I told a girlfriend of mine at the university that I was going on a quest, but never said what it was. We just laughed about it, and even went out for a celebration dinner. It's not often the grunts, like us, get a chance to participate in a quest, let alone head one up. That's it. No one but Dr. Bart even knows of the existence of Dr. Scott's note."

"Who is this Dr. Bart?"

"Dr. Terrence Bartholomew. We all call him Dr. Bart. He's the head of the Archaeological Department at the U of A, and my boss."

"Didn't it strike you as strange that Dr. Bart simply allowed you to venture off to locate what might be the most significant archaeological find in decades?"

"At the time, I didn't think much about it. But now you mention it, yes. Yes, it does seem strange. I guess I fully expected him to insist I give him the note so he could try to find it himself. When he didn't, I wasn't going to look a gift horse in the mouth. I thanked him for the vacation time, and took off!"

So, what you're saying is, other than yourself, only Dr. Bart knew there might be directions to where Dr. Scott hid the tablet. You're sure you never mentioned it to anyone else?"

"No. I never spoke about what my quest was, or how I came to be on it, to anyone. So, yes, only Dr. Bart knew. Oh, crap! It had to be Dr. Bart who told Carver!"

The blood drained out of Jenna's face when she realized the full impact of what she just said. The very person she trusted most was the very person who was now having her tortured for information. She looked up at Robert with tears in her eyes.

"Oh, RJ! That's how Carver found out. Dr. Bart must have called him the moment I left his office. That explains why they were onto me so quickly. They probably even followed me home, and to dinner. RJ! They might know we're together. Oh, what have I done to you?"

Robert reached out and touched Jenna's hand softly, and then took both her hands in his. She was trembling with fear. Jenna felt the steadiness of Roberts hands, and took heart. Robert was fully aware of the position they were in. If he felt any fear at all, he never betrayed it to Jenna. Robert smiled at her softly, his face full of intensity and confidence.

"Don't worry, Jenna. We're in this together, and together we'll succeed. Neither of us is a dummy. We're both intelligent and resourceful, and that's what will get us through this. With me on board, we have access to resources you probably don't have—like money, for example. I have plenty of that, and I think it'll come in very handy. One lesson I'm sure you've learned is we can trust no one except each other."

Jenna felt the strength in Robert's hands, and saw the resolve in his eyes. Again, she was very grateful to have been rescued by such a decent man. It was obvious he had courage—and not foolish courage either. All his questions had purpose. She could see it now. She could also see that Robert was bringing many things to her consciousness. Her heart swelled in her breast as she held his hands.

"So, Jenna, there's no time for tears or fears now. The fact that Carver's gang didn't get anything out of you tells me you're one tough lady. It's time for both of us to be tough. If Carver wants to play rough, we can play rough too! I'm not an advocate of violence—hate it. But we'll be on the defensive the whole way."

Jenna smiled at Robert and took great courage from his. She straightened up. Confidence and resolve filled her. *What a man!* she thought, *What a man!*

"Jenna, do you still have possession of the map—since that's what it really is? There wasn't anything on your person when I found you."

"I don't have the map on me. I always try to find an

inconspicuous spot to hide it, and it's always close by. Something tells me if I had given those crooks the location of the map, we wouldn't be having this conversation."

"I don't think Carver's goons are onto the fact we're together. I have a pretty sophisticated security system here, and I'd know if anyone was roaming about the property. I'll take a look at the cameras covering the road, but I don't think anyone will be there. No, I think they'll be staking out the motel, and maybe your room."

"You said you were missing in action for a couple of days. Do you think the motel would pack up your things to make the room available?"

"No, RJ, I don't think so. When I booked in, I said I might want the room for a week. I booked in on Monday, and today is Thursday, so I should be okay."

"Is the map hidden somewhere in your room?"

"No. That would've been too easy. You'll think I've watched too many spy movies when I tell you where it is. I taped it underneath a large flower vase in the hallway leading to my room."

"Brilliant! It's highly unlikely they would even think of looking there. Hopefully, the vase is still there, and no one has found the map."

"You mean like cleaning staff?"

"Yeah!"

"Somehow, I don't think so."

"Is there anything in your room you just gotta have?"

"Well, there's my clothes, and personal hygiene stuff. Nothing of great significance. Why?"

"As for clothes, you're the exact same size as Chris, and there's lots of clothes for you to choose from in boxes upstairs. I have several suitcases, so you can pack what you like in those. As you've already noticed, there's quite a selection of personal hygiene stuff here as well. I think our first plan of action is to retrieve the map. If we don't have to go into your room, so much the better. There might be an armed goon or two waiting for you to return. What about a passport and other ID?"

"Ah, that *would* be in my room. I can't see them taking it along when they drugged and moved me. RJ, are you sure you want me to take some of Chris' clothes?"

"Chris would want it that way. I'm sure of it. After all, they're just sitting there doing nothing. Maybe that's why I never had the heart to give them away. I knew, someday, a beautiful damsel in distress would come along who would need some nice clothes."

"Thank you, RJ. You're very generous."

Robert was lost in thought. How could he get into Jenna's room without arousing suspicion? He needed to get her passport and ID if they were going to be travelling to the Middle East, or anywhere else on the planet. The map should be easy enough.

"I suppose you don't happen to have your room key handy."

"Sorry, RJ."

"Do you know exactly where your passport and other documents might be in the room?"

"I hid them underneath the spare blankets on the shelf above the coat closet. Why?"

"When you checked in, did you mention your affiliation to the U of A, or what you do for a living?

"No, just the usual check-in banter, nothing else. Wait...I may have mentioned that I was working on a research project for the U of A."

"Okay. This is what we'll do. I want you to call the motel. Ask them to go to your room get your passport and wallet under the blankets. That should satisfy them it's really you calling, since you know the exact location. Tell them to put your things in an envelope. Mention you're stuck in meetings, and you're sending an assistant, yours truly, to get the envelope. When I pick up your stuff, I'll tell them you'll need the room until next Monday. If they want some payment, I'll pull out your credit card and pay to Monday. They should already have the imprint anyway from when you checked-in. Will your credit card bear the strain?"

"Oh yes. I always keep my credit card paid up, so there's no problem with the room charges."

"Good. Now, what floor is your room on?"

"I'm in room 207, so the second floor."

"Okay, I'll first go up to the second floor, and retrieve the map from the vase. Next, I'll go to the desk to get your documents, and pay the room. Then I'll return here."

"RJ, isn't that kind of dangerous?"

"The danger should be minimal. They don't know who I am, and that we're working together. I should be able to move freely without suspicion. When I think about it, it's not likely they'll take the chance to actually wait in your room. It would be hard to explain their presence to the housekeeping staff. Besides, if you escaped, or they let you escape, you might go to the police, and be escorted back to the motel. The last thing they would want is a run-in with the law. No, I think they'll be waiting for you to make an appearance at the motel, either staking the place out from a vehicle, or maybe sitting in the lobby. Since you've been gone for some time, just sitting around in the lobby would attract attention, so a vehicle stakeout is most likely. We'll have to chance it. There's no other choice."

Jenna sat there amazed at what Robert just said. She could see how he was sorting out all the facts and possibilities in his mind—logically and methodically. She couldn't help being impressed. A calm resolve began to settle upon her now. This man knew what he was doing, and she could trust him completely. She considered Robert's plan. It was audacious. What he proposed made sense. There really was no alternative she could think of. She was worried that something might happen to Robert, and yet she had every confidence that he'd pull it off. She looked at Robert, and a broad grin brightened her face.

"Well, the game is afoot then!"

"Yes, it is, Jenna! "Yes, it is!"

Chapter 6 - Plan A

Robert sat quietly now, mulling things over in his mind, running his index finger slowly around his coffee cup. Jenna sat immobile in her chair; her breath soft and shallow; not wanting to do anything that would distract him. She knew he was very far away, working out his scheme to retrieve the map.

She was startled when Robert broke out of his reverie, and asked her if she wanted another cup of coffee. Robert laughed when she jumped, and grasped at her heart with a short shriek.

"Oh, my gosh, RJ, you scared the very devil out of me!" Robert laughed even harder now. The tension of the last hours had obviously caused both reactions. Jenna finally started laughing herself.

"Coffee?" Robert asked again, with a smile as he held up the pot.

"Yes, please."

For some reason, she felt very giddy—like at a funeral, when a funny thought passes through your mind, and you just can't help yourself. She was doing everything she could to stifle her giddiness, but it wasn't working. She began to giggle uncontrollably. The heavy stress of the last few days was finally being shed as she felt totally safe and secure with Robert. In less than twenty-four hours, Robert went from rescuer, to confidant, to full-blown confederate in the quest—and maybe something more?

Robert filled their cups.

"I'll be back in a minute." He stood, moved away from the table, and into the house. He walked quickly to his study. Robert pulled a few sheets of blank paper from the desk, grabbed a mechanical pencil, an eraser, and a ruler. Before Jenna even had time to wonder what he was up to, he was back again, sitting next to her.

He placed his little treasure trove on the table in front of Jenna. She looked at him quizzically. Robert smiled. "Do you think you can remember the layout of the motel inside and outside?"

"Ah, you want me to draw you some plans."

"As accurately and you can. First, the outside of the motel showing approximately where the entrance is along the building, and where the car park is located relative to the entrance."

Jenna closed her eyes, trying to remember the Super 8's exterior, how she turned into it, how far she had to walk. Slowly, it was coming back to her, as the mists of her mind began to dissipate. She picked up the pencil and began to draw. Robert sat quietly sipping his coffee, watching her intently.

"I think this is pretty close." The drawing showed the entrance close to the south end of the building, and parking along the entire front.

"Well, there's certainly no way to sneak into the building without being seen. It'll be a full-frontal assault, complete with onlookers. If they're staking out the building, they'll probably use more than one car and team, otherwise someone might notice—especially if motel staff are checking outside cameras. Shouldn't be a problem. They don't know me, and as long as I don't look suspicious, they'll have no reason to take much note of me."

Jenna listened attentively. She smiled to herself, wondering how many spy movies Robert had watched.

"OK, now the inside, as best you can remember. The front lobby area, elevator, stairs. Then along the corridor to your room, especially the approximate location of the vase you taped the map to."

Again, Jenna carefully considered the inside of the building. She noticed Robert had quietly moved away again. She returned to her thoughts, and began to draw. Before she finished, Robert had returned, this time with a laptop computer. She continued to draw, but couldn't help being curious about what Robert was doing on the computer. When she finished her sketches, she passed them to Robert.

"What are you looking up, RJ?"

He turned the laptop around, so she could see. He had googled the Super 8, and photos of the motel were now displayed on the screen. "I thought this might help jog your memory a bit."

They compared her sketches to the photos on the screen.

Jenna was amazingly correct in her recollections.

"Remarkable memory you have there, Jenna!"

"It comes with the job. In *my* line of work, *I* have to remember a lot of details, so I can compare drawings, photos, physical artifacts, and a lot of other stuff.

Robert considered the sketches carefully. His mind was a whirlwind of strategies. To himself, he thought, *God, do I ever feel alive!*

"How about this for Plan A? You call the motel, and ask them to hold your things at the desk. I'll try to park around here...as close to the entrance as possible so as not to be in view of Carver's thugs for any length of time. If I'm careful, I'll be able to move into, and out of, the motel with a minimum of face time. They may be taking pictures of everyone who enters and leaves the motel. If all they get is a profile, it'll be hard to make me out again later. It'll be a quick in-and-out, so they don't have any reason to be suspicious.

"It would be nice to know the cleaning schedule for the hallways, so I'm not delayed getting the map on the second floor. Just have to chance it. First thing is to quickly, but nonchalantly, get to the stairs, make my way to the vase, and get the map. How did you stick it on, by the way?"

"I put the paper in a small envelope to protect it and folded it a couple of times. I used some heavy, clear tape with two strips in a cross shape."

"That should make it fairly easy and quick to pull off. Next, I'll move back to the lobby and ask for your envelope. Then, I just trot out with no one the wiser. What do you think?"

Jenna considered Robert's plan. "What if the lobby staff question you about I.D., or what you were doing on the second floor."

"Hmm, good point." Robert winced, and tightened his jaw. "Then, I should get the envelope first. When I go to the stairs, lobby staff will probably think you sent me to your room to get something else. As I think about it, there's probably a security camera in the hallway. I'll have to stop, and pretend to examine the vase with interest, to keep suspicion down. Then, I'll go to your room door, pull out my phone, and pretend to be taking a call from you telling me to skip going to the room."

"Sounds good to me, RJ. So, what's Plan B?"

With a wry smile, Robert answered. "Grab the stuff, and run like hell!"

They both laughed, although they knew this was no laughing matter.

"What do I do in the mean time?"

"Enjoy yourself here, and pray that all goes well."

"I think I'll be sitting here scared stiff that something awful happens to you. What if they follow you?"

"Been thinking about that. I don't want to show up as your assistant driving a Land Cruiser. That's bound to attract attention. I think I'll stop off at a car rental place, and rent something a bit more modest. If they notice it's a rental, it'll just add to my cover. Once I'm back in my SUV, I can probably outrun anything they might have, since they'll have to use a nondescript car too, if they want to avoid attention. I know my way around these parts, and can take a very circuitous route back here. I think this is probably the easiest, and safest part of our little quest."

"RJ, I'm worried that they might be cruising around this road looking for me. What if they recognize your SUV?"

"That's unlikely if I use a rented car, and they don't know you're here, or who I am. I'll keep my eyes open, and make sure no one is tailing me."

Robert sat there looking very serious. "What's wrong, RJ?"

"It would be normal for you to tell motel staff that a Mr. So-and-so will be picking up the envelope. I want to avoid using my real name. That would link me to you if anyone asked. If Carver is as well connected as you say, it would be a piece of cake to get my location. It would be really nice to know a forger right now." Robert sat quietly considering.

Jenna sat strait up in her chair, and spoke with some excitement. "Forger, of course! You have a computer and a printer here, right?" She didn't wait for an answer. "We can go online to the U of A site, snag an image of the U of A logo, make a few fake cards under another name you can present to lobby staff."

"Total genius! Well, why are we sitting here, let's go to my study, and get started."

They rose quickly, and made their way to the study. Jenna said she was pretty good at this kind of stuff, and could put something together in a few minutes. She wasn't kidding! Within fifteen minutes, Robert had a few cards, cut from some old card stock, in the name of Richard Carter, Research Assistant, Department of Archaeology, U of A. To add a bit more credibility, she even took a picture of Robert, and incorporated it into the card. She knew that many U of A personnel had picture I.D. cards.

By the time they finished concocting their plan and making arrangements, it was already lunch time. Carmen ventured out to see if they were still sitting on the terrace. When she saw no one there, she wondered where they had gotten to. As they came out of the study, Carmen caught sight of them, and asked if they cared for some lunch. Robert and Jenna looked at one another, and nodded. They were famished. It was very hungry work being on a quest!

They soon found themselves sitting in the dining room, enjoying a scrumptious meal, and talking over the afternoon's planned activities. Robert suggested they pack for a quick getaway, in case things went sideways on them. He also gave Carmen some very specific instructions, should Carver's goons come calling—something he seriously hoped would not happen.

Chapter 7 - In and Out

It didn't take Robert long to pack two suitcases, and prepare all his travel documents. Jenna, on the other hand was sitting on the edge of Robert's bed looking at a bewildering array of designer clothes, lingerie, shoes, and unmentionables. Robert took all the boxes of Christine's clothing out of the closet, and opened them. He noticed the deer-in-the-headlights look on Jenna's face.

He laughed. "Well, you won't be able to say you don't have a thing to wear."

She just looked at him—tears welling up in her eyes. This was a wardrobe she could never imagine in her wildest dreams, and here it was spread out in front of her. She was speechless. She wasn't sure if she wanted to laugh, or cry, or both! She looked lovingly at this man who was about to put his life on the line for her—*for her*—and was offering up this treasure trove. She just sat there holding back the tears. Robert began to feel rather embarrassed as he realized what was happening. But this was not a time for blushing, it was a time for action.

He went to the door of the bedroom, and called out, "Carmen, would you come here please?"

"Sí, señor, I come." She made her way up the stairs quickly, and practically ran to the bedroom. "*¿Que pasa, señor?*" She immediately noticed Jenna sitting there in shock, looking at the boxes, and understood.

"Carmen, could you please help la señora to pack some clothes for a long trip? She will need some comfortable clothes for a warm climate, and some comfortable shoes for walking long distances. It would be good to have a sweater or two, and a couple of jackets. She will also need something for formal evening wear. Don't forget bras, panties, and other things."

Jenna was now in the capable hands of Carmen who would

quickly help her sort through the boxes, and pick out the most appropriate and becoming outfits.

He looked earnestly at Jenna. “You need to be packed and ready to go immediately on my return. I don’t expect to be more than 60 to 90 minutes—if all goes well. If we’re lucky, we’ll have time to plan our next steps here, rather than in hiding, or on the road.”

“Thank you, RJ! Thank you so much!”

Robert stood in front of her, squatted down, and held her arms firmly in his hands. Jenna couldn’t hold back any more. The floodgates of her tears burst forth. With a full heart, she threw her arms around his neck, and kissed him hard on the lips for a long time. His arms slid around her waist, and he responded with a long and tender kiss of his own. He did not feel the slightest bit embarrassed or guilty. Instead, he felt a surge of energy pass through his entire body along with an odd sensation that he just wanted to jump up shouting, *YES!* This latter passion he managed to stifle, and retained some sense of decorum.

Robert now moved quickly to his walk-in closet, and closed the door. He changed into a suitable business suit—nothing fancy or expensive. He wanted to look the part of an archaeological researcher. He chose an old grey suit, plaid shirt, a tie that didn’t match at all. He set aside his favourite soft-leather Gucci shoes, and chose more business-like oxfords. When he emerged, he tossed his Guccis into his carry-on bag.

Jenna laughed as she looked up at the transformed man standing before her. “All you need now is a pair of black, thick-rimmed glasses, and no one would ever know you!”

“Wait a minute!” Robert dove into his closet once more, and began rummaging around through some drawers. “Got em!” Again, he emerged from the closet a changed man. This time, he indeed had a pair of glasses with a heavy frame. “Got these for a silly costume thing Chris and I did ages ago. I knew they had to be in here somewhere.”

Jenna looked appraisingly at “Richard Carter,” the U of A’s new Research Assistant. She walked all around him, as he took an air of erudite smugness.

“Yes! Yes, I think this will work! I’ve seen plenty of people around campus dressed just like this. Love that smug look you have too. Perfect!” For the first time, she truly felt her quest would come to a fruitful end. This man could make it happen! With courage and confidence filling her, she now stood tall and strong. *Yes, we will succeed*, she thought. Carver would have his hands full with this pair of opponents.

"OK, *h*-hour is here. Time to get things moving. Jenna, Carmen, you both know what to do—right?" They both nodded quietly. "Then off I go, into the lion's den."

Jenna moved close, and put her hands gently on his shoulders, and pressed her lips softly on his. "For good luck, RJ. Come back to me in one piece."

Carmen stood by, and looked away. She knew when not to make her presence known. It was obvious to Carmen that whatever was going on, there was much danger involved, and she was struggling with nerves of her own. This was her employer of more than 20 years, and never had she feared for his safety before. After a few moments, with Robert and Jenna still in a locked gaze, she spoke. "Sí, señor, come back safely. Now, señora, there is much to do while señor Robert is away."

If ever there was a signal—that was it!

Robert turned away, and walked out of the bedroom, down the stairs, and out the front door. He was surprised to find his SUV still sitting there. Of course, with the events of the previous day, and today, he never moved it to the garage. Out of curiosity, he opened the back tailgate. He chuckled as he saw the grocery boxes sitting there, stacked just as he had left them. He wondered if anyone had gone for groceries yet. In a quick motion, he took the boxes out of the SUV, and put them down on the front porch of the house. For an organized man bordering on OCD, this was unheard of for Robert. *Amazing how a chance meeting can affect a man*, he thought.

During their lunch discussions, Robert decided to use the Budget car rental centre because it was farthest from the hotel. He climbed into his powerful Toyota, and started it. Even the SUV knew something was up. He was sure the engine roared with more gusto than usual. Every muscle was strained now—ready for action.

He roared away, kicking up stones in the process, down the lane to the road. Jenna and Carmen stood at the window watching him drive away with obvious intent. When Robert disappeared from sight, they turned, looking at one another.

"All will be well, señora. Señor Robert is strong, and has the heart of a lion," Carmen offered, as much to console herself as Jenna. They returned to the task of picking out clothes, and packing.

Robert turned down the dirt road towards the highway. The adrenaline was pumping something fierce. He realized he was speeding, and forced himself to slow down. He had the plan all laid out in his mind, and was confident it would work. He began to focus on what was going on around him. He checked his mirrors many times to make sure no one appeared to be following, and no oncoming vehicles were making a U-turn to come around behind him. So far, so good. Everything was normal.

As he arrived in Airdrie, he stayed on the 567 until he passed Highway 2, then turned south to get to Budget Car Rental. He parked his SUV about 100 metres from the agency. He hadn't made a reservation, but knew they would have something available. For a moment or two, he sat in his vehicle thinking of Jenna, and the past 24 hours. He shook his head, realizing that she definitely hadn't had a chance to fully recuperate from the pummelling she suffered at the hands of Carver's goons. The thought of her beating burned on his face.

Robert took a deep breath, exited his SUV, and walked casually, but with purpose, to the car rental agency. At the counter, he asked for a compact car, nothing special, just something to get around in. They offered him a Hyundai Elantra. He accepted the offering, and proffered his I.D. for the rental. Because he had no other official I.D., he had to rent it in his own name. He wasn't too worried about that. Some 20 minutes later, he was driving out with his low-key vehicle.

Not having seen anything suspicious, he drove directly to the Super 8. Luck was on his side, and there was a parking space almost directly opposite the motel entrance. He stood there, fussing a bit with the glasses he was now wearing, looking through them and giving them a quick wipe with his tie. He made no effort to surreptitiously scan the parking area. In fact, he was turned away from the largest part of the lot. Finally, he began to walk with mock pomp to the front entrance.

In a late-model Ford Fusion, parked some way off in the parking lot, a man and a woman watched him closely through the telephoto lens of a camera, and a pair of binoculars. By the time he finished with his glasses, they decided he was nothing special, and returned to the conversation they were having about Jenna, and how their boss was furious she had managed to get away from their team. In fact, he was in an absolutely foul humour, and ripped them apart on the phone. They had all left the building they used for the interrogation, thinking she was still too drugged and weak to do anything. When they returned a couple of hours later, they found her gone—without a trace. They had driven up and down the road in three different vehicles, checking the ditches for any sign of her. Nothing! She simply vanished into thin air! Now, the only thing they could do was to stakeout the motel, in hopes she would return. She didn't have the directions to the Emerald Tablet on her person, and they had checked her hotel room thoroughly without success.

Robert, a.k.a Richard Carter, entered the lobby area, and moved casually to the front desk.

"Oh, hi. My name is Richard Carter." He handed his card to the clerk. "My associate Ms. Carpenter called earlier to have some items of hers held for pickup."

The clerk looked at the card and then at Robert. "Ah, old card, new glasses." He removed the glasses so she could get a good look.

Without any further hesitation, the clerk turned around, picked up a large manila envelope from the counter behind her, and handed it to him with a smile.

"Ms. Carpenter asked me to make sure her room will be available until next Monday."

The clerk checked the registration. "Yes sir, that's correct. Housekeeping staff said her room hasn't been slept in the last couple of nights." She looked at him closely.

"That happens quite often in our line of work. We get rather caught up with artifacts, and accuracy of dating. These little get-togethers can go on for days. This time, I got lucky, and she was dragged into a big mess."

The clerk seemed satisfied at his answer, seeing he was a Research Assistant with the Department of Archaeology. "Thank you, sir."

Just to cover his movements, Robert asked, "Can you tell me at which end of the corridor I'll find her room—207, I believe. She asked me to get a couple of other things at the last minute."

"Of course, sir. If you take the elevator, turn left when you get off. It's about half way down the corridor."

"Thank you very much."

Robert now walked with purpose to the elevator. It was available right away, so he simply walked in. As the doors closed, he took a deep breath. *So far, so good,* he thought. He made no show of looking for a security camera. He'd already seen it in the reflection of the mirror panel at the back of the elevator.

A moment later, Robert found himself walking down the corridor towards Jenna's room. He spotted the table with the vase, where she had hidden the map. There were two housekeeping carts in the corridor—obviously, a tag team of cleaners. *This might get rather dicey*, he said to himself. They were at the farther end of the corridor, and he hoped they wouldn't poke their heads out while he was getting the map. As he walked up to the door of room 207, he pulled the phone out of his shirt pocket. As he did, one of the cleaners exited the room she was cleaning to get supplies from the cart.

"Can I help you sir?"

Robert, held up his hand as if to ask her to wait a moment. "Yes, Ms. Carpenter, I'm here now." Standing still now, he pretended to be listening to the person on the other end. "So, you don't want those papers after all?" Another pause. "Sure, I'm heading back right away, then." Another pause. "You're quite welcome."

He turned to the cleaner and said, "I guess not. But thanks for asking." He flashed a genial smile at her, turned, and began walking toward the elevator. He stopped by the table with the vase, and turned to look at it carefully. He picked it up and took it to a window as if to get a better view. As he did so, he felt the taped envelope underneath the vase. While he stood in a way that he wouldn't be noticed, either by the cleaner, or the security camera, he deftly pulled the map off, and stuffed it in his jacket breast pocket.

The cleaner walked up eying him suspiciously. "Sir?"

"Oh, I'm in archaeology." He pulled out another Richard Carter business card and handed it to her. "The motif on this vase is very similar to pre-Columbian pottery found in South America. See here how the pattern repeats, and has a very fine line above and below? It always amazes me how ancient patterns pop up in modern objects. Some things never seem to get old."

The poor woman he was talking to had no idea what he was talking about. Of course, neither did Robert. He counted on a bit of mumbo-jumbo to cover his tracks. He smiled at her, and put the vase carefully back in its place. He walked casually to the elevator to return to the lobby.

The desk clerk gave him a smile as he left the building. Carver's thugs watched him leave, but had no particular interest in him. Robert got back into his rented Hyundai, and drove off.

Instead of turning north, directly back to Budget, he turned south, driving at normal speed down the road. He watched carefully in the mirrors to see if anyone followed him from the motel, or pulled in behind him. The street was fairly busy, but he noticed nothing out of the ordinary. Having watched lots of spy movies, he knew to drive around in a circle to see if the same car would be following. He did this a few times, and decided all was clear. Finally, he took a different route to the car rental agency, so as not to pass by the Super 8 again.

The agent at Budget was a bit surprised the vehicle was being returned so soon. Robert explained he had an errand to run that needed a vehicle, and he no longer needed it. Since he looked a bit nerdy, the clerk just shrugged his shoulders, and processed the return. Robert then walked casually back the way he came until he reached his SUV. He didn't stop though. He walked right past it, giving it a quick look to see if it had been tampered with. He stopped ten metres past his vehicle, pulled out his smartphone, and snapped a picture. He turned, and satisfied nothing was out of place, climbed into his Toyota.

He drove south at first, and made a wide circuit of Airdrie. He kept a sharp lookout for anyone who might be following. Again, everything was clear. "Phone home," he spoke to the unseen woman who was the voice of his SUV. His phone automatically connected to the voice-activated Bluetooth system when he entered. He heard the phone ring. Carmen picked up instantly. She and Jenna must have been sitting by the phone waiting to hear from him.

"Hello, Jackson residence."

"Put me on speaker please, Carmen."

"We're here, RJ. Is everything alright?" Robert could hear the strain in her voice.

"So far, so good. I have your travel documents, *and the map*. I don't know if anyone was watching the motel, but I imagine they were. I'm hoping I gave a stellar performance as Richard Carter, and no one took much notice of me. I did a bit of driving around town to see if anyone is following, but nothing—thank goodness!"

Both Carmen and Jenna let out an audible sigh of relief. "Are you on your way back then?"

"Yes, I'm heading down the 567 now, and there's hardly a car in sight. I'll be keeping my eyes open, especially on the stretch of road where I found you, to make sure there's nothing suspicious. Should be there in 20 minutes or so."

"That's wonderful to hear, RJ. We've been worried sick."

"With a bit of luck, we'll have time to plan our next move carefully. We have to be canny, and not do the expected."

"We're all ready at this end. Everything is packed. Carmen is an absolute gem. She had me sorted out in no time at all."

"That's my Carmen!"

True to his word, Robert drove down his lane about 20 minutes later. He wondered if he should leave the big SUV in front of the house, ready for a quick getaway, or if he should put it out of sight in the garage. Since there shouldn't be anything perishable in the suitcases or carry-ons, he decided the best course of action would be to put all the luggage in the SUV, and back it into the garage.

He pulled up at the front door. Jenna and Carmen came out quickly to greet him. Jenna unabashedly threw her arms around his neck, kissed him, and held him tight. "I don't think I've been so worried about anything, or anyone, in my life!"

Robert, put his arms around her, and held her tight. This felt good, way too good, he thought. Carmen just stood a bit away from them. Robert could see the deep worry lines on her face. He gently and politely let go of Jenna, and took a step to Carmen, and gave her a big hug. There was no embarrassment on either side.

"What next?"

"We put all the luggage into the SUV, and I'll park it in the garage. Then, we'll watch the security cameras at the front of the house to see if there are any suspicious vehicles lurking around. If there's nothing, we should be able to stay here for another day or so before leaving. It would be good to have a clear idea of where we need to go next."

Before a word more was said, Carmen began hauling out the suitcases. As Robert took them from her, and placed them in the SUV, he thought to himself they certainly weren't travelling light. Then again, travelling with lots of luggage might be good for their cover as tourists. With the SUV packed, Robert quickly backed it into the garage, and closed the door.

Back in the house, he and Jenna headed for his study, where they could watch the comings and goings along the front of his property. Motion alarms around the estate would sound if anyone dared to cross the fence and wander about.

Chapter 8 - A Flash of Green

Dr. Ambrose Scott, the greying head of the archaeological dig site Tel Al Hajiwa, near Aqaba, Jordan, sat in his tent, starring in awe at the strange artifact laying on the table before him. He ran his fingers lightly, almost reverently, over the surface, feeling each symbol of the raised inscriptions that covered both the front and back of the artifact. Except for the movement of his right hand, he sat quite still and totally silent in the half-light offered by a single glowing bulb over the table. He had twisted the other bulbs out of their sockets to keep the light low. This was one artifact he did not want to call attention to. In his mind, he played back the events that led to this artifact greeting the light of day once again.

Tel Al Hajiwa was not large, as archaeological sites go. The mound was only about 100 metres square and stood about 6 metres above ground. It's a wonder it hadn't been surveyed and examined long ago. It was considered to be a site of little importance in the grand scheme of things in the Middle East. Most of the major, news-making sites had been, or were now being, excavated. Small sites like this one were parcelled out to universities around the world. It was more by luck of the draw that Dr. Scott found himself heading up this dig. The Department of Antiquities of Jordan (DAJ) contacted the University of Alberta to offer them the new site they named Tel Al Hajiwa. They worked with the U of A before, and were very satisfied with the results. Dr. Bart asked Dr. Scott to head up the project. Neither expected to find anything significant at the site, but felt another good cooperative effort between the university and the DAJ couldn't hurt. The DAJ felt the same way, and offered a generous license to the U of A, allowing them to transport approved artifacts back to Canada for study, and eventual return to Jordan.

"Oh well, it'll give me a chance to get out into the field again," Scott told Dr. Bart.

Scott was a digger, and felt himself going stir crazy in his campus office, examining artifacts, preparing for lectures, and correcting papers. He hated working with students who seemed not to care, and asked the most ridiculous questions, just to get a reaction from the others. This was a chance to slip into his khakis, and feel the hot desert sun on his face again.

He arrived in Amman with three research assistants in tow. All three were post-graduate students working towards their PhD. He was glad to have them. They could do the grunt work, leaving him to survey, and choose the best locations to dig first. With a small site like this, he expected to have the complete top uncovered in a few months. With such mounds, the chances of finding anything more than the odd potsherd, and a lot of petrified sheep poop, where slim to none for the first 30 centimetres or so.

The DAJ would be their first stop. They would meet with antiquities officials, and receive all the necessary permits and licenses. This was never a short meeting. In fact, with all the formalities and traditional protocols, it could take days. And so it was, with Tel Al Hajiwa!

Once all the paperwork was in order, Scott could now turn his attention to obtaining equipment and supplies. The DAJ had given them a list of reputable dealers they could count on to get decent quality goods. They would need tents, electrical generators with a large fuel tank, a water cistern since there was no water at the site, folding tables, shelving, cupboards, mobile kitchen that used propane appliances, electrical wire, posts, shovels, picks, screening, lumber, and on, and on. Some of the materials could be had locally in Aqaba, but most of the big stuff would need to be transported from Amman to the site. Scott's fluency in Arabic, Hebrew, Greek, and few other languages made it much easier than trying to work through translators. But they did hire a good translator to work at the site, to allow the research assistants to communicate with the diggers, as they were limited to some Greek and Hebrew.

Almost two weeks after their arrival, the little band of U of A archaeologists along with several large trucks arrived at Tel Al Hajiwa—a bump in the middle of nowhere some 20 kms from

Aqaba. Scott had the trucks stand off until he could take a quick drive around the mound to decide on the most suitable location for the camp. He finally settled on a spot on the west side, and radioed the trucks to move toward his location. He was glad the sand was quite well packed in most places, which allowed the trucks, in particular, to move safely and easily to the camp site.

He drew a plan of how the camp was to be laid out, and left his senior research assistant, Meadows, and his colleague, Madison, in charge of unloading and starting the setup. He and Michaud, the third assistant, went to Aqaba to arrange for food supplies, as well as smaller equipment. (He was always amazed at how he ended up with three research assistants whose names all had the same first letter: *M*! He often referred to them as "the Three Musketeers.")

Scott had never been to Aqaba before. The DAJ provided him with letters of introduction, and the names of contacts he could use to obtain whatever he needed. Although it had been a while since there was any serious dig work around Aqaba, hiring a team of diggers was easy. Many men were glad for the opportunity to get away from wives and bratty children to earn a decent wage. The women too were happy. There is nothing more surly than a man who is idle because he can't find work! Once wages and work rotations were nailed down, Scott found himself with about 40 men ready to dig. It was unusual for women to work for pay, but in the present circumstances, no one made a fuss when Scott hired six middle-aged widows to work as cooks.

Back at the site, Scott was amazed at what had been accomplished. Meadows and Madison, with the help of the translator, Mr. Ahmed, had mustered the team of workers that accompanied the equipment. With great efficiency, they paced out all the camp and equipment locations. They started with the most important—the cistern, and the electric generators. Scott was impressed. He hoped they would be as good with the digging.

Before the sun set, the camp was in full swing. Water had been trucked from Aqaba and the cistern was now ¼ full. The main electric generator was purring away, and long extension cords snaked their way to the four U of A staff tents, and the kitchen tent. The kitchen was completely setup and his six new cooks began to make a simple meal for everyone. Scott smiled to himself and thought, *I love it when a plan comes together!*

It wasn't long before the diggers removed the top 30 cm across most of the top of the Tel. A surprising number of potsherds were found that seemed to predate the usual finds in Jordan. They were all meticulously catalogued, and placed in groupings according to colour and pattern. The site could sometimes get quite windy, and given this was a mound, it might explain why there was so little loose sand at the top.

Scott busied himself during the day wandering around the site, talking to the diggers, examining artifacts they carefully pulled up from the earth. As he did so, he decided there were three areas that might yield something significant, and organized some deeper trench excavations at those locations.

His nose didn't let him down. Before long, diggers were pulling out some beautifully carved artifacts that were distinctive, like no other found in the area. Again, these seemed to predate anything else found in Jordan. He began to wonder if he had stumbled upon a significant site. For now, he would just continue to dig, sort, and catalogue the artifacts as they were discovered, and keep a low profile.

It was his habit, at the end of the day, to climb into one of the deeper pits, and scratch away gently to see if he could find a little gem of his own. Most of the time, his only reward was dirt. The odd time, he would come across something nice. He was careful to record it in his notebook, take a picture in-situ, and return to camp. It was on the last of these little explorations that he found what was now sitting in front of him.

He climbed down into pit 14A. With his small trowel, he began to scrape away some dirt in a spot he chose quite at random. After a few minutes of careful scraping, the metal blade hit on something. He smiled, and felt the usual excitement of making a find. He kept scraping carefully. Finally, the corner of what appeared to be a somewhat large object appeared. It glinted green as he wiped the dirt away. He shined his little flashlight on it for a better look. Emerald? Quartz? Now his curiosity had been piqued. He continued to carefully scrape away the dirt on either side, top and bottom of the artifact. He peered into the large cavity he cleared. The flashlight revealed it was still much larger. He wondered if he should wait until morning to uncover his treasure. The adrenaline was pumping, and his heart was racing at the thought of making a significant find—and this one would be *his*!

With his flashlight firmly clenched between his teeth, Scott continued to scrape away all around this artifact. He didn't want to disturb it too much in case he might damage something else. The dirt yielded easily, and he was careful not to scratch against the shiny green surface. His mind was racing, wondering what it might be. When he thought he had gone deep enough, he gently used his two hands to wiggle out this unexpected find. *Oh, please don't break!* he prayed earnestly. Finally, it came free. He found himself looking at what was obviously a stone or quartz tablet of some sort with raised markings. He knelt in the bottom of the pit, carefully removing the remaining dirt with a little brush.

The light reflected brightly off the tablet. It was utterly beautiful. It was a bit larger than a letter-size piece of paper, and about 2 cm thick. There were raised markings on both sides, and the edges were smooth. He didn't recognize the markings at all. They looked different from anything he'd seen in his career. He knew instinctively his little treasure was a treasure indeed. He took off his shirt and wrapped the tablet in it. He carefully documented exactly where he found the artifact. He knew he should place it in the cavity he had carved out, and take an in-situ photograph, but he didn't want to risk scratching or breaking the tablet. Although it seemed quite sturdy, he worried that it might break into pieces at any moment.

Against all his instincts as an archaeologist, he climbed out of pit 14A with the artifact carefully tucked under his left arm, still wrapped in his shirt. He had been there longer than he thought. There were no workmen in sight anywhere—probably at supper. He nonchalantly crossed the top of the Tel, and made his way to his private tent. He didn't want to arouse suspicion, so he unwrapped the tablet, and hid it in plain sight, laying on a cupboard shelf with some papers strewn on top. He donned his shirt, and made his way to the mess tent.

The food smelled good, and he was ravenously hungry. He sat down with his colleagues.

"No treasure to show us tonight, doctor?" asked Meadows, with a smile. "You're later than usual."

"Thought I had something, and got all excited. Kept scraping away, and it looked immense. In the end, just a rock! That was disappointing!"

"Did a nice job on your shirt, though," piped in Michaud.

Scott chuckled. "OK, don't rub it in! I see we had a good haul today, though. Looks like you all did well, especially in the pits."

"Yes, we catalogued over 150 great pieces today from all over the site," announced Meadows. "Madison, here, gets the prize for today—an almost intact vase. Doesn't look like it was for storage, more decorative, and the lip is quite different. Think it might have been ceremonial."

"Excellent! I'll be wanting to take a close look at that tomorrow. What are your thoughts, Madison?"

Madison considered for a moment. "Why is it that whenever something ornate is found, it's almost always considered to be ceremonial? Why wouldn't the folks living here just want a nice vase to put something decorative in? There might have been a lot of nice flowers here in their day. Flower vase."

Scott looked at him with a big, broad smile, and nodded. "You're absolutely right, Madison. We archaeologists tend to jump to conclusions because it happens to suit us better that something be ceremonial rather than simply decorative. It's a lot more interesting to report finding a ceremonial bowl rather than a simple wash basin, don't you think?"

The four burst out laughing at the absolute truthfulness of what Scott just said. They lingered there for some time after eating, discussing finds of the day, and the possibility of opening-up another deep pit in the southwest corner of the site. Michaud had noticed a veritable trove of objects being unearthed in an area about 7 metres square, and thought it might yield even more if they started going straight down. They discussed the possibilities, and how they would rearrange the workers. In the end, Michaud got the green light to dig his pit. They all toasted to a new pit, and more interesting finds.

It was getting late. The jovial group broke up, and everyone headed to their private tents—including Scott. When he entered, he unscrewed some light bulbs leaving only one over his desk/table. This was commonly done to save power. And this is where he sat now, in wonder and awe, caressing his gleaming, green treasure.

When he finally came out of his reverie, Scott had no idea how long he'd been sitting there, stroking his prize find. He quietly collected his thoughts. The clear-thinking and methodical man who was Ambrose Scott had returned.

He looked hard at the tablet on the table in front of him. He examined it closely now. The inscriptions were definitely not decorative in nature. No, this was a form of written language. It was different from anything he'd seen in his career. From the shape of the characters, it appeared to be written right to left, and top to bottom. The close proximity of the characters gave him the impression the information density was quite high—there was a lot written on this fairly small tablet. He couldn't really tell which side was front, where the writing started, and which was back, where the writing ended. Lines on both sides completely filled the surface of the tablet and were all full width, with no obvious paragraph endings—assuming this language had paragraphs, of course. It was as though the entire tablet was one big long sentence, but he had no way of knowing.

He walked to his cupboard, took out some thin velum, and a cylindrical piece of soft charcoal. He cut a piece that would span both sides of the tablet, taped one end over the visible side of the tablet, and began to gently rub the surface while pressing it down. With the raised inscription, it was a quick and easy job to make a very clear rubbing of the writing on the surface He repeated the process on the other side. There was now a complete record of what was written on the tablet. He carefully folded the rubbings and placed them among other rubbings done at the site. He would quickly recognize them again, but others might miss them completely. By putting them with the other rubbings, he knew they would make their way either to the U of A or the DAJ, if anything happened to him. In either case, they would probably be put in a box placed in storage for many years, before someone would dig them out for closer examination.

He returned to his table. Gently, he picked up the tablet, and held it up to the light. This was not opaque stone. The light shone through the tablet, showing it was translucent. He examined it carefully. He could see streaks inside the material, but nothing that would give an indication there were some kind of key markings needed to decipher the inscription. Not being a gemologist, he couldn't tell if this was a type of quartz, or if it was real emerald. Either way, he knew he was probably holding an artifact of great historical and financial value. This was an artifact that would be the envy and desire of every museum and private collector on the planet. He didn't mind if museums vied for the privilege of displaying the tablet in their collections. It would be an incredible draw no matter where it was.

No, it was the private collectors he worried about most. Some would stop at nothing to obtain this prize. There were a handful who would covet this object greatly: Carver, Mikkelsen, de Santos, Calbarri, Botha. Of all of them, he knew that Carver would be the one to fear most. Many have lost their careers, their health, and even their lives trying to stand in his way. He was also the most well connected. He had to find a way to protect the tablet.

Well, I can't just bury it again, Scott thought. *Or can I?*

Slowly, a plan was beginning to take shape in his mind. Scott was a very clever man. He nodded gently, and then smiled to himself—a scavenger hunt. Of course! He would know where the tablet was hidden, but no one else could know. He had to take it away from the site as quickly as possible. Since no one knew he dug it up, it gave him some time and flexibility in terms of getting it out.

As a good and honest archaeologist, Scott knew he had to report his find to the proper authorities, in this case, Dr. Bart, at the U of A, and Dr. Shareef El-Amin, at the DAJ. When it came to Carver, and the others, he knew he could trust no one. Once his report was filed and read, it would get to Carver and the others within days, if not hours! All these collectors paid handsomely for information about new finds. They would pay huge sums to appropriate authorities to have artifacts redirected to them. He would have to disappear as soon as the report was sent.

A scavenger hunt! Yes, that's what it would be. He would have intrepid seekers travel far away from the tablet before bringing them back to its hiding place. It was time for Dr. Scott to go on a little journey. He knew he would have to keep a very low profile while travelling. It would be overland, as much as possible with air travel only when necessary, and then to unexpected destinations. It would be tricky, but he could do it.

For each location, he would have to come up with some kind of riddle pointing to the next location. If the riddle was not correctly interpreted, it would lead the seeker to a dead end. It would take the right kind of person to sort out his little clues. The rubbings were safe enough. He was satisfied with that. It would be the initial starting point he would have to conceal cleverly so it *could* be found—but not *likely* to be found. He had plenty of time to think of how he would accomplish that while he was travelling. What he had to decide now was where it would all begin.

The biggest problem wouldn't be getting the tablet out of Jordan. He was confident that could be accomplished easily. It was getting it into Egypt—the nearest Arab country—that would be the biggest difficulty. He had already decided it would be hidden in Egypt. Scott considered this dilemma carefully. His mind was racing through various alternatives. As always, in the end, the most straightforward plan would be the best. He was well aware that plaster casts of artifacts were often carried around from one country to another for close examination by experts.

He put the tablet in its hiding place again, then took a little stroll to the work tents. He entered one, turned on the lights, grabbed a bucket, some plaster, some gauze, a pair of scissors, and a stir stick. He filled a second bucket with water. He casually made his way back to his tent. He met a couple of workers on the way, and exchanged pleasantries. No one took any notice of what he was doing, simply because it was a common occurrence.

Back in his tent again, Scott mixed some plaster, and soaked the gauze strips. He put some newspaper on the table, and placed the tablet on it. Methodically, he began to wrap the stone in plaster soaked gauze. He pressed it all firmly in place in a thin layer. He wanted the inscription to be as visible as possible to make it look like a plaster impression. He smoothed out the plaster as best he could. The plaster dried quickly because of the heat and dryness of the location. It took about an hour to get it just the way he wanted. When it was all done, he was quite pleased with his handiwork.

He took the leftover plaster, and other materials to the work tent. There, he put everything back, and cleaned out the plaster bucket. No one around this time as he made his way back to his tent.

Scott moved about his tent, quietly and casually. He didn't want the shadow cast by his wanderings to call any attention as being out of the ordinary. He pulled out a suitcase and packed some clothes, his usual notebook, his iPad (which he now plugged in to bring to full charge), and a few miscellaneous items. There must be nothing to raise suspicion. He carefully wrapped the green tablet in thick cloth, and tied it all together with some sturdy nylon string. He would bring with him a few sample potsherds to explain that he was travelling to Egypt to compare with some samples in the museum in Cairo—a common occurrence that would keep the Egyptian border authorities satisfied.

Once everything was ready, Scott stripped to his shorts, grabbed a fresh pair, and headed to the communal shower tent. The female staff lived in a separate area of the camp, so he wouldn't be offending anyone while roaming around in his underwear. He took a nice hot shower with a cool rinse. He grabbed a towel off the top of the pile to dry off. As he did, Meadows entered the tent.

"Getting ready to call it a day, boss?"

"For some reason, it's been a long, hot day." In the spur of the moment, he added, "Oh, by the way, I may have to go into Amman to meet with Dr. El-Amin, and his cronies of the DAJ tomorrow. That find of Madison's will raise a few eyebrows. Don't be surprised if I end up being away for a while. These things can go on forever down here. They'll argue, bring out a ton of previously unearthed artifacts to compare to Madison's find, before they rule it to be something special."

"What do you think doctor? Is this stuff really so different from anything else?"

"So far, I've seen nothing like it. I've checked some online catalogues for any similarity to anything found in Jordan, and other places in the Middle East, but nothing. I think we've stumbled onto a unique site. Whatever this place was, it was different from anything else. I get the impression this place is a lot older than other sites in the region. That's what I'll be presenting to El-Amin. It may change the entire complexion of the dig. May change our licenses too. I just hope they don't decide to kick us off the site to take it over themselves, or worse still, bring in some hotshots from the States."

"Maybe we should just keep it quiet, sir."

"We could, Meadows, but we wouldn't be doing our job. The U of A has a good reputation for honesty and integrity here, and we don't want to destroy our relationship with the DAJ, or the proverbial shit will really hit the fan. And you can kiss your PhD goodbye in the process!"

"Damned if you do, damned if you don't!"

Scott laughed. "Welcome to the wonderful world of archaeology, my boy. I'll be calling El-Amin in the morning. If he gets all excited, I'll be out of here very quickly. So, don't be surprised if you see me tearing away like a bat out of hell. By the way, you don't have any problem taking over while I'm gone, do you?"

"No problem at all, sir. I'll keep things running smoothly. I'm sure Mr. Ahmed will get my instructions across to everyone. It's sure great to have him around!"

"Great! Then I'll bid you a good night. I'll want to get together with you, Madison and Michaud, first thing tomorrow. I'll need to put together a report of our findings here, and send it off before I leave."

"I'll let the others know, sir. What time?"

"Breakfast at 6 a.m., so let's say we talk about it then. Shouldn't take more than an hour."

Scott then strode out in fresh underwear back to his tent. *Yes*, he thought as he lay in bed, *This will work*.

Chapter 9 - Welcome to Taba

Ambrose Scott awoke with a start. It was still dark. He reached for his trusty Timex Indiglo watch and pressed the crown to display the time. It was 5:17 a.m. It would be more than an hour until sunrise. He breathed a deep sigh; he felt well rested, and surprisingly very alert. His jaw was set; his eyes fixed ahead at nothing in the darkness. His mind was meticulously going through every detail of his plan to safeguard the tablet he unearthed less than 12 hours earlier.

He swung his legs over the cot bed, and switched on the reading lamp on the table beside him. He could glimpse his packed suitcase in the shadows just beyond the pool of light. He got up and moved swiftly now. He pulled the string that lit the main tent lights. Reaching up, he screwed in the bulbs he twisted out the previous night. He placed the iPad and charger in his briefcase. He would need these. He went to the wash basin, splashed some water on his face, and rubbed some through his short greying hair. Looking in the mirror, he quickly shaved with an electric shaver. When finished, he tapped it gently to clean it. This too, he threw into his briefcase. *Got to make it look good*, he thought.

He pulled on a pair of casual dress pants, plain shirt, dress shoes. This would pass muster for a man preparing for a trip to the big city for a business meeting. He walked from one pool of electric light to the next on his way to the research and cataloguing area. The camp was buzzing with activity. The mess tent was already brightly lit. The ladies would be preparing breakfast, which was served from around 6 a.m. until 7:30 a.m. Workers would be on the dig site as soon as the sun was up, while it was still cool. In the research tent, he turned on the lights, then moved to shelves filled with binders. He picked out two containing photos and descriptions of the artifacts found the previous day. With these under his arm, he made his way directly to the mess tent. It was now 5:40 a.m.

Scott sat down at the usual U of A researcher table. He opened the binders on the table in front of him. He wanted to glance at the information before the "Three Musketeers" arrived. As he perused the pages, he was still in awe of the artifacts recovered at this site. Like nothing else. He was rather surprised that the DAJ had not reacted with more curiosity at the reports being sent to them regularly. Obviously, potsherds just didn't pique their interest much. Since there were no visiting strangers to Tel Al Hajiwa, he assumed the private collectors weren't interested either.

He shook his head with a wry smile, thinking, *That'll all change in a hurry, when today's report is sent out.*

The "Three Musketeers" entered the tent in unison, and sat down at the table. They weren't surprised to find Scott there already, intently looking through the binders. They waited patiently for him to acknowledge them before anyone spoke. Finally, he looked up, glancing at each in turn.

"Good morning, gentlemen," he greeted them with a broad smile.

"Good morning, sir," they replied in unison.

Scott placed his hands on the binders. "This will definitely stir things up a bit. Maybe an abundance of unique potsherds hasn't excited them much, but Madison's find will blow their minds—an almost intact vase."

Madison felt a surge of pride. Scott knew the other two would be just a bit envious.

"Shall we grab some grub before we get down to business?" Scott asked rhetorically.

They all got up and made their way towards the food trays, where they took their place in line. The workers were filing in quickly now. They each picked up a plate on which they heaped a good portion of eggs, beef bacon, hash-browns, toast, and poured themselves a large cup of fresh coffee. All the comforts of home!

Back at the table, they munched away at their food. There was some idle chatter while they ate. When they finished, they stacked their dirty plates on the end of the table. Mr. Ahmed quickly picked them up, and took them away. He knew this would be a high-level discussion amongst the top men of the dig, and wanted to make sure they didn't end up pushing the plates onto the floor, as happened before at these early-morning meetings.

After about 45 minutes of intense discussion and debate about Madison's vase, and how it compared in pattern and material to what they had already unearthed, they all settled back. They reached a consensus—very important in any branch of science. They all agreed the vase was definitely of the same quality and origin as all the pieces they already found. In fact, it confirmed that all the pieces were of the exact same make and manufacture. Whatever this place was in the past, there was no deviation in pattern, material, and general styling in earthenware. Even the metal pieces they uncovered bore the same overall design. In any normal settlement, there is always variation, but not here. This was not a normal place. In fact, they had no clear idea of the period when this location was settled. They all laughed when Meadows suggested it was a ceremonial site, remembering their conversation the previous evening about the vase. Scott couldn't help thinking about his secret find. Was this indeed a special place?

"Well, here we are, then," Scott said. "We have something special here. Was it ceremonial? A place of worship? Could this be the residence for priesthood, male or female? Was it a royal residence? So far, the artifacts only conjure up more questions, and no answers at all."

"Doctor, do you think we'll be able to answer some of those questions as we dig deeper?" asked Michaud.

"It would be nice to think so. But my gut's telling me this is a one-use site populated during a very brief time span—a few years or decades. I haven't seen anything yet to suggest this site was in use over an extended period."

"Why is that, sir?" chimed in Madison.

Scott carefully considered his response. "If you look at all the artifacts we've uncovered so far—all of them—there is no variation whatever in design. None. In any settlement, there is always change over time, whether it comes from within, or through trade with neighbouring settlements. And even when we look at royal or priestly residences that have a known history, there is always change, even if the general pattern is very similar, there is *always* change. It could be a new group in ascendancy, new materials, new ideas, experimentation, and many other factors. But there is always change. This is the first site I've seen where, so far, we've found absolutely no change. The artifacts from the higher strata have exactly the same design as those from the lower strata. I believe, as we dig deeper, we'll quickly run out of artifacts, and signs of settlement."

The others listened intently to Dr. Scott's little dissertation. They sat there quietly mulling over what he just said.

Madison was the first to speak. "So, maybe it's more than just a flower vase!"

They all looked at Madison, and burst out laughing.

"So, it really looks like we found something after all," commented Meadows.

"All the more reason to make sure we're very careful about what we do, and how we do it. There can be no question about the integrity of the site and the cataloguing of all artifacts. (A pang of guilt ran through him as he thought of the tablet.) I'm going to make a copy of some of these pages for my report. I'll be calling Dr. El-Amin as soon as my report is finished, and I've sent it off to Dr. Bart and the DAJ. This will get the wind up in Amman. I've asked Meadows to take charge while I'm away. Don't know how long I'll be."

With that, Scott stood up, grabbed the binders, and headed for the research tent. He scanned several pages to attach to his report. Back in his tent, he sat down at his laptop, and composed a very carefully-crafted report. He included a casual mention of the green translucent tablet he found, but did not include any photos, since he hadn't taken any. This was the moment he dreaded. He sent the report with attached documentation. It would be late in Alberta, and he didn't expect Dr. Bart would see this for another 10 to 12 hours. It was the DAJ he was worried about. They would be looking at it in the next few hours. It was 8 a.m. He picked up the satellite phone, and called Dr. El-Amin.

Dr. Shareef El-Amin was already at his desk. He picked up his phone, and answered in Arabic. Scott identified himself, and El-Amin greeted him warmly. After a bit of idle chit-chat, Scott got down to business. He told El-Amin that he just sent a report on some new finds at Tel Al Hajiwa. El-Amin listened intently, as Scott gave him the gist of the contents. Scott suggested he come up to Amman to meet with El-Amin in a few days to discuss the contents of the report, and the site in general, with him. This would give the DAJ a chance to read the report, and mull it over before his arrival. El-Amin agreed to the meeting based on what he heard, and the urgency in Scott's voice.

After Scott rang off, he took a deep breath. *This'll give me at least a few days head start. If I play it right, I might be able to stretch this out. The only thing that will mess me up is if they find something else of significance, and they try to contact me at the DAJ.*

He picked up his briefcase and his suitcase. At the door of his tent, he looked around for the staff cars. He spotted one parked nearby. With his luggage in hand, he headed casually to the SUV. Meadows caught his eye, and he gave him a wave. Meadows responded likewise. He placed the luggage gently in the back of the vehicle, climbed in, and drove off in the direction of Aqaba. Since this was a common occurrence, he knew no one would take particular notice of his leaving. Now, it began!

First stop—Aqaba. Although Aqaba was new to Scott, he became good friends with Jamal Hussein, a local supply merchant, thanks to his frequent purchases for the site. When Scott arrived at Hussein's warehouse, Hussein immediately came out to greet him, when he spotted the U of A emblem on the side of the vehicle. Scott got out and they embraced—in a manly fashion. Hussein invited him to his office for a libation—non-alcoholic, ofcourse.

"What brings you into Aqaba today, my friend?"

"I need your help Jamal. I have a few things I need to check out in Cairo, some pottery and a plaster cast, but I'm feeling like a little boat ride across the Gulf to Taba first. I've always wanted to take a look around Taba, and this is a perfect excuse to go there."

"Ah, so you want a little cruise to Taba then. Several choices come to mind, but I would recommend only two. You may take a boat from the marina here in Aqaba, cruise down the coast, and then across to Taba, staying out of the way of Israeli gun boats. Or, you may drive down to the docks further south on the highway and cross by boat from there."

"I suppose you have transport available in both places," laughed Scott.

With a broad grin, Hussein replied, "But of course, my friend. What would my business be without alternate means of transport?"

Scott considered for a moment. Taking a boat from Aqaba meant not leaving the SUV far down the road. His concern was that someone might see him, and report his movements.

"Would the departure from Aqaba be discreet, Jamal?"

"I am the soul of discretion, Dr. Scott. I can assure you that no one will know of your departure, or your destination."

"This little side-trip is totally unofficial, and I'd like to keep it that way."

"Not a problem. When would you like to depart?"

"As soon as arrangements can be made, I suppose."

"It will be a journey of a couple of hours. Something comfortable, or something inconspicuous?"

"Whatever will be most likely to avoid a search by the Israelis."

"Then it is best to use a cargo vessel that makes the run across the Gulf often, and is known to them. With your permission, I will make the arrangements now."

With a nod from Scott, Hussein picked up the phone and made a call. After some quick conversation in Arabic, Hussein rang off. Even with his fluency in Arabic, Scott couldn't follow.

"It is arranged, then. The *Star of Aqaba* will be leaving in about 90 minutes. Until then, you are my guest." For the next hour, they engaged in friendly conversation, with Hussein being quite interested what was being unearthed at the site. Although he trusted, Hussein to a point, Scott was not inclined to give him too much detail, in case he was on the payroll of any of the private collectors, or site robbers.

At the appointed time, Scott and Hussein drove to the docks. Scott retrieved his luggage from the back of the SUV, and asked Hussein to take care of the vehicle for him until his return. He didn't indicate any specific date, but suggested it might be several weeks. Hussein amiably agreed. Scott was introduced to Captain Awad of the *Star of Aqaba*, who turned out to be a second cousin of Hussein's.

Scott assured him he was not carrying any contraband, or illegal items. He opened his briefcase to display some papers, his personal items, a few pieces of wrapped potsherds (with paperwork). Next, he opened his suitcase to reveal clothes, and the mock plaster tablet. The captain was satisfied. He explained the last thing he wanted was to be boarded, and anything illegal found. The Israelis, he said, did not have a sense of humour when it came to searching Arab vessels. He assured Scott that, for the most part, they didn't bother him. He often made the run between Aqaba and Taba, and was well known to them.

Without further delay, the Captain had Scott's luggage taken aboard. He and Scott boarded, and the gangway was retracted. A few minutes later, Scott found himself steaming south along the Jordanian coast in the Gulf of Aqaba. It was much hotter now.

Captain Awad appeared at Scott's elbow, and leaned against the rail. "I never tire of cruising down this coast. To me, there is much beauty here."

"Yes, Captain, I see what you mean. You're a man of the sea then."

"I am that, Dr. Scott, I certainly am that."

Just as suddenly as he appeared, he straightened up and announced, "There are soft drinks and water in the dining room." He motioned to one of the crew, and told him to show Scott to the dining area. This he did immediately.

Scott was glad. He felt parched—partly the heat, and partly nerves. With a large bottled water, he made his way to a shady part of the deck and found a place to sit down. As he watched the coastline drift by, he thought of what would happen when he would pass through customs in Taba. He knew it wasn't a big non-Arab tourist draw. He hoped the customs officers wouldn't be too inquisitive about his plaster tablet. This was the most dangerous part of his plan. Although it was hot, there was a nice cool breeze coming off the Gulf. He closed his eyes, and drifted off into quiet slumber.

He awoke with a start to find Captain Awad standing over him. "We are almost at Taba, doctor."

"Thank you, Captain." Could he really have slept the whole way? He drank a long pull from his water bottle, then poured some into his hands which he rubbed on his face. He could see ahead the Egyptian coast, and a small dock. This was Taba. Before he knew it, his luggage was brought to the gangway, ready to disembark.

Fifteen minutes later, Scott found himself in a small shed where customs and immigration officials were examining his documentation. He declared the artifacts he had with him. They could see from his credentials he was an archaeologist, so his artifacts were no surprise. They quickly scanned the paperwork that accompanied them, were satisfied, and all manner of stamps were applied. He was welcomed into Egypt, with a smile from the officials who appreciated he could speak Arabic. They seemed inclined to chat with him about his dig site, and what they were finding. He took the opportunity to find out where he could rent a vehicle, and get a room for the night. He was directed to a small hotel nearby. There were other larger, modern hotels if he preferred. He could rent a vehicle at the local hotel.

With that, Scott grabbed the handle of his suitcase, picked up his briefcase and headed out the door. The heat was stifling! The small local hotel was only about 50 metres away. He strode quickly to get out of the sun. As he walked in, the young woman at the desk looked at him curiously. In Arabic, he asked for a room for the night, and to rent a vehicle. The desk clerk was even more surprised to hear him speak excellent Arabic. Scott understood, and handed her his U of A business card in Arabic. She smiled and understood. She pulled out the necessary forms, and got to work.

"Do you want the room for only one night, sir?"

"Tonight, for certain, and perhaps tomorrow."

She nodded, wrote on the registration form, then asked for his passport, which was customary.

Picking out a room key, she handed it to him. "Our best room, doctor, number 14, upstairs."

"What type of vehicle are you needing, sir?"

"A 4-wheel drive suitable for a quick run into the dessert."

"That is not a problem. How long will you be wanting it?"

"Is it possible to rent it one-way? I'm planning to drive to Cairo afterwards."

"It is possible, sir, but there will be a one-way charge."

Scott nodded his ascent. "That's fine."

"Do you want the additional insurance as well?"

"Yes, please."

He pulled out his international driver's license, and credit card, which he handed to her. She completed the paperwork. With a flourish, she placed the documents in front of Scott for signature. After swiping his credit card and receiving an authorization, she handed him the keys to a Toyota Land Cruiser. The car was around back, she informed him.

"Oh, and could you please return the vehicle to this garage in Cairo when you are done with it?"

"Of course. Thank you very much for your friendly service."

She beamed a great smile at him. He moved to the stairs, and walked up to the first floor. Number 14 was at the front of the building, offering a nice view of the Gulf. It was mid-afternoon. He turned on ceiling fan, and the air conditioner. He stripped, and took a cool shower. After dressing, he made his way downstairs. He asked the desk clerk if they served food at the hotel. Again, she beamed at him.

"I am Zahra. If you need anything, I am pleased to serve you."

She walked around the counter, leading him through a doorway into a small restaurant. A menu in Arabic was placed before him. He scanned it quickly, and ordered an entrée. Zahra, now the waitress, took his order, advising him it would be a few minutes, then disappeared into the kitchen. Scott chuckled to himself, wondering if she was the cook as well.

As he waited for his food, he spotted some magazines on a small table. He rummaged through them, and found a car magazine in English. He sat down again, and began flipping through the pages. It was about 15 minutes later when Zahra brought out his meal. His mouth was watering. It looked delicious. She stood by him to get his reaction to the food she had prepared. It tasted as good as it looked. She could tell by his face that he was pleased. Her face beamed with pride.

"If there is anything else you would like, please tell me."

Scott thanked her, and dug into his wonderful meal. When finished, he sat back and relaxed. He felt very mellow now. Gone was the tension of earlier. He was in Egypt. Barring something unforeseen, he would be burying the tablet in the morning. Now, he had to think of a riddle, and a place to hide it. He remembered seeing some brochures on the table with the magazines. He went over and sorted through them. He found one describing a popular coral reef diving spot not far away—Pharaoh's Island—on which stood a fortress used by crusaders, and expanded by Saladin. What a wonderful place to hide a cryptic clue!

He wandered back to the lobby. Zahra was all smiles again. He asked if he could hang onto the brochure. She was only too happy to offer it to him. He asked where he might find some paper and an envelope to write a note. With a laugh, she ran off to what was probably an office, returning with several sheets of sand-coloured paper and matching envelopes. He thanked her politely, and made his way back up to his room.

It dawned on him that he would have to know exactly where to send treasure seekers before leaving his clue. He pulled out his iPad. To his surprise, there was Wi-Fi available. He called down to get the password, which was provided quickly and efficiently. He wondered if she was married. *Oh, to be young again!* he sighed. He brought up a map of Egypt and scanned it. Where to? Suez caught his eye, and held it. *Right then, Suez it is. But where?* He began to look for some landmark, or monument, where he could hide the next clue, so it would not be easily found without the clue he would leave here in Taba. After a while, he came upon the War Memorial. *Of course! What better place?* It was permanent, and there would be few people around. He could choose a suitable grave, and place the note carefully under some gravel, or tucked in behind the grave marker. Now, all he needed was to pick a grave. He looked through the names of the fallen. He settled on a Canadian at site 2 E 10. He would craft a clue pointing to that location. After thinking about it for while, he came up with something that should work:

> Where ships through the desert sail, look where heroes rest.
> A+1 B+3 K-1.

It wasn't a very difficult code to crack, but giving the grave location from right-to-left would add some measure of difficulty, so he reversed the numbers and added: See from the east, not from the west.

Surely, he wouldn't write in plain English! No, it had to be something more unconventional. He thought of Arabic, too obvious; Hebrew, again, too obvious; Yiddish, better, but too common. *Ah, I know exactly what to use!* When he finished, he had his note:

> *Kie ŝipoj tra la dezerto velo, rigardi kie herooj ripozi.*
> *K-1 B+3 A+1 Vidi de la oriento, ne de okcidente.*

This he wrote carefully on a sheet of notepaper, and placed it in the envelope. As an afterthought, Scott realized he would need to somehow weatherproof his clue to some extent if it was to last. He casually sauntered back downstairs. The young Zahra was sitting there reading a book, looking rather bored until she looked up to see him.

Scott asked if she might have some plastic wrap, or sealing plastic bag—nothing too big. The young woman smiled brightly, and ran off to the kitchen. A minute later, she returned with a sampler of zipper bags. Scott laughed, and picked one out of the bunch she spread out on the counter. He asked if she might have a few more of the same size. Without hesitation, she was off again, returning with at least a dozen bags. He smiled broadly at her, and thanked her generously, offering her a small tip for her trouble. She blushed, and wasn't sure whether or not to take the money. He insisted, and she finally accepted.

Back in his room, Scott carefully placed the envelope in a zipper bag. These were good sturdy freezer bags, should last for some time, and not be prone to tearing when he hid the clues. Now that he had his first clue settled, and the location of the second, this might be a good time to look for other places to leave clues. He wanted to spread them out as far and wide as he could. He didn't want to make them too obvious either. Then again, he realized he wasn't all that clever when it came to riddles. It would have to do.

After several hours of peering at his iPad, Scott was becoming somewhat bleary-eyed. The time spent was worth it. His journey would take him across Egypt, to Cyprus, Greece, Italy, and France, before returning to Taba. He wondered if he would be able to pick up the same SUV he rented here, for his return trip.

Evening had crept up on him. He was getting hungry again, and was hoping dinner would be just a good as lunch. After stretching and twisting for a minute or two, he made his way back down to the lobby. He was surprised not to find the lovely Zahra at her post, but found her waiting tables in the restaurant. She saw him enter, and immediately bade him sit down at the best table in the house. The other diners were obviously locals who enjoyed good food. She handed him the same menu as for lunch. The others obviously arrived well before him, as they all had delicious looking platters in front of them.

After a few moments, he called Zahra to his table. She came instantly. He closed the menu, and asked Zahra what she recommended. She blushed—flattered he asked her opinion. She said she could make him an excellent Kusherie or Faatah. With a smile, he said the Faatah sounded wonderful. Zahra trotted immediately to the kitchen, oblivious of the others in the restaurant. Scott shook his head, breathed a sigh, *Oh, to be young again!*

He recognized the diner at the next table as one of the officials he met when entering Egypt. The man seemed friendly enough, and they engaged in a lengthy discussion alternately about the sad state of the economy in Egypt, and what was being discovered in the various sites around the Middle East. The conversation was easy and friendly, with much joking and laughing. When Zahra arrived with an absolutely scrumptious looking Faatah, talk was curtailed while he revelled in his meal.

As the customers finished, and sat back with a cup of strong black tea, there was a general air of comfort and contemplation. Scott finished his fine meal with the look of a man satisfied. Zahra cleared away the dishes, and asked if he wanted anything else. Scott asked if it would be possible to have a pot of tea sent to his room, citing he had some documents to work on. Zahra said she would bring a pot up as soon as he returned to his room. With that, he thanked her and made his way back. About ten minutes later, Zahra was at the door with a fresh carafe of tea, and two cups. To his surprise, she also brought along a hotplate to keep the tea warm. She smiled at him tantalizingly as she left.

"If you need anything at all, just dial 1-0. I will be happy to serve you."

Chapter 10 - Sweet Zahra

Scott had the distinct impression Zahra was flirting with him—and none too subtly. He looked at himself in the mirror. Well, not too shabby, he thought. Ruggedly handsome, still some charm and appeal. It was a long time since he had been with a woman. Staying busy allowed him to keep his mind off female affection. Still, there were some lovely graduate students at the university who showed definite interest. He found himself feeling rather warm as he thought of the beauty who just left his room.

There's no fool like an old fool, Scotty, he told himself. *But I can't risk it now.* The thought of getting the tablet sorted out flooded to his mind. *Maybe when I get back, if I get back, and she's still willing.*

He scowled at himself, turned away, and walked toward the table. A quick glance around showed that nothing had been touched while he was out of the room. He plugged in the hotplate, poured himself a cup of tea and placed the carafe on the hot plate. He looked at the two cups curiously. Another invitation? Saucy little thing, and yet he found himself quite attracted to her. He shook himself back to reality, and sat down in front of his charging iPad.

Now that he had hiding places for all his clues, he needed to come up with the clues themselves. This would be a tough slog. And so, again for hours, he poured over the locations, and worked on cryptic clues. If this was archaeology, it would a breeze! But this was more difficult than he thought. Hours later, the carafe was still full, his brain was mush, but he finally had all his clues neatly written on notepaper, inserted in envelopes, with each finding its way into a zipper bag. He tossed everything in his briefcase. After pouring another cup of tea, he stood and stretched. He was mentally tired, but physically craved some exercise. He thought of going for a walk around town to get the blood flowing again. He just wanted to clear his head for a while, and forget the darn tablet he so urgently wanted to dispose of before it could be stolen.

He heard a soft sound at the door. The hair on his neck bristled! His whole body stiffened with tension! The door handle moved gently. *Damn! Never locked the door!* There was no time to do anything. His breathing became quite shallow. He looked for something to use as a weapon. He could always use the sturdy carafe, and throw the hot liquid on the intruders. Before he could act, the door opened.

Zahra, silently slipped in. Scott didn't know whether to shout at her, or kiss her. Her intentions were obvious when she closed the door behind her. It was late now. Zahra wasn't wearing her work outfit anymore. Instead, she was wearing something rather more casual and comfortable. She was biting her lip, and her eyes were wide open—half hopeful, half frightened. She swallowed hard. Scott smiled broadly at her, a soft gentle smile. She responded likewise. No words were spoken. No words were needed. They moved quietly towards one another. She slipped her arms around his neck, and they kissed deeply. Scott totally gave in to his manhood, as Zahra offered him her womanhood.

It was early in the morning when Scott opened his eyes. Zahra was still beside him, propped up on one elbow with her head resting in her hand. The other hand lay gently on Scott's chest. She was simply looking at him with a gentle smile on her face. He smiled back. He turned his head and saw the perfect beauty of her body. He looked at her face, and their eyes locked. She leaned over, and kissed him gently on the lips.

"I must get ready for work."

"I know."

Zahra snuggled up to him. "When are you leaving?"

Scott held her tight. "This morning, I must go away for a while."

Her eyes moistened. "Will you ever come back to Taba?"

"I hope so. Maybe in two or three weeks."

"I can wait for you?"

He closed his eyes, and nodded gently. "Yes, I would like that."

"You will not forget me?"

"I will not forget you, Zahra. I will *not* forget you," was his gentle, and heartfelt, reply.

"Then I will be happy until your return!"

As she was moving to go, he held onto her gently. She smiled.

"I...don't want to go, but I must, or I will be in trouble."

"Zahra, if I don't return in three weeks, it will be because something has happened to me, otherwise, I will see you again."

"I believe you." She kissed him passionately.

In less than a minute, she was gone—as quietly as she arrived the night before.

Scott slowly let out a long breath. *What on earth just happened?* he thought, as he lay in bed. His whole body was weak. His gut was churning. They made love for quite some time the night before—both lost in each other—for different reasons, obviously. But something happened between them he couldn't explain. Was she just a local prostitute on the side? Well, if she was, she certainly wasn't good at it. She never asked for money. She seemed so genuine. This was impossible! She was half his age! She was Muslim; he was Christian.

He shook himself out of his reverie. *There's no time for this right now.* Yet, the emerald tablet seemed trivial compared to Zahra. *Enough!*

He jumped out of bed, walked quickly to the bathroom where he took a brisk shower. There was still plenty of tea in the carafe, so he poured himself a cup. It tasted terrible, having been left all night. He drank it down quickly. He chose something casual from his suitcase, and dressed. He packed the rest of his things. With suitcase and briefcase in hand, he made his way with purpose down the stairs.

Zahra Amari was at her post at the desk. She beamed her special smile for him, and he smiled back. He asked her to choose something nice for him for breakfast, along with some strong coffee. Looking very happy, she quickly made her way to the kitchen. There was one other person in the restaurant, but she walked right past. She would make Scott's breakfast first. After putting his luggage in the SUV, Scott was at his table with a new car magazine sitting next to his plate. She had noticed.

Scott ate his meal slowly. He was not in a hurry. The other diner had left. Zahra hovered over him. Neither seemed to know what to say. Scott slowly stood up, facing Zahra, very close. Her eyes were moist. Something *had* happened. They both looked around. Finally, he put his arms around her waist, and pulled her towards him. They kissed long and hard. They heard someone moving about, and parted.

In a very officious tone, too officious, Scott asked Zahra if it was possible for him to have the same SUV he would be dropping off in Cairo, when he returned there. She smiled and gave a little laugh. "Of course, sir, but there will be a reservation charge." Scott stifled a laugh, and agreed to the charge. Once the paperwork was done, it was time to leave. She put her hands on his.

"In two to three weeks."

"I will wait." She gave his hands a final squeeze and moved away.

Scott's heart was pounding as he left the hotel. For several minutes, he sat in the SUV wondering what he was doing. It all seemed so straightforward a few days ago. Days? It was only some 36 hours since it all started! And now, a stolen emerald tablet, a pounding heart, a churning gut, crazy in love with an Egyptian beauty that must have cast a spell on him! He didn't want to go!

Zahra looked out the window. She could see Scott sitting in the SUV. He kept looking towards the hotel. Why was he torturing her by staying so long? Did he not realize the sooner he left, the sooner he would return to her? For the first time in her life, Zahra felt incredibly happy, and incredibly sad at the same time. She was surprised to find herself completely in love with this Canadian archaeologist who speaks flawless Arabic. She had little love pangs before—but this was an explosion! Never, never, had she gone into a strange man's room to offer herself for love. She still couldn't believe it. And yet, it was a night of magic, a night of bliss, a night of the greatest happiness in her life. She trusted Scott completely. If he said he would come back—he would come back. But first, he needed to *leave*!

As if on cue, Scott started the big SUV. He already picked the spot where he would bury the tablet. He took the portable GPS unit out of his shirt pocket, and set the destination coordinates. He had to remember to erase them after burying the tablet. He drove off in a flurry of flying gravel.

Zahra smiled as he drove away. *Now, he can return to me*, she thought.

Scott was used to driving in the desert. The sand there was well packed. He wouldn't leave any deep tracks. When he arrived at his predetermined coordinates, Scott pulled out binoculars, and took a good look around. There was absolutely nothing out here to draw any sightseers, or anyone else, for that matter. He grabbed a shovel, a standard accessory in all SUVs in the dessert, and began to dig. He dug furiously for a good 20 minutes, resulting in a hole some 75 cm deep. This should be deep enough not to be uncovered in the event of a sandstorm. With luck, it would be covered even more. He gently placed the plaster encased tablet at the bottom of the hole, and covered the hole using all the sand he dug up. He smoothed the area as well as he could. Again, he looked around with the binoculars. Nothing. With everything back in the SUV, he headed in a long arc to the Nuweibaa-Taba Road on his way south to the hiding place of his first clue.

Over the next 18 days, Scott travelled more than 7,000 kilometres, hiding clues in nine cities around Egypt and Europe. It was a gruelling journey with few stops along the way. The whole time, he was very careful to watch for the presence of anything out of the ordinary—besides him, that is. He was ever vigilant to make sure he was not being followed. He constantly wondered if anyone picked up on the emerald tablet yet, and if they did, why they weren't out looking for him. Surely, Carver, and others, had confederates spread throughout the world. Of course, he wasn't exactly taking a normal tour. He kept very low key, staying in modest hotels—not the most expensive, nor the rundown hovels where they might look for him. So far, there was nothing. He even took the battery out of his cell phone to make sure no one could track him that way. He felt relatively safe using his iPad occasionally as it would be harder to trace. So far, everything looked promising for a safe return to Taba, and his beloved Zahra.

Scott arrived in Cairo at 1:30 a.m. and found himself a comfortable hotel room by 3 a.m. He slept in late, and enjoyed a hearty breakfast. Later, he picked up the SUV originally rented in Taba. As he climbed in, he was overwhelmed by thoughts of Zahra. She was never far from his mind, but he was concentrating on distributing his clues. Now, it was done, and he was "back home" in Egypt. Without wasting time, he headed out of Cairo for the five-and-a-half-hour drive back to Taba.

Zahra was working at her desk in the lobby area. Yet again, she looked up at the calendar. Scotty told her two to three weeks. Eighteen days had passed since he left. It was late afternoon. For some reason, she had circled today's date. She felt sure that Scotty would be back today. So far, only two tourists wanting directions to the fancy hotels farther south. The day was dragging, but she was hopeful and happy inside.

Since there was no one around, she decided to check the kitchen to make sure there was enough food for the restaurant. After a quick inspection, she decided there would be enough for dinner and breakfast, but tomorrow would require a trip to the grocery store. It was just before 5 o'clock.

Scott was a man on a mission! He drove as fast as he could without risking problems with the law. He wanted to get to Taba as quickly as he could. Only Zahra filled his thoughts now. Several slow sections held him up. He finally rolled into Taba, and parked outside the hotel.

Just as Zahra was returning to the lobby, Scott walked in. They both stopped, looked at each other, and didn't know quite what to do next. There were tears in Zahra's eyes—tears of joy. They both just stood there, trembling, looking at each other.

Mustering up all his courage, Scott asked, "Would Room 14 be available?"

Throwing all caution to the wind, she ran to Scott, and threw her arms around his neck. He embraced her tightly. Obviously, Zahra had not forgotten him. Without a word, she broke free of him, reached behind the desk, and grabbed the key to Room 14. She took his hand, almost dragged him up the stairs to the room. Once inside, they closed and locked the door. The world melted away in their absolute love.

Fortunately, no one noticed that Zahra was not at her post for some time. But then, no one really noticed Zahra. Scott spent the next several days and nights at the hotel. Each night, after work, Zahra would slip into his room. They spent their time talking, playing games, making beautiful love.

They both knew Scott couldn't stay at the hotel indefinitely. He would eventually have to return to his work in Jordan. Neither wanted to talk about it. On the fifth night, as they lay quietly together, Zahra broached the subject first.

"You must go back to your work one day."

"Yes," was all Scott could think of saying. "I would rather stay here with you."

"I know that. You love me, yes?"

"Yes, Zahra. I love you very much."

"You are a very intelligent, and wise man, Scotty. I know you can think of something we can do to stay together."

Scott thought maybe Zahra could be hired-on at the dig, but discounted that idea almost immediately. The women there were carefully segregated from the men. She rested her head on his chest. He ran his fingers through her long black hair.

"Would you come to live with me in Canada?"

Zahra pushed up excitedly. "Is that possible?"

"Yes, it's possible. You would have to be my wife, though."

"Your wife! You want me as your wife?"

"Yes, Zahra, I want you to be my wife, if you will have me as husband."

"Do not play with my heart, Scotty, or I will die."

"I mean it, Zahra. I want you to marry me. I know it might be difficult since you're Muslim, and I'm Christian, but I think we can make it work."

"But I am not Muslim, Scotty! I am Christian, like you."

"You are! You really are!"

Zahra laughed. "Yes, it is why no one notices me, or has much to do with me here."

"So, will you marry me?"

"Yes! Yes! Yes, my darling Scotty!" Tears began running down her cheeks.

She rolled onto his chest and began kissing him deeply. Their next hours were spent in absolute bliss.

In the morning, they awoke still clinging together. Both were happy. There was no doubt about that. Zahra told Scott she would get up and make him a wonderful breakfast—one suitable for her betrothed. He smiled, and asked if they could eat together in the room. She agreed, but it would have to be quick, so she could get back to work. Some twenty minutes later, Zahra appeared at the door with a tray of food. After closing the door, they sat together, and began eating.

She could see that something was troubling her Scotty, and asked what it was. Scott felt he could trust her, but didn't want to tell her too much. The less she knew, the better. He told her about finding a special artifact at the dig site. One so special, it had to be hidden quickly before it could be stolen. He told her of the men that might be looking for him to find out where he hid the artifact. He worried about Zahra because these men could end up beating her to find out what she knew. Zahra listened attentively to everything Scott told her. She was concerned for him, and not for herself. Scott asked her to keep their betrothal a secret for now, until everything was safe. That way, no one would bother her. She agreed, but with reservation. She wanted everyone in town to know she was betrothed, and very happy.

Zahra was deep in thought. Scott didn't want to disturb her concentration. He knew she was a very smart lady, and probably thinking things out. After what seemed an eternity, she smiled, and looked hard at Scott.

"You are worried that bad men will take you, and torture you, perhaps even kill you, to find this artifact, yes?"

Scott nodded.

"You are worried these bad men will try to find me to torture me for the information, if they know we are betrothed, yes?"

Again, Scott nodded.

Zahra broke into a sly little smile. "So, the best thing is for you to be taken away by force, to be tortured, yes?"

Scott was beginning to understand where she was going with this. "Go on."

Zahra placed her hands firmly on her hips, and spoke with the air of a woman who was making a pronouncement, rather than a suggestion. "I am the happiest woman in all of Egypt. I am betrothed to a wonderful man. I will marry you. No one will take that away from me, *no one*! This is what will happen. You will return to Tel Al Hajiwa. Shortly after, you will be taken away by terrible men—*my* terrible men—men I know and trust. They will bring you to Taba. From here we can go to a place where we can be happy together, a place where no one will find us."

Scott thought about this. "It could work! I will need some time to make preparations before you kidnap me. I must move money where I can get at it, but no one knows about. I also need to prepare the last instructions for finding the artifact, and hide them at the dig among my papers."

Zahra's response was quick. "Can you prepare your instructions here before you go? It would be best. If you are right about these thieves, you will not be long at the dig before they take you. They are maybe already waiting for you to return."

"You're right. Zahra, can you arrange for your men to kidnap me, and take me to Suez a couple of days later? I'm not known there, so I could move around freely, and do my banking. Then we can go wherever you feel is safe."

Zahra considered this for a moment. "Yes, my Scotty, that is possible. Perhaps we could be married in Suez as well. There are Christian churches there, and it would not be suspicious."

"Sounds like a plan! You get to work. We don't want to arouse suspicion. I can get you a nice engagement ring in Suez too."

With that, Zahra gathered up the dirty dishes, kissed her man, and left the room as she would any other room on any other day.

While Zahra went about her daily routine, Scott got to work. He would have to translate, and place his initial instructions in such a way they would be eventually found, but not obvious. He looked through his briefcase, and found his trusty notebook. He looked at it carefully, turning it around, this way and that. Finally, he nodded. He went down to the lobby, and asked Zahra if she had a long slender knife, and some glue. She looked at him curiously, but produced a suitable knife from the kitchen, and glue from the office. Back in the room, Scott used the knife to carefully slice open the cardboard back cover of the notebook. He took the paper with the instructions, and slipped it into the cover. Leaving the tiniest corner of paper showing, he glued the top edge of the cover together. The lamp on the bedside table made a handy weight to keep the cover together while the glue dried.

When finished, he brought the knife and glue back to Zahra. She was talking quietly to three rough-looking men at the front desk. She smiled at Scott, and introduced him to his kidnappers. They eyed him suspiciously. Zahra assured them he could be trusted. After all, he was her betrothed. They didn't look convinced.

With an impish grin, Zahra told Scott, "There will be an extra charge for the additional services," and they all laughed, which relaxed everyone.

There was no one in the hotel, or the restaurant, so the men sat at a table while Zahra, playing waitress, was pretending to take their order. She brought out some tea she already had brewing. Scott explained that security at the dig site was quite lax. No one would challenge them if they were carrying a shovel, pick, or bucket. The trickiest part would be to get Scott out, making it look like a kidnapping while at the same time not arousing enough suspicion to be challenged by security, or any of the workers. They discussed many ways of doing this. *Men!* Zahra thought, as she rolled her eyes. Scott noticed, and asked her what she was thinking. She smiled sweetly at him. She told them that the best plan is always the simplest one. Their complicated plans could go wrong at any moment.

Her plan was simple: her boys would go in looking like workers; they would say nothing to anyone, because their Egyptian Arabic would be spotted immediately; they would make their way directly to Scotty's tent, where he would be waiting for them at the appointed time; they would leave together with one man on either side of Scotty, and one behind; they would go to the closest staff car, get in, and drive towards Aqaba, as normal. Her Scotty would bring nothing traceable, like his cell phone—only his passport and visa. In Aqaba, they would board the fishing boat the men used to cross the Gulf. The customs and immigration officials in Taba would be bribed—something rather common, if not acknowledged. Scotty would have his passport stamped, and a long-term visa waiting for him when he landed. They knew Scott now, and wouldn't suspect any foul play—maybe a bit of hanky-panky.

Scott looked at Zahra in awe. *What a woman!* he thought. She flushed a bit, and looked lovingly at her Scotty. They all agreed it was a good plan—simple, straightforward, no fuss. The only thing that would foil it would be if others were waiting to take him right away, as he arrived.

Before anything was put into motion, Scott had to get an idea of what was happening in Jordan. He picked up his reconstituted cell phone, and called Jamal Hussein. All was quiet in Aqaba, and at the site. Apparently, Meadows was having the time of his life, and didn't really care where his boss had got to. The staff car was claimed by Meadows, but Hussein would be delighted to drive him out to the dig personally. Hussein wondered if Scott needed another lift across the Gulf. Scott thanked him, but declined, saying he already made arrangements in Taba.

Scott packed his suitcase and briefcase. He had all his travel documents for Jordan in order. He took his luggage down to the lobby. He settled his bill casually with Zahra. She was very excited. She knew he would be back again in the evening, if all went well, and he would be all hers. Soon, she would be happily married. Zahra's three kidnappers were waiting. They took his luggage to their fishing boat. They all boarded, and headed off. They crossed the Gulf of Aqaba often, never following any predetermined schedule. The Israeli patrols knew them, and never fussed. It was only 8:30 a.m.

When they arrived in Aqaba a couple of hours later, Scott called Jamal Hussein. In a few minutes, Hussein arrived. Scott's luggage was placed in Hussein's SUV, and they drove quickly to Tel Al Hajiwa. The conversation was easy and friendly. Scott explained he needed a break, and was rather misleading to the staff there about where he was going. When Hussein asked him about any romance, Scott couldn't help but smile broadly as he thought of his beautiful Zahra. Hussein laughed heartily, exclaiming it was, then, a successful little vacation. Scott agreed.

They arrived at the dig without fanfare. Scott invited Hussein to his tent for a nice cigar before returning to Aqaba. Hussein was glad to accept the invitation. He loved the cigars Scott offered him on his little trips. Hussein noticed a couple of lounging workers, and called to them to take Scott's luggage to his tent. They immediately complied. Once in the tent, Scott busied himself unpacking, throwing clothes in the laundry hamper, putting his things away, including the documents and his notebook. Everything had to look ordinary. All the while, Hussein sat back puffing on his cigar, chattering about nothing in particular. An hour or so later, Hussein bid Scott a fond goodbye. Scott pressed several cigars in Hussein's hand, begging him to keep his little secret. The appreciative Hussein laughed, and promised it was between gentlemen.

Scott left his tent and began to make his way about the site, greeting workers and staff as he did his round. Everyone welcomed him back without any seeming alarm as to his absence. He came across Meadows outside the research tent. Meadows welcomed is boss back, but looked just a little disappointed. They entered the tent where Scott greeted Madison and Michaud warmly. They burst out laughing as they told him that Hussein informed them not to worry about their boss—he was on a little vacation. Dr. El-Amin called a few times wondering where Scott had gotten to. They told him what Hussein told them. Apparently, Dr. El-Amin was very understanding, and was no longer concerned for this friend.

They all talked shop for a while. Scott received a good ribbing from his "Three Musketeers." Not much to report from the DAJ, they asked. Scott must have looked particularly happy and content, because they all commented on it. Madison said he looked like a man in love. Scott blushed deeply, and everyone in the tent laughed. They teased him mercilessly about it too: asking her name, what she looked like, what they would name the baby, and on, and on. Finally, Scott could take no more. He looked at his watch, and said he would return to his tent for a rest. They all laughed heartily. It wasn't often they could tease their boss, as he was so straight, and self-assured.

Back at his tent, Scott waited impatiently for his kidnappers to arrive. If all went to plan, it would only be another 30 minutes. He tried to sit, but couldn't stay still. He paced slowly across his tent with thoughts of Zahra running through his mind. Every two or three minutes, he looked at his watch again. So far, all had gone well. Suddenly, he heard a commotion outside. He stepped out of his tent to see what was happening. There was some sort of scuffle going on near the gate. The blood drained from his face. Was it his kidnappers? He stood there wondering if he should go check it out.

Keep to the plan, Scotty, he told himself.

If it was Zahra's men, he'd know soon enough. He re-entered his tent. He didn't have to wait long. A minute or so later, Zahra's kidnappers entered looking suitably fierce. They told him to move quickly, and as planned. They took advantage of the disturbance to grab Scott. They proceeded to the first available staff vehicle. They put Scott in the back seat with one man on either side, and the third driving. They casually drove out towards Aqaba. Scott waved to a security guard who was watching the vehicles. There was no chase, no panic. The only deviation from the plan was to put local clothes on Scott, so he wouldn't attract attention at the port in Aqaba. Thirty minutes later, Scott, along with his papers were on the fishing boat, heading back to Taba.

During the crossing, they noticed an Israeli patrol boat. It was moving on a parallel course, but in the opposite direction. As it passed by to their starboard side, the patrol boat began a turn, bearing down on them. The three fishermen, plus one, became rather concerned. The patrol boat pulled up beside them, and waved them down. At least a dozen sailors stood at the rail with automatic weapons at the ready. A sailor, who looked like a cook, asked if they had anything nice and fresh to sell them. They had some fresh fish in the hold, so they bargained a price. A basket was lowered and the fish placed inside. The cook looked satisfied, and waved them off. The patrol boat turned, accelerating away. No one had noticed the new fisherman in the boat.

Zahra was waiting at the dock in Taba. She could hardly contain herself. Neither could Scott, for that matter. The officials greeted Scott warmly. Since he had nothing to declare, and no luggage to search, they simply stamped all his documents, and let him pass. No one took much notice that Zahra and her Scotty walked together with arms around waists.

It was evening now. Zahra prepared them a wonderful meal.

They talked about what to do next. It was agreed they would leave for Suez early in the morning. Scott knew he couldn't use his credit card anymore. Zahra had some money saved up, not much, but enough. Scott had withdrawn several thousand dollars as he travelled around stashing his clues. He knew he might need some cash in a hurry if he was being tracked down.

Early the next morning, Zahra slipped out of bed without waking Scott. She prepared a nice breakfast, and some food for the trip to Suez. Scott was still asleep when she returned to the room. She gently climbed in the bed and kissed him gently on the lips, and on his eyelids. He woke up to see a very happy young woman. He held her close. She told him breakfast was ready, and they should leave soon.

Scott didn't remember ever feeling the way he did now. Happy, content, with a joy and vigour that filled his entire being. He looked at Zahra, and felt he could weep with joy. She felt much the same. She knew nothing is ever written in stone, but this man was her rock. He would be true. She just *knew* it.

They ate quickly. Scott took a shower, and dressed in clothes set out for him. To his surprise, they fit perfectly. Again, he felt nothing but awe for this incredible woman. Before long, there was a knock at the door. Zahra peeked out. It was two of her henchmen. She smiled, and let them in. Scott was ready to go. They took Zahra's suitcase from the room. He was surprised to see another sitting there, which they took as well. Zahra thought of everything.

A little over four hours later, they entered Suez. Zahra already arranged for hotel rooms. The first order of business was to get Zahra an engagement ring. On their fourth jewellery store, they found the perfect ring—and the right size! Zahra was elated. This made it official. Now, they obtained the necessary papers to get married. With everything in order, all they had to do was to find a minister willing to marry them. Tonight would be tough. Scott and the boys would stay in one room while Zahra would be in another room. They needed to maintain propriety, so as not to attract attention.

The next day, they began calling protestant churches. A United Church minister said he would be delighted to marry them. Later that afternoon, wearing a new dress, Zahra walked down the aisle to her beloved. The boys had cleaned up nicely. When they were pronounced husband and wife, neither needed an invitation to kiss. Scott wondered if he was in some sort of dream. But this was very, very real. The minister gave them a signed certificate complete with the names, and signatures, of the witnesses.

At the hotel, Scott moved into Zahra's room. It was alright now. They showed the marriage certificate to the desk clerk to confirm they were now married. Surprisingly, the hotel upgraded them to their best suite for the night. This was unexpected, but welcomed. Mr. and Mrs. Scott thoroughly enjoyed their first night together.

Scott had a sizable bank balance, owing to the fact he was rarely in a position to spend his earnings. He also did quite well with his investments. He knew he would probably have to go into hiding at some point, so he began quietly liquidating all his investments while travelling to hide his clues. While he was at it, he made several inquiries regarding offshore bank accounts. He settled on two banks in particular, where financial transactions were secret and secure. While in Nice, he transferred all the funds from his Canadian accounts to a numbered account at the first offshore bank. By now, the funds would have reached the new bank. On their third day in Suez, Scott made some calls to transfer these funds into numbered accounts in the second offshore bank. The first transaction would be recorded on the Canadian side, but the second transaction would be secret, and hidden from prying eyes.

After another few days in Suez, they headed to Zahra's secret location. Her men acted as body guards until Scott and Zahra were dropped off. Zahra was no fool. After they were dropped off, they bought an old car, and headed to their hideaway.

Back at Tel Al Hajiwa, it was late in the evening when Meadows, Madison, and Michaud discovered Scott was nowhere to be found. A check with Jamal Hussein in Aqaba came up empty. They searched the camp, and the entire dig site. Only one security guard remembered seeing Dr. Scott in a staff vehicle with three other men. A month later, after many inquiries, Scott was declared missing under suspicious circumstances.

Randolph Carver, stood at a window at his opulent home looking out at the rain. His mood was as black as the clouds. Dr. Bart had not read Scott's report for an entire month—*an entire month*! It sat on his desk buried under a mountain of other documents. Now, it appeared one of his competitors had taken

Dr. Scott. No one reported finding an emerald tablet at the site. They were all surprised with the revelation that Scott reported such a find. There must be an error. *No,* he thought, *there was no error.* Carver prided himself on being ahead of the game against all his competitors. How could any of them have found out before him? It was inconceivable! The only information he was able to gather was that Dr. Scott was driven away from the site sitting in the back seat of a staff vehicle, accompanied by three men. He was not sighted again. Scott had vanished. None of his competitors admitted to any knowledge of the Emerald Tablet's whereabouts. He turned, smashing his fist on his desk, just as a clap of thunder shook the house!

Chapter 11 - The Note

Robert and Jenna sat close to one another in his study. On the large monitor, they watched recorded video from security cameras positioned at the front of the estate. Although they were oriented along the perimeter, they still afforded a view of the road at the edge of the frame. They were looking intently to see if they could find vehicles that appeared too often along the road. Dutifully, Carmen appeared after a short while with a fresh pot of coffee and two cups. Robert would have preferred something stronger to settle his nerves, but didn't want to impair his mind in any way.

For more than an hour, they examined the videos carefully. Finally, they looked at each other shaking their heads.

"Nothing!"

"Nothing!"

They both sat back, and took a deep breath which they blew out slowly.

Robert stood strait up in his chair. "Good grief! I completely forgot about the focus of today's little escapade–the map!"

Jenna jumped at Robert's unexpected exclamation. Robert swung around to reach for his jacket, which he had thrown on top of a small table. Instead, he found himself knee-to-knee with Jenna, as they were both sitting on swivel office chairs. Whether it was a release of tension, the surprise of Roberts comments, or something inside, she didn't know, but an inexplicable giddiness caught hold of Jenna who burst out laughing hysterically. This surprised Robert who looked at her curiously. Her laughter was infectious. Before long, he began to laugh as well. They sat there, facing each other, knees touching, killing themselves laughing. They were so loud Carmen came to see what was happening. When she appeared in the doorway with a concerned look on her face, Robert and Jenna just laughed louder. Carmen frowned, shook her head and withdrew. This just fuelled their crazies. Tears were rolling down Jenna's cheeks from laughing so hard. Finally, they both calmed down. Jenna leaned in towards Robert, caressing his face with her hands, and kissed him.

Robert swallowed hard. This was so right. Everything inside was feeling very strange. He was confused, happy, sad, amazed, aroused, nervous, unsure, too sure—just a jumble of thoughts and feelings. He thought of Christine for a moment. Strangely, he didn't feel guilty at all. It was as though Christine was happy to see him like this—obviously falling in love. Of course, that's what she would want for him. Finally, he pulled Jenna hard to him, and kissed her passionately. She didn't resist. She slid easily into his strong arms, her heart pounding. There was no way she would let go of this man.

Eventually, they disentangled, her hands slipping softly down his arms to hold his hands in hers. No words were spoken, nor needed to be. Their eyes were locked. The only thing to be seen there was the love growing in their hearts.

Robert broke the silence. "Shall we look at the map?"

Jenna nodded. Robert reached past her to his jacket. He pulled out the envelope complete with tape, which stuck to the inside of the pocket. He gently pealed it back as Jenna held down the jacket. With the envelope finally freed, they turned back to the desk. Robert handed the note to Jenna.

"It's your map. To you go the honours."

Jenna pulled the tape gently from the envelope. She didn't want to rip the note inside. Robert handed her a letter opener with which she slit open the envelope.

"Well, here goes." With that, she pulled the note out of the envelope. The paper was not large by any means. It looked like a page out of a small notebook. Of course, why wouldn't it be? It probably came from the very notebook in which it was found. Jenna unfolded it and pressed it flat on the desk.

It read:

La smeralda tablet estas grandvalora kaj netaksebla preter kredo.

Post raportado lia fajna, Mi sciis min devis kaŝi ĝin.

Mi scias ke ili venos al Mi.

Mi neniam malkaŝi lia loko kvankam ĝi povas kosti mian vivon.

Se vi legas tiun, mi ne plu kun vi.

Sekvi la spuron trovi vian premion.
Spekti vian dorson kaj fidu neniun.
Tio estas via nura vojo al la tablojdo.
Direktoj restis de loko al loko.
Jen via unua tasko:
En Egiptio, trovi la lokon Pura.
Saladino, ho Saladino, kie estas via potenco?
Kie Aqaba levas, noto atendas.

"What on earth?" Robert stared at Jenna with a puzzled look on his face.

"Did I not mention I couldn't make heads or tails of the note?"

Robert looked down at the note again. "It's no language I've ever seen before. This is quite the new twist."

"I suppose it makes sense. He wouldn't want his note to be that easy to decipher. It might be one of the languages he spoke."

"Do you know what those languages might be?"

Jenna thought back to what she knew about Dr. Ambrose Scott. "He's a Middle East expert. He's fluent in Arabic, Hebrew, Greek, Latin, could read and interpret hieroglyphics, hieratic, demotic. Maybe a couple more languages."

Robert stared at the note again. "This text doesn't look like any of those except maybe Latin. The others all use their own alphabet styles. Arabic and Hebrew are written right-to-left and the same goes for hieroglyphics, and probably the others too. I know a bit of Latin, and this doesn't look right for Latin."

"RJ, that's why I came to Airdrie in the first place—to consult with a linguistics expert I met at the university. I figured if anyone could decipher the text, it would be him."

"Airdrie isn't exactly the obvious place to begin a quest, so we can assume Carver knows exactly why you're here. Either he has your linguistics friend under his control, or he's being carefully watched."

They both looked rather crestfallen as they stared at the small sheet of paper before them. They stared at it long and hard. Neither spoke. Both were obviously wondering what to do next. Robert broke away, and reached for the coffee pot. He poured them both a fresh cup. Jenna turned her head slowly, and watched as he performed this little ritual. He pulled his smartphone out of his shirt pocket, switched on the camera app, and took a close-up picture of the note. He checked the result to make sure it was clear. Jenna watched with interest, but said nothing. Robert looked around his desk. A book caught his interest. He reached for it and placed it carefully on the note. He took a couple of mouthfuls of coffee. He turned, and smiled at Jenna.

"Let's go for a little walk."

"A walk?"

"It's a lovely day, nice and warm outside. Let's walk in the back garden."

"Okay," was all she could think of saying.

Robert pushed back the chair, and stood up. He extended his hand to Jenna who took it willingly.

"There's nothing like taking a little walk to clear the head, and get the blood circulating again."

They walked casually out of the study, along a short corridor into the main part of the house. Robert offered his arm. Jenna slipped hers through his as they walked out to the terrace. They continued down the lawn, and towards the formal garden with its many colourful flowers. The air was full of their fragrance.

Carmen spotted them from the kitchen window. Despite her loyalty to her late mistress, she was glad to see her señor Robert so happy. It was about time. He had been mourning for long enough—too long. She approved of la señora Jenna. She was a good match for him. She looked like señora Christine, but had a completely different personality. She wondered why they were walking in the garden. Taking a nice little break from the difficulties, perhaps. She remembered the coffee she had brought them some time ago, and hurried to retrieve the coffee pot and dirty cups before they returned. It would be time for dinner soon. She would prepare something special for them.

In the garden, Robert and Jenna walked happily looking at the flowers, and engaged in some idle chit-chat. They didn't discuss the note or the Emerald Tablet. They enjoyed the sun, the fragrance, and each other's company. Both felt deliriously happy, but didn't discuss that either. Robert stretched and twisted. Jenna laughed. Her wonderful man looked more like a little boy now—a little boy without a care in the world. At that moment, neither did she. She felt as though she was wandering in some sort of dream, and had no desire to even think about waking up.

Robert took Jenna by the hand, leading her to a bench. They sat down close to one another. Robert placed his arm around her as though it was the most natural thing to do. He too was enjoying this moment.

Finally, he spoke. "Jenna, you intrigue me at every turn. From the instant you appeared in a cloud of dust until this very moment. You've told me stories of hidden treasure, unscrupulous collectors, corrupt officials, beatings, a lost map. I can hardly wait for the next instalment."

Jenna smiled, biting her lower lip. "What can I say, RJ, I'm a complicated girl!"

They both laughed. "I'll say you're complicated! And you've really complicated my life. I don't know whether I'm coming or going, in a wonderful dream or a nightmare. I'm not complaining, mind you. I've just never felt like this before. I've always been in control, you see, and now I'm not the slightest bit in control of much of anything."

Jenna placed her hand on his arm, and comforted him. "Well then, you're doing a great job of pretending to be in control. You keep us on track all the time; you comfort me, and give me a total sense of security; you're fearless, focused, funny, fantastic, and lots of adjectives I can't think of right now. I know—*I know*—we'll get to the bottom of the Emerald Tablet mystery. And I know we'll get through it in one piece."

"Thank you for your kind words, Jenna, but we're not going anywhere until we can figure out that note of Dr. Scott's."

"What do you suggest, RJ?"

"We need to find out what language Scott used to write his note. Obviously, he decided to use something that others around him would probably not understand. Maybe it's a made-up language, and we need some kind of key to break his code.

"I hope not, RJ. All I brought with me was the note. I didn't think I might need his notebook too. I certainly can't casually waltz into the U of A archaeology archives to sort through Dr. Scott's other dig notes.

Robert looked at her, considering what she said, and especially about the note, and where it was located. "No! Let's think about this for a minute. He hid the note in the cover of his notebook. There was nothing else there. You mentioned before that everything else in the notebook was notes about the dig. Jenna, was this notebook spiral bound or glued pages?"

Jenna frowned, took a deep breath, and threw her mind back

to when she examined the notebook. She finally exhaled. "It wasn't spiral bound. No, it was sewn and glued. Very sturdy so it could be opened wide without breaking. They're a special kind. All Dr. Scott's notebooks were the same type. Why is that important?"

"When you examined the notebook, do you recall if there were any pages torn out? If it was sewn and glued, there would be bits of paper left in the binding."

Again, Jenna thought about the notebook. "I don't know, RJ. I can't recall any pages torn out. When I saw the corner of the note, I was focused on it. If he tore a blank page from the back of the notebook, I wouldn't have noticed at all. I stopped checking where the writing ended."

"Did you read through all his notebooks?"

"Yes, I did. Just scanned them, really.

"Did you notice any strange writing, like the stuff we have here?"

"No, nothing stood out or appeared curious. Why. What are you driving at, RJ?"

"I was thinking if he used this language before, then it would be something that others would know about. That he used it only for the map kind of tells me he used a language that was unusual, or rare enough that few would be able to know what it is. He was being very careful and cagey. It's almost like he left the note for himself, and yet he would already know its contents."

They both sat there pondering the latest theory expounded by the good Dr. RJ.

"What would Indiana Jones do?" he finally murmured.

"What?" Jenna laughed.

"Seriously, what would Indiana Jones do if he was confronted with the same problem?"

"He'd probably dig into the university library looking for something that looked like the language on the note, I suppose."

"Brilliant! Absolutely brilliant! Jenna, you're a genius!" With that, he bent over and kissed her.

Robert grabbed Jenna's hand, and almost dragged her behind him as he hurried back to the study, leaving her speechless.

When they sat down again at the desk, Jenna cried out, "What is it?"

"What's the biggest library in the world?"

Jenna started thinking about libraries that she new about in universities, independent libraries, private libraries, but had no idea which one Robert was referring to. Finally, she looked at him and simply shrugged.

Robert was excited. He pulled the computer keyboard forward and began typing. "The Internet, my dear, the Internet!"

Jenna was still none the wiser, even if Robert thought she was somehow a genius.

Robert looked at her, and pointed at the screen—Google Translate! Finally, she understood. Look for a language that matches the note.

"With Google Translate, I can choose any of a hundred or more languages as source or destination. The translate language, of course, is English. First, we type in a line. Hmm, let's pick a short one with no accented characters. This one: *Mi scias ke ili venos al Mi*. Now, we start picking out source languages. Eventually, we'll have to find one that makes sense."

Robert typed in the line, and Jenna double-checked to make sure he had it right. Robert set the destination language to English. Before going any farther, he copied the text and pasted it in a text app on the computer. Now, he began the process of elimination. At first, he selected randomly, but had no luck. He decided to just go through all the languages in alphabetical order. He laughed to himself as he thought Murphy's Law would dictate it would be the very last one, and was tempted to try Zulu.

After working through the first 20 or so, the translated text shouted out from the monitor: *I know they will come for me*.

Jenna bounced up and down on the chair shouting, "RJ, RJ, that's it! That's it!"

Robert looked incredulously at the monitor. "Esperanto! It *is* a made-up language! No one uses Esperanto!"

"Quickly, RJ, let's translate the whole note!"

Some thirty minutes later, they stared at the translated note. Robert placed the text in an app on the computer, and printed it out.

> *The emerald tablet is precious and priceless beyond belief.*
> *After reporting its find, I knew I had to hide it.*
> *I know they will come for me.*
> *I will never divulge its location though it may cost my life.*
> *If you are reading this, I am no longer with you.*
> *Follow the trail to find your prize.*
> *Watch your back and trust no one.*
> *This is your only way to the tablet.*
> *Directions have been left from place to place.*

Here is your first task:
In Egypt, find the place Clean.
Saladin, O Saladin, where is your stronghold?
Where Aqaba rises, a note awaits.

As they read the note several times, a chill ran down their spines. It was obvious that Dr. Scott feared both for the safety of the Emerald Tablet, and for his life. Their quest quickly took on a serious and sinister air. This was not going to be a frolic in the park. Dr. Scott had gone missing, presumed kidnapped, and had not been heard of since. Had he given his life to protect this artifact? If Carver's people were chasing Jenna around, they hadn't found the tablet. Scott had not talked—at least not yet.

Chapter 12 - First Riddle

Neither Robert nor Jenna were laughing now. Gone were the soft and tender feelings of romance that brightened their day only moments ago. Both sat stiffly on their chairs. Slowly, they turned to face each other. Only sombre looks greeted them this time.

"I guess we forgot just how we got here in the first place—with you staggering around on a country road after having been drugged and beaten!"

"Somehow, that seems so long ago, RJ, a million years ago. And yet, you just returned from masquerading as a research assistant to get my documents, and the note."

"Jenna, just how important is it to find this Emerald Tablet?"

Jenna smiled sweetly as she recognized what Robert was really saying, but answered seriously. "Important enough for a seasoned archaeologist to risk his life to protect."

They sat looking at each other for several minutes. It was Robert who broke the silence. "Do we have any idea what we'll do with this thing if, and when, we find it?"

It was a good question. If they found the tablet what *would* they do with it? The private collectors like Carver had connections everywhere, and deep pockets to bribe anyone they wanted. Was there a museum somewhere—anywhere—that could safeguard the tablet? Or would it be stored in some drawer deep in a museum or university archive just to quietly slip away to a private collector?

"Another question comes to mind, Jenna. How do we stay safe—before and after? You narrowly escaped Carver with your life. We can expect him, and others, to be looking for you all over the world, as we search for the tablet. If we make any arrangements for safeguarding the tablet, will we ever be safe from Carver? Will we need to live in hiding the rest of our days?"

Jenna gave him a sheepish look. "I really hadn't thought about any of that when I excitedly ran off on my quest, RJ."

Robert suddenly laughed. "Well, we're up to our armpits in alligators now! Let's try not to get bit, shall we?"

Jenna looked at Robert in awe—her own private Indiana Jones—ready to dive into danger with both feet—fearless and confident. *Wow!* she thought.

"If they knew we were together, we wouldn't be sitting here undisturbed trying to figure out our next move. We've noticed nothing suspicious on the security monitors, and nobody has come knocking at our door. That buys us time, time to figure out the riddle, and make arrangements to travel."

Jenna listened attentively to what Robert said. She caught one phrase that had a strong impact on her. He said "*our* door," not "my door," or "the door." He said "*our* door." A warm feeling washed over her as she thought of this. Nothing else seemed to matter at that moment. She suddenly realized she was staring into space, and refocused to find Robert looking at her curiously.

"You okay?

"Yes. Yes, I'm fine. Um, you're absolutely right, of course." She hoped this banal response would be fitting, because she could remember nothing of what he said. *C'mon girl, focus! This is important and dangerous!* she admonished herself.

Robert wasn't so sure what to make of her reply.

"Let's get down to figuring out this riddle."

In Egypt, find the place Clean.
Saladin, O Saladin, where is your stronghold?
Where Aqaba rises, a note awaits.

Jenna wanted to make herself useful. "Well, we know it's in Egypt, and Aqaba might be a reference to the Gulf of Aqaba."

Robert focused his attention on the computer monitor while murmuring. "Okay, let's get a map of Egypt up on the screen to see what we can find. Here we go. Good old Google! Gulf of Suez...nope."

"Other side of the Sinai Peninsula, go east." She pointed on the monitor. "That's the one!"

"There's not a whole lot along that coast. I'll zoom in to see what we can find. Write down the names of the places we can see along the coast. Starting at the top, there's Taba, The Castle Zaman...seems to be a restaurant, Ras Shaitan...a beach resort, Wasit, Nuweibaa, Mamla-Ras Abu Galum...says it's a protectorate, Blue Hotel, Dahab, Le Méridien...a resort, Nebk,

Nabq, Sharm El Sheik. That's about it. Not much really."

Jenna read out the first line. "*In Egypt, find the place Clean.* Find the place Clean. So, are we supposed to look for a place that's clean then?"

They both read the first line of the riddle several times. Each time they read it, the more puzzled they became. They looked at the short list of place names on the Egyptian coast of the Gulf of Aqaba, and back at the riddle. They both pondered this little problem in silence glancing back and forth between the names, and the riddle.

"My head hurts, RJ. None of this makes any sense. What's clean? And what about our friend Saladin?"

"Your Dr. Scott is a very cagey man, Jenna. Would you say that Scott was meticulous?"

"Judging by his very careful notes, and his dedication to proper archaeology, I'd say he was very meticulous. That's why none of this makes any sense. Dr. Scott is a man of high integrity. It's just not like him to take off with a priceless artifact, and hide it somewhere."

"Then we have to assume his clue is written meticulously, and leaves nothing to chance. Every word was carefully selected. We just need to think like an archaeologist, and take each word for its exact meaning."

Jenna smiled, and looked teasingly at Robert. "RJ, you seem quite fond of Indiana Jones. Can you think of how he would approach our little puzzle? Some movie snippet or bit of dialogue?"

"You're making fun of me now," he sniggered.

"No, RJ, I'm really not. It's just that this whole Emerald Tablet thing is right out of an adventure story. Maybe there's some sort of correlation, as weird as that might seem. And you're the big Indiana Jones fan."

Robert didn't look convinced. He sat there in silence for several minutes with his eyes closed. He played back the movies in his mind, as best he could remember, in fast forward. Then suddenly he exclaimed, "That's it! Of course!"

"Jenna, look at the first line of the riddle carefully. Do you notice anything strange, or out of place?"

Jenna looked again at the words: *In Egypt, find the place Clean*. Robert was grinning ear-to-ear. Jenna looked at him. She knew Robert had figured it out, but was giving her a chance. Was this an Indiana Jones thing? Finally, she shook her head.

"Sorry, RJ, I can't really see anything but a misspelled word."

"You hit it on the head!" Robert was ecstatic! "You said Scott was meticulous. He wouldn't make a spelling mistake like that. Then why would he write *clean* with a capital *C*? I think the name of the place is 'Clean' but in another language—probably Egyptian."

"Of course! That makes a lot of sense! Let's look at that list again. There's Taba, Wasit, Nuweibaa, Dahab, Nebk, and Nabq. All these are only one word. Can you Google these to see what we can find out about them?"

Robert began what turned out to be a not-so-arduous task. He searched for the name Taba. It was only a minute or two later when he pointed at the monitor. "Taba is a girl's name: it means *clean* in Arabic. Got it on the first try."

"Wow! Now we have the first part of the riddle solved. We need to go to Taba, in Egypt."

"But *where* in Taba do we need to look for the next clue? Let's look at that map again."

"Can you zoom in real close?"

Robert zoomed in. As he panned the map along the coast, they looked carefully to see if anything jumped out at them. Nothing seemed to catch their eye.

"*Saladin, O Saladin, where is your stronghold?*" Jenna read it over quietly. "A stronghold can be a castle, or fortress, or any kind of fortified city, or town."

"Okay, let's find out who Saladin actually was. This might give us a clue to his stronghold. Big, long, real name...first Sultan of Egypt and Syria...fought against the crusaders. Nothing here about Taba."

Robert tried a new tack. He typed in "saladin taba" in the search box. They both jumped excitedly when the search engine offered "saladin castle taba."

"Oh, my gosh, RJ, can it really be that easy?"

"Here it is. He took over a fortress on Pharaoh's Island in the Gulf of Aqaba, just south of Taba. He expanded the fortress, and it was taken over by crusaders, and others. It's a popular diving spot now. This has to be it, Jenna. This *has* to be it!"

They looked at each other. Both were shaking with excitement.

"Oh, what the heck," stammered Robert. And with that, he leaned over, and kissed Jenna hard on the lips. Jenna's heart leapt in her breast. She could scarcely breath. This wasn't their first kiss by any means, but this one was different somehow. She reached around Robert's neck, and returned his kiss passionately. As they tried to pulled away, their lips kept meeting in gentle pecks, and little tugs. Jenna was barely breathing. Her body was warm with desire. She wanted this man. From the look on his face, he wanted her too. Was this the moment?

Suddenly, they became aware of Carmen standing at the door, looking down, being very quiet, with an impish little grin on her face. "Dinner, señor, señora!"

After a delicious dinner, they returned to the study.

"What do you think he means by: *Where Aqaba rises, a note awaits.*" Jenna asked. "It's the last part of the riddle."

Robert considered for a moment. "Well, Pharaoh's Island is in the Gulf of Aqaba. The Gulf has tidal ebbs and flows. My money says he's talking about the high-water mark, somewhere on the outside of the fortress."

"That makes sense. So, we're going to Taba in Egypt to look for a note at the high-water mark on the outside of Saladin's fortress on Pharaoh's Island."

"Looks that way. Ever been to Egypt?"

"Only in my dreams, RJ. Can't go gallivanting around the world on *my* salary."

"Now that we know, what do you think we should do with the note?

Jenna exhaled slowly, almost whistling as she did. "Should we destroy it?"

"If we fail in our quest, and the note is destroyed, the Emerald Tablet may be lost forever. I doubt it's anywhere near a dig site where it might be found again."

They sat quietly considering what to do with the note. Robert finally suggested, "Scott hid the note in a notebook. Maybe we can hide it in a book of our own in this room."

The study was a combination library and study. There were floor-to-ceiling bookcases on three walls of the room. Robert stood up and wandered around looking at the books on the shelves within easy reach. He stopped, and pulled out a book. He motioned for Jenna to join him.

He handed her the book. "Well, what do you think?"

Jenna laughed when she saw the title. "Perfect!" It was a copy of *Around the World in 80 Days*.

Robert returned to the desk, and pulled open a drawer. From

a roll of sticky tape, he cut off four pieces, which he used to stick the corners of the note, placed back in its envelope, to the inside of the dust jacket of the book. He then carefully put the book back in its place on the shelf. For some reason, they both felt relieved.

"Now the fun part," announced Robert. "We need to figure out the best way to get to Taba.

They both sat down at the computer again. Robert began checking for flights from Calgary to Taba. After searching for a while, there seemed to be nothing.

Jenna watched him quietly.

"There's only a small non-commercial airport near Taba. It looks like we'll have to fly into Cairo and then drive to Taba." Robert continued his research. "We'll need visas for Egypt. According to the government web site, we can get them on arrival, but that might mean a long delay. The recommendation is to get one at the embassy in Ottawa, or the consulate in Montreal. They're valid for 30 days, so we should be good. We also need to get a bunch of vaccines before we leave."

Jenna had drifted into another world. She initiated this quest, and somehow figured she could accomplish it all on her own. Now, as she listened to Robert, it was obvious she could never have even gotten this far. Robert was incredible. Without him, she knew she was dead—not just figuratively, but in very real terms. *What a fool I was to just launch off on my own,* she thought. She slowly returned to the study in Robert's home.

"How long will all that take?"

"The shots we could get in Airdrie, but that would be too risky. We could drive to Calgary. It's only about a half hour away. It should be safe enough, as long as we stay away from the airport, and maybe bus and train stations. As for the visas, I think we should get those either in Ottawa, or Montreal."

"Will we drive all the way there?

"It would be a long drive." He considered for a moment. "I think we need to avoid the close airports. They'll be watched. Vancouver might be a good bet. It's a long day's drive, but it's unlikely Carver and his agents will be expecting us to go west. From there we could fly to Ottawa. What do you think?"

Jenna was still in a bit of a haze. Things were moving so quickly. The quest, of course, but mostly Robert. Although she just met him, it was as though they'd been together for years. She felt she knew this man intimately, and trusted him implicitly.

"Jenna, are you alright?"

"Yes, darling, of course. Just a bit tired, that's all."

"I must be crazy! It's hardly been a day since I found you wandering in a drugged stupor. No wonder you're tired. You've hardly recovered yet."

"It's alright, RJ, I'm fine, really."

He offered his hand as he stood up. "Come on. Let's go sit somewhere comfortable. I'll ask Carmen to make us some hot chocolate, and then it's time to hit the sheets. Tomorrow, we can go to Calgary for the vaccines. Unless there's a good reason, we can stay here and take it easy for a couple of days while you get your strength back. We can leave for Vancouver on Monday."

Jenna, graciously took his hand as she pulled herself up. Once out of the study, Robert offered his arm, which Jenna took willingly. They made their way to the living room and plopped themselves down on a comfy couch.

"Carmen..."

Chapter 13 - Take a Breath

It was seven o'clock on a bright, beautiful, Friday morning as Carmen made her way to the kitchen. She wasn't sure, but she thought she heard someone moving around. Once in the kitchen, it was obvious. The Keurig coffee machine had been pulled out with a used K-cup of Robert's favourite flavour still sitting in the machine. She thought to herself that señor Robert must have been very distracted to just leave the used K-cup sitting there, and not throwing it out.

Carmen walked quietly to the study. There, she found Robert sitting at the computer intensely studying the information on the screen. She looked at him curiously. He had a bathing suit on, and a towel around his neck. He still hadn't noticed her.

"*Buenos días*, señor Robert."

Robert jumped at the sudden interruption. "Carmen, you scared the devil out of me!"

"*Lo siento, señor*," she apologized. "Would you like your breakfast now?"

Robert caught his breath. "Sí, Carmen, on the terrace please."

"*Muy bien, señor.*" Carmen immediately returned to the kitchen.

Robert was checking out clinics in Calgary that might offer travel vaccinations. He found one, and would call later to see if they could get the vaccinations today. Then he looked for flights from Vancouver to Ottawa, and from Montreal to Cairo. As much as possible, Robert wanted non-stop flights. He hadn't travelled for a while, and found air fares to be somewhat outrageous. Thankfully, he had the funds necessary to undertake this little quest.

Robert put his computer to sleep, and headed to the terrace within a couple of minutes after Carmen left. He tossed the towel over the back of a convenient chair, and jumped into the pool.

The cold water felt refreshing. He began swimming laps, as he normally did, almost every day. It was his favourite fitness exercise. About twenty minutes later, Carmen came out with Roberts breakfast, which she placed on the table. She walked over to the pool, waiting for Robert to finish a lap.

"Breakfast is waiting, señor."

Robert pulled himself out of the pool, grabbed the towel and wiped himself down. He sat at the table, and devoured his breakfast. He was famished. As he ate, he pushed the pesky Emerald Tablet out of his mind. Instead, he turned his thoughts to Jenna.

What on earth had happened? In less than three days, this woman totally transformed his life, blown his mind, and stolen his heart! She was definitely *not* a Christine replacement. No, Jenna was very, very different. He realized he had completely fallen in love with Jenna. He thought he should somehow feel guilty—but he didn't. He knew it had to be crazy to be so madly in love with a woman he barely knew—but it didn't seem all that crazy. Certainly, Carmen's behaviour, and comments, made it clear she approved of Jenna, and their growing romance. Last night, when they finished their hot chocolate, and headed for bed, Robert wanted to take Jenna's hand to lead her to his bedroom. He felt she would have willingly followed. For the sake of propriety, he didn't, of course—or was it propriety? Maybe he knew she still needed time to recover physically from her assault. Maybe he knew nothing at all! He felt both dazed and alive—alive for the first time since his beloved Chris died. He just sat there, completely lost in thought.

Jenna woke up in her comfy bed wearing wonderful blue silk pyjamas, that had been laid out for her. She looked at the clock. It was just after eight. She knew somehow, that Robert must already be up planning their movements for the next few days. She threw the covers off, lay back, and stretched. Who was this man who swept her off her feet, literally, in the middle of a dirt road? He swept her heart away too. She felt the warmth of love wash over her entire body. She thought of that moment yesterday when she would have gladly given herself to him. She became acutely aware she was quite aroused. She felt no shame, no embarrassment. She was completely in love, and she knew it. She wanted to feel his strong arms around her, his warm lips, his hard body against hers.

"Time for a cold shower, girl!" she admonished herself out loud.

Jenna slid out of bed, made her way to the bathroom, slipped out of her pyjamas, and walked into the shower. After drying herself, she shook out her hair. She looked at her reflection in the big mirror above the vanity. She scanned her entire body, turning around to try to see her back as much as possible. The welts, from her beating of a couple days ago, were still quite visible. She touched a few of the bigger ones. They were still tender, but she felt great, invigorated. She wondered if it was the time she had to recuperate, or if it was Robert.

Returning to the bedroom, she found a nice blouse and skirt laid out on the bed, which was already made up. She was amazed. She heard nothing. It was obvious Carmen knew she was in the shower, and took the opportunity to quietly, and very efficiently, sort out the bedroom. Jenna wondered if Carmen selected clothes for her former mistress as well. She laughed, and pinched herself, *Ouch! No, this isn't a dream.*

As Jenna arrived at the bottom of the stairs, Carmen welcomed her, and pointed out to the terrace. "*Benos días, señora.* Señor Robert is on the terrace. Your breakfast will be out in a few minutes."

"Thank you, Carmen."

When she reached the large patio doors, she stopped. There was Robert, sitting at a table, in his bathing suit. His hair was all mussed up from rubbing it with the towel. He seemed lost in thought, with his head resting in his hands, elbows on the table, staring out into Neverland. She quietly walked up behind him, and kissed his neck. Robert, startled again, jerked up, and turned to see Jenna there with a big smile on her face.

"Good grief, Jenna, this is the second heart attack I've had this morning!"

Jenna laughed to see the look on his face. He was definitely startled. It only took a few seconds for him to compose himself again. He stood up courteously, and bid Jenna sit down.

"Please forgive my casual attire, but I really needed a good swim to clear my head.

She ran her eyes over him approvingly. "Hmm, you look pretty buff for a real estate mogul." What she was really thinking was, *What a hunk!* Robert blushed deeply.

"So, what was your head full of that it needed to be cleared?"

"Just going through all this Emerald Tablet stuff, and the very real dangers involved. I've been wondering how many clues our friend Scott stashed, and where on earth we'll end up. Then there's you."

"Me?"

"Yes, you."

She tried to hide her nervousness with an awkward smile. "What is it about me that you're thinking about?"

Robert realized he was about to spout off his love for Jenna. He was not a man to mince around. No, he was a straightforward, full guns blazing, kind of guy. But this was different. It had only been two days since they met. He was worried she would think him to be an old fool. He wanted to tell her how he felt, but maybe now wasn't the moment. He blew out a long slow breath as he considered what he would say. He took a deep breath, and swallowed hard.

"Darn it, Jenna, I'm really worried about your safety! First, Scott leaves a note of concern, then he's kidnapped—never to be heard of again, then you're taken! I don't want anything to happen to you. You're import..." He cut off there abruptly, and averted her eyes.

Jenna was listening intently for what Robert would say. He seemed terribly uncomfortable. When he cut off where he did, she knew what he really wanted to say. But, why didn't he say it? Should she just come out with it, and clear the air? It was obvious they were in love. Then she smiled sweetly at him. She understood. He didn't want to come onto her too heavy, so soon. She also knew he would have to be the one to declare his feelings first. She would try to keep her thoughts to herself, but she would do all she could to facilitate the process for Robert.

Jenna, reached over, taking Robert's hand in hers, and said softly, "I understand, RJ. I understand completely." Robert returned her gaze. "I have to admit I'm a bit scared of what's going to happen. I've already been beaten once, and I don't want to be beaten again. Next time, they won't be so nice to me. But, I started this whole thing. I'm already in it up to my neck. I can't back down now. I'm all in. I can't do it alone, and you're not going to do it alone either. We're a team, you and me. We work well together. Quite frankly, I really enjoy being with you, and what's happening." *Will he take the bait?* she wondered.

Robert listened carefully to everything Jenna said. What did she "understand completely?" Was she trying to tell him she knew how he felt? What was happening that she enjoyed? Maybe he didn't have to spell it out. Maybe he could just let it happen. *Dang! Why is love so complicated?* he thought. He placed his hand on top of hers.

"You're a real trooper, Jenna."

They sat there for a minute or two, gazing into each other's eyes. They heard Carmen arriving with Jenna's breakfast. They slowly slipped their hands away. Carmen placed breakfast on the table.

"Oh, Carmen, it looks absolutely delicious!"

Carmen visually puffed up a bit. Robert had to stifle a laugh.

"More coffee, señor?" Her words had a slight frosty tone.

"*Sí, Carmen, por favor*. My breakfast was wonderful, as usual!"

Carmen turned, and walked away rather haughtily. Both Robert and Jenna, had to keep from laughing. Whatever tension had developed earlier, was now dispelled with this little comic relief.

As Jenna ate her breakfast, Robert explained, "We need to get vaccines before we travel. Normally, we would get these a few weeks before leaving, but we don't have that luxury. I found a clinic in Calgary, where they offer travel vaccinations. I'll call when they're open, to see if we can get our shots today. If we can, we'll head out as soon as you're ready. Take your time, though, they don't open until nine.

"The drive to Vancouver will take 12 to 13 hours. I thought we could head out on Monday morning. That would give you time to get fully recovered. I thought we'd take a day off, and just tour around Vancouver, if you want. On Wednesday, it's off to Ottawa. I've booked the tickets. I managed to get us on a non-stop flight.

"We'll apply for our Egyptian tourist visas early Thursday morning. Hopefully, we'll be able to get them by the end of day Friday. We could drive to Montreal that evening, or Saturday morning. Next Saturday night, we fly out of Montreal to Cairo,with a two-hour layover in Paris. We should be in Cairo by Sunday evening."

Jenna was happily munching her breakfast as she listened to the itinerary that Robert described. She nodded her approval occasionally. Robert had certainly been a busy boy this morning, she thought. She was very thankful for Robert, and his efficiency, and determination. She finished eating and took a sip of coffee.

"Wow! I can't believe it! Paris! Cairo! Dream destinations. Places I would probably never get to if it wasn't for this! Sounds to me like you've got it all planned, RJ. All I have to do now, is tag along."

"Jenna, I'm so sorry! I should've waited for you."

"No, no, RJ! That's not what I meant at all. I'm *glad* you have everything in hand. All I'm saying is you seem to be doing most of the work. Then again, I'd be totally lost without you! I'm so out of my depth here. When you told me a couple of days ago that I needed looking after, you were absolutely right! And I'm really glad you're the one who's looking after me."

Robert looked rather sheepish. He wasn't sure how to broach the subject. Again, he took a deep breath, and breathed it out slowly to calm himself. Still, he found himself stammering, and looking down at the table.

"There's just one thing, Jenna—the accommodations."

Jenna didn't know whether she should laugh or cry. This poor man—such a gentleman—was torn about whether they should share a room, or have separate rooms.

"I'm fine with sharing a room, RJ. It might be more believable than if we have separate rooms, since we're travelling together, and it's kind of obvious we're kind of sweet on one another. I think it would also be safer if we didn't split up too much." Would he take the bait this time, she wondered?

Robert's mind almost exploded! His thoughts scattered everywhere. He tried to compose himself. He picked up his coffee cup only to find it was empty. His hand was shaking. *Can't hide anything in a bathing suit*, he thought. He prayed silently that Carmen wouldn't return now with his coffee, but to no avail.

Carmen appeared with a fresh cup of his favourite brew. Robert was beet red; his whole body glowed. Carmen wondered why he was so red. Jenna caught her eye, with a pleading look on her face. She was also biting her lip hard. Robert was looking down at the table. As she approached, she saw the problem. She too bit her lip. The two women exchanged glances. Robert was mortified. Carmen placed the fresh cup before her master, and immediately withdrew.

It was obvious to Robert that Carmen had seen it all. He wanted to leave, but that was impossible at the moment. He found himself wondering how long it would take. He said nothing.

Jenna leaned towards him, reached over, gently touching his shoulder, and whispered, "RJ, please don't be nervous about it. I'm not."

She was very close. He could smell the scent of her perfume. Her hair brushed, ever so softly, against his temple. Robert leaned in, kissed her gently, and then with increasing passion. Jenna responded with her own passion. Tablet or no tablet, she knew she would never let this man get away from her.

They heard some scuffling by the patio doors. Carmen was averting her eyes from the couple. She could feel the "heat" from where she stood. It pained her to interrupt them. She had the cordless phone in her hand. Robert and Jenna fought hard to regain their composure.

"*¡Lo siento mucho, señor!* The telephone, señora Matheson," she croaked.

"It's alright, Carmen. I'll take it here. *Gracias*."

Carmen approached, and handed him the phone. She glanced at Jenna. Women seem to be able to communicate without words. It was obvious that Carmen had interrupted at a crucial moment. Jenna didn't convey to Carmen that she was upset in any way, just that the timing was terrible. Carmen understood.

"Carmen, there's a sticky note on my desk with the number for a clinic. Would you bring it out here please?"

"*¡Sí señor, pronto!*"

Robert took Jenna's hand. He placed the phone on speaker. For a few minutes he spoke to Sonya Matheson, a good friend of his and Christine's. She inquired about Robert's health, and some other chit-chat. She was concerned that Robert wasn't getting out, and socializing. Robert assured her he was fine, and in fact, planning to do some travelling. Sonya was glad to hear it, and asked if he'd chosen a destination. Maybe a trip around the world, Robert offered—in 80 days. They both laughed. He decided to tell her his trip might be a long one, and not to worry if he was out of the country for some time. They finally rang off.

Carmen placed the sticky note on the table in front of him. Robert dialled the number, and inquired about the possibility of obtaining travel vaccines that day. The receptionist replied in the affirmative, and advised they would have to come in before four o'clock.

Robert was back to normal now. He smiled at Jenna. They held hands. He kissed her gently. "I'll go get ready, then we can head out to get those vaccinations."

They were back by lunchtime. After lunch, they spent the rest of the day just taking it easy. It was another beautiful sunny day. Jenna wanted to catch a bit of sun, so she picked out an available bikini from Christine's clothes boxes. When Robert saw her, he almost dropped! It was the very bikini Chris used to drive him to distraction. Jenna looked fabulous, and very sexy in her long blond hair.

Robert jumped into the pool. Under the circumstances, it was the only thing he could do. Jenna understood. She jumped in seconds later. She swam over to him, put her arms around him, and as she kissed him, pressed her body firmly against his.

It was a very leisurely Saturday afternoon. Robert and Jenna were enjoying the sun out on the terrace. Jenna found a black string bikini to sunbath in. Robert was only too happy to apply lotion to her back and legs. They didn't seem to have a care in the world.

Carmen appeared, carrying the cordless phone, and looking concerned. She handed the phone to Robert. The caller-id displayed *RCMP*. Robert turned the phone to show Jenna. They looked at one another with mounting tension. The phone continued to ring. Robert nodded to Carmen.

"It's okay, Carmen, I'll get this."

Robert answered the phone, and placed it on speaker.

"Hello."

"Hello, sir. This is Constable Willows with the RCMP Airdrie Detachment, could I speak to Mr. Jackson, please?"

"This is Robert Jackson."

"Mr. Jackson, we're following up on a reported missing person in your area."

"I see. Do you have a description?"

"Yes sir, female, Caucasian, mid-40's, blond, between 162 cms and 170 cms, about 50 to 60 kgs, last seen wearing a light blue blouse, and short black skirt."

Robert sat quietly and did not respond. His mind was cast back to when he was informed Chris was involved in a road accident. The description the constable had given was exactly what Chris would have been like back then, right down to the clothes she was wearing.

"Sir, are you still there?"

In a gruff voice, Robert finally answered. "Connect me with your detachment commander, please."

"I don't understand, sir."

"Do it now, Constable, or I'll have your badge," Robert demanded, obviously restraining himself.

"Sir, you had best be warned..."

"No, Constable, *you* had best be warned. Connect me to your detachment commander, *now*!"

"One moment sir."

"This is Staff Sergeant Arnold, what is the problem, Mr. Jackson?"

Robert could barely contain himself. “Staff Sergeant Arnold, I am not amused by your constable’s little joke.” The strain in his voice was palpable. Jenna looked at him with great concern. “The missing person’s description your constable just gave me is the exact description of my late wife, who was killed violently in an accident not far from here—right down to the clothes she was wearing! What kind of game are you playing at, Sergeant, because I don’t find it funny?”

“I’m terribly sorry sir. I’m very sorry for your loss. However, this is the description of the missing person reported to us, sir,” replied the sergeant, in a very conciliatory tone.

“Who reported this person missing?”

“She was reported missing by staff at the Super 8 motel when they noticed her bed hadn’t been slept in all week.”

“And what does that have to do with me?”

“We’re checking with everyone in the area around Airdrie, sir, in hopes someone has seen her.”

“Forgive me for being so rude, Sergeant. If you look up the file for the death of my late wife, Christine Jackson, you’ll understand. As for your missing person, I’m afraid you’ll have to keep looking.”

“Thank you, sir. Very sorry to have upset you, sir.” The sergeant hung up.

“Oh, RJ, I had no idea!” Jenna said softly, with tears in her eyes.

Robert took Jenna’s hand in his, and smiled at her tenderly. “It’s okay, Jenna. Some hurts take a long time to go away. I miss Christine, to be sure, but it’s the way I lost her that hurts the most. Maybe, one day, I’ll be able to tell you about it. But that won’t be today.”

Robert sat deeply in thought for a couple of minutes. “In a way, this came in handy. I was able to throw off the police without causing any suspicion. We also found out the search for you is local, at least for now. And we know it was the motel that called it in. I would’ve been a lot more worried if it was the university.”

“Why is that?”

“If it was the university, I imagine your Dr. Bart, and his buddy Carver, would be involved, in which case we could expect a countrywide search.”

Robert looked at Jenna quizzically. He had a little smirk on his face. Jenna smiled, but had no idea what Robert was looking at.

"How do you feel about being a raven-haired beauty?"

"They're looking for a blond. Of course! Just like in a movie! What an adventure! I'd love to! I know this could be very dangerous, RJ, but let's have some fun with it too!"

"I think we're okay going to Calgary, as is. Hmm. Let's take some of the heat off us. While we're in Calgary, I want you to call the Super 8. Explain that you've been dragged from one meeting to another—goes with the cover. Ask them if they can send your things to you at the U of A in Edmonton. Have them charge your credit card, of course. That should squash the missing person report, and it should completely throw off our detractors."

Chapter 14 - Mistaken Identity

It was six o'clock on Monday morning. Robert was having an early-morning swim. Jenna was just rolling out of bed. How strange to hear an alarm clock again. It seemed like ages since the last time she was awakened to the sound of beep-beep-beep. Robert looked at his watch to check the time. He pulled himself out of the pool feeling refreshed, and wide awake. Jenna lay there for a moment smiling. She knew this would be a long day of driving.

The night before, Robert asked Carmen if she would mind getting up to prepare breakfast early. She gladly agreed, and was now dutifully in the kitchen making a nice "travelling" breakfast—nutritious, but not too heavy, since they would be sitting all day.

Robert was walking down the hallway just as Jenna emerged from her room. Both were dressed and pressed, and ready to go. Without hesitation, Robert slipped his arms around Jenna. They embraced warmly. Both were happy. Both were a bit tense. No more planning—this was it. There would be no turning back now.

They descended the stairs arm-in-arm. Carmen greeted them, announcing breakfast was served. She too understood their quiet time together was over. They would be leaving today. She realized only too well the dangers Robert and Jenna would be facing on their quest. She put on a brave face, but inside, her gut was churning, and she was frightened for them both. Jenna didn't only captured Robert's heart, but Carmen's as well. She didn't want to lose this happy couple now—not ever!

Breakfast this morning was a quiet affair. Robert and Jenna sat across from one another at the big dining table. They concentrated on their meal, both lost in thought. When they finished, they sat there leaning forward on their elbows, blowing on their hot coffee. Robert put his cup down and slid his hand across the table. Jenna looked up to see his confident smile. She reached to take his hand, and squeezed it tight.

"Well, this is it then."

"This is it, Jenna. The Emerald Tablet, or nothing!"

"Nothing but a very big headache!

"The other day, you said we should have fun with this. I agree. We need to be cagey, canny, and always ahead of the posse. Maybe half the fun will be how we can do that creatively. Above all, we need to be on our toes all the time, without being obvious about it."

Jenna pressed Roberts hand in hers. "RJ, I still don't know what possessed me to tear off on this quest on my own, in the first place. For years, I fantasized about going to exotic places I read about in dig journals, and making some incredible find of my own. But this isn't a fantasy! This is real! This is downright dangerous! Now, I've dragged you into this mess, not to mention expense. It's not lost on me that you'll be spending a lot of money—money I don't have. What was I thinking?"

To Jenna's surprise, Robert burst out laughing. He reached his other hand across the table. "Jenna, my sweet Jenna, for way too long I've been moping about the house feeling sorry for myself. I withdrew from society, from my friends, from everything. Meeting you was the best thing that could ever happen to me! I have no regrets. It's high time I had an adventure, and who better to have an adventure with? As for the money, it's just been sitting there growing, but doing nothing. It's time I did some spending. The danger of this quest is not lost on me—particularly for you. As long as there's breath in me, I'll gladly give my life for you."

Jenna didn't know what to say. Maybe the tears rolling down her cheeks said it all.

Carmen entered the room. She accepted the fact there would probably never be a good time to interrupt.

"Can I get you anything else, señor, señora?"

They both shook their heads. One final squeeze of the hands. They both stood up from the table.

"You know, RJ, I really think we'll pull this off!"

She took Robert's hand as she rounded the table. They walked resolutely to the front door. All the luggage, and travel documents, had been checked, and were sitting in the rented SUV, a Chevrolet Tahoe, sitting in the driveway. On Saturday, Robert, Jenna, and Andrea, his gardener, had slipped into

Calgary in his Land Cruiser. He decided it would be better to do a one-way rental from Calgary to Vancouver, rather than take his own vehicle.

Carmen stood on the front porch with tears in her eyes. *What will happen to them?* she wondered. *Will they ever return?* Robert was acutely aware of Carmen's distress. He wrapped his strong arms around her, embracing her tightly. He gave her a great big smooch—right on the lips! Carmen blushed deeply. When Robert moved away, it was Jenna's turn. She too gave Carmen a big hug, but dispensed with the kiss. She whispered in Carmen's ear, "Thank you for everything, for being so nice to me. We'll be back soon. Robert will see to that." Carmen tried to smile, but the intensity of her emotions was too much. Tears began streaming down her face, so much so, she had to pull her apron up to dry them.

Robert and Jenna got into the big SUV.

Suddenly Carmen shouted, "Wait, *momento, señor*! Your coffee mugs!" And with that she ran back inside. A minute or two later, she ran back out with two large insulated travel mugs. She handed them to Robert, who opened his window.

Robert took them, and laughingly said, "What will we do without you, Carmen?"

"Exactly, señor Robert. What *will* you do without me?"

Robert waved and drove off. He knew he could trust Carmen to tell any nosey visitors the story they agreed upon.

On the road now, they made their way along the Trans-Canada Highway, heading west. Robert and Jenna talked the whole way. They talked about anything and everything. They often laughed as they realized they had a lot in common. Conversation was easy, never strained. They were both enjoying the trip immensely. Although, they were both feeling comfortable and relaxed, Robert kept checking his mirrors to see if there was anything suspicious, particularly when they stopped for fuel and food.

Twice along the route, another SUV pulled in to fuel up, and eat, at the same time they did. Was it coincidence, or were they being tailed? At the second such stop, Robert told Jenna what he was noticing. Jenna, casually, looked at the three passengers of the SUV—two women and a man. They didn't look familiar to her as being involved in her previous abduction. This was the first test of their mettle. It was very possible they were being followed by these people. They had to show no concern, just two people in love who were on vacation.

Jenna was becoming rather nervous. Robert noticed, and decided to do something about it. He got up from his seat in the booth, and slipped in beside her. She slid over go give him space. He was smiling teasingly, which got her to smile. With his arm around her, he leaned in, and began to kiss her softly on the lips—little pecks and pulls. Jenna responded. She was much more relaxed now. The threesome they had noticed were chatting amongst themselves, while laughing quietly at the goings on between Robert and Jenna. There appeared to be nothing sinister about them.

The waitress came to their table, and asked if there was anything else. She too had a teasing smile. It wasn't usual to find an "older" couple being so lovey-dovey. Robert pointed to their two big travel mugs, and asked for a refill. A few minutes later, they paid the bill, and left.

Robert and Jenna sat in their vehicle for a few minutes, curious to see if the suspicious threesome would follow. They were not disappointed. They left the restaurant walking quickly to their vehicle. They looked surprised to see Robert and Jenna still there, intently studying a map. Robert saw immediately they had the deer-in-the-headlights look. Busted! The threesome entered their vehicle and delayed as well.

"Looks like we've got company, Jenna."

"I see that. What do you think we should do?"

"Act like a couple of love birds on a trip. Darling, I think you forgot your purse in the restaurant."

"You're quite right, dear. Should I go get it now?"

"Not just yet. Let's see what they're up to."

They folded the map. Robert started the Tahoe. He drove off as any normal person might. A few moments after getting back on the highway, the SUV with the unknown threesome followed—close enough to keep them in sight, and hopefully far enough not to be noticed.

A short way down the road, Robert pulled onto the shoulder. Jenna made as though she was searching for something. She got out of the SUV, opened the back door, and rummaged around. Their suspected tail had no choice but to drive past, anything else would cause suspicion. After they passed, Jenna got back into the Tahoe. Robert waited for a break in traffic, and pulled the SUV to the far-left lane where they made a U-turn at a nearby break in the centre median. They headed back to the restaurant, where Robert parked behind the building, out of sight.

In the black SUV, the woman sitting in the back seat watched helplessly as their prey was pulling a U-turn, and heading in the other direction.

"Are you sure she's the one we're after?" asked the driver.

The woman in the passenger seat chimed in. "Yeah, like where would she pick up a guy, and be all kissy-kissy with him in just a few days?"

"She fits the description, but you're right. Where the heck would she get herself a man, unless they already knew each other?" replied the woman in the back seat.

"Should we turn back and see where they're headed?" wondered the driver.

"It might be risky," said the first woman. "If they notice us, we're blown."

"If they're just regular tourists, will they even notice?" suggested the driver.

"Okay, let's go back," ordered the back-seat woman.

They had no choice but to continue to the next break in the median before they could make a U-turn of their own. They headed back at speed. They slowed as they passed the gas station/restaurant to check for the presence of the large white Tahoe. It wasn't an easy vehicle to hide. The two passengers scanned the entire lot, and service station area. Nothing. They must have gone back. They picked up speed, heading east, hoping to catch-up their prey. Thirty minutes later, it was obvious they had lost Robert and Jenna.

The woman in the back seat took a deep breath as she dialled a number on her mobile phone.

"Yes!" It was Randolph Carver.

"I'm sorry sir. We lost the couple we were tailing."

"What do you mean, you lost them?" he barked into her ear.

"Quite honestly, sir, we don't think it was the Carpenter woman."

"And why not?"

"Well, sir, she was with a man, and they were all over each other. It's only been a few days, sir. Where would she find herself a man? And why would they be travelling so openly. Carpenter would know we're looking for her. The last thing she'd want is to be out in the open."

Carver considered this carefully. He still wasn't happy. "How did you lose them?"

"It's actually a common occurrence with women, sir. It looked like she forgot her purse in the restaurant. They stopped a short distance down the highway. She was looking around their vehicle, got out, and looked in the back seat. We had to drive past, or arouse suspicion. When we looked back, they made a U-turn to return to the restaurant. They had a few minutes on us. She could easily have gotten her purse, and then taken the crossroad north or south. They were checking the map when they left the restaurant, sir."

"Were you made?" Carver growled.

"I don't think so, sir. They didn't take any notice of us. Like I said, they were totally into each other."

"I will call you back."

Carver hung up the telephone, then he dialled another number.

"Bartholomew," was the response on the other end.

"Did this Carpenter woman have a lover?"

Dr. Bart knew the voice. Carver was a man to fear, and not one to cross. "Not that I'm aware of. She was divorced a few years ago. No campus gossip about her with anyone else since. Maybe the odd date. I can make some discreet inquiries, if you like. Why do you ask?"

"Do your inquiries, and let me know within the next hour."

An hour or so later, Carver called his tracking team, and spoke again to the woman in the back seat.

"I don't like it, but you may be right. No one knows of any man in her life. Where is the damned woman? Very well, return to Airdrie, and start a house-to-house in the area where she disappeared."

When Robert and Jenna saw them pass by, they new for sure they were being followed. Robert wondered how they were discovered. Had they known all along that Jenna was at his place? Somehow, that was unlikely. He touched Jenna's hand, and nodded. They got back into the Tahoe, and drove quickly west. With some luck, they gave their tail the slip, but probably not for long.

Robert kept his eyes open for the black SUV that was following them. Even though Jenna didn't recognize any of them as her captors, didn't mean they weren't Carver's henchmen, or someone else's. The rest of the trip to Vancouver was uneventful. Robert made a lot of fuel stops to see if anyone else pulled in or pulled up on the highway. There was nothing suspicious. They both knew they dodged a bullet, but not by much.

When they arrived in Vancouver, Robert programmed the GPS to take them to the Rosewood Hotel Georgia—an historic 5-star hotel in the downtown area. Jenna had no idea where Robert was taking her except for the name of the hotel. She knew this would be their first night together. Outwardly, she was still confident and conversational, but on the inside, she was a bit anxious.

When they arrived at the hotel, Jenna couldn't believe her eyes. It was incredible! Her normal stays were at basic hotels, in basic rooms. This place was nothing short of opulent. It wasn't long before they were shown to an Executive Suite, which Robert booked after they decided to share a room. She couldn't believe her eyes. After the porter left, she just walked around the sumptuous suite touching everything. Finally, she turned to Robert, threw her arms around his neck, and kissed him hard.

Robert bowed low. "Well, Ms. Carpenter, will you do me the honour of joining me for dinner this evening?"

"Why, Mr. Jackson, I would be delighted," she sniggered.

"I suppose we should unpack some things. We'll be here at least two nights." He shuffled nervously, not to sure what to do next. "Well, I suppose you should get ready first."

"There's no reason why we can't get ready together, RJ." She too was nervous. She didn't know why. It wasn't as though she'd never been with a man. After all she was married for almost 15 years. Robert hadn't been with a woman since Christine died, five years earlier. Jenna took Robert by the hand, and led him into the spacious bedroom.

Jenna laughed as she contemplated the king-size bed. "With a bed this big, I may never find you."

Robert let go of his nervousness, and laughed along with her. They both started unpacking their bags.

"How on earth did Carmen manage to get all this stuff in two bags," she wondered out loud.

"Carmen is incredibly efficient when it comes to packing. Look at mine. The only problem is getting it all back in again!"

Before long, they both unpacked what they wanted. After a few more nervous moments they accepted they each had bodies, and went about their business. Robert wasn't sure if he should avert his eyes, or just stare at the stunning beauty in the room with him. On her part, Jenna found herself very attracted to

Robert.

They were both in just underwear now. Jenna noticed Robert in a deep blush, and kept turning away from her, as she moved around the room. Finally, she took him by the arm, to keep him from turning, and moved in front of him. Robert wasn't sure where to look. Jenna simply looked straight into his face, until he finally looked at her. She smiled sweetly. He swallowed hard. She reached back, unlatched her bra, and slipped it off. She moved closer to him.

"Make love to me, RJ," she whispered softly.

When it was all over, they both lay in bed, amazed at the sheer passion they demonstrated towards one another. There was no going back now. Robert knew this was the woman he wanted to spend the rest of his life with. Jenna would hang on tight to this wonderful man.

Robert made a reservation in the main dining room, so they decided to dress formal for the occasion. Jenna found four beautiful formal gowns packed in her bags, and chose a white shimmery dress with spaghetti straps, and completely backless. Robert's jaw dropped when he saw her. Jenna spotted the look on his face in the mirror. *Oh, Carmen, thank you, thank you, thank you!* she thought. He knew she would turn heads, especially sporting her new long black hair. Robert looked dashing in his standard black tuxedo.

In the dining room, Jenna did indeed turn heads—both male and female. She looked absolutely gorgeous! Robert felt proud to have her on his arm, and stood a little taller than usual. After a wonderful meal, they decided to check out the Prohibition Bar. They were glad they did. It was great fun, and they didn't feel out of place in their formal attire. The bar's lively music was great for dancing, and they danced the night away. It was magic. It was a dream.

After a late breakfast the next morning, Robert and Jenna spent a leisurely Tuesday in Vancouver. They simply wandered around openly, playing the part of star crossed lovers touring the city. Of course, the star-crossed part wasn't much of a stretch.

A large black SUV pulled up at the Jackson estate. A pleasant-looking lady got out and made her way to the front door. Carmen answered, as usual.

"Hello, my name is Linda Cavendish, and I seem to have misplaced a friend," the lady said.

"*Por favor, señora,* I do not understand...misplaced," responded Carmen in her officious tone.

"Forgive me. A friend of mine is staying in this area, but I've lost the exact directions, and I'm not familiar with the area."

"*Perdon, señora,* but there are no guests here at present. Since señora Jackson died, señor Jackson has not had any guests."

"Perhaps you have seen her then." The lady, showed her a photo of Jenna.

Carmen made a show of thinking about it when she saw the photo. "Maybe at *señor y señora* Nicholson. They often have guests."

"Which way, please?"

"It is about 4 kilometres in that direction," replied Carmen, pointing to the right.

"Thank you so much."

"*De nada, señora.*"

With that, the nice lady climbed back into the SUV. Carmen closed the door, and quickly made her way to the kitchen. She picked up her phone, and dialled Robert's number.

"Señor, a very polite lady just left. She asks about señora Jenna, and has a photo."

"What kind of car was she driving?"

"A large black SUV, señor."

Wednesday morning, found Robert and Jenna, along with all their baggage, at the Vancouver airport. Their non-stop Air Canada flight to Ottawa departed at 9:40 a.m., and was on time. Jenna was a bit surprised that Robert booked business class seats. Nothing but the best available, it seemed. Their flight was comfortable and smooth. It was about 5:30 p.m. by the time they deplaned. It was another thirty minutes before they had their luggage. They certainly weren't travelling light!

Pushing their two luggage carts, they made their way to the car rentals. Again, they chose to rent a large SUV with plenty of power. This time, it was a Range Rover. They were given a map of Ottawa, and some quick directions to the Fairmont Château Laurier Hotel in the downtown area. When they claimed their vehicle on the lot, the attendant showed Robert how to use the Range Rover's GPS, and set it for the hotel.

Jenna couldn't believe it. She would be staying at the Château Laurier! It wasn't long before they were shown to an Executive Suite. She couldn't believe her eyes. Again, she was in awe of the opulence of the room. Robert was obviously determined to show Jenna a good time, sparing no expense. After the porter left, she turned to Robert, threw her arms around his neck, and kissed him hard.

They decided to dress formal for dinner. Jenna looked, and felt, like a queen in the clothes Carmen picked out for her. Robert never complained when Christine wore them, and somehow, Jenna looked even better.

This time, there was no nervousness as they both prepared. After showering, they dressed. Robert in his usual black tux, while Jenna selected an off-the-shoulder black satin gown—tight in all the right places. Robert surveyed her approvingly. After dinner, they decided to relax in Zoé's Lounge, where they could listen to the very talented pianist. There was no talk of the Emerald Tablet.

The next morning, they made their way to the Egyptian Embassy, where they quickly found themselves at the visa application desk. There wasn't much of a line-up. Not too many people heading to Egypt these days—too many travel advisories. Nevertheless, the intrepid duo was not to be put off. They applied for a standard tourist visa. When asked, they told the person reviewing their application they were planning to travel to some of the main sights in Egypt, and maybe some smaller places—they didn't have a set itinerary. They answered all the usual questions, and a few more. Most importantly, the official looked at all the pages of their passports to see if they'd been to Israel. They were told their visa applications would be reviewed, and to return the next day.

They spent the rest of the day visiting the sights in, and around, Ottawa. They were having a great time. But all the while, they both watched for any signs they were being followed. So far—nothing! As he hoped, no one would expect them in Vancouver, or Ottawa. Why would they? What Robert didn't know was that Carver had people watching major airline gateway airports—which didn't include Ottawa.

On Friday, they did some more sightseeing before going to the embassy. When they arrived, mid-afternoon, the Egyptian passport officer greeted them cordially. He advised them that they were granted a 30-day tourist visa, which he then stamped in their passports. He gave them some additional literature about dos and don'ts while in Egypt. Much of this applied to Jenna, more so than Robert. There was the usual warning about liquor in a Muslim country. The official informed them there were a few unstable areas, especially in the Sinai Peninsula. If they stayed on main roads, they should be safe. He highly recommended they hire a guide to help with travel and translation.

They now had a choice. They could stay another night in Ottawa, or leave that day for Montreal. Their flight wouldn't be until Saturday evening. In the end, they opted to drive to Montreal, and overnight there. And, so it was. They checked out of the Château Laurier, and drove the two-and-a-half hours to Montreal.

Robert called ahead, before leaving Ottawa, to book a deluxe suite at Le Westin Montréal. Again, Jenna was in her glory. This was all a dream for her. She'd never stayed in the opulence of such hotels and never in a suite, with the exception of her wedding night. With all the wonderful clothes Carmen chose for her, Jenna could fit in anywhere, and feel comfortable, beautiful, and sexy. Robert approved wholeheartedly.

Robert arranged for a late check-out, so they didn't have to hurry in the morning. They ate a wonderful breakfast in the Executive Club Lounge. There was no doubt, to anyone watching them, that they were in love. Everything they did was wonderful. They enjoyed each other's company immensely. From time-to-time, Robert had to remind himself, and Jenna, they needed to be very watchful. Carver's people could be anywhere. They thought back to the drive to Vancouver when they were being followed. They both wondered why no one seemed to try to catch up to them after they gave the first trio the slip.

In the late afternoon, Robert and Jenna repacked their bags, with much difficulty, and checked out of the hotel. It was only four in the afternoon, and the flight for Cairo wasn't leaving until 9:40 p.m. They had a good four hours to kill. They wandered about, stopping at small shops to look at some of the interesting things for sale. Jenna would laugh, thinking of all the stuff she'd love to buy. Robert told her to get whatever she wanted, they could mail the items back to Alberta. In fact, Robert found some crazy aprons to send to Carmen.

Finally, they were at the airport, where they dropped off their rented SUV. They would travel to Cairo via Air France, with only one stop—at Paris Charles de Gaulle airport—for two hours or so. Since they were travelling business class, they had priority check-in, and could wait in the Air France executive lounge.

Jenna caught sight of the cost of a ticket, and almost fainted. Robert was certainly sparing no expense!

A solitary bearded man was wandering nonchalantly back and forth along the lines of passengers waiting to check-in at the various airline counters. He looked rather tired and bored. It had been almost four hours, and he was looking forward to the end of his shift. Soon his replacement would arrive.

He watched the comings and goings of the passengers, looking for one in particular—a woman named Carpenter. Why she would fly out of Montreal, he didn't know. All he knew was his mysterious big boss was paying him to be there, and he knew better than to complain. He had long ago memorized Carpenter's photo. There was no indication of her travelling with anyone, so he was looking for a good-looking blond with a furtive look. There were several close calls, but all of them false alarms.

As Robert and Jenna made their way to the check-in counter, he noticed Jenna right away. *What a stunner*, he thought. She was certainly better looking than the gal in the photo. Both she, and the man she was with, looked confident, and were obviously married, or at least lovers. He sighed. He thought it would be nice to have a great looking gal like that on *his* arm. He tore his eyes off Jenna, and continued looking around for his target. As far as he was concerned, the woman he was looking for was far away from Montreal.

Carver was pacing back and forth in his large study. He was not used to being denied what he wanted—and he wanted the Emerald Tablet. The emerald alone was worth a fortune, but it was the content of the tablet he was after. It was said it contained the secrets of alchemy and immortality.

He had dozens of people on the lookout for this Jenna Carpenter. He still fumed over the fact she escaped his interrogation team in Alberta. *What buffoons!* he thought. How had she managed to get away so cleanly? What sort of training did she have? She was not heard of for days, and the hotel filed a missing person report. Then, out of the blue, she calls the hotel from Calgary to have her bags forwarded to herself at the university, which effectively cancelled the search. But no one had seen her! Was it really her who called?

"Damn!"

The only probable explanation was that one of his competitors somehow found her. But how? Still, he couldn't take a chance. He had major airports watched around the clock. There were just too many bus stations. In Canada, trains are impractical, and have limited destinations, so there was no point wasting manpower there.

If she was on her own, she certainly knew how to lay low. He would have to find out if she has any friends in Calgary she might call on for help.

"Double damn!"

She had to be somewhere! She's a research assistant! This was not going well! He should've had the Emerald Tablet months ago! And *where* was Ambrose Scott? Disappeared without a trace—abducted! But by whom?

"Double, double damn!"

Carver slammed his fists on the desk.

Robert and Jenna boarded at about 9 p.m. It would take a while to fill the plane. First class, and business class, boarded first. Hundreds waited in the main hall for their turn to board. Jenna scrunched herself down in the generous seat next to Robert. She took his arm and squeezed it tight. Robert couldn't help thinking about the dangers, but they seemed so far away with Jenna at his side. While waiting to depart, the flight attendants passed around drinks, and some snacks. This was an overnight flight, and he knew he should get some rest. But he felt so invigorated, and happy. He wasn't tired, and by the look of it, Jenna wasn't tired either. Her face reflected the pure bliss she felt inside.

They talked quietly all the way to Paris. Now, though, the conversation was different. They wondered what would await them in Cairo, and in Taba. The Egyptian Embassy official mentioned the area around Taba was not so secure, and further down on the peninsula. Still, they had to risk it. It was obviously safe enough for Scott to place his first clue there. Jenna asked if they should make some kind of emergency plan in case things went badly. Robert considered this for a few minutes, and said it would be difficult to make such a plan now, not knowing what lay ahead.

In Paris, they changed planes. Their luggage would be automatically transferred, or maybe automatically lost altogether! Who knew? Today's modern technology left a lot to be desired. They were glad to walk about, a chance to stretch their legs. Jenna looked out the windows of the transit lounge. She told Robert she so much wanted to see the Eiffel Tower. Robert promised he would take her to Paris for a real trip after all this was over. She kissed him tenderly, knowing he would keep his word.

Before they knew it, they were back in the air, en-route to Cairo. Now, they were tired. They slept most of the way.

It was almost 7 p.m. local time when they arrived in Cairo. As with boarding, they deplaned before the masses. The Cairo airport was quite efficient. Before long, their passports were checked and stamped, and their luggage was waved through customs, as they had nothing to declare, and the eagle-eyed customs officials thought this was a nice couple. The men looked longingly at Jenna, with her long jet black hair, looking more like a goddess than a tourist. They all smiled, and gave a little bow.

Jenna was becoming rather self-conscious about the attention she was getting. Robert told her that it came with the territory—she was drop-dead gorgeous! She was glad Robert thought so, but worried that all that attention might attract the wrong crowd—meaning Carver's agents. Robert told her the last thing Carver, and anyone else, expected was a stunning beauty who stood out from the crowd. They would be expecting someone who would be trying to be as self-effacing as possible.

"The best place to hide," Robert told her, "is out in plain sight."

They wheeled their luggage to the taxi/limousine service desk. Robert ordered a limousine, indicating the destination as the Four Seasons Cairo at Nile Plaza Hotel. Jenna was truly appreciating Roberts, efficiency and ability to plan ahead.

When they arrived, they walked directly to the front desk. Jenna thought she must be in a dream. As with the other hotels, this was one of the best. Her mind almost exploded when they were shown to the Royal Suite on the 30th floor. She looked around at the luxury in a state of near shock. Then, she looked out the window. In the distance, she saw the pyramids at Giza, all lit up. That's when she simply broke down and cried. Robert walked over to her and put his hands on her arms. She turned, looked at him, tears streaming down her face, and began to sob in his arms.

"Looks like I got this one right," Robert said softly.

"RJ, darling, is this *real*? Are we *really* in Cairo? In Egypt?

Am I *really* seeing the pyramids?"

"Yes, Jenna, it's all very real."

"This must be costing you a fortune."

"Can't think of a better way to spend my money. Besides, it's all part of our cover."

"Oh, God, you're wonderful!"

Robert opened the doors, leading Jenna out to the private terrace. For a while, they just stood there, looking at the pyramids, the Nile, and the city lights around them. Jenna calmed down. They went back into the suite, and began unpacking.

"How long will we stay in Cairo, darling?"

"I booked this room for three nights. We'll leave on Wednesday for Taba. That'll give us a couple of full days here. You'll get to see the pyramids up close, and even touch them, when we visit Giza tomorrow—assuming you *want* to go to Giza, of course."

"I can't believe it! I'll actually be standing on the Giza Plateau!"

For the next two days, Robert and Jenna did the sights. They spent the better part of a day on the Giza Plateau. Jenna was busy acting as tour guide, as she led Robert all over the plateau. She knew it well from her studies, and work. They spent some time in the Cairo museum. Jenna was a fountain of knowledge. They were having the time of their lives. They didn't care if anyone was following them. They were a couple in love, doing what tourists do. On Tuesday afternoon, Robert rented a Toyota Land Cruiser. It was just like his own. He knew this vehicle well, and was happy to have it. Tomorrow, they would leave for Taba.

Wednesday morning, they repacked their bags. Jenna bought several nice outfits as they toured around. Both picked up some nice Egyptian souvenirs. The problem was what to do with them. They thought about buying another suitcase, but Robert said their four suitcases, and the carry-ons were plenty. In the end, they carefully packaged their new purchases and sent them off to Robert's place.

Robert called down to the Concierge, and asked if his Land Cruiser could be brought around, and a porter sent up for their luggage. This was done quickly and efficiently. Robert travelled enough in his life to know that booking a high-price suite came with certain perks not available to regular guests. Staying in the Royal Suite came with priority treatment.

Robert set the GPS in the Land Cruiser to get them to Taba. To be on the safe side, he had a road map of Egypt. The Concierge at the hotel showed him the route to take to get to Taba, but warned it could be dangerous in that area—particularly for non-Arabs. It would be a six-hour drive, once out of the city. There were often delays on the road which might stretch it out.

It was nearly 5 p.m. when they finally arrived in Taba. Robert booked a suite at the Swiss Inn Dream Resort on Nuweibaa-Taba Road just south of Taba itself. It was only a few kilometres away from Pharaoh's Island. In fact, they passed Pharaoh's Island on their way up to the hotel. They were shown to a nice suite with a large terrace overlooking the Gulf of Aqaba. They were booked for two nights, but were assured they could stay longer if desired.

Along the way, Robert was careful to watch for anyone who might be following. So far, there was no one. It was looking like his plan of hiding in plain sight was working well. They had either eluded their hunters, or they had some incredibly good luck.

"RJ, come here for a moment." When he arrived beside her, she added, "Look over there. The city of Aqaba is on the other side of the Gulf, and the Tel Al Hajiwa dig site is only 20 kilometres or so from there. This is so surreal!"

Robert smiled at her, with his arm around her waist. He was thinking this was indeed surreal. He was in some strange little place on the Sinai Peninsula in Egypt, just a few kilometres from the Israeli border, with the most incredible woman he'd ever known. Christine was never far from his mind, but Jenna now filled his heart.

"I'm not going to argue with you. This is not where I expected to be a couple of weeks ago. It's still early. I noticed when we checked-in they have a spa here. Maybe you want to check it out to see if you can get a nice something-or-other before we have dinner."

Jenna thought this was a great idea, and phoned the number for the spa. She was in luck, and she could come down now. After a quick shower, she made her way to the spa area. She must surely be in a dream!

Robert did some unpacking of his own, and took a shower. He was tired after the long trip in the hot sun. He donned swim trunks, and headed for the pool. After a few laps, he felt refreshed, and invigorated. In his robe, he walked to the lobby area where they had many brochures. He spotted one he wanted—snorkelling at Pharaoh's Island. He inquired at the desk where he might be able to get some snorkelling gear, and was informed he could either purchase or rent some gear at a small shop across from the island. Robert returned to their room, slipped off the robe, and sat down in a shady corner of the terrace. He closed his eyes, and dozed off.

Robert awoke with a start as Jenna kissed him on the neck and shoulders. They laughed about it. She looked radiant. *How could she be more beautiful than before*, he wondered.

Jenna had changed into a bikini, and sat on the chair beside him.

"Well, darling, this is it. Tomorrow, we go to Pharaoh's Island on a pretence of snorkelling. Somehow, we'll have to make our way around the entire fortress without arousing any suspicion. Hopefully, we'll be able to find the next clue."

"If we keep up our love-birds cover, we should be able to rummage around without too much trouble. Do you think there will be someone watching the island?"

Robert considered this for a moment. "It's unlikely. They wouldn't know where Scott hid his note, unless he cracked, that is, in which case there won't be a note to find."

"RJ, they were following us a few days ago. Wouldn't that mean they still didn't have the Emerald Tablet?"

"True. What concerns me more is whether or not they have people in Taba watching out for anyone out-of-place. After all, this would be a likely spot for Scott to ditch the tablet."

At the Mövenpick Resort, four of Carver's men were stationed to watch Taba, and the surrounding area. There are many hotels in the Taba area, and they were going around casually gossiping with hotel staff and guests to discover any new faces.

That evening, one of the men was lounging in the lobby of the Swiss Inn, talking to one of the staff. He was told of a foreign couple arriving in a big SUV.

"The woman is as beautiful as Cleopatra, and has the bearing of a queen," said the porter. "The two are obviously very close.

"Americans?"

"No, I think they're Canadians."

"They keeping to themselves?"

"Not at all. The woman went to the spa for a treatment almost as soon as they arrived. I saw the man in the lobby a bit later looking at brochures. I think they're in the dining room now."

Carver's man thanked him and sauntered towards the dining room. Through the door, he scanned the guests seated at the tables. A waiter asked if he wanted to be seated. He accepted and went in. As he did, he noticed Robert and Jenna sitting at a table hidden from his original view. From the vantage point of his own table, he could watch the two of them. The woman was certainly very beautiful. The man seemed fit, and somewhat older than the woman. It was obvious they were in love. He could see it on their faces. They certainly were not keeping a low profile. He pulled his phone out, and looked at a photo of Jenna he was texted days ago. The face was similar, but the hair was very different. She didn't look like a woman who was being hunted. He ordered, and ate his meal quietly. At an opportune moment, he snapped a picture of them with his phone. He texted a number with the photo attached.

Randolph Carver's mobile phone buzzed. It was the one he used for this project. He always destroyed the phones he used when an item was finally acquired. He picked up the phone, read the text, and looked at the photograph. The picture was rather small, and he couldn't tell much from enlarging it. He walked over to a large monitor, and connected his phone using Bluetooth. Now, he could see the photo clearly. He stood back, and looked at the two people in the photo.

This looked like the couple his Alberta team lost on the Trans-Canada highway. They hadn't taken a photo, so he had nothing to compare to. If this was the same couple, what were they doing in Taba? What a strange place to be. They certainly weren't in a hurry. It was almost a week-and-a-half ago when they were lost. They weren't hiding. They didn't look frightened, nor on their guard. Who was the man, and where did he come from? Is he an acquaintance of Carpenter's from Calgary?

"Damn!"

There were just too many questions!

He texted back: "Keep an eye on them, but carefully."

Jenna caught the man taking a picture of them. She never turned to challenge him. She kept her focus on Robert the whole time.

"Darling, a man over on my left just took a picture of us with his phone."

"Big guy, looks Egyptian?"

"That's the one."

"Noticed him come in, and scan the room. He's looking for someone, alright. Don't take any notice of him. If they've made us, they'll keep a watch on us. If they don't know we know, we have the advantage."

They finished their meal, signed the receipt, and casually made their way back to the room. Carver's man had no idea he was now under suspicion.

Carver's men set up a four-man rotation. They would watch the hotel from a vehicle parked nearby. They couldn't watch the room itself, because it was on the Gulf side of the hotel. They figured as long as their targets were in the hotel, they wouldn't be able to escape.

In the morning, Robert and Jenna had breakfast in the restaurant. They didn't want anyone to have the impression they were being evasive in any way. They took a walk around the hotel, looking at the nice flower beds, and the scenery around them. To keep up appearances, Robert brought an expensive camera, which he had around his neck. He took lots of pictures of Jenna all around the building. He would also take pictures of the surrounding area with his lens in full telephoto. He saw an SUV parked a short way down with a good view of the hotel driveway. When they finished their little tour, they returned to the room to discuss their next move.

"Well, Jenna, my dear, we're definitely being watched. I saw an SUV parked near the front of the hotel with one man in it. He has binoculars, and is watching the hotel. No one will go in or out of here without being noticed."

"Do you think they know we were doing recon as we walked around?"

"Don't think so. I think we were doing the tourist thing well enough, but not overdoing it. I still think we have the upper hand."

"Are we still going out today to Pharaoh's Island, then?"

"I think we proceed exactly as planned, sweetheart. We're just a couple in love wandering the world together having fun."

"RJ, I know this is getting serious, but I *am* just a woman in love wandering the world with the man I love. I know we have to be careful, but I can't get my head around it."

"I know what you mean. I feel the same way. Maybe that's

how we have to keep it. The more we act naturally, the less they'll be interested. If they were sure about who you are, they'd come grab you, like they did in Airdrie."

"Then I just continue living in a dream?"

"Yes, and no. We still need to keep our wits about us. We both seem to be naturally observant, so we can see what's going on around us without it disturbing whatever we're doing."

Robert went to the table to fetch the brochure about Pharaoh's Island. It had a nice picture of the fortress. He sat back down by Jenna, and spread open the brochure.

"This is Pharaoh's Island. According to the brochure, it's a diving hot spot—especially snorkelling. There's a shop across from the island where we can get the gear we need."

"How do you know that?"

"Spoke to the desk clerk. He told me about the shop.This is Saladin's fortress. It takes up much of the island. We'll need to scout it out when we're there. If Scott was clever enough to get the tablet away from the dig site, out of Jordan, and put clues to its hiding place in different locations, he was just as clever with the hiding place. His note said we'd find the next clue at high tide, so it's on the outside of the fortress. He would pick a spot where few people go. He wouldn't want anyone to see him hide the clue, and not likely to find the clue either, unless they were looking for it."

"You're right, R.J. Scott's one of the best we have. He has a sixth sense on where to find things. That means he's probably just as good at hiding them."

Now, they prepared to go on their first clue hunt. They both dressed very casually, with bathing suits under light clothing. They waved at the front desk staff as they left the hotel. They drove slowly down the driveway to the road. They made their way, without haste, to their destination, without a care in the world. Carver's watcher followed behind them at a safe distance. Robert noticed him right away. They slowed and turned off the highway when they reached Pharaoh's Island. There were already several vehicles parked there.

Hand-in-hand, they walked to the small shop near the beach. They were amazed it was a full dive shop. Not only could they get snorkelling gear, they could also rent tanks, and wet suits. Robert bought two new snorkels, but rented the fins and masks. To make it look good, he bought a small waterproof camera. The dive shop operator, who spoke passable English, said the battery was fully charged, and it had an SD card already in place. He told them there was a boat that shuttled back and forth from the beach to the island, as required.

Carver's watcher shook his head. If this couple was looking for something, they sure weren't hiding the fact, nor did they seem pressed for time, nor furtive for that matter. He'd followed people before. He knew how they acted—always looking around. This couple didn't seem to give a damn. He phoned his colleague back at the hotel.

"This is a dead end," he said. "These guys can't be who we're looking for..."

"They're just getting snorkelling stuff to go out to the reef around Pharaoh's Island..."

"We've followed people before, and they were always trying to slink around so as not to attract attention. These guys haven't thrown a suspicious glace, and they're certainly attracting attention. That woman is a real beauty. Can't miss her. They're just out having fun..."

"They're either very brave or very stupid..."

"Yes, I know what the boss said. Still think we're wasting our time..."

He disconnected, sat back and waited.

The boat arrived a few minutes later. Robert and Jenna boarded, and were soon on the island. They waved to the boatman as he left. They didn't see many people, but then, they would be out on the reef, diving. For now, they found a spot where they could leave their clothes in a cloth bag they bought at the hotel. They donned their gear and flapped out into the Gulf of Aqaba. Jenna asked Robert to take a picture of her standing in the water. This was an absolute must. They laughed about it.

The watcher peered through his binoculars, and shook his head.

They splashed in the water, and did some diving. They shared the camera, taking lots of pictures of the fish, and each other. As they swam around the island, they would scan the shoreline for a likely location to find the clue. Robert spotted what he thought was a great place. Scott would probably have snorkelled here too. He reached out, and touched Jenna's arm. In an embrace, he told her of the spot. They rotated slowly while in a clinch. Jenna saw what Robert was talking about, and agreed.

Jenna began swimming towards the spot. She swam fast, and laughed. Robert swam after her. When they got to the shore, they tossed off their gear, and picked their way gingerly across the rocks. They pressed up against the wall of the fortress, in a lover's clinch. As they moved around, they looked for some sort of crevice where the clue might be hidden. The high-water mark was obvious on the fortress wall. Jenna let out a little shriek. She pretended to be biting Robert's ear.

"About a metre away...a crevice with a stone that looks oddly placed," she whispered.

They rolled around along the wall to the crevice. Jenna had her arms around Robert's neck. Robert had one arm around her waist while the other hand was groping around just behind her. He managed to dislodge the stone, and reached in. He felt what seemed to be a plastic bag with something in it. Jenna leaned forward to give Robert more room to manoeuvre. He pulled the bag out, folded it behind Jenna's back, and with the folded note in his palm, placed it in his bathing suit pocket. He was always grateful men's bathing suits have a pocket.

They walked along the fortress wall, looking up, cocking their heads back and forth. Robert took a picture straight up the wall, and one of Jenna standing next to the crevice where he found the note. They laughed, and smiled sweetly at one another. They walked back to their gear, and entered the water again. Robert hoped the bag was well sealed. They kept swimming around the island enjoying the view.

Back at their clothes, they grabbed their shoes from the bag, and stuffed in the diving gear, after shaking off as much water as possible. They climbed up the staircase to check out the fortress.

The watcher looked through his binoculars again, just in time to watch Jenna, in her bikini, heading to the staircase. *What a beauty,* he thought. *Just tourists.*

Robert and Jenna were dying to see the contents of the clue.

"We can't chance taking it out here," Robert advised.

"I know, and it's probably in Esperanto, as well."

They lingered at the fortress, taking in the sights, and taking lots of pictures. They would have plenty to bore Carmen to death with when they got back, Robert thought.

It was three hours later, when they made their way down to

where the boat would pick them up. They sat there for a few minutes, and waved towards shore. The boat headed out to fetch them. Before they knew it, they were dressed again, and driving back to the hotel.

The watcher took out his phone, and dialled.

"Yeah, they spent about four hours here swimming, and wandering around the fortress. Lots of sexy stuff, but they're not looking for anything. They're just tourists. What do you want me to do?"

"Okay, I'll be there in five or six minutes."

Chapter 15 - Off to Suez

It was mid-afternoon when Robert and Jenna walked through the lobby of their hotel. The desk clerk greeted them with a smile, asking how they enjoyed their time at the reef. They both looked elated. Robert told the clerk they had a wonderful time, and it might be worth a return visit to do it again.

Back in their room, they dropped all their things just inside the door. Robert took off his slacks so he could get at the note in his bathing suit pocket. They sat, full of excitement, at the small dining table. Robert quickly took the clue, in its zipper bag, out of his pocket, unfolded it, and pressed it flat on the table. They both sat there quietly, looking at the mysterious note they retrieved a few hours earlier from an innocuous little crevice at the base of Saladin's fortress.

"I don't see any water in the bag," remarked Robert.

"So, the note should be intact, then."

They just sat there, looking at the note.

"This one is yours to open, RJ."

For whatever reason, Robert was very nervous about opening the clue. Finally, he picked up the bag, unzipped it, and pulled out the envelope. It was sealed.

"Do you have something in your make-up case we can use to open the envelope?"

Jenna sprang up, and ran to the bedroom. Robert asked her to bring in his iPad while she was there. Jenna was gone for less than a minute, returning with a nail file, and Robert's tablet. Robert took the file, and carefully slit the envelope open. Inside, he found a folded note. He pulled it out, unfolded it, and pressed it flat on the table. It contained only 2 lines, written in Scott's hand:

Kie ŝipoj tra la dezerto velo, rigardi kie herooj ripozi.
K-1 B+3 A+1 Vidi de la oriento, ne de okcidente.

As with the first, Robert pulled out his smartphone to take a clear photo of the note.

"What do you think it means, particularly the equation on the second line?" wondered Jenna.

"The Wi-Fi connection looks good. I'll fire up Google Translate, and we'll see what Saladin has to offer us."

Robert carefully typed in the Esperanto. He had a few issues with the accented character, but finally got it.

> *Where ships through the desert sail, look where heroes rest.*
>
> *K-1 B+3 A+1 See from the east, not from the west.*

They read the note out loud several times.

"The only places I know where ships sail through the dessert would be the Nile river and its tributaries, and the Suez Canal," offered Jenna.

"The word 'ships' is the key here. I can't see ships cruising Nile estuaries, and the Nile is one long river—just not specific enough. Suez, on the other hand, is a specific place where you might hide something."

"I'll go along with that. But what about *where heroes rest*?"

"We need to be careful. We've been out for hours. I'm famished! We need to keep up our cover, remember. I think we should change, head to the dining room, and have a nice meal. We don't want anyone to think we got back from Pharaoh's Island, then secluded ourselves here right way."

"You're right, sweetheart. Come, let's shower and go. Maybe we can try to work it out over lunch."

They walked together to the bedroom, and prepared—but not before Robert slipped the note between the cover and first page of the room service menu. It wouldn't be a place where anyone would look, should their room be searched while they were out.

In the dining room, they sat at a table near the window. After ordering, they gazed into each other's eyes, holding hands, speaking low, just as any couple in love might do. But now, the conversation was not about being in a dream world, it was about trying to decipher Scott's riddle.

"So, we're agreed that Suez it the place," confirmed Jenna.

"Yes."

"Where do heroes rest, darling?"

Robert considered. "Heroes are usually dead—at least most of those I've heard of."

"Cemetery?"

"Sounds right, but not just any cemetery; it has to be a special cemetery."

"War cemetery?"

Robert looked at Jenna lovingly. "Again, I think you've got it. We need to check out war cemeteries in Suez."

"What about that equation? What do you think it means?

"The only thing I can think of, is that it points to the grave site in the cemetery."

He changed places to sit next to Jenna at the table. He pulled out his phone, and brought up some pictures they took while in Cairo. If anyone was looking, it was obvious they were looking at pictures. They looked, laughed, and commented on each one as they flipped through them. Finally, they arrived at the equation, which they considered for a few moments.

Jenna looked thoughtfully at Robert. "Letters can stand for numbers too, can't they?"

"Yes, of course they can! Let's see. K is the 11th letter of the alphabet, so K - 1 would be 10."

"B would be 2 + 3 is 5. I'll let you do the last one because it's really hard."

"Very funny! Okay, A is 1 + 1 is 2. So, we have 10, 5, and 2. That would be the grave number."

"That's way too easy, RJ! Scott was trying to make things at least a bit difficult for us. The grave number is just way too easy. There's got to be something else. Could they be mixed up?"

"Look at this last part of the riddle. *See from the east, not from the west.* That has to be the key."

Jenna repeated, "*See from the east, not from the west.*" She put her arm around Robert, turned, and gave him a long passionate kiss. "To help keep our cover," she sniggered, "and to help me think."

The waiter arrived with their food. He was about to place Robert's food where he sat, but Robert told him to put the plate across the table. When Jenna kissed him, he flipped the photos back to a Cairo picture. He didn't want anyone to see what they were *really* looking at.

He moved back to his seat across from Jenna. He liked the view much better. They ate, quietly smiling at each other. From time-to-time, they spoke love talk. It was time to have fun. When they finished, Robert stood up, offering his hand to Jenna. They walked out the door to the pool area, where several fountains were splashing happily. They had their arms around each other.

"I see it's time for a walk to clear the head, and get the blood flowing again," chuckled Jenna.

"You're absolutely right, my dear. And to simply enjoy your wonderful company." Robert was thoughtful for a few moments. "Most middle-eastern languages are written right to left, aren't they?"

"I believe so. What are you thinking?"

"Right to left—from the east, which is on the right on a map compass, to west, which is left on the compass."

"Of course! Now it's your turn to be brilliant! The grave number is written from right to left: 2, 5, 10. That'll be it!"

"Now, all we need to figure out is which cemetery. We'll check them out on the Internet when we saunter back to our room."

During all this time, they both kept a weather eye out for the watchers. They didn't follow them to the hotel, and there was no one suspicious hanging about. Had they dodged a bullet once again? Or, were they preparing for something more sinister?

Carver's watcher from the previous evening was on the phone with the hotel porter, who was given money to keep an eye on Cleopatra and her man.

"They arrived at the hotel a little over an hour ago," advised the porter.

"Did they seem excited about anything?"

"Not really. They looked happy, as usual, and said they really enjoyed the reef; said it might be worth another trip back to Taba to do it again."

"Did they stay in their room after returning?"

"Only for a few minutes. They changed, and came out for lunch. Looks like they were looking at pictures on his phone. They were laughing, and kissing. The usual. After that, they wandered around the pool area looking at the fountains. I don't see them anywhere, so they're probably in their room making love."

The watcher rolled his eyes at this. He thanked the porter.

Turning to his confederates, he said, "Told you it was a waste of time. Just two lovers having an Egyptian adventure—nothing more."

Back in their room, love once again took centre stage. Robert quickly checked the room service menu. The note was still there. He had visions of making sweet love to Jenna amongst the splashing fountains, and admitted this to her. She laughed, held him tight, and told him maybe they could sneak out in the middle of the night, just for fun. For now, their cozy suite would have to do.

It wasn't until the following morning that they turned their thoughts back to Scott's clue. Robert pulled out his iPad, and began searching for war graves in Suez. The obvious choice was the Suez War Memorial Cemetery. They even found an online document showing the layout of the graves.

"Look, RJ, they use letters and numbers for grave locations."

"You're right, darling. Looks like we'll have to rethink those calculations. A + 1 could either be section 2 or section B, I suppose; B + 3 could be E or 5; and K -1 could be J or 10."

Jenna pointed to a link on the page. "There's a link here for casualty records, if we take a look at that, we might be able to figure out the grave numbering for the lettered sections to see how it compares to what we have."

Robert displayed the casualty list. "Great idea! Look, the numbered sections contain three parts, like our number, while the lettered sections are consecutive numbers."

"Then we're looking for grave 2, E, 10, right?"

"Looks like that. Let's find out who that is... Cagey old Scott, he picked a Canadian casualty's grave, being a Canuck himself. I think we've got it! Let's find a nice hotel in Suez and book for tomorrow. We'll just enjoy ourselves visiting the sights around here for today. If this is the Sinai Peninsula, then Mount Sinai must be here somewhere."

"RJ, are you kidding me? We can actually go to Mount Sinai?"

"Let's go for breakfast first, and we can ask at the front desk."

Jenna threw her arms around Robert's neck, kissing him hard. Robert accepted the sweetness of her lips, holding her tight. He was in heaven. When Jenna finally let go, they spent another 15 minutes perusing the hotels in Suez. There wasn't much to choose from. In the end, they booked a terrace suite for two nights at the Jaz Little Venice Golf Resort in Ain Sokhna, south of Suez on the west side of the Gulf of Suez.

Robert secured their belongings, and they headed to the dining room. On their way, they stopped at the front desk to inquire about Mount Sinai. They were informed it was a popular destination for pilgrimages. It would be about a three-hour drive each way. There was the St. Catherine's Monastery, as well as several guest houses where they could get food, and some fine crafts could be had at a few local shops. If they wanted to go to the top, it was almost a three-hour trek by foot, or on a camel.

Robert and Jenna decided they would go for it. After a quick breakfast, they grabbed a few bottles of water, and returned to their room. They changed into something suitable for the long day of travelling, and grabbed Robert's good camera. Jenna was very excited, so they almost ran to their vehicle. Jenna practically dragged Robert, who was laughing heartily. He looked around, but didn't see any sign of watchers. Needless to say, they had a marvellous time on their little side trip to Mount Sinai. Jenna was in her glory!

"Nothing much to tell you," reported the porter, "They had breakfast, then left in a big hurry to visit Mount Sinai. The woman was obviously excited, and dragged her man along. They'll be gone most of the day."

It was late in the evening when Robert and Jenna returned to their hotel. They were tired, but happy. They took a shower, and changed into some fresh clothes. Robert checked the room service menu. Nothing was disturbed. The porter was just going off shift. He asked them how they enjoyed their day at Mount Sinai. They both reported it was a wonderful experience. At dinner, they enjoyed their meal, quietly talking about all the great experiences they were having together. Jenna was still living in a dream. Robert wasn't far behind.

Back in their room, they sat close to each other on the sofa. It was only now they decided to talk about the Emerald Tablet. They would leave in the morning after breakfast. It would be a long drive to Suez. They would be retracing their steps along the same highway they took to get from Cairo to Taba. It would be about an hour drive from their hotel to Suez city. They could visit the canal, and the War Memorial Cemetery, on a day outing. With some luck, they'd quickly find the clue, decipher it, and get to their next destination.

They decided to make an early night of it, and snuggled close in absolute bliss. Sleep came easily to both.

Robert and Jenna cuddled in bed for a while after they awoke. Finally, Jenna couldn't resist, and began teasing Robert with little kisses, and gentle caresses. Robert was truly enjoying this, and resisted for as long as he could. In the end, they both lost themselves in pure love.

After showering together, Jenna began packing her cases. Robert donned his swim trunks, and headed to the pool, where he swam a couple of dozen laps. He returned and showered again. He felt refreshed and invigorated—ready for the drive to Suez. He retrieved Scott's note, and slipped it in the pocket of one of his pants, then quickly packed his case. If Carmen saw the mess he made, she'd be totally disgusted. They both laughed at the thought of what she'd say when they returned home. Jenna stopped a moment to think of what they just said. She now simply assumed she would continue to be with Robert after their quest was completed. Robert felt the same way. He couldn't imagine life without Jenna.

When they finished a hearty breakfast, they asked if it was possible to have some food prepared they could take with them on their journey. The waiter checked with the chef, who was happy to make something nice for their road trip. Robert stopped at the front desk to check-out while Jenna continued to the room. When he finished settling the bill, he asked for a porter to help get their luggage into their vehicle. Within a few minutes, they were off to Suez.

The porter gave his report to Carver's watcher. Cleopatra and her man left after breakfast. They weren't secretive about their next destination—Suez. They wanted to see the canal, and might take a cruise up the canal to Great Bitter Lake and back.

Carver's watcher made a call.

"Yes," answered Carver.

"You wanted to know where that couple was heading to."

"Yes."

"Suez, to see the canal. Just tourists, sir."

Carver hung up the phone, and wondered. Were they really just tourists? They certainly acted that way in Taba. Was it a coincidence? He would be a lot happier if he knew who she was.

"Fools never checked their passports to get names!" he spat out loud.

He placed a call to the Taba watcher.

"Get their names from the hotel register!"

Two hours later, the watcher called back.

"Mr. and Mrs. Robert Jackson is what is on the register, sir."

Carver hung up. He was shaking with fury. He wanted to know

what was on their passports. As far as he was concerned, Robert Jackson was an alias. Who was he? Was it the Carpenter woman with him? Why were they so absorbed in each other? Why no concerns? Why pop up in Taba when they were cruising around in western Canada? Why go to Suez from Taba? Things just weren't adding up.

"Damn! More questions! No answers!"

In their Egyptian hideaway, Scott and Zahra were blissfully happy. Scott never felt so wonderful in his life. He thought back to all the digs he worked. He loved digging. But there was no love to compare to what he felt for his delicious and awesome Zahra. On her part, Zahra often thought of their first night together—the night she knew beyond doubt that Scotty was the man she wanted. Never before had she felt such intensity. It also surprised her it would be a foreigner. She didn't care. This man loved her, and would be faithful to her always, and she would be faithful to him until death.

Scott would find, once again, that Zahra had a cunning, and organized mind. One day, in late June, a stranger showed up at their door. Zahra spoke to him quietly for a few minutes, then closed the door.

"Who was that, Zahra?"

"A messenger from Taba," was her nonchalant reply.

He looked at her in amazement."You have a courier network back to Taba?"

"Yes, my dearest husband. You did not think we would vanish without knowing what was happening in Taba, did you?"

"What did he have to say?"

"He reported there are some things happening in Taba. Four strange men are staying at the Mövenpick. They are going around looking for someone—a woman who works at your university. They show a photo to people. Her name is Carpenter. They have been asking at hotels. He said these men began watching a couple staying at the Swiss Inn, but gave up when it was obvious they were just tourists."

"Carpenter? Jenna Carpenter? Is that the name?"

"Yes, that is it. Do you know her?"

"She's a research assistant who works only on campus. She must have found the directions hidden in my notebook before I was so gently kidnapped. She was able to translate my note. Good for her!"

"She is in danger, then. If your real kidnappers are looking for her, they will take her, and beat her for the information she has."

"You're right, my love," agreed Scott sadly.

"You might be interested to know the couple they were watching are going to Sucz."

"So, they found the first clue on Pharaoh's Island. Why else would anyone go to Suez from Taba? Did your messenger say if the couple being watched went to Pharaoh's Island?"

"He said they spent many hours there. They were being watched. They stopped watching after they left the island."

"I wonder who the man was she was with."

"Whoever it was, she is very much in love with him. The messenger said they were always together, and very loving. They were registered as Mr. and Mrs. Robert Jackson, a man older than you."

"Jackson? Don't know anyone named Jackson."

"He reported that the woman is more beautiful than Cleopatra, with a wonderful figure, perfect skin, and long black hair. Do you think, my Scotty, that I am more beautiful than Cleopatra?" asked Zahra demurely.

Scott smiled as he answered, "Cleopatra could not stand in your shadow. Your beauty is perfect. She is dead. You are alive, and warm, and I love you."

Zahra gave him that special smile she only gave her man. She jumped on his lap, kissed him, and looked longingly and teasingly at him. Her invitation was not rejected.

Later, holding Zahra in his arms, Scott thought, *So the search begins. It didn't take as long as I thought.*

Chapter 16 - Grave Robbers

It was a long hot trip to Suez. Robert and Jenna were delayed along the way for over an hour, owing to an overturned semi-trailer that left much of its contents strewn all over the road. A large tow truck was needed to drag the unit off the road, to get traffic moving again. Robert decided to turn off the engine of his rented SUV so as not to risk it overheating. The Land Cruiser is a hardy vehicle used heavily across arid plains and deserts, and would probably not have problems, but why take the chance? With the sun beating down on the vehicle, it became very hot in no time at all.

They were glad they had some good food, and lots of water, for their journey. After five hours, they finally reached Suez. It would be almost an hour before they reached Ain Sokhna to the south on Route 65.

It was just after four in the afternoon when they rolled in at the Jaz Little Venice Golf Resort. Within seconds of pulling up to the entrance, a porter was already there to take their luggage. Robert and Jenna made their way directly to the front desk. It was a lovely hotel, and worth the extra drive. Before long, they were shown to an Executive Suite with a nice view of the pool area.

Moments after the porter left, they closed the curtains, stripped, and had a long refreshing shower. Afterwards, they stood at the foot of the bed, and simply fell backwards. They lay there, staring at the ceiling, with their legs hanging over the edge. Jenna started laughing. Robert took her hand in his.

"This must be the most exhausting trip I've ever made!" exclaimed.

"I've had worse, but not by much."

Jenna turned to Robert, and said teasingly, "It'll be a while before dinner."

Robert turned to look at her, appreciating her beauty. She was looking at him sweetly, biting her lower lip. Robert didn't need a written invitation.

It was nearly seven when they were suitably dressed, and made their way to the main restaurant. They were shown to a table by the window. Sitting at right angles to one another, they held hands, entranced with the beauty of the scene before them in the sunset. The colours were beautiful. Neither spoke. Their mutual contentment showed clearly on their faces. There wasn't a crease of concern to be found there. The Emerald Tablet was in some other galaxy. It was just them now, happy and in love.

Their reverie was interrupted by the waiter who arrived with their food. They slowly turned to look into each other's eyes. The world was at peace this night. The food was wonderful. They ordered dessert and coffee to end their meal.

Now, they wandered out of the building, heading for the pristine beach. They both kicked off their shoes, and walked barefoot on the sand, holding hands. Very little was said. They could just enjoy one other quietly, each lost in their own thoughts. They sat in the sand hugging their knees, looking at the moon's reflection on the water. When they spoke, it was in hushed tones, almost a whisper, as if they were afraid of shattering the dream.

"It's so beautiful and peaceful here, RJ. I'm not sure this can be real. I'm sitting on a beach on the Gulf of Suez, in Egypt, with the man I love. I've been to Vancouver, Ottawa, Montreal, Paris, *Cairo*, Taba, and now here. I've stayed in wonderful hotels, and even a Royal Suite, stood on the Giza Plateau, touched the pyramids, *and* the Sphinx, explored a coral reef in the Gulf of Aqaba, and wandered through a fortress where Saladin once lived. And all in less than three weeks! I feel like a princess on a world tour, and we've only just *begun* our quest."

Robert smiled as he listened to her. She was right. This was indeed surreal. Three weeks, was that all? Sitting here now, it seemed ages ago, like he'd been with Jenna forever. He felt alive, content, happy. But, for Robert, being quite a practical man, the dangers of the quest were never far away.

"Your more than a princess, Jenna. You're a queen—the queen of my heart, and my whole being. I hope you'll allow me the privilege of being your knight in shining armour."

"Oh, RJ, you're so much more than a knight. You're my king,

and I'm your very humble consort. Without you, without your courage, without your wisdom, without your money (she sniggered), there would be no quest at all. I would be dead in some awful little place in the back of beyond of Alberta."

"Which brings us back to reality, I'm afraid. In the next day or so, we need to go to the war cemetery to look for Scott's next clue. There may not be many people there, but I don't think it'll be a cake-walk."

"We'll find it, and we'll get it too, R.J. I know in my heart we'll be successful in our quest."

"We still need to figure out what we'll do with it when we find it."

"What'll we do tomorrow?"

"I think tomorrow we keep our cover intact—just tourists in love in a surreal dream." He smiled at her. "Our little ruse has worked so far. Look at Taba! We were being watched, and they gave up on us because of our romantic ramblings."

Jenna laughed. "We certainly have been acting rather like a couple of teens on school break!"

"Call it what you will, darling. It's working, and I'm really enjoying it!"

"No complaints here either, my love, no complaints."

When they returned to the hotel, still barefoot, they attracted a bit of attention, but they didn't care. They walked over to the Concierge to inquire about the possibility of taking cruise up the Canal to Great Bitter Lake and back. He told them about a luxury cruise that departs at 8 a.m., returning to Suez at about 8 p.m. Meals and drinks were served on board. He said they were likely to pass many different types of ships cruising up and down the Canal—from pleasure craft to large naval vessels. He offered to make a booking for them, if they wanted to take the cruise. They accepted, and returned to their room.

As always, Robert took a quick look around the suite to see if anything was disturbed. Everything looked fine, so he breathed a little easier. Neither noticed anything unusual during dinner, and on their walk. Robert decided to call home, knowing Carmen would be worried sick about them. Although he could make the call on the hotel phone, he decided to incur the outrageous roaming charges, and called on his cell phone, feeling it would be more private.

Carmen was happy to hear from her boss, and breathed an

audible sigh of relief when she heard their voices, particularly as there was no sign of stress, only happiness. Jenna excitedly told Carmen about their wonderful adventure so far. Carmen reported there was some activity going on in the Airdrie area. Some of her friends, who work in other households, told her they too had been visited by a "nice lady in a big black SUV" using variations on the story she used on Carmen. There were also "road crews" beating the bushes along the dirt road leading to the highway. The were pretending to be picking up trash in a beautification effort, but they were wandering quite far from the road to find their trash.

After they rung off, Robert said, "Looks like they're still looking for you in Alberta in a big way."

"So, they think I dropped dead in the bush."

"Carver is covering all his bases. He had us followed, but he's not sure if you're really you, or if you perished after escaping. The house visits the 'nice lady in a big SUV' is making tells us he still thinks you're alive."

"Do you think they'll stop trying to follow us here, then?"

"Carver would be a fool to drop us completely. He's got to wonder if we're the same couple they were following on the way to Vancouver. The descriptions would match. We know the watcher in Taba took a picture of us, but we don't know if the watchers on the Trans-Canada took a shot of us or not. I didn't notice anything, did you?"

Jenna thought for a moment. "No, RJ, I don't recall anyone taking our picture when we were on the road, unless they did it from inside their vehicle."

"Carver is spending a bundle on finding you, that's for sure. We'll have to keep our eyes open. Carver is actively looking for us now. It's only a matter of time before he gets my name, if he doesn't already have it."

"Do you think Carmen is in trouble?"

Robert considered Jenna's question carefully. "You're right, it's time to get Carmen out of the house."

Robert made two calls. The first was to a security company in Calgary that Robert used in the past to watch the house when he and Christine were away for an extended period. He arranged for the house to be patrolled several times per day. He could also monitor the whole estate from his cell phone or tablet. The second call was to Carmen.

"Carmen, Jenna and I talked about what you told us. We feel

things are getting too dangerous for you to stay at the house."

"But señor, I am not afraid of a woman in a SUV!"

Robert and Jenna smiled at one another. Good old Carmen!

"I know, Carmen, but it's not the woman in the SUV I'm worried about, it's the gang they'll send when they figure out who I am. Carmen, I want you to pack, and go visit someone. You may be gone for a few weeks or more, so prepare for a long vacation. Of course, I'll pay whatever costs you'll have."

"Señor Robert, is it truly necessary?"

"Yes, Carmen, it *is* truly necessary. You must also tell Andrea and Jake to go for a vacation as well. No one is to return to the house until I contact them. You must all leave as quickly as possible. Stay in a hotel somewhere in Calgary tonight until you can make arrangements."

"Is it truly so dangerous, señor? You and señora Jenna sounded so happy before."

"Yes, it's very dangerous for all of you."

"But who will take care of the house, señor?"

"Call the usual cleaning service and arrange for them to come in once a week. We've done this before, so it shouldn't raise any suspicion. I've already arranged for the security service to patrol the house until we return."

"*Bien, señor*, if you command it, I will tell the others. We will leave quickly."

"Call me when everyone is out of the house. I'll turn off this phone when I know you're safely out, so they can't trace it back to us."

"Sí, señor."

With that, Robert rung off.

Jenna noticed the deepening furrows on Robert's face."You're very worried, darling."

"Better to be safe than sorry. This way, they'll have no one to push around. If they try ransacking the house, they'll find nothing, and might get themselves caught in the process."

The sky was dark, thunder cracking, lightning streaking to earth, and rain pouring down, where Randolph Carver paced in his grand study. The same was happening in his head. He was furious! He was not accustomed to this kind of foolishness. Never before was he denied his prize quickly and efficiently. He had connections—important connections—and yet he had no idea where Ambrose Scott and Jenna Carpenter disappeared to so completely.

There were too many unanswered questions. How could an unattached university research assistant simply vanish? Was the woman on the Trans-Canada actually Carpenter? If so, where did she acquire a lover? Was this couple chasing the elusive Emerald Tablet? If so, why were they travelling openly, not covertly? Why were they not concerned about attracting attention to themselves? Was the couple on the Trans-Canada the same couple who popped up in Taba? Why were they now headed to Suez? Did they find anything in Taba? Who *are* they? Is Jackson a real name or an alias? Who was funding their travel? Where *are* they *now*? Questions, questions, questions!

Carver found himself knowing precious little about his quarry. Carpenter was described as a hard-working, divorced, research assistant who dated infrequently, and was not known to have a lover. She had a few good friends—all female—who didn't have a clue where she was. They tried to reach her several times, without success. As for Robert Jackson, no one at the university seems to have heard of him. He was the dark horse; Carver was sure of it. But he had absolutely no information about him.

It was time he had some answers. He picked up his mobile phone, and dialled the "nice lady" who was looking for her wayward friend in the Airdrie area.

"Report!" he barked into the telephone.

She described the progress so far—nothing! No one remembered seeing the Carpenter woman anywhere in the area. No one heard of any woman wandering in the area, or being picked up. The search along the roadside found nothing—not even a shred of clothing. The woman simply vanished.

Carver slammed his fist on the desk. He wanted to shout at the woman, but knew it would be a waste of breath. On the other end, the "nice lady" was trembling with fear. She was one of the few people her boss used consistently for his little projects. She knew he too would be trembling, but with anger, not fear. She waited for him to speak first. Carver was trying to calm himself down. His myriad of questions floated around in his mind.

"Find out if there's anyone in the area named Jackson!"

"Jackson, sir?"

"Yes, Jackson! Are you deaf?"

"Just a moment, sir." She quickly went through the interviews she had with various people during the house-to-house search. "Yes, sir, there is a Jackson in the area. I remember a housekeeper telling me that since her mistress, Mrs. Jackson, died, Mr. Jackson had not entertained any guests."

"Do you remember which house?"

"I didn't take any particulars down unless I thought they would be useful, but I'm sure I can zoom in on the house again in a few minutes, sir."

"Then I suggest you get zooming, and find out *where in hell they are*!" shouted Carver, and immediately disconnected the call. *Ah, for the good old days, when I could slam a phone down on the receiver*, he thought.

The ever-efficient Carmen called Andrea and Jake to the main house as soon as she disconnected from her call with Robert. She explained that señor Robert told them to pack, and go on vacation immediately. There was to be no arguing, or debate. They looked at Carmen quizzically, wondering if she'd gone completely mad. What they saw was a face of stone. They'd seen that face before, and knew not to question her orders. If the boss said get out of the house now, he meant it.

It was less than an hour later when Carmen, Andrea, and Jake left the Jackson estate. Carmen made the housekeeping arrangements. The service had keys to get in, and were given the latest guest pass code for the front gate. Carmen knew she could count on them to keep the place clean. Just before leaving, Carmen made the call to Robert, to let him know that everyone was gone.

Carver answered his ringing cell phone. "Yes!" he growled.

"I found the Jackson house, sir. It's a large estate a few kilometres from the highway, and from where the Carpenter woman disappeared."

"Are you staking out the house?

"Yes, sir, but we have to be careful. There's a security company patrolling around the estate. The gates are closed, and they have the code to get in to check the house. We don't want to be spotted."

"When you first visited the Jackson place, was the gate open or closed?"

"Open, as I recall, sir. Why?"

"Do you remember seeing any security people in the area?"

"No, sir."

"Have you seen anyone entering or leaving the property?"

"Only the security people, sir."

"He must be onto us. Gates are closed, security patrol, and probably no one home."

"Do you want us to take a quick look inside, sir?"

"Are the patrols at regular intervals?"

"Too early to tell, sir."

"See if you can find a place to get in—without being seen—and take a look around. Don't leave a mess for the security people to notice. Let me know if you find anything relevant."

Finally, Carver thought, *we're getting somewhere!*

Robert and Jenna woke early on Sunday morning. They needed to leave by 6:30 to make sure they were at the Canal docks in time to board the cruise ship. It would be a long, leisurely, day on board, and they were sure to see some interesting sights. They quickly showered, and dressed casually. Robert grabbed his camera while Jenna stuffed some things in a cloth travel bag. The breakfast buffet was just being set out when they arrived in the dining room. They ate quickly, and were on the road.

At that time of the morning, there wasn't much traffic on the road to Suez. The GPS led them directly to the docks in plenty of time. This was an upscale cruise. The *Queen of Suez* was a nicely appointed boat. She was quite clean, with no obvious rust showing. She sported a fine dining room, and two bars—one at either end. The crew were dressed in well-pressed whites, and were courteous and efficient.

The passengers already aboard, and those who arrived shortly after Robert and Jenna were well dressed, and perhaps a little haughty. Jenna's choice of outfit for the outing was perfect. She would definitely fit in with the other ladies. Robert figured there were between 25 and 30 passengers aboard when it looked like everyone had arrived.

On the docks, not far from the *Queen of Suez*, stood two men. They were carefully watching the passengers as they boarded. As usual, Jenna's beauty attracted attention. They looked again at the photo displayed on one of their mobile phones. They decided that Robert and Jenna were the pair they were looking for. One of the men dialled a number.

"Yes!" growled Carver.

"We have found them. They just boarded the *Queen of Suez* for a luxury cruise up the Suez Canal."

"You're sure it's them?"

"Yes. They're the same two from the photo you sent. What do you want us to do?"

"How long is this cruise?"

"All day, 12 hours. It leaves in a few minutes."

"Are there any stops on this cruise?"

"I don't know. We've never taken the cruise. Too expensive."

"Then get aboard, and keep an eye on them. And try not to be too obvious about it!" barked Carver.

"But sir, we are not dressed appropriately. This is a luxury cruise!"

Carver was on the verge of exploding. "Just follow them, you idiots! That's what I pay you for!"

After disconnecting, the watcher told his companion they needed to get aboard. They both looked incredulously at each other. They had dressed down to be inconspicuous among the dock workers. The first man shrugged, and told the other to get moving. They almost ran to the counter where they could buy tickets for the cruise. The ticket seller looked at them with a certain loathing, but their credit card was good, so they were given tickets, and told to hurry. Once the gangway was up, they wouldn't be allowed to board.

Just as the crew was about to raise the gangway, Robert saw two badly dressed men running quickly, shouting at the crew to wait. They made it aboard in the nick of time. An officer went over to check their tickets. Finally, he had no choice but to let them stay aboard.

Robert was watching this with interest from his vantage point at the upper rail. Whoever these men might be, they were certainly in a fluster, almost in a panic. Robert smiled, and turned to Jenna, who was having a delightful conversation with a couple of American ladies. He gallantly waited for a break in the conversation before taking Jenna by the elbow, leading her away.

"Sorry, darling, but I think we've got company." They moved to the rail where Robert nodded his head towards the two awkward-looking men who just boarded.

Jenna chuckled as she observed the two newcomers."You'd never know it from their attire. It certainly won't be difficult to spot them."

"We need to be very careful, Jenna. They could be the comedy team meant to get our attention while the real watchers are very close to us."

"Did they come on at the last minute, RJ?"

"Yeah, fairly ran up the gangway just as they were raising it."

"If Carver, or his minions, made us earlier, they wouldn't be so blatantly obvious about coming aboard."

"True enough, my dear. True enough. So, we need to keep up our cover without getting too close to our new friends. We'll have to find a way to lose them when we get off."

"I just love keeping our cover!" Jenna sighed, as she squeezed Robert's arm.

So do I, he thought, *so do I!*

As though they didn't have a care in the world, Robert and Jenna schmoozed their way around the boat, chatting with the other passengers, and gazing passionately into each other's eyes. They enjoyed the scenery passing by, with either Robert or Jenna taking pictures, often asking other passengers to take their picture together.

Meanwhile, Carver's two watchers were seriously shut out by the others. No one wanted to associate with them, as though they knew these men were up to no good. Whenever the watchers approached Robert and Jenna to try to steal a snippet of conversation, they casually moved away, arm-in-arm, and engaged other passengers in conversation. For some strange reason, the watchers never felt they'd been made. Robert and Jenna took no interest in them, except for the odd curious look because they stood out so much. But the intrepid duo took great notice of them, and never let down their guard.

Occasionally, one of the officers of the *Queen of Suez* would mingle with the passengers, as was their custom. It was obvious that several of the passengers were put off by the watchers, judging by the disparaging looks the officers gave them.

Near the end of a wonderful cruise, the 1st Officer was chatting with Robert and Jenna. Robert casually mentioned that he thought these men were taking far too much interest in Jenna, and was concerned they might have something nasty in mind. The officer offered to have the men detained below, if they were bothering them. Robert said that might cause a needless stir, and ruin an otherwise pleasurable cruise. Instead, he suggested that, perhaps, these men might somehow be gently delayed while the passengers disembarked, and left the docks. The officer was glad to accommodate them.

And so it was, at the end of their wonderful cruise, Robert and Jenna disembarked amidst the other passengers. The two watchers were taken aside by an officer and two crew members for a private discussion, and told they were banned from ever setting foot on the *Queen of Suez* again. By the time they finished, all the passengers had left the dock area. Robert and Jenna were long gone.

"Glad you're making the call," the second watcher said to the first.

Very nervously, the first watcher dialled the number.

"Well?" barked Carver at the other end.

After a long pause, "Well?"

The silence at the other end said it all. Carver flew into a rage. "You *lost* them! You were on the same boat all day, and you *lost* them!"

"Yes, sir. Sorry, sir. Please let me explain..."

"I don't want explanations; I want to know where they are!" Carver shouted furiously into his phone. "Find out where they're staying, or you'll both be taking a very long vacation! Do you understand?"

"Yes, sir!"

Carver disconnected.

"Idiots! Complete idiots! Why have all my regular people suddenly become idiots?" he shouted out, in the confines of his study. "These two are out there, without a care in the world, all over each other, not hiding, not sneaking around, and no one can find out anything about them, or where they are! You'd think they were trained undercover agents, or something! They're making me look like a fool!"

He picked up the phone, and called the "nice lady" on speed dial.

"Yes, sir."

"Gina, get yourself, and your team, to Egypt ASAP! I need you to be on the ground in Suez within 24 hours."

"You've tracked them down, then, sir?"

"Yes, but the buffoons in Suez had them all day, then lost them. They did a luxury cruise on the Suez Canal. They must be in Suez somewhere, or at least close by. I want you to tag these two, and stay with them. They shouldn't be hard to find again, they're out in the open, and apparently, the Carpenter woman is attracting a lot of attention."

"We'll need to get visas, sir."

"You can get those when you arrive. Use my private jet. I'll have it in Calgary in the next couple of hours. I'll make some calls to make sure your visas are waiting for you when you land."

"And the search here?"

"Put the second team on it. Tell them to be careful. Give one of them this number, and make sure he knows to report in regularly."

"Yes, sir. I'll have everything arranged within the hour. We should be at Calgary airport in by the time your plane lands."

"Good girl! Don't mess this up! We need to find these two, and find out what they're up to."

"Yes, sir. I'll let you know when we're in the air, and when we arrive in Egypt."

"I want regular reports of what you're doing out there, do you understand? And be careful of those two idiots already on the ground in Suez, or they'll expose you. You need to stay low."

"Got it, sir."

Robert drove at a leisurely pace back to their hotel in Ain Sokhna. They were both happy, having thoroughly enjoyed their day-long cruise. They knew of the dangers of having Carver's watchers so near them, and yet they never felt in danger. The watchers were so obvious they couldn't even get close.

Robert checked many times for any sign they were being followed. There was no one on the road behind them. In the hotel lobby, a quick glance around showed nothing out of place. Almost as an afterthought, Robert went to the front desk to ask if there were any messages. There were none. If anyone inquired about them, Robert figured the desk clerk would've mentioned it. After a light snack, they talked for a while about the interesting sights and sounds they encountered on their cruise. They decided to call it a day, feeling very mellow.

It was seven o'clock on Monday morning. Jenna was still sound asleep. Robert slid out of bed gently, so as not to wake her. For a few moments, he looked at her lying there so peacefully, with a smile on her face. She looked like an angel. He was surprised to find a tear running down his cheek. He wiped it away, smiling.

He quietly donned his swim suit, and padded barefoot out of the room. It was time to get some real exercise. There was only one other person at the pool, another lap swimmer like himself. He jumped in. The water felt fresh and rejuvenating. After fifty lengths of the pool, he pulled himself out, dried off, and returned to the room.

He found Jenna awake now, lying on her front with her chin resting on her hands, which rested on a pillow at the foot of the bed. She was waiting for her man to return. She knew he would. When Robert appeared at the door, Jenna smiled broadly at him. She lay there uncovered, in all her radiant beauty. Robert responded, and they made beautiful love.

Later, over breakfast, they spoke, for the first time since they arrived, about the Emerald Tablet, and the next clue. Robert told her the cemetery was open between 7 a.m. and 2:30 p.m. They would have to go immediately after breakfast.

"Do you think the clue will be hard to find, RJ?"

"It's hard to say. I think it'll be easily accessible, like the first clue, because he wouldn't have much time to stash it without being noticed."

"I don't imagine there'll be too many other visitors, since this is a war cemetery, and most of those buried there are from foreign countries."

"You're probably right, darling. That's a two-edged sword, though. If we're the only ones in the cemetery, we'll stick out like a sore thumb. If there are lots of people, it'll be difficult to find the clue."

In a way, Robert was thankful for the hour drive to Suez. This gave them a chance to discuss strategies to cover various scenarios that might develop at the cemetery. To watch them now, anyone would have said they were operatives from some sort of secret agency. Except for Jenna placing her hand on Robert's arm while he drove, there was little sign of affection. It was all business now. These were two intelligent people on a mission. Each was glad for the other's insights. They were ready; neither was nervous.

As they arrived in Suez, Jenna spotted a flower shop, and suggested they get some flowers for the grave. It would seem odd for them to visit a grave without something to place on it. Robert pulled over. Jenna went alone into the flower shop. She chose a nice bouquet, which she paid for on her own credit card. Back in the vehicle, she happily showed Robert her little purchase.

"Even put it on *my* credit card! It's not much, but now I can say that I contributed *something*."

They both laughed. This helped ease the tension built up during the intense strategizing on the way there.

"My darling Jenna, you've contributed significantly to this little quest, and don't you forget it!"

Fifteen minutes later, they were at the cemetery, and parked close to the gate.

"Ready if you are, darling."

Always the gentleman, Robert walked around to open the door for Jenna. She emerged, holding the flowers, with a sweet smile on her face. She put her free hand on Robert's face, leaned in and kissed him gently.

"Got to keep up appearances," she sniggered.

Robert smiled, and offered his arm as they walked through the gate.

Gina, and the rest of Carver's elite team, arrived in Cairo by Carver's private jet at 6 a.m. on Monday morning. It was another hour before all the paperwork was completed, despite Carver's connections, and money. There was no use complaining. Nothing moved very quickly in Egypt at that time of the morning. This was, after all, a private jet, not an airliner with hundreds of passengers. It was 7:30 a.m. by the time they rented two SUVs. Although it was normally a two-hour drive from Cairo to Suez, unexpected road works slowed things down considerably. They finally entered Suez at nearly 10:45 a.m. They were given an address where they would meet up with the two watchers who lost Jackson and Carpenter the previous day.

The watchers carefully explained their dilemma on the cruise, and how they were delayed from disembarking until all the passengers had left. There was no way of knowing where their quarry had gone. As others before them, they described Jackson and Carpenter as just two tourists. They weren't nervous in any way, or showed any concern about them—at least, no more so than the other passengers.

Gina listened attentively. It was obvious these men were rank amateurs—more of a liability than an asset. In a separate room, she placed a call to Carver.

"Sir, it's 11:15 a.m. local time in Suez. We've met with the local guys. I'm afraid you're right, sir, they *are* idiots. I suggest cutting them loose, and letting us take care of things here."

"They may be idiots, but they know the Suez area better than you do. Keep them handy for now, if for no other reason than to provide local information and scuttlebutt. Do you have a line on our two wandering lovers yet?"

"Not yet sir, but we have some ideas on where to start."

"Don't drag your feet, Gina. These two may be out in the open, but they sure have a habit of disappearing in a hurry!"

"I understand *exactly* what you mean, sir. I won't quickly forget how they vanished in front of our eyes on the Trans-Canada."

"Don't remind me of that. I can't believe that you, of all people, would be hoodwinked by a couple of amateurs. Find them, but don't touch them. When you find them, keep a multi-person watch on them around the clock. You have *carte blanche* on this one in terms of expenses. I want to know what they're up to; don't want to pounce just yet."

"Yes, sir. Thank you for your confidence, sir."

"Don't let me down, Gina! This may be the biggest prize ever."

Robert and Jenna casually made their way around the cemetery. They stopped to look at the Cross of Sacrifice, directly across from the entrance. They made their way slowly to the Stone of Remembrance, where they stood solemnly for a minute or two. As they turned around, they glanced across the entire cemetery. They were the only visitors. They could see the gardener working quietly at the far end.

Jenna took the cemetery layout from her purse. Robert looked at it carefully. They could walk directly ahead of them, down the alley between groups of graves. When they arrived at the second group, they continued on, counting rows as they walked. It would be the fifth row. When they reached it, they turned left, slowly walking, looking at the names on the graves as they went. At the tenth grave, they stopped.

"Where do you think he hid the note, RJ?"

Robert was surveying the grave. "The only place I can imagine is somewhere in the small patch of earth around the gravestone."

"RJ, there's a small flower planted just next to the grave. I don't see many others with a planted flower."

"You're right; and it looks recent. I don't see the ground disturbed anywhere else, do you?"

"No. It all looks like the other graves."

"I'll go around to the right side of the grave, and crouch down. Move around to the other side, and crouch down to place the flowers on the grave, against the stone. With any luck, I'll be able to pull up the plant without the gardener noticing. Hopefully, the clue is just below the plant, and I can push it in again quickly."

The gardener noticed the raven-haired beauty, and her escort, entering the cemetery. Out of the corner of his eye, he saw them walking around. To him, they seemed to be a dignified couple who would cause no trouble. When he saw them crouching beside a specific grave, he wondered if he should go over to see if everything was in order.

Robert dug his fingers around the new plant, and gently pulled it out of the earth, trying not to be noticed. He plunged his free hand into the whole. Got it! Another envelope in a zipper bag. This he handed to Jenna reaching across the gravestone. He quickly replanted the flower, and was compacting the earth around it just as the gardener arrived.

"Is everything in order, sir?" The gardener watched Robert pressing down around the plant.

"Yes, everything is fine. This flower was planted recently, and I was just digging up the soil to make sure the roots can spread."

"This man was my great-uncle," Jenna told the gardener. "We wanted to see his grave while travelling in Egypt. Do you know who planted this lovely flower?"

"It was at least a couple of months ago, madam. A man came to ask me if he could plant the flower next to the grave. I think he would be my age, and very fit. I offered to plant it for him, but he insisted on planting it himself."

Both Jenna and Robert were standing now.

"It was very nice of him. Do you know his name or address? I would like to write a thank-you note to him."

"No madam. He left no name."

"What a shame," said Jenna. "Do you have any idea whom it might be, darling?"

"I'm afraid not, dear. You have a big family. It could be anyone."

"You keep the cemetery in very good condition," Robert told the gardener. He took out his wallet, and pulled out some money, offering it to him. "A small token of our appreciation for your excellent work here."

The gardener wasn't sure what to do. No one ever offered him a token of their appreciation before.

Jenna smiled sweetly at him. "It would please us greatly if you accept our little gift."

Slowly, the gardener took the money, thanking them profusely.

Robert and Jenna continued to tour the cemetery, sometimes

stopping to look at a gravestone. There was no hurry. Finally, they turned towards the entrance. Just before leaving, they waved to the gardener, who was back at his work.

Outside the gate, they walked casually to their vehicle. It was 11:15 a.m. They would be back at their hotel shortly after noon. Robert's smartphone began sounding an alarm tone. He pulled the phone out of his pocket, feeling rather remiss that he forgot to turn it off. It was the house alarm from his estate.

Jenna curiously looked over his arm to see what was going on. He turned the phone so she could see. The app he used showed which zone(s) were triggered, so he could quickly select the appropriate camera. They watched with interest as four men dressed in dark clothes, with ski masks pulled over their heads, climbed over the wall on the far side of the estate. Within minutes, the security people had them under surveillance, waiting for the police to arrive. Some sixteen minutes later, what appeared to be a contingent of armed police surrounded the house. Zones all over the property were showing red now. The four thieves, undoubtedly Carver's men, were trapped. One managed to escape by throwing himself into some thick bushes, waiting there for an opportunity, and finally sneaking to the wall, which he climbed in a great hurry. Robert and Jenna sat there in amazement watching the goings on as Robert switched from one camera to another.

Jenna looked at her man with admiration."That's one heck of a security system, you have there, RJ!"

"Works like a charm. The security company has access to the entire system. Those guys were made the minute they scaled the perimeter wall. Too bad one of the beasties got away."

"I don't think Carver will be a happy camper."

"No, he won't. I'm sure we've thoroughly ticked him off now. He obviously knows who I am, and where we live. We'll have to keep our guard up—more than ever."

"Thank goodness Carmen, and the others, are gone, and safe," she said. And to herself, *He said, where we live.* Her heart fluttered. She touched his arm, looking at him with great tenderness, and moist eyes.

When they arrived at the hotel, Robert again inquired if there were any messages. Of course, there were none. Needless to say, he would've been very surprised if there *was* a message. They walked, holding hands, down the corridor to their room.

Once inside, Jenna threw her hands around Roberts neck,

kissing him passionately. Robert responded with equal passion. And yet, there was something needling him. He somehow felt there was an urgency about deciphering the note, and leaving the Suez area quickly. He imparted as much to Jenna. By now, she had come to trust his intuition implicitly. Without argument, she pulled the note from her purse, offering it to Robert.

They moved to the small dining table in their suite. Robert dashed to the bedroom where he retrieved his iPad, and the nail file from Jenna's make-up kit. With both seated at the table, Robert opened the zipper bag, extracted the note, and slit it open. With a wry smile, he passed it over to Jenna.

"It's your turn, darling."

Jenna, unfolded the note, and pressed it flat. Robert took a photo with his smartphone. It read:

> Loko de tomboj grandaj kaj malgrandaj punktoj la vojo;
> Kie konstruistoj ripozi, rigardu suden kaj kalkulu 1.2.3;
> Balai la plankon ĉe la muro bisekcita.

They looked at one another.

"This looks like a long one, RJ."

"Let's get it translated."

A few minutes later, they had the clue in the clear:

> *Place of tombs great and small points the way;*
> *Where builders rest, look south and count 1.2.3;*
> *Sweep the floor at the wall bisected.*

Jenna was bouncing with excitement. "I think I know what he's saying!"

"Go for it!"

Jenna explained her theory. "*Place of tombs great and small.* That has to be Giza where there are pyramids for the Pharaohs and wealthy, and burial places for the lesser folk, like those who worked on the pyramids. *Where builders rest.* RJ, do you remember me dragging you all across the Giza Plateau? Do you remember me showing you the small homes where the craftsmen lived, and sometimes worked? That fits right in with the Giza Plateau."

"Go on," encouraged Robert.

"I think the *look south* part means we have to face south to count. It's doing the right-to-left thing again. I think he means the 3rd worker house from the right end of the dwellings. The last one is so easy, I'll let you give it a try."

They both laughed at this as Jenna looked sheepishly at

Robert. He responded by leaning over, and kissing her.

"Okay. Let's see. *Sweep the floor at the wall bisected.* Well...bisected means cut in two, so maybe the middle of the wall. I don't think he meant for us to bring a broom to sweep with. Sweep can mean look around, scrutinize, observe. I think we're looking for a hiding place in the floor about half way along one of the walls. What say you, O Queen of the Nile?"

Jenna sniggered. "See, I told you it was easy, and I think your absolutely right."

"So, it's back to Cairo we go. Do you want to stay at the same hotel, or a different one?"

"Oh, darling, I so loved the suite we had there last time. Could we stay there again?"

"There are only two Royal Suites in the hotel. If one is available, I'll get it for you, with pleasure. If not, will something a bit lower down the scale be acceptable, O Queen of the Nile?" Robert bowed low in mock homage.

He checked the Internet for the travel distance and route from Ain Sokhna to Cairo.

"Hmm, the Four Seasons has a second hotel, just as beautiful as the one we stayed in. It has the advantage of being on the Giza side of the Nile. The rooms there are gorgeous, too. What do you think, O Queen of the Nile?"

"RJ, stop with the 'O Queen of the Nile' thing, or I'll have a swelled head so big it won't fit through the doors of even the Royal Suite!"

He took down the phone numbers for both the Four Seasons Cairo at Nile Plaza Hotel, and the Four Seasons Hotel Cairo at the First Residence. Robert called the Nile Plaza hotel using his smartphone. This way, no one would know their destination. Both Royal Suites were booked. He tried the First Residence property with the same results. He decided to mix things up, and reserved a Presidential Suite at the First Residence hotel.

"I'm very sorry, O Queen of the Nile, but Royal Suites at both hotels are booked up. You'll just have to settle for a Presidential Suite." Robert ducked as he told her.

Jenna took a mock swing at him. They laughed heartily, embraced and kissed passionately. *I so totally love this man*, Jenna thought.

"It looks like there's a pretty good road directly from here to Cairo, so we don't have to drive back up to Suez again. Estimated time is an hour and a half. I give it a couple of hours. If we get ready, and pack now, then have some lunch, we should be in Cairo by late afternoon at the latest."

"Then let's get ready, and get out of here. I'm starting to feel like you, RJ. Something is coming our way we need to avoid."

They showered, and changed quickly. After a hurried lunch, Robert settled the bill at the front desk while Jenna returned to take care of the final preparations. The note found its way into Robert's pants pocket to keep the first one company. In a few minutes, their luggage was stowed neatly in their rented Land Cruiser, and they were off to Cairo. It was just before 2 p.m.

Gina, with her team in tow, were heading at speed down Route 65 towards Ain Sokhna. Being a good-looking woman had its benefits. She was able to charm the ticket salesman for the *Queen of Suez* cruise. She was told the booking came from the Concierge at the Jaz Little Venice in Ain Sokhna. It was no wonder no one could find them in Suez—they were staying almost an hour away to the south. She placed a call.

"Yes!"

"I've tracked down their hotel, sir. They're staying at the Jaz Little Venice Golf Resort in Ain Sokhna. It's about an hour's drive south from Suez. Guess they couldn't find anything to their liking in Suez proper."

"Where are you now?"

"We're on our way there now. It's 2 p.m. here, so I'm hoping they're still there, since they obviously didn't go hunting for anything on the all-day cruise. If they're in the Suez area, I'm assuming they'll be looking for something here today, which means they'll probably stay put in the same place tonight."

"Don't assume anything with these two. They're either very lucky, or very cagey. Either way, you'll need to be extra diligent on this project, my dear."

"Yes, sir. I'll keep you posted on our findings in Ain Sokhna."

Carver disconnected. *With Gina on the ground in Egypt, I'll finally get some results*, he thought.

Gina's team arrived in Ain Sokhna just before 3 p.m. She told the group to remain with the one vehicle while she and a driver went to the hotel.

Gina casually walked into the hotel with total poise and confidence. At the front desk, she inquired about her good friends the Jacksons. She was told they checked out about an hour earlier. Maintaining her composure, she asked if they mentioned their next destination. The desk clerk told her there was discussion about Karnak. She thanked him warmly and left.

Back in the vehicle, she took a deep breath as she dialled Carver's number.

"Give me some good news, Gina!"

"Sorry, sir, we just missed them. They checked out an hour ago. The desk clerk said they mentioned Karnak as their next destination."

"Damn!" Carver spat into the phone. "If I didn't know better, I'd say they know when we're getting close, and hightail out of town. Damn!"

"It's a six-hour drive to Luxor, sir. If we leave now, we might catch them up."

"Do you know what they're driving?"

"Yes, sir. A rented grey Toyota Land Cruiser."

"Sounds like the same vehicle they had in Taba. The only way into Egypt is through Cairo. I'll make some discreet inquiries to see if I can get more information about Jackson and Carpenter from the car rental companies there. In the meantime, Karnak is our only lead, correct?"

"Yes, sir. It's all we have. They told the hotel in Taba they were heading to Suez, so it's a good bet they're headed to Karnak. There would be no reason to deviate from what they did before."

"Very well, get down to Karnak, and keep an eye out for that grey Land Cruiser."

He disconnected. "Damn!" he shouted. "They've done it again. Always a step ahead of us. Damn!"

Carver's phone rang again. It was the Airdrie secondary team.

"Yes!" he barked into the phone.

"Sir, we entered the Jackson premises to do a recon. This guy must be paranoid. I think they knew we were there before we did. The police picked up three of us. I got out by the skin of my teeth. Been laying low ever since."

Carver was shaking with fury.

"Get the hell out of there! Destroy all phones, and anything else that might connect you to me." Carver's voice was filled with dread.

He immediately dismantled his phone, threw it on the floor, and stomped on it with rage.

"What the hell is going on? Who is this Jackson character? He's making a mockery of my whole organization! No one does that!"

Carver walked over to a cupboard. From within, he pulled out a box—another burn phone. He made note of the phone number on the box. He returned to the plush chair in which he was sitting before, and began making calls to all his active teams to notify them of the change in phone number. This was the first time he ever had to change numbers mid-project. He was trembling with rage.

Chapter 17 - Deception

Once they were under way, both Robert and Jenna were relieved. The tension they felt during lunch had fallen away. Their love once again came front and centre. They spent most of the trip to Cairo in light conversation. Jenna often placed her hand on the driver's seat near Robert's back, sometimes unconsciously tracing little patterns on his right shoulder. Robert enjoyed this little quirk of Jenna's.

As they entered Cairo, Robert smiled broadly. Jenna looked at him curiously. *What is he up to?* she wondered. He gave her a quick look, and a wink. Obviously, he was about to do something Jenna would like. Although they'd been together only a short time, she was quickly becoming wise to his little ways. She knew he must have arranged something special. She began questioning him narrowly, but Robert would say nothing—just kept grinning from ear-to-ear.

Even with the GPS showing the way, it was a nightmare driving through Cairo. Jenna noticed Robert drove over a bridge across the Nile. She didn't remember crossing a bridge when they left the hotel to go to Taba. They were now on the west side of the Nile, and she distinctly remembered the view from the Royal Suite looking across the Nile, with the pyramids in the distance. She crinkled her brow as she smiled at him. *Where's he taking me?* she thought. *Just sit back, girl, and you'll soon find out.*

Finally, Robert pulled up to a very modern hotel; it was the second Four Seasons. She remembered Robert mentioning it when he made the arrangements. When he arrived at the entrance, a doorman was opening Jenna's door even before their vehicle was completely stopped. A porter was standing by at the back of the Land Cruiser to get their luggage. Robert left the keys in the SUV as he exited. With the porter bringing up the rear, they made their way to the front desk.

"You have a reservation for Jackson, Mr. and Mrs.," announced Robert. Little tingles always ran through Jenna whenever Robert referred to them as husband and wife. She closed the gap between them, taking Robert's arm, and squeezing it tight.

"Yes, of course, sir. We have the Presidential Suite prepared as you requested, sir," replied the desk clerk, with deference.

They made their way to the 18th floor. The porter led the way out of the elevator, and down the hall to the doors of the Presidential Suite. He unlocked the door, and with flair, swung open the double doors of the suite, then moved aside. Robert positioned himself behind Jenna, so she could have a full view of their suite.

As Jenna slowly walked in, she couldn't believe what she saw. Not only was it huge, and beautifully appointed, it was full of flowers. Vases full of flowers—everywhere! To say she was blown away would be an understatement. She held her hands to her face, her eyes filled with tears. Robert took her by the elbow, and walked her to the huge window at the end of the suite. In front of them, closer than before, she could see the Giza Plateau stretch out before her. Robert already tipped the porter, who retreated quietly to give them privacy.

"Oh, RJ, you always find a way to blow my mind!"

"It's a challenge I hope to have for a long time, darling."

"Now, I know why you stood up, and turned away, when you made the hotel reservation. You were ordering all these beautiful flowers," Jenna whispered. She looked into his smiling face, with tears running down her face. "RJ, how on earth will I ever be able to keep up? What can I possibly do to bring you the happiness you've brought me since you whisked me off my feet on a dirt road, so long ago?"

"With every loving look, tender caress, gentle kiss, and the tremendous passion you pour out to me." He held her tightly in his arms, and they kissed tenderly. They remained in an embrace for several minutes.

"I truly hate to bring everything crashing back to reality, Jenna, but we have work to do. We have about two hours of daylight left. I'm feeling very strongly that we need to find that clue today, and leave early tomorrow morning."

Jenna looked positively crestfallen. "So soon?"

"I'm hearing the baying of the hyenas in the distance. We need to ditch the vehicle we have now, and get something else. Carver's watchers know what we're driving. If they took down the plate number, it'll be easy to track us down. We were lucky in Suez, and lost them, but they're not far behind."

"I so hate reality right now! And I don't much care what happens to the Emerald Tablet anymore, either, to be quite honest!"

Robert laughed, in a kind way. "And so says the woman who started it all! Come on girl, we can't quit now! Besides, like Indiana Jones, I've got to see this through. I'm incredibly curious of where Scott will send us next, and what wonders we'll behold."

Jenna eventually smiled. She new he was right. They'd come this far; they couldn't simply let it drop now. It was supremely annoying that they were being hunted down, as it put a severe crimp on what the two of them could enjoy together.

"How quickly do you think you can find the builder's house Scott was talking about?"

"Let me see." Jenna closed her eyes, casting her mind back to their last visit. "When we were there last, we drove in from Cairo. Then we walked along a road that passed the Great Sphinx on the left, then Khufu's pyramid complex on the right. Next was Khafre's pyramid complex on the left. A little further the road turns down along the builders' quarters. That's where we have to go. If we're lucky, we might be able to park very near the particular enclosure we're looking for."

"Good girl! You have an incredible memory! You're absolutely wonderful!" He caught her up in his arms, and kissed her hard.

"I'm not the Queen of the Nile for nothing, you know," she sniggered.

"And you even got your head through the doors of the suite with no problem at all."

"Do you feel a need to change, or are you okay the way you are?"

"I'm fine the way I am, sweetheart."

Robert called down to the Concierge, and asked for a car to take them to the Europcar rental agency not far from the hotel. He was told a car would be available as soon as they came down. Robert explained to Jenna there was no time to return their current vehicle, get the new one, and then go to Giza. They would take the Toyota back later, but for now, he wanted a fresh set of wheels that wasn't known to the watchers.

Thirty minutes later, they were driving towards the Giza

Plateau in a newly rented, shiny-white, Range Rover. It was close to 6 p.m. when they arrived at the complex. There were a lot more people than Robert expected. Jenna explained there was a fabulous light and sound show after sunset, and these people were probably here to get a good seat. *Note to self*, Robert thought, *light show on the Plateau, when this is all over*.

Vehicles were moving slowly along the road described earlier by Jenna. It was 6:25 by the time they reached the builders' quarters. They managed to pull off almost directly in front of the section Scott mentioned in his clue. They casually walked towards the ruins, poking their head in, here and there. All the while, they'd look past each other to see if they might be challenged.

"Okay, RJ, this would be the one." As with the others, they poked their heads in, and casually entered, looking all around. While Robert turned taking everything in, Jenna was "sweeping the floor."

"I think it'll be along the back wall." Her instincts were right. About half way along the wall, there was a crack in the floor. There were some small loose stones stuck in the crack that didn't seem to belong.

"I think I found it. Keep a lookout while I check." It took less than a minute for her to dislodge all the loose stones. She gingerly stuck her fingers down the crack, hoping there was nothing else there but a note in a zipper bag. Her fingers touched the edge of the bag.

"It's in there deep, RJ. I can touch it, but just can't seem to grab it with my fingers."

Robert noticed a few long slivers of wood in the corner. "Here, try a couple of these."

Jenna slipped the sticks down the crevice as far as they could go, and squeezed them closed. She finally managed to pull out the note. Breathing a sigh of relief, she hiked up her skirt, and tucked the note inside her panties. If they searched her bag, they'd find nothing. Hopefully, they wouldn't do a full body search.

"Got it, sweetheart! And it's safely tucked away where none but you can go!"

Robert looked at the crevice where she was standing. "Quick, put the stones back in. We don't want anyone to drop by to see loose stones that shouldn't be there."

Robert was moving towards the entrance just as a security

guard wandered by, looking in.

"You know, darling, I can't imagine how people could live in such cramped space," Robert said aloud, for the guard's benefit. "Look, it's only about two arm-spans wide, and maybe four or five long. What do you think? Maybe four metres by eight or so?"

"It's not much bigger than a standard bedroom, dear."

Robert reached for her hand. She extended hers to take his. They smiled at the guard.

"Do you speak English?"

"Yes, sir. It is required to work here. There are many foreign tourists, you see."

"It must be amazing to work here, among the pyramids of pharaohs, and so much history!" exclaimed Jenna.

He shrugged. "When you have been here for years, as I have, it wears off. You might believe that the builders who lived in these small homes would be amazed also, but to them, it was a job, a very hard job. Failure was not tolerated, and could result in instant death. To visitors, there is much wonder and mystery here. To those who live and work here, the wonder becomes boring."

They were amazed at the wisdom offered by this humble security guard. They nodded.

"If you visited the majestic mountains, and the vast green plains where we come from, you would probably find them amazing, but as you say, they are simply mountains and fields that are very ordinary to us. You are a very wise man," Robert told him earnestly.

"For tourists, like us, who came here to enjoy the wonder and awe of this place, thank you for your service in keeping it safe for all to see," added Jenna.

The guard felt a surge of pride. He stood straight and tall, with his chest out. It was a rare occasion when a tourist showed any appreciation for the work he did. He touched the brim of his cap with the tips of the fingers of his right hand in salute. He stepped back to allow Robert and Jenna to pass by.

"That was close," whispered Jenna, as they walked back to their vehicle.

"Where exactly did you put the note 'that none but I can go?'"

Jenna smiled broadly as she gave him a coy look. "Perhaps you'll have to do some exploring to find it."

On the way back to the hotel, Jenna leaned in towards Robert. She took his arm, squeezed it tight, and let out a deep sigh. "It's so wonderful being with you. I'm really glad we can still have some fun on this quest."

"You might find that everyday life with me will be terribly boring, after this is over. "

"I seriously doubt that, RJ. And, I'd love nothing more, right now, than to be laying on the terrace sunning myself, with you by my side, spreading lotion all over me."

"Don't say things like that, my love, it makes it difficult to focus on my driving, and I'd like to get back to the hotel in one piece!"

They both laughed, and Jenna squeezed all the tighter.

When they arrived at the hotel, they parked their new vehicle in the car park. Back in the lobby, Robert asked at the desk if there were any messages. Thankfully, there were none, and nothing was mentioned about anyone inquiring about them. He advised the desk clerk they would be checking-out in the morning. Sadly, they needed to leave, but didn't specify where to.

They asked the Concierge to have their car brought around, as they hadn't parked it themselves. It would be done immediately. The Presidential Suite came with its perks. In a few minutes, their Toyota was waiting at the front entrance.

Robert set the GPS for the Cairo International Airport where they dropped off the Toyota, and took a limousine back to the hotel. When they arrived, the doorman looked confused as he opened the limo door to find Robert getting out, followed by Jenna. Robert smiled at him, shrugged, and gave him a good tip. The doorman shook his head, thinking, *Tourists!*

Back in their suite, Jenna did a little dance, flinging her skirt about, smiling coyly. Robert watched with interest.

"Wondering where I hid the note?" Jenna enticed him, twirling her hips to-and-fro, with her skirt flying up.

"You didn't!"

With a flick or two of her eyebrows, Jenna hiked up her skirt. The note was plain to see tucked in her panties. "Wanna come get it, lover?" She flirted, still twisting her hips around.

Robert moved close. *Not yet, RJ, me laddie! Later! Get a grip!* he thought. He reached out, and very slowly pulled the note out. He felt the heat of her body, and could hardly contain himself. Jenna could plainly see that Robert was holding himself back. He was trembling slightly. She could feel it in his fingers as he pulled out the note.

"Jenna, you drive me absolutely to distraction." He closed his eyes, and breathed deeply.

Jenna let her skirt fall, reached around his neck, and kissed him deeply. He held her tight. They gazed into each other's eyes. There was nothing but love there. After a few minutes, they parted. It was time to get back to work.

Robert handed the note to Jenna. "I'll get the iPad."

"I'll get the nail file."

With their tools at hand, they sat at the dining table. Jenna opened the zipper bag, and pulled out the note. With the nail file, she slit open the envelope. After carefully pulling out the note, she smoothed it down on the table. It read:

> *Centro de lernado de antikva tempo, lumturo por ĉiuj vidi;*
>
> *Tempoj raraj kaj valoraj troviĝas.*
>
> *Rigardi al Britannica por kie vin trovas.*

After Robert took a photo of the note with his phone, he carefully typed in each line of the clue to get its English translation. This was becoming routine now, only taking a few minutes. In the clear:

> *Centre of learning of ancient time, a beacon for all to see;*
> *Tomes rare and valuable can be found.*
> *Look to Britannica for where you are.*

"The first line is an obvious reference to the place," offered Robert.

Confidently, Jenna began. After all, Egypt was her bailiwick. "Assuming Dr. Scott was still in Egypt, there's only one place this might describe. In ancient times, the greatest centre of learning was Alexandria. The beacon must be a reference to the great lighthouse built there."

"If we ever get out of Egypt, maybe *I'll* get a chance to put a pin on the map!"

Jenna laughed. "Somehow, I think Alexandria will be our last stop in Egypt. See how he's moved from Taba, to Suez, to Cairo, and now to Alexandria. I can't see him doubling back."

"My gut says you're right."

"RJ, can you lookup libraries in Alexandria? I know the original was destroyed a long time ago. There must be a modern equivalent."

Robert did some digging on the Internet. Jenna watched as he pulled up various web pages. She asked him to stop when they reached the Bibliotheca Alexandrina. She quickly scanned the articles on its web site.

She pointed on the iPad. "Here! They have a rare books section, which just happens to contain several copies of the Encyclopaedia Britannica. And I'll bet my panties Dr. Scott put the next clue in the oldest one, rather than a random one, under the topic: Alexandria."

Robert chuckled. "You know, Jenna, you're right. We do make a great team. I arrange travel and accommodation, while you solve all the clues! So, it's Alexandria next."

"Once we're out of Egypt, I'm sure you'll shine, sweetie." She gave him a coquettish peck on the cheek.

Robert checked the hotels in Alexandria. The accommodations and service at the Four Seasons hotels were impeccable, so he saw no reason to change. He didn't think it would matter much if he mixed the properties. If Carver's people were going to find them, it would be in any hotel they stayed at. Interestingly, they hadn't seen any watchers in Cairo yet. He hoped it would stay that way. He made a reservation at the Four Seasons Alexandria at San Stefano, and was able to snag the Presidential Suite overlooking the Mediterranean. He booked for two nights, hoping they could have some time to roam around.

Gina instructed her drivers to go as fast as possible, without risking a run-in with the law. As they drove, they overtook a couple of grey Toyota Land Cruisers, but neither was Jackson and Carpenter. Of course, they departed an hour before them, and if their prey drove as fast as they were, they would never overtake them.

Carver's new project phone rang. It was 8 p.m. local time in Egypt.

"Yes!"

"We've checked the car rental places as discreetly as we could. The vehicle you described was returned to the Cairo International Airport in the early evening. They didn't leave a forwarding destination," reported the voice on the other end.

"What? *This* evening? In *Cairo*?" spat out Carver, in a fury.

"Yes, sir. That's correct."

Carver disconnected. "Damn! Damn! They've done it again!"

Carver dialled Gina's number.

"Yes, sir."

"They've done it to us again!" Carver shouted into the phone.

"Done what, sir?"

"Given us the slip, that's what! They're in Cairo! Turned in their vehicle at the airport early this evening, your time." Carver was in an absolute rage!

Gina closed her eyes. No wonder her boss was furious. She waited.

"How soon can you be in Cairo?"

"We're only an hour out of Luxor, and there are no decent roads that cut to the main road up to Cairo, sir. Just a moment please while I check something."

"Hurry up about it!"

"Sir, we'll be rolling into Luxor at about nine local. It's almost eight hours to drive up to Cairo; say nine with stops. That would have us there at 6 a.m., but we'd all be beat. I suggest we overnight in Luxor, and fly out on the 5:50 a.m. flight to Cairo. That will get us there at seven, fresh, and ready to track them down."

"So, there dead at six, or bright-eyed and bushy-tailed at seven."

"Sir, is it possible that someone else took their vehicle to Cairo? Maybe a swap of some sort?"

"Nice try, Gina, but no. The description fits. It was them alright." *What I don't understand is why they're travelling around so much. We know she had a map of some sort, but why all the travel? Could it be a deception?* he wondered.

"Their *M.O.*, so far, seems to be staying at each destination two or three nights. With any luck, they'll spend tonight, and tomorrow night in Cairo. That should give us all day tomorrow to track them down."

"You may be right. Carpenter's rich boyfriend is obviously showing her a good time while they try to find the artifact. Very well, you, and your team, can get some rest in Luxor. I have a feeling you'll have your hands full tomorrow."

"Very well, sir. I'll let you know when we're on the ground in Cairo."

Robert and Jenna showered, and changed. It would be formal again tonight. Jenna loved wearing Christine's beautiful gowns. They always made her feel super-sexy. For his part, Robert loved to see her all dressed up, as well. He often wondered why he never saw Jenna as Christine, when she wore her clothes. He was sure Christine was looking down on them with a happy smile on her face. There was no guilt, no pangs. He was totally in love with Jenna—period!

After a sumptuous dinner, they sauntered slowly back to their suite. As Jenna turned on all the lights, Robert watched curiously. She wandered about the suite, stopping at each flower vase to admire their beauty and scent. She twirled around holding out the flowing skirt of her gown. She was radiant, beautiful, sexy. She stopped across the living room from Robert, and looked at him with pure love. She slowly unzipped her dress, and let it fall to the ground. To Robert's surprise, she was completely nude. With a very sultry walk, Jenna went to her man. Lost in their love, the outside world evaporated.

Gina and her team arrived on schedule at the Cairo airport. It was another 30 minutes before they secured two rental SUVs. Since Jackson and Carpenter were using only upscale hotels, Gina dispensed with checking anything that was three stars or less. No, it would be a 4- or 5-star hotel. That would make it easier to find them. The previous evening, the team made a list of hotels they would need to visit in Cairo.

She chose to wear something elegant that spoke money. She would again try the ploy of looking for her good friends, the Jacksons. It was still too early to visit hotels. It would be unusual for a tourist to be looking for friends at 7:30 in the morning. They would have breakfast at the airport, and wait until nine before starting.

Looking very chic, Gina entered a hotel, moving casually to the front desk, where she inquired about her good friends. At every hotel, she was informed they had no guests named Jackson registered there. This included both the Four Seasons where Robert and Jenna stayed. The front desk clerks were a little suspicious of an elegant, rich woman inquiring about her friends, Mr. and Mrs. Jackson, when she would've known they weren't really married. The Royal Suite and Presidential Suite included a certain amount of discretion.

When Gina finished her round, she was surprised, and a bit stressed. If they were in Cairo, she thought, they would surely be known somewhere. The team discussed their lack of success so far. Could it be their prey changed their pattern, and were staying in a cheaper hotel? Gina knew she needed to report back to Carver, and wasn't looking forward to it. He would be furious.

Carver's phone rang. "Give me some good news, Gina."

"Sir, something's not right here."

Carver felt his blood pressure rising. "What do you mean, 'not right'?"

"Jackson and Carpenter have been staying in expensive suites in upscale hotels. We've done the round of all the 4- and 5-star hotels in Cairo and Giza. They're not registered as guests at any of them, or at least the staff aren't saying," reported Gina. She held the phone away from her ear, expecting a tirade.

"Go on," Carver said quietly.

"There are three possibilities: they're using another name, which would be difficult unless they're now using different credentials; they're staying at a cheaper hotel in Cairo, which doesn't sit right with me; or, like Suez, they're staying somewhere outside of Cairo/Giza, which is where I'd like to start looking."

"I take it there are no other leads at this point?"

"He obviously threw us off with Luxor, sir. Finding out they're in the Cairo area was surprising. It demonstrates premeditated deception. They know they're being tracked, and they're being very cunning in their movements. Dropping off their original vehicle at Cairo airport could be a ruse. They could still be here with another vehicle, or taken a flight out. We can check hotels further afield, and make discreet inquiries with airlines at the Cairo airport. If they haven't been seen, I recommend posting watchers at the airport here. My intuition tells me it won't be long before they leave Egypt. If we don't know where they're going, it'll be difficult to find them."

Carver took a deep breath. He considered what his top agent just told him. He shook his head.

"I don't know how they could elude you Gina. You command my top team. It can't be the Carpenter woman. And by all accounts, this Jackson fellow is a real estate agent. Can it be dumb luck?" He was relatively calm, a sign to Gina that he would stop at nothing now. She only saw him this way once before, and death was not far away for anyone who stood against him.

"I still have confidence in you, Gina. You have full *carte blanche* now. Do whatever you feel is necessary to make progress—full force, if required. I want results. Use whatever strategies you feel will get us these two people. They, of course, must be taken alive, and in good condition. Do you understand?"

"Yes, sir. I'll get them for you, sir."

"You had better," croaked Carver. He disconnected.

Gina closed her eyes. Carver's not-so-veiled threat was not lost on her. Not only her job, but her very life now hung in the balance. She *had* to find her prey, and *fast*!

Robert and Jenna awoke early in the morning. Considering they had a rather late night, they felt well-rested and itching to get going. Robert enjoyed starting the day with a good long swim, and today was no exception. He always felt invigorated after his swim, and built strength, and stamina. Today, Jenna decided to join him. She realized it had been a while since she had any real exercise, not to mention it meant being close to her man.

They donned their bathing suits. Jenna knew Carmen packed several bikinis—from conventional type to very sexy string bikinis—but she also packed a nice one-piece, which she chose this morning. With their robes on, they made their way down to the pool, which they had to themselves. They both dove in, and swam laps. Robert was way ahead of her. Jenna made a mental note to get back into shape again. She'd been living the high life since meeting Robert. After some 30 laps, she gave up, and contented herself to sit on the edge of the pool, watching Robert tirelessly go back and forth. It was no wonder he was so buff. He really took care of himself. Robert swam at least double the laps that Jenna managed. When he finished, Jenna wrapped him with a towel, and pat-dried him.

"It would be great to have this lovely, little service every time I swim."

"It will be my great pleasure, O Great Pharaoh, God of the Sands." With mock humility, she bowed low before him.

"Now, don't you start!"

They both laughed, and made their way back to the suite.

After a nice shower, they dressed casually for the trip to Alexandria, after which, they repacked their luggage. They wanted to be ready to go after breakfast. The sooner they were out of Cairo, the better Robert would feel. Still, they didn't rush. There was probably time for a bit more fun.

They enjoyed a wonderful buffet breakfast in the hotel's Tea Lounge. Everything was fresh, and very tasty. They sat back afterwards, sipping a cup of strong coffee.

"Well, there's no chance of me falling asleep at the wheel, not with this coffee. One more cup, and I'll be buzzed for the day!"

"I know what you mean, RJ. I'm already buzzed, but it's a good buzz."

Robert asked one of the passing staff what time the shops opened in The Residence. He was told they would be open in a few minutes, at eight.

"Are we doing some shopping before we go?"

"I don't want to take too long. But I'd like to find something nice for you, and some things to send back home."

They finished their coffee, and wandered down the corridor towards the shops. Although they didn't want to spend much time shopping, it was plain to see they could spend an entire day exploring the shops in this complex.

As they walked by a jewellery store, Robert noticed something in the window. He smiled, and pulled Jenna into the shop. He took the clerk aside, and told her what he wanted. She walked to the window to fetch the stunning emerald earrings he saw displayed there. Jenna was astounded when Robert asked her if she liked them. She was speechless. Robert figured this meant yes, so he nodded to the clerk who beckoned Jenna to come close. She carefully removed Jenna's earrings, and placed the new ones on her ears. Looking in the mirror, Jenna could still say nothing, but only looked at Robert with tears in her eyes. Again, Robert nodded to the clerk, pulled out his credit card, and paid for his purchase. He told the clerk to place the old earrings in the box. His lady would wear the new ones.

They quickly explored a few other shops, and found some souvenirs for Carmen, Andrea, Jake, and Jenna's friends. He also picked out a couple of things for his friends, the Mathesons. Because there was no one at the house, he would courier their new purchases to the Mathesons for safekeeping.

It was nine in the morning now, and time to go. As usual, Jenna returned to the suite to make sure everything was in order when the porter arrived. Robert settled the bill, and asked the Concierge if his vehicle could be brought around, giving him the keys, and the stall number. Without further ado, it was done. By 9:15, they were on the road.

Gina was between a rock and a hard place, and she knew it. Her team needed to get something concrete on Jackson and Carpenter. After her failure to acquire any information from hotel desk clerks, she decided to try with the doormen. Doormen saw everyone who entered, or left the hotel. They would know if Jackson and Carpenter were staying at their hotel. Carpenter, in particular, was very attractive, and would be remembered easily.

Gina had several copies made of the photo taken of them by the watcher in Taba. Two of her best men dressed-up in suits to look somewhat official. They began to canvass the luxury hotels again. Gina stayed in the vehicle, as she might be recognized, and cause suspicion.

Finally, at the Four Seasons Nile Plaza, the doorman remembered the couple very well. They stayed in one of the two Royal Suites while they were there; very nice couple, and very much in love, but they left almost a week ago. He told Gina's man to maybe check their sister property in Giza. The group in the second car was dispatched there immediately. Within 30 minutes, Gina's man reported back that Jackson and Carpenter checked-out early that morning, and driving a white Range Rover. The doorman had no idea where they were going, but they seemed in no particular hurry, only stayed one night.

Gina reassembled her team for a meeting. Obviously, Jackson and Carpenter left Cairo with perhaps a six- to eight-hour head start, and they knew what kind of vehicle they were driving. She placed a call.

"Report!"

"We have a lead, sir. It's a slim one. The doorman at the Four Seasons in Giza remembers Jackson and Carpenter very well. He said they checked out early this morning, driving a white Range Rover."

"Do you know their destination," he asked anxiously.

"Not exactly, sir. If you look at where they've been—Taba, Suez, Cairo—it gives us an idea of where they're probably going. There aren't too many places they would go. The places they've been to are large cities, with the exception of Taba, which is suspected to be where the object is buried. There are only three more places they might go using that scenario: Luxor, Alexandria, and Port Said. We can rule out Luxor, since they used that to throw us off the scent. I recommend having watchers keep an eye on all luxury hotels in Alexandria, and Port Said, for a white Range Rover."

"You'll need rotating watches on all those properties. This will require a great deal of manpower. I think you're right, though, so I'll make arrangements through some Egyptian connections. Do you have a preferred location?"

"Yes, sir. Alexandria. I don't think there's anything much in Port Said. With your approval, sir, my team will head up to Alexandria immediately."

"You're in control. Do what you feel is right," advised Carver.

After hanging-up, Gina told her team, "Alexandria. Let's get going!"

Chapter 18 - Chameleon

A few minutes after leaving the hotel, Robert swung the car right, and crossed a bridge back to the east side of the Nile. Jenna noticed this right away. At first, she said nothing, but the curiosity was eating at her.

"Isn't Alexandria that way?" she finally asked, pointing in a general north-westerly direction.

Robert had a wry little smile on his face. "Yes, my darling, it certainly is."

"Did I miss a meeting, RJ?"

"Didn't miss a thing, dear."

"Um, okay; I give up, where are we going? I thought you wanted to get out of Cairo early."

"We're headed to the airport." Robert was enjoying his little secret.

"Are we flying to Alexandria?" Jenna was full of curiosity, more from Roberts little smile than their destination. "You're teasing me, aren't you, sweetheart?"

"Yes, I am. You know how I love throwing you off balance, just for fun. Can you think of a good reason why we might be headed back to the airport?"

Jenna thought about this carefully. She knew Robert wouldn't do anything to put them in danger. She also knew he was always thinking ahead, even if he didn't let her in on his little plans. So, now the question became: what was so important at the airport that Robert would delay driving straight to Alexandria? It was something Jenna grew to love about Robert. He always seemed to be one step ahead of the game, and always invited Jenna to try to guess what it was.

Robert sat there, quietly waiting for Jenna to work it out in her mind.

"It has something to do with the vehicle, right?"

"Yes, you've got it. Now, can you think what it is about the vehicle?"

Jenna considered the question for a moment and smiled. "This flashy, white, monster would be noticed by anyone trying to track us down. You're going to get rid of it."

"Bingo!"

"I knew it! I knew it! When you rented this vehicle, I wondered why you picked something so obviously visible."

"Exactly. I got rid of the previous vehicle because it was known to our detractors. We narrowly escaped being made in Taba. We were definitely under surveillance in Suez, and I'm sure they weren't far behind us when we left the hotel."

"That's why the deception with Karnak. Of course! You thought they were getting close, and you wanted to get them going as far away from us as possible."

Robert continued his explanation. "That's right. It would only be a matter of time before someone would get smart, and check the car rentals. They would suspect we entered Egypt at Cairo, and would probably rent a vehicle here. When we returned the vehicle, they would know they were duped, and get someone to Cairo in a hurry. That's why I wanted to get out of the hotel early. There's less urgency to get out of Cairo. I'm sure they'll be checking hotels, and hotel staff, to try to get a lead on us."

"So, you rented a big, flashy vehicle that everyone could remember, and Carver's goons would be looking for. Pure genius, my love." With every day, Jenna grew in admiration of this wonderful man.

"At the airport, we'll get something quite different, normal, and more low key. But that's not all we need to do. We know Carver's people are tracking us. At the beginning of this quest, I mentioned we need to be cagey, and cunning. We did that early by making you a raven-haired beauty."

Jenna bristled with excitement. "Are we going to disguise ourselves, RJ?"

"Yes, Jenna. You're going to need yet another metamorphosis. You're the centre of attraction. No one takes much notice of me. All eyes are drawn to you. I could stand next to a Carver watcher, and he'd never know who I was. No, they'll be looking for you. I think we'll do another job on your hair—different colour and style."

"And a big, broad-brimmed hat, with huge sunglasses?"

"Stylish sunglasses, perhaps, but the hat would be a dead

giveaway. Remember, we want to maintain our cover of hiding in *plain* sight."

"What will we do with my hair, then?"

"I think you should be...a redhead, for a while. It would go well with your green eyes."

"It's just as well we didn't use permanent dye in my hair then. I can wash this out easily with the stuff I got when we bought the dye. Do you think we'll be able to get the same kind of dye here?"

"I'm sure we can. We need to do something with your beautiful, long, flowing, hair. I was thinking about that. What do you think of putting it in a French braid?"

"It *would* make quite a difference. I've worn my hair in a French braid before, so I can do it up that way easily. But shouldn't we do something for you, too?"

"I'm thinking a white hat, or something like it. Not a ball cap—hate them. Something dignified that wouldn't look out of place in a luxury hotel, or cause undo attention."

"Why do I get the impression you already have everything planned out?" Jenna had no doubt whatever that Robert *did* have everything well planned, which was a great comfort to know.

"Because, I plan, and you decipher!"

"You forgot one thing, RJ. You plan, *and pay*!" chuckled Jenna.

"I have a little idea about that, but I'll keep that one to myself, for now."

At the airport, they found two luggage carts, and placed their luggage on them, just like any tourist might do when leaving. He checked the car in with the attendant. They pushed their carts into the airport, heading for the car rental agencies. At each agency, except the one where they rented the Range Rover, they asked about available SUVs. The third agency down the line offered different size Toyotas—Rav4, Highlander, and Land Cruiser. They decided on a metallic, dark-red Highlander. It was common enough not to be noticed, yet wouldn't look out-of-place at a luxury hotel. It was 10:15 a.m.

When they were settled in their new vehicle, Robert took a piece of paper from his shirt pocket. He entered the coordinates into the GPS. Jenna knew these would probably lead to a hairdresser where she could get her hair colour changed. She was right. Less than half an hour later, she found herself sitting in a chair having the black washed out of her hair. Robert called ahead to make sure they had easily removable hair dye, like the one they used before.

Jenna laughed when she was shown so many different shades of red to chose from. In the end, she chose a red that was bright enough to be a striking change, but not bright enough to cause undo attention, and suspicion on the part of possible watchers.

When it was all over, and Jenna appeared as a redhead, complete with French braid. Robert was amazed at the change. *No wonder spies do this all the time*, he thought. No matter what Jenna did with her hair, she was still, in his mind, the sexiest woman on the planet!

“You look terrific! All I can think of is finding a cheap, by-the-hour, motel where I can make passionate love to you!”

She slipped her arms around his neck, kissed him softly, and whispered in his ear, “Do you have GPS coordinates for that?”

They both sighed deeply. Robert quickly paid, and they left. Jenna wondered why, suddenly, Robert was in a hurry to get to the vehicle. She looked at him, and stifled a laugh. She hurried too. Robert seemed to struggle with his manhood at the worst moments, and this was one of them. Jenna was flattered. Without a word, Robert punched in the coordinates for a hat shop, and drove off. Nothing was said. They both felt it; they both wanted it.

At the hat shop, they couldn’t believe all the different hat styles available. Robert looked around, and fancied a white fedora. They both agreed it suited him. Jenna thought he looked quite distinguished, but not before she teased him that it should be brown with a well-worn, brown, leather jacket.

It would be a three-hour drive to Alexandria, once they crossed back to the other side of the Nile. As they drove through Giza before turning north, Robert spotted what appeared to be a nice, cozy restaurant in the hotel district. They stopped for some lunch.

They enjoyed the drive to Alexandria. Rather than take the faster route through the desert, they opted to drive the slower route through the delta region. It was a welcome change from the arid conditions prevalent throughout their travels, so far, in Egypt. It was nice to see the lush, green fields and waterways. It was almost a different country.

Still in her dream world, Jenna rolled down the window, and rested her head on folded arms on the window sill. She looked out in awe and amazement at the scenery passing by. It still hadn’t sunk in they were travelling through Egypt—so far away from her home in Edmonton. In three weeks, she travelled across

Canada, and now across Egypt, with the Nile Delta spread out before her. Where else would she go? What other wonders would she see? And she was doing this with a man she was utterly in love with. The Emerald Tablet was far from her thoughts. She was totally at peace.

Robert occasionally glanced at her. This was definitely a welcome change, but traffic was heavy. He had to concentrate on his driving. Sitting there next to Jenna, he thought he could actually feel her love reaching out from her heart to his. He was happy to see her so content. This calm was like an oasis in the desert. He knew things would change when they reached Alexandria. He knew the hyenas were converging on them. He had no way of knowing how narrowly he eluded Carver's people. He would be glad when all this was over.

Jenna noticed the countryside change when they turned towards the final stretch to Alexandria. She sat back in her seat, closing the window. She reached over to the driver's seat, looking at Robert tenderly. Robert glanced at her, smiling. He waited a moment, and wasn't disappointed, as she began tracing her little patterns on his shoulder.

"What do you think will happen when we arrive at the hotel."

"I imagine they'll be watching hotels where they think we'll stay. No doubt, they'll have a watcher or two at our hotel. Hopefully, they'll take little notice of us with the change of vehicle, and your matching hair colour. They'll still be looking for a big, white Range Rover, and a raven-haired beauty."

"So, we should at least get into the hotel without a problem."

"I think that's a good bet."

"Will we still stay hidden in plain sight?"

"That's a good question. I've been trying to put myself in their shoes on the drive out here, since conversation was a bit sparse," he said teasingly.

"I'm sorry, lover. I was lost in a dream. My brain is still fuzzy. Do you know we've driven all over Egypt?"

Robert looked around in mock seriousness. "Is that where we are? That would explain the sand dunes."

"RJ, you're terrible! And I love you so much for it. *Please*, never stop being terrible."

Robert swallowed hard. He looked at her for a moment. She could see the softness in his eyes.

"Getting back to your original question, they know that we know they're tracking us. They'll expect us to lay low, and change our strategy. The changes we've made will buy us time, but not much, I'm thinking. Carver knows who we are for sure now. He'll put his best trackers on us. I booked the room for two nights. The library is open between 11 a.m. and 7 p.m. There won't be much time tonight to go searching the rare book collection. We'll do that tomorrow. Tonight, is for us. We should be safe enough. It's tomorrow I'm worried about."

"By the way, they have full spa services there. We should be in our room by five or so. If you want, we can see if we can get a massage, or some other treatment. They have a full menu."

"Did you notice if they do body waxing?"

Robert laughed. "On the list I saw, the only thing they don't wax is your butt!"

"Excellent! Thank goodness I don't need a butt wax! Now, you, on the other hand..."

"Hey!"

They both laughed. Yes, tonight was for them. To blazes with Carver, and his minions; they weren't invited!

It was just before five in the evening when they arrived at the Four Seasons. Keeping with their normal tourist cover, neither scanned for watchers. They behaved like any other tourist. The Alexandria hotel was just as efficient and beautiful as its sister properties in Cairo and Giza. As usual, they handed over their passports when they registered. Robert asked if they could register under another name—Mr. and Mrs. Green. He explained they had some pesky people they met in another hotel, who were following them around. The front desk clerk smiled, and said this would not be a problem, as they had their real passports. So, Mr. Edward, and Mrs. Tanya Green it was. Robert gave him a generous tip for his trouble. Again, Robert knew this would be one of the small accommodations offered to those who occupied the premium suites.

After being shown to their room, Jenna chuckled, "Edward and Tanya Green. You have some cheek, my darling! *E* for Emerald, *T* for Tablet, and Green, of course, for the colour."

Robert laughed heartily. "You wanted to have fun on this little quest of ours, didn't you? I think the humour, and the pun, will be lost completely on the opposition, my dearest."

Robert went to the desk, where he pulled out a thick, leather-bound folder containing dining menus, and lists of available amenities. He offered it to Jenna who was standing, entranced, at the huge floor-to-ceiling window, looking out over the

Mediterranean Sea. She never tired of the wonders Robert provided her. She turned to find Robert standing close. He gathered her in his arms, kissing her deeply. He pulled away, offering her the folder once again. She scanned the spa pages.

"This! Yes, this is what I want, RJ! It sounds so strange and interesting—a volcanic clay treatment followed by a 60-minute massage."

Robert considered the offerings. "I think it'll be a Pharaonic Massage for me. It's been a long time since I've had a nice massage."

Jenna called the spa to make the appointments. She was told there were openings in about 30 minutes. This was fine with both, so they confirmed their treatments. It would give them time to shower, change, and relax a few minutes out on the balcony overlooking the sea.

It took some time for Carver to get in touch with his contacts in Egypt to arrange around-the-clock watches on the luxury hotels in Alexandria, and Port Said. He stressed that the main focus was Alexandria. He sent a photo to each of them, and advised that Jackson and Carpenter were driving in a white Range Rover. Unfortunately, he had no idea when they would arrive in Alexandria, and they may already be there.

It was about 6:30 p.m. when Gina's team arrived in Alexandria. She felt in her bones they were close now. They would have them before the end of the day, she was sure of it. A short time later, her phone rang.

"The watchers should be in place," Carver informed her. "Where are you now, and what are your plans?"

"We arrived in Alexandria, and arranged accommodations here. If they left Cairo early this morning, they've arrived long ago. My first stop will be the Four Seasons to check for the white Range Rover. If it's not in the car park, I'll have one of the boys talk to the doorman. Hopefully, it's the same guy who was here around the time they would've arrived. He might be able to tell us if Jackson and Carpenter are there, or not. If they're not there, we'll do the rounds of all the luxury hotels. I'm very confident we'll pin them down before the end of the day, sir."

"Don't make any promises, Gina. These two are as slippery as eels, and a lot smarter. They've managed to give all our teams the slip, even when we had them in our sights."

"Yes, sir. Unfortunately, I'm very well aware of that. My ego is smarting a bit. It's a matter of pride now, sir."

"Remember, you have full control, *and* full responsibility. I expect results, and quite frankly, I don't give a damn about your ego. Just pin them down. No rough stuff—understand?"

"Yes, sir! Absolutely." Her stomach was beginning to churn now. The reproach was not lost on her.

"Gina, I want to put a hypothesis to you. That archaeologist, Scott, who found the item in question, went on an unscheduled, secret vacation for a little over three weeks. I'm beginning to wonder if he was actually going about leaving clues to the location of the item. I can't see him taking that long to find a place to hide it. He must've been doing something else. What do you think?"

Gina thought about this, mulling it over in her head. Carver waited patiently, knowing what she was doing. He wanted her best opinion.

"Sir, what you're suggesting makes a lot of sense. If Scott was trying to keep the item out of the hands of private collectors, he would hide it, to be sure. He would want to make it difficult to find, so that only a certain calibre of person, or group, could follow clues he left in various places. Already, our pair has been to Taba, Suez, Cairo, and now Alexandria. It could very well be they're finding Scott's clues, and moving on to the next. We're always one step behind them, because they know where they're going to next, and we don't. They've also started to vary their movements, and leaving false trails for us. They know we're after them. They're watching for us, and they've been very good at making us without our noticing."

"Everything you say rings true. The question I'm struggling with now, is whether to pick them up when we have them, or follow them, letting them do all the work. After all, it appears they've been successful so far."

"Ah, good question, sir. You're right about their success. It looks like they can find the clues right in front of us, and we don't even notice. The watchers in Taba had them under careful surveillance, saw nothing unusual, and poof, they're off to Suez. They were so open and into themselves, the watchers noticed nothing. It was the same in Suez. They obviously found the clue there, under our noses too. They spent less than 24 hours in Cairo, and they're gone to Alexandria. It's either a big spoof to throw us off, or they're very, very good at finding and deciphering Scott's clues."

Her tone was not lost on Carver. He reminded her, "It's plain from your tone, Gina, that you're beginning to admire them. I've come to both hate *and* admire Jackson and Carpenter. They've cost me dearly, not only financially, but my ego is bruised as well. I must admit they're the most formidable opponents I've come across in my years of collecting. Admire them if you will, but remember they're the opposition; they're the prey; they're the means to the prize; they'll also make, or break, your career." Gina paled with fear at this last comment.

"I'm well aware of that, sir."

Carver rang off.

Gina was still white when she entered the room where her team waited for her. None had ever seen her like that. They instinctively knew that Carver must've made some serious threat to her, and, by extension to them also. They knew they were under the gun. She didn't have to say much.

"We need to find them, and keep them pinned down. We're not to take them, but keep them on a very short leash. The boss thinks they're following clues left by Scott when he disappeared, and thinks they're doing such a great job, we should let them do all the heavy lifting.

One last thing. If we fail—we're dead, quite literally!"

The team knew she wasn't kidding. They saw it her face. For several minutes, everyone was preoccupied with their own thoughts. No one spoke.

So far, none of the watchers in either Alexandria, or Port Said, reported a sighting of Jackson or Carpenter, or their vehicle. Time was ticking away. Gina was becoming very impatient.

"They've got to be *somewhere*!" she shouted.

Robert and Jenna were back in their room feeling mellow after their spa treatments. They were sitting quietly on the balcony, holding hands, watching the sun setting in the west, throwing its last colourful rays across the water in front of them.

Robert turned to look at Jenna. "Formal, or casual, tonight, darling?"

"I don't want to move from here. It's so beautiful.

"Dine in, then?"

"Mmmm, yes, that would be wonderful."

Robert rose to get the menu. Jenna wouldn't let go of his hand. Tears filled her eyes. "I love you, Robert Jackson, more than you could ever imagine."

He swung his legs around on the lounge chair to face her. He felt pathetically inadequate to respond to such a deep admission of love. He reached out with his free hand to gently wipe the tears from her cheeks. The reds in the last rays of sunset highlighted her red hair, and somehow caught the green of her eyes, causing them to sparkle. What a picture she was. He thought his heart would explode. Without noticing, he too had a trickle of tears running down his cheeks. He was surprised to see Jenna smile, reach out to him, and brush his tears away.

Robert went to retrieve the dining menu, turning on the balcony lights, as he returned. They quickly chose something that sounded good. Back in the suite, Robert called room service to place the order. He was told it would be about an hour. He relayed this to Jenna on the balcony. She rose, re-entered the suite, turning off the balcony lights. Taking Robert by the hand, she led him to the master bedroom. She didn't say a word. She slipped off her dress and undergarments, letting them fall to the floor. She gently kissed Robert, and undressed him. They made love.

When the doorbell rang, announcing supper, they donned bathrobes with a chuckle. Jenna had a silly thought; she wondered if people answered the door in the nude. The waiter pretended not to notice. This was, after all, rather common. When Jenna entered the main room, he was dazzled by her beauty. Robert cleared his throat, and the waiter got back to the business at hand. He asked if they wished to dine inside or at the dining table on the balcony. Jenna nodded towards the balcony. So, the waiter set the table, and laid out their meal. After receiving a generous tip, he retreated.

Robert and Jenna had a quiet conversation over dinner. They wondered what those in Canada were doing. She felt badly for Carmen, who was ready to defend her stronghold at all cost. Robert laughed, saying she would be a formidable enemy indeed. It was an easy conversation between two lovers who were very comfortable together. Yes, tonight was for them.

Gina was pacing up and down the room, deep in thought. No one dared interrupt her. To do so would result in a stern rebuke, and the back of her hand across the face. They respected and feared Gina. She was tough as nails. Everyone waited.

It was already nearly midnight. There hadn't been any sightings of Jackson and Carpenter anywhere. There was one white Range Rover picked up, but it turned out to belong to a group of 20-something jet-setters. This was not going well.

"Nothing!" Gina finally spat out. "Nothing here; nothing in Port Said! Where the hell *are* they? There's no way they would head down to Luxor. I'll stake my reputation on them being here. I feel it in my bones."

The other five on the team, three men, and two women, had nothing to say. They already discussed possible scenarios to death. They followed up on the plausible ones, and even some of the less plausible, with no success whatever.

"Listen up, people. There's something I read in a book once. Sherlock Holmes said something like this: 'If you have eliminated all the probable solutions, then the correct solution is the improbable one.' Well, we've eliminated the probable scenarios. Let's look again at the improbable ones, and see where they lead."

Their list was short:

- Cunning disguise—it would have to be theatrical quality as Carpenter was hard to miss.
- They changed vehicles again—what were they driving now?
- Blatant change of M.O.—staying in a cheap hotel and/or moving around every night.
- They were somewhere else—where?
- They hadn't arrived yet due to some detour, or unexpected delay.

Gina opened the floor up to her team. They discussed each alternative in detail.

When it came to disguise, the men felt it would have to be extreme. The ladies, on the other hand, disagreed. They knew that a simple change of hair colour, hair style, and/or makeup could completely change the look of a woman. Although Jackson was ruggedly handsome, he wasn't pulling attention. Carpenter, on the other hand, attracted a lot of attention. Gina took out some copies of the photo taken in Taba. She took a yellow highlighter, and coloured in Jenna's hair. On another, she took a red marker, and did the same. They looked at the two pictures along with an original. Everyone could see the change. With different sunglasses, a hat, hair up in a bun, there was no way you would ever tell they were the same woman. The big problem would be to figure out what Carpenter looked like now.

The team discussed again the possibility that Jackson and

Carpenter changed vehicles between the time they left the hotel in Cairo and the time they reached Alexandria. They all agreed that it was possible, but couldn't come up with any viable reason why they would do so. It meant delaying their trip to Alexandria. Given they spent less than 24 hours in Cairo, there was obviously some urgency to their trip. Why waste time switching vehicles? If they did switch, the team felt it would be done in Alexandria, rather than Cairo, before arriving at the hotel. Gina decided they would check on the availability of a white Range Rover at all the car rental agencies in Alexandria.

A covert check of luxury hotel registers showed no Jacksons. If they were using an assumed name, how were they accomplishing it? Hotels are quite strict about names on the register. It would have to be the name of one of the people registering. For completeness, they checked for Carpenter as well, but there were no Carpenters either. A respectable real estate agent, and a respectable university research assistant would not have the resources, or contacts, to have fake documentation made up. It was decided to toss out aliases.

There were many cheaper hotels in Alexandria. They could mobilize the watchers to check them out at the cost of leaving the luxury hotels blind. But that wouldn't include the myriad small places that offered a bed for the night. Jackson and Carpenter were obviously cunning, and know it would be difficult to watch all such places. Gina threw her mind back to Jackson's house in Alberta. It looked very rich, and sat on a huge estate with manicured lawns, and formal gardens. This man enjoyed his wealth, and used it. No, it was inconceivable to her that they would "slum it" in something cheap and tawdry—no more so than her boss would. So, they threw out low-cost accommodation again.

They all agreed it was quite possible Jackson and Carpenter hadn't arrived yet. Gina didn't think it would be vehicle problems. If anything, it would be a scheduled detour, someplace special they wanted to see before continuing. After all, Carpenter's expertise, according to Bartholomew, was Egypt and the Middle East.

Gina's phone rang. She knew it was Carver.

"Yes, sir."

Carver stood at a window, looking out on a sun-drenched day. He had a wry smile on his face.

"Well, Gina, it's after midnight your time. Do you have your quarry in your sights?" he asked calmly.

Gina swallowed hard. "No, sir."

"Thought as much. Here's a word of wisdom for you, my dear—don't overthink these two. Generally, when you're brought in, it's because we're up against a person or persons who are well trained in covert operations, and have access to associated resources. These two are just plain folks. They don't have any training. They don't have access to document forgers, safe houses, or any sort of covert resources. They're out in the open."

"You have a point there, sir. We've been knocking ourselves out looking at scenarios, and following up on them, for hours. It's gotten us nowhere. In fact, we don't even know if they're in Alexandria at all. None of the watchers in Alexandria, or Port Said, have reported seeing a white Range Rover, or anyone fitting their description. I hate to say it, sir, but I may have jumped too soon."

"Don't beat yourself up too much. You'll need to think 'normal' on this assignment. What would two normal people in love do? Remember, to them this is an adventure, and they seem to be enjoying it."

"Yes, sir, I see what you mean. It's a whole other mindset."

"I haven't lost confidence it you *yet*, Gina. You're the best there is when it comes to tracking down your prey. Sometimes, the prey is right in front of your nose, but you're too busy beating the bushes to see them. Keep me posted."

"Yes, sir."

Gina relayed the gist of the conversation to her team. At first, they had a look of consternation, but slowly they began to realize the wisdom of Carver's words.

It was another beautiful morning. Robert and Jenna knew they had work to do. They cuddled together for a while, discussing what adventures the day would bring. Finally, they got up, showered, and headed to the pool to swim laps. Jenna knew Robert would want to "clear his mind," and wanted to join him. She was beginning to enjoy her morning swims. Afterwards, they had a leisurely breakfast at the Kala Restaurant.

"The library opens at eleven. We should be there first thing, when there'll be fewer people. That might allow us the luxury of picking a spot away from others."

"I think you're right, RJ. A quiet spot is best, but we'll have to keep an eye out for security cameras. You can be sure a library like the Bibliotheca Alexandrina will have very good security."

"Hadn't thought of that. Do you have a strategy in mind?"

"Depends on where the cameras are located. We don't want to be too obvious in scanning the room for them, but we need to be aware of those covering wherever we sit."

As Robert considered the security issues, a sudden thought came to mind. "I wonder if they might have microphones hidden to detect any conspiratorial conversations."

"Now, *I* hadn't thought of that. Interesting possibility. I've never heard of that before. Maybe we could check the Internet after breakfast to see if there even is such a thing. Better to be safe than arrested."

"And somehow, I don't think Egyptian prisons will be very hospitable to a couple of foreign Christians."

"So, we'd better come up with strategies for the various possibilities we might encounter."

They spent the next thirty minutes sipping their coffee, discussing how they could block the view of security cameras in various positions, just long enough to retrieve Scott's note, but not long enough to raise suspicion. They took heart that Scott was able to place the note in a book without being noticed.

At about 10:45, they made their way to the lobby. At the entrance, they asked the doorman for a taxi, which he waved over immediately. Robert was wearing his new hat, while Jenna sported high-fashion sunglasses. It wasn't long before they were dropped off at the entrance to the Bibliotheca Alexandrina.

Once inside, they paid their entrance fee, and Jenna checked her purse, which is mandatory. They found themselves in a vast repository of books and artifacts. They wandered around in wonder and awe at the sheer size of the building. They asked an attendant the way to the Rare Books Collection. She offered them a folded map of the facility, showing the way to the collection. Once oriented, they found their way easily. When they arrived, they needed to pay an additional entry fee.

They looked around at the seemingly endless rows of books. They already knew they couldn't just fetch the book they wanted. This was always done by staff. At a service desk, they asked for the oldest and newest versions of the Encyclopaedia Britannica they had for the volume that contained the topic *Alexandria*. The man at the desk didn't show any surprise at their request. He nodded politely, and searched his computerized catalogue. After a few minutes, he wrote some reference numbers on a piece of paper. He invited them to select a reading table anywhere in the immediate area, and he would bring the books out to them.

Robert and Jenna looked around, in a touristy way, checking for cameras. They must've been well hidden, because they saw nothing obvious. Robert pointed to a reading table with no one around, close to the window wall, which provided plenty of light. They sat down facing the outside. If there were any cameras, they would be mostly at their back. Hopefully, this would hide what they were doing. In less than ten minutes, the attendant was at their side with the two volumes they requested. He advised them that, because of the condition of the books, if they wanted to photocopy any pages, they would need to get one of the staff to do it for them. They thanked him, and he left them to their research.

Jenna stared down at the two books before them. "Well, darling, what do you think we'll find?"

"Hopefully, the article we're looking for."

To make it look good, they placed the volumes side-by-side, as if to be able to refer to both books at the same time. Jenna opened the new volume to the entry for *Alexandria*. They both looked at the entry with interest, even running their finger down the article as though they were reading it. In fact, both were very nervous. They turned to the old volume which Robert carefully opened to the desired entry. They looked at the page. Nothing! There was no envelope, no clue. They looked at one another.

"Oops," whispered Jenna.

"Where did we go wrong?"

Since they were permitted to keep their phones, Robert took his out, and brought up the translation for the clue they found in Cairo.

Centre of learning of ancient time, a beacon for all to see;
Tomes rare and valuable can be found.
Look to Britannica for where you are.

"I'm still confident, the place is Alexandria. The second line must refer to this library. I don't think there's another library that compares to this one for rare books."

Robert heaved a heavy sigh. "I guess we'll have to get volumes from all the Britannica's."

Robert went over to the same attendant who served them earlier. He asked how many copies of the Encyclopaedia Britannica they had in the Rare Books Collection. The man checked his online catalogue again. They had six full copies, each being a different edition. Robert asked if he could have the volume associated with the topic *Alexandria* from the other editions as well. The man looked curiously at Robert. Robert laughed, pulled out his wallet, and showed the man one of his fake research assistant cards. He explained they were both research assistants who worked together, and were doing some comparative research while on vacation. The man understood immediately. He smiled, and told Robert he would bring the other volumes to him in a few minutes.

Robert returned to the table where Jenna was studying the entries from both volumes. He was chuckling to himself.

"Thank goodness for those cards you made up for me."

"You brought them with you!"

"Never know when you need to be a research assistant. It worked, though. They have four more sets of the Encyclopaedia Britannica—all different editions. Damn that Scott!"

"I just hope his clue will be in one of the other volumes. I'd hate to have to sit here, and go through all the volumes of each set."

"Don't even say that, Jenna!"

A few minutes later, the attendant returned with four heavy volumes on a cart, and placed them on the reading table. If they needed anything else, they only need to ask, he told them.

More for show than anything else, they stood, and moved the newest volume to the far left, and the oldest to the far right. They placed the other volumes by order of date in between. They opened each volume to the entry for *Alexandria*. Nothing! They still made a show of looking at the various entries. Robert took out his phone, and took pictures of each page.

"We've got to be missing something!"

"*Look to Britannica for where you are*," read out Jenna. "We're here, in Alexandria."

She looked at Robert. She knew that look of intense concentration. He was picking apart each word. She remembered Robert telling her that Scott was being very careful with his wording. She tried to think of what that might be.

Robert stared out the window, lost in thought. He knew it was in the wording of the last line. "*Look to Britannica,*" seemed obvious. No, it wasn't there. It had to be the last phrase, "*for where you are.*" *Where are we?* he asked himself. He closed his eyes, and a broad smile covered his face. Jenna knew he must've figured it out.

He looked softly at Jenna. "Where are we?"

"Alexandria."

"Where's Alexandria?"

Jenna scrunched her face as the realization of what Robert just said hit home. "Egypt! We took the obvious meaning. How could I be so stupid?"

"Don't kick yourself too hard, sweetheart, I thought exactly the same thing."

Robert walked back to the service desk with the look of a man who just discovered something important. He asked the attendant for the oldest volume that contained the entry for *Egypt*. The man smiled, and seemed to share Robert's excitement. He hurried off to the shelves. A few minutes later, he handed the volume to Robert, who was still waiting at the desk.

Back at the table, Robert and Jenna looked at one another excitedly. They opened the book to the page for *Egypt*. There, carefully wedged into the binding, was Scott's note. There was no need for a plastic bag here. It would've made the presence of the note obvious. There wasn't even an envelope, just a small piece of paper folded in two. They bent over the volume, pretending to read. Robert pulled out the note, and began using it as a rule to move down the column of text as they read.

The attendant was curious to know if they found what they were looking for. He saw Robert moving the note down the column of text, and thought nothing of it. He'd seen this technique used by countless patrons. Jenna told him they indeed found their little treasure. She explained that the oldest article on Egypt made some glaring errors based on false assumptions by archaeologists of the time. The attendant returned to his station.

"Wow! That was close," she said, letting out a long slow breath.

"You're not kidding, but we have the clue, and I can just tuck it into my pocket anytime."

They remained at their reading table for some time. Jenna was genuinely interested in the changes in the articles from edition to edition, explaining how knowledge progressed slowly in the earlier editions, and more rapidly in the newer ones.

It was three hours later when they entered a taxi at the library for their return trip to the hotel. As they got into the taxi, Robert took one long last look at the building and surrounding area—just as any other tourist might do. He was doing a quick scan of the area for anyone who might be a watcher. He saw nothing.

Back in their suite, they brought out the iPad to get a translation. This clue read:

Sur insulo dividita, kie mastrino de amo naskiĝis;
Spektu teatraĵo de sidejoj de ŝtono, sxtono supren.

It was the shortest yet. They wondered if this meant it would need more work to decipher. With the trusty Google Translate, they quickly came up with the English version:

On island divided, where mistress of love was born;
Watch a play from seats of stone, one stone up.

They looked at each other with concern. They read and reread the note many times. Nothing came to mind. This clue was going to be tough!

Jenna was the first to venture an opinion. "I think we're out of Egypt with this one, darling. Absolutely nothing Egyptian remotely comes to mind."

"This one was a bit more stressful to find, and will be more difficult to crack. I think it's time for a walk."

"A walk?"

"Let's take our mind off this for a while. Let's have some lunch, chill out, and come back to this later."

"Actually, I *am* famished. I never thought clue hunting could be such hungry work."

They headed down to the restaurant, where they enjoyed some wonderful seafood. They switched gears completely, letting their love shine through again. As they did, they relaxed, enjoying the incredible view they had of the blue Mediterranean flowing out to the horizon before them. Neither saw anyone suspicious, though they both knew the watchers were out there. Perhaps their new look would keep them hidden for long enough to make it to their next destination undetected.

Back in their suite, they took the note from its hiding place. Nothing in the room was disturbed. They got down to working out the clue.

"It would've been so much easier if Scott simply left GPS coordinates to the next clue," murmured Robert.

"But it wouldn't be nearly as much fun! RJ, let's make this fun. Maybe if we do, we'll stay loose, and our minds will be more creative."

"You're right, as always, my dearest. So, let's see what we can do with this little riddle."

Jenna squeezed Roberts arm, and kissed him tenderly.

"Okay, we're looking for a divided island. It would have to be nearby, so Mediterranean Sea. It could be physically divided, or politically divided. What does a map show for divided islands?"

Robert scanned the map on his iPad. "Well, there are a lot of islands in the Aegean. A couple could be said to be divided physically, but each part has a different name. The only thing close to Egypt would be Cyprus. It has a Greek part, and a Turkish part. Nothing else."

"Okay, let's tentatively go with Cyprus as our choice. Now, for the mistress of love, or goddess of love. See what you can find."

"Ah, Aphrodite is the Greek goddess of love, and her Roman counterpart is Venus. Let's see what Wikipedia has to say about Aphrodite."

"Look here, RJ, in the Birth section. Her usual birth place is said to be Paphos, on Cyprus. Imagine that!"

"Well done Jenna! I think we've got the first line."

"Thank you! But you're the one doing the searches. I'm just a fast reader—comes with my job. Another kiss for good luck?"

Now it was Robert's turn. "Watching a play from seats of stone tells me it's a natural amphitheatre. Let's take a look around Paphos to see if they just happen to have one. Yep, there it is. Very interesting setup. Looks to be in decent shape, too."

"You see, lover, I told you it would be your turn to shine once we leave Egypt."

"I don't think I'll feel too shiny until I figure out the last bit—one stone up."

"A stone's throw? A stone length? One row up, maybe?"

"Oh, no. This is another of Scott's little tricks. It's the wording again. The key word is stone. He's not in Egypt anymore, so I don't think there's any Egyptian meaning here."

"Well, let's look up 'stone' and see what Google gives us."

"Good old Google!"

"Oh, my gosh! Can it really be that simple?"

"I wonder if your friend Scott realized that his clues could be rather easily deciphered using the Internet? One stone weight is 14 pounds. 14 rows up."

Jenna summarized: "To recap, then, we need to look in the 14th row of the amphitheatre at Paphos, Cyprus."

"I'll start looking for flights from Alexandria to Cyprus, and arrange accommodations—my job, you know."

They both laughed. Jenna wrapped her arms around Roberts

neck, and kissed him hard. "You're a wonderful man, RJ. You shine bright for me all the time."

Robert returned to his iPad, checking for flights. "Well, I might not be so shiny today, sweetheart. There are no direct flights from Alexandria to Larnaca, Cyprus. They all have two stops minimum. They all seem to end up in Cairo, and it's a short hop to Cyprus. That flight leaves Cairo at 16:10 and arrives at 17:20. Maybe the best would be to drive back to Cairo tomorrow, and leave directly from there. We don't need visas to get in, but we do need to book a return ticket. What do you think?"

"16:10, that's 4:10 p.m., so it's too late to head out now, right?"

"I don't think we'd make it, drop off the vehicle, and catch the flight in time."

Jenna stretched herself out. "I guess, we'll just have to rough it here for the night, then."

"I'll book for tomorrow afternoon, but I'm afraid we'll be flying with the riffraff."

"Do you think I could chance another spa treatment, RJ? I so enjoyed the one I had yesterday."

"Might not be a bad idea. It would help pass the time, as if we needed something to help us pass the time."

"Of course, that *is* a wonderful option." She rose, and flirtatiously made her way to the bedroom.

Robert quickly searched hotels in Larnaca. He finally settled on The Golden Bay Beach Hotel. Surprisingly, at this short notice, he was still able to book the Presidential Suite for a couple of nights. He heard Jenna calling him from the bedroom. He flipped off his iPad. He found her laying nude on the big bed. He stood at the door in awe of her perfect beauty. She saw him there, almost frozen. She smiled, stretching her hand out to him, beckoning. He practically tore off his clothes. Their pent-up passion exploded.

"No, sir, no sightings yet. All our inquiries were unproductive."

Silence at the other end, said it all. The connection was terminated.

Chapter 19 - Face-to-Face

Robert and Jenna awoke early to another bright, sunny, day. They lay in bed cuddling for a few minutes, talking quietly about what the day might bring. Both felt an urgency to get going. They had a long drive ahead of them, and wanted to be sure of arriving in Cairo in plenty of time to check their luggage. Robert felt strongly that they needed to leave Alexandria by 9 a.m. Jenna sighed deeply, and finally agreed. They enjoyed a bit more tenderness before Robert swung himself out of bed. Jenna groaned, not wanting to break the mood. Robert reached down from the foot of the bed, grabbed her hands, and pulled her up, and into his waiting arms. They laughed, and teased one another as they prepared to go down for their morning swim.

Jenna noticed that Robert was more tense this morning than at any other time since they arrived in Alexandria. He became more introspective. They walked quietly to the pool. Robert jumped in with great vigour. Jenna settled for a lady-like, elegant dive. Robert swam like a man possessed. Jenna couldn't hope to keep up with him. As usual, when she ran out of steam, she sat at the end of the pool, watching her man. Something was eating at him. After a few more laps, she noticed he was beginning to return to his usual form. With every lap, his strokes became longer, more controlled. His body didn't seem as stiff. Finally, he stopped near Jenna. She could see the tension had left his face, replaced now with solid confidence.

"Sorry, darling. I could really hear the baying hyenas getting very close now. It got to me. Thanks for coming down with me. It was important that you be here with me."

"I know they're close, but I know we're better than they are. You've been brilliant, RJ. It's thanks to you—your organization, your forward thinking, and your *sang froid*, that we've been a step ahead of them at every turn. My head's been in the clouds since we left for Vancouver, I'm afraid."

"Nonsense, Jenna. You've been a pillar of strength for me—my muse, if you will. Not to mention you've been the one to decipher those clues."

"Do you think we've been made?"

"I think if we have, we would've noticed something out-of-place, but I haven't seen anything to indicate that. Let's get back to the suite, pack, and have a nice breakfast. I don't want us to appear to be in a hurry."

"Just a couple of tourists in love," sniggered Jenna.

Back in the room, they chose their travel clothes, and packed everything else. There were a few items they left out they would want available while they drove. Robert's confidence bolstered-up Jenna's. They were back to being their normal selves again.

After breakfast, Robert made his way to the front desk. As he was checking-out, he asked if anyone had come asking for them. The desk clerk told him a lady had indeed come looking for her friends, the Jacksons. An officious looking man even asked the doorman if anyone arrived in a white Range Rover. Such an inquiry was unusual, and he asked Robert if this meant anything to him.

Robert couldn't help displaying a broad smile. "We decided to change rented vehicles to throw them off."

The desk clerk chuckled. "Then, sir, your little ruse obviously worked."

"Out of curiosity, have you seen any strangers hanging around the lobby?"

The desk clerk considered the question for a moment. "I believe there was mention of someone spending a lot of time in the lobby last night, drinking only mineral water."

"Is that person here now?"

"No, but there are two nice-looking ladies, also drinking only mineral water, sitting at the far end of the lobby."

"Unbelievable! They're even staking out the hotel because we tend to use Four Seasons properties when we travel. Which way are they facing?"

"Away from you, sir, as though they are watching the elevators."

Robert was laughing quietly now. "Is there another way out of the hotel, so we can escape these people?"

"You are ready to go, sir?"

"Yes, we're packed, and ready."

"I will send a porter to your suite, and instruct him to take *Mrs. Green* down the service elevator, which will bring you to the other side of the building. If you leave through the entrance, they will not see you. Bring your vehicle around to the back of the building. The porter will meet you there. They will be completely unaware of your departure."

"Thank you so very much!" Robert offered the clerk a hefty tip for his services.

"Always a pleasure, *Mr. Green*," he said, handing over Robert's and Jenna's passports.

"May I make a quick call to *Mrs. Green*?"

"But of course." The clerk slid his phone towards Robert.

Robert dialled the number of their suite. It rang several times before Jenna picked it up.

"Hello."

"Jenna, darling, our new friends are waiting to snag us in the lobby. The porter is on his way up, and he'll take you down the service elevator to the back of the building. I'll bring the car around, and meet you there."

"You scared me to death! Okay, I'm all ready to go here. See you out back in a few minutes, then."

It only took Jenna and the porter five or six minutes to get to the back entrance. It took Robert extra time to take the long way to the car park, pay the parking attendant, and make his way to the back of the building. He breathed easier when he saw them waiting there. The porter had all the luggage in the vehicle in no time at all. He received a good tip, too.

Robert concentrated on getting back on the main road out of Alexandria, and to the highway back to Cairo. Once they were on their way, things loosened up, and conversation flowed again.

"They were staking out the hotel. One man last night, and two women this morning. Thankfully, they weren't facing the front desk. They were watching the elevators, figuring we had to use them to get out, at some point."

"Do you think they know we were at the hotel?"

"I don't know, Jenna. It could be they were checking out everyone who used the elevators to see if we'd show up. It could be they were watching the elevators because they knew we were there, and they didn't want to lose us."

Jenna looked out the back window of their vehicle. "Do you think they're following us?"

"I've been watching for that, even did a big circle on the way out. Didn't notice anything suspicious."

"You knew they were very close, didn't you, RJ? That's why you were so tense earlier."

"Could be. It's only a matter of time before they pick us up again. Jenna, when they were questioning you, did they ask about a map, or a note?"

"They always asked for a map. I don't recall anyone mentioning a note. What's going on in that devious mind of yours, my love?"

Robert sat quietly, mulling things through, as he avoided an errant donkey on the road. Jenna didn't interrupt.

After a few minutes, he gave her a glance, smiled, and reached out to caress her arm. Jenna couldn't believe what this loving touch was doing to her. She was instantly aroused. She wondered if Robert would notice. Robert heard a quick intake of breath, and felt her shift in her seat. When he glanced over again, she was looking straight out the window. *Glad to see I'm not the only one who has unexpected reactions,* he thought.

"You see, darling, it appears they think you're in possession of a map leading to the Emerald Tablet. They want the map so *they* can find it. I don't think they know it's not a map, but a note that leads to a series of clues stashed around different places. They're probably wondering what in the world we're doing, travelling around so much, and so quickly."

"They've only been searching for me, because they think I have a map leading to the tablet. Until they suspected I snagged myself a wonderful man, they thought I was alone."

"Now, they know we're together, and they know where I live, and they know I've got money. They know, to some extent, we stay only in the best hotels, and book the best suites. For all they know, we might simply be on a whirlwind trip around the world. If you know where the tablet is, you might already have it, or you might not have a clue, or you're waiting until the end of our love journey to claim the prize."

"Oh, RJ! That makes so much sense! They're confused, very confused. This could change their whole strategy."

"Exactly! If they're finally getting wise to the fact we're following clues, they may decide to simply try to find us, keep us in their sights, letting us do all the work. They may want to take us out, and try finding, and deciphering the clues themselves, but my gut tells me they won't do that."

"If they think we're following clues, they'll know we've been pretty good at finding them, and moving on quickly. You're right. Why stop us, since we're doing so well. Why not let us dig up the tablet, and then take it from us?"

"Which brings up that nagging question again. What the heck do we do with the Emerald Tablet when we find it?"

"Dr. Scott wanted it protected, studied, and displayed for all to see."

"That's all fine, but with Carver's connections, is there a museum anywhere that's safe?"

Jenna looked at Robert softly. She knew this question was nagging him a lot. They wouldn't be safe until they could resolve this issue. She had no idea what could be done to safeguard the tablet, *and* get Carver off their backs. She wanted the Emerald Tablet to just go away. She took Robert's right hand in hers, bringing it to her lips, kissing it gently.

Gina, and one of her female colleagues, sat in the lobby of the Four Seasons Alexandria, pretending to read magazines, and drinking mineral water. They'd been sitting there for an hour. They were bored. Stakeouts were always boring. They sat in a way to focus their attention on the elevators. Gina felt in her bones that Jackson and Carpenter were here. They would eventually have to take the elevator down to the main floor to go anywhere. The watcher from last night saw no one remotely resembling their quarry.

There was a large group of people who exited the elevators at about the time they arrived, but no one stood out. They weren't interested in the comings and goings at the front desk. Gina felt this would only be a source of distraction, and they would have to turn to watch the elevators, which might raise suspicion. They were oblivious to Mr. Green who was checking-out behind them, and that he casually walked out of the main entrance of the hotel.

By 10 a.m., Gina's instinct told her they were gone. She wasn't feeling it anymore.

"Damn!" she cursed, quietly.

Her colleague looked at her curiously. "What?"

"I don't *feel* it anymore. They're gone. Somehow, we missed them." Gina was frustrated!

"We didn't see anyone who even looked remotely like them."

"I felt their presence earlier. I had shivers going up and down my spine, they were so close. Now, it's gone! And they're gone too!"

Gina pulled the cell out of her purse. She placed a call to the leader of one of Carver's watcher teams, and ordered that he get someone in the lobby at their location, to replace them. They needed to leave. Within five minutes, a middle-aged man walked in, and ordered mineral water from the lobby waiter. He positioned himself to watch the elevators. Gina was advised that her replacement was in place.

Gina, and her companion, casually left the building, and returned to their command centre. Gina was livid! Jackson and Carpenter did it again—snuck out from under their very noses—from under *her* nose! This was the third time this pair gave her the slip. How were they doing it? How could they know they were being watched? What was her team doing that gave them away? No one had answers, but they all knew that if Gina said they were gone, they were gone. They knew she had a sense about these things, and she was *always* right.

Jackson and Carpenter had the advantage, of course. They knew where they were going. Gina didn't. She remembered what Carver told her—these are normal people, think like a normal person. So, what would a normal person do? They knew they were being tracked. They would want to move on as quickly as possible to their next destination. She was very confident their tour of Egypt ended in Alexandria. This would mean air travel to go anywhere. It was unlikely they would skulk around looking for secret passage on a cargo ship. In Egypt, most air travel routes through Cairo.

Gina knew she had to report in. Each call was becoming more difficult. Carver was extremely calm and quiet—which meant big trouble! She dialled; Carver picked-up.

"Report!"

"They gave us the slip again, sir."

"How do you know this?"

"I, and another of my team, were staking out the lobby, watching the elevators. They had to come down sometime. I knew they were there, sir. No sighting, but I *knew* it. By ten, I couldn't sense their presence anymore. We left a watcher there in case, but I just know they've left Alexandria."

"Your plans?"

"I'm confident Alexandria was the end of the line in Egypt, sir. Remembering what you said about thinking 'normal,' they'll need to fly out of here. Cairo is the air hub in Egypt. Practically everything routes through Cairo. We're heading to the Cairo airport immediately. They don't have much of a jump on us. If we boot it, we shouldn't be far behind them. I'm requesting 20 watchers placed at the entrance, and on the departure concourse. With some luck, we should be in place in two-and-a-half hours, sir."

"I'll make calls. Watchers will be in place within the hour. So, you were so close you could smell them."

"Yes, sir. While sitting in the Four Seasons lobby, I felt their presence very close by. An hour or so later, that feeling was gone. They didn't exit any of the elevators while we were there. Even in disguise, I would've felt something."

"I'm well aware of your sixth sense when it comes to tracking, Gina. I agree with your conclusions. I'll have people all over the Cairo airport. I want to know what they're up to. They're moving quickly now. This is not a nice lovers' vacation. They're finding and following clues left by that damned Scott. Eventually, they'll lead us right to the item. Find them, and stick to them like glue!"

"Yes, sir."

The drive back to Cairo was more enjoyable than the trip to Alexandria. There was less traffic, so Robert could relax. Jenna was still enthralled with the fact they were driving around in Egypt, but was content to admire the scenery while chatting with Robert. They were about half way, when an interesting thought popped into Jenna's head.

"RJ, why do *you* always drive? I can drive too, you know."

Robert knit his brows, and thought about this for a moment. "I have no idea. I guess I've always been the one to drive whenever Chris and I went anywhere; force of habit, I suppose. Then too, I want to let you enjoy your dream trip, and I want to be able to keep an eye on what's coming up behind us. Why do you ask?"

"I was just thinking it must be rather tiring for you to drive for hours without a break. If you tell me what to do, I can watch the mirrors too."

"Do you want to drive?"

"Yes, of course. I love driving."

"Well, then, you'll be the chauffeur in Cyprus. Does that work for you?"

"Yes! I think that'll be fun!" She grabbed Roberts arm and squeezed it.

Robert laughed. He never even thought about it. He knew

Jenna felt she wasn't contributing much. The more he considered what she said, the more he realized he almost completely took over the quest. He started to chuckle. Jenna looked at him curiously.

"You going to share the joke, sweetheart?"

"Robert looked at her with a broad smile. "It just dawned on me that I've been hogging your quest—just like my alter ego always did."

"RJ, don't even *think* that! I certainly don't feel that way. We both have different strengths, and we've been working extremely well together. It just seems you're doing all the tedious physical stuff, while I spend my time floating in the clouds. I need to do my share too. You're just too much of a gentleman to even ask. And one last thing—this is *our* quest, not just mine."

"Lean in here, you vixen, and kiss me!" he commanded. Jenna was happy to comply, even though it almost resulted in an accident.

By noon, the Cairo airport was crawling with Carver watchers. All entrances and concourses were covered by several agents. They all had a photo of Jackson and Carpenter. It would be Carpenter who would attract their attention rather than the nondescript Jackson.

Robert and Jenna rolled into the Cairo airport about one in the afternoon, after a very pleasant journey. Their first stop was the car rental return, where they disposed of their vehicle. As the attendant was completing the paper work, Robert looked around for anything out-of-place. He noticed a man leaning on a car, with a magazine in his hand. He smiled as he turned to Jenna.

"Guy with a magazine, to your left."

Without moving her head, she looked out the corner of her eye. Yes, there he was. As they took their carts of luggage to the terminal, they saw two more loitering at the entrance, this time, a couple.

"Looks like they have the whole airport covered."

Jenna saw them too. "They're so obvious, I can't believe it."

"Let's try to keep our cover. We have three hours to kill before we board the plane. We'll make our way to the EgyptAir counter right away, then head for the departure level. We can have lunch there."

Jenna laughed. "I'm going to try to count how many watchers we see."

Robert too, thought it was rather funny, but it wasn't lost on him either that this could be dangerous. They still had the advantage of knowing their destination. They wondered if Carver's people would try to take them, or would be content to follow them.

At the EgyptAir counter, there were at least six more distributed across the area. Robert remembered at the last minute they were flying tourist, so they lined up with the throng of other travellers already lined up. They dressed down a bit for travelling, allowing them to blend in better with the other tourists. Robert was glad they were buried in the crowd. If they were flying business class, they'd be spotted immediately. Jenna busied herself looking at a brochure she picked up in the hotel. She slid her sunglasses to the top of her head. They spoke quietly about their chances of slipping through Carver's net.

Finally, they moved to the counter. The attendant told them they had to pay a surcharge for their second checked luggage, and for being overweight. They explained they wanted business class, but there were no seats available. The attendant checked her computer. There were, in fact, two business class seats available. It was obviously a late cancellation, because the seats were together. Robert said they'd take them. She efficiently switched their booking to the business class seats. Robert offered his credit card to pay for the upgrade. The attendant was all smiles, and happily sent their luggage down the conveyor belt into the bowels of the terminal building. She let them know the executive lounge was available for their pleasure.

As they turned to leave, Jenna scanned the area quickly while Robert sorted out their travel papers. She saw at least two more possible watchers. True to their cover, they happily made their way to the departure concourse.

If they had this many watchers, they were sure the executive lounge would be watched as well. They decided to have lunch in one of the restaurants on the concourse. This was a time to blend in, rather than to stand out, so they chose a restaurant with plenty of patrons. They also chose to sit with their backs to the concourse. They ate a leisurely lunch, showing no hurry, no concern.

As they left the restaurant, they used a large group of travellers for cover, and ducked into a store. There were some beautiful things there. Robert and Jenna were having a lot of fun wandering through the shop. In the end, they couldn't resist buying a few items, which they placed in their carry-on bags. As they left the shop, Jenna caught the eye of a woman walking slowly against the flow of traffic—another watcher.

"RJ, I think we've just been recognized," she whispered to him. "A woman walking by looked straight at me. I'm sure she recognized me."

"No need to panic, they won't risk a takedown here on the concourse—way too much security. All they could do is threaten us to go with them. Carver wants the Emerald Tablet badly, or he wouldn't have so many people out looking for us. He also knows we're the only ones who have any clue where it is. If we resist, they can't very well shoot us, or stab us, or that puts an end to finding the tablet."

"So, really, the best they can do is find out where we're going, and follow us there."

"Yep! It's when we get to Cyprus that the fun will begin. In the mean time, let's be in love."

Jenna held his arm tight. He was right. They were safe—for now. In Cyprus, they would quickly find out if Carver wanted them, or was content to follow them around. If the latter, they needed to come up with a plan to safeguard the tablet, and save their own skins!

Gina, and her team, finally arrived at the Cairo airport. It was 1:45 p.m. So far, none of the watchers reported a sighting. All her instincts told her Jackson and Carpenter were here. The adrenaline was pumping, her mind was sharp, and her team was ready.

"Possible sighting, departure concourse, outside duty-free shop. Woman has red hair with braid, man is similar to photo," came the report over the phone.

"Stay with them. Do *not* lose them!"

Gina's team moved quickly to the departure concourse. Once there, they split into pairs moving in the direction of the duty-free shops.

"Where are they, now?"

"Walking slowly towards the departure gates."

"Did they make you?"

"It is possible. The woman and I locked eyes. I sensed she knew I was watching for them."

"Damn! What is she wearing?"

"Jeans, short-sleeve, light-red, blouse."

"Stay back, blend in, don't let them see you."

"They are not looking around; they completely ignored me; but I am certain I was made."

"Have they taken any evasive action?"

"No. Walking casually, laughing, looking at things in store windows, normal tourist behaviour. If it was not that I think something passed between me and the woman, I would think it was a false sighting."

"We're very close now, when we spot them, we'll let you know."

Gina's heart was pounding. She knew she was going in for the kill. She scanned the area carefully, but quickly. Then, she spotted the target. She contacted her colleagues, telling them where to position themselves. *These two must have ice water in their veins*, she thought. She walked past them far to the left. She wanted to see their faces. They were taking no precautions, behaving like any normal tourist with some time to kill before boarding. If it wasn't for her instinct, she would say they weren't the pair she was after. *Turn around, damn you, turn around!*

Out of the corner of her eye, Jenna caught sight of Gina, who was intently looking at her.

Jenna smiled. "We have company, my darling, someone we know already."

"Oh! Who might that be?"

"Remember our three friends on the Trans-Canada?"

"Ah, the nice lady with the big black SUV, that paid Carmen a visit."

"Yes, dear, the very one. She's trying to figure out if I'm really me, or just a lover on a dream tour."

"If she's here, then she has a team with her, you can count on that. I'm guessing she's one of Carver's elite squad, given we've seen her in Canada, and now in Egypt."

"You said earlier that we're pretty safe here, do you still think that's true?"

"Yes, I think we're safe as long as we stay in the airport."

"We've been playing cat-and-mouse with Carver's people for weeks. I think it's high time we meet, and set some ground rules, don't you?"

"Aren't you the brave girl!" With great admiration, he turned to face Jenna. He saw the look of determination in her eyes. He reached out, caressing her face with his hand. "You know, I think there's method to your madness. I'll follow you're lead."

They grabbed the handles of their carry-on bags, and began moving again. They made a slow turn towards Gina. At first, they paid no attention to her. When they were about three metres away, Jenna looked up, directly at Gina. Robert did the same, scanning quickly for others who might intervene. His adrenaline was pumping fast now. He was preparing to protect Jenna at all cost.

Gina was taken completely off her guard as Jenna moved with purpose directly towards her, staring strait into her eyes. Her colleague began moving to block the way, but Gina pushed him back. She knew nothing would be done in the airport. Jenna stopped about a metre in front of her. Robert and Gina's team member were staring each other down, and there were no winners.

Jenna extended her hand. "Hi, I'm Jenna Carpenter, but you know that already. Might we have the pleasure of knowing who you are? After all, you've been dogging our tracks for weeks." Her tone was neither hard nor soft, but very business-like.

Gina took her hand, introducing herself, "Gina Archer. I'm glad we've finally met. You've given us a very good run."

Jenna retracted her hand gently. "You can give this message to your boss, Carver: I don't scare easily, the beating his people in Airdrie gave me only strengthened my resolve to keep the Emerald Tablet away from him; and if he ever wants to get even a peek at the tablet, he'll keep out of our way."

"My employer extends his apologies for your treatment in Airdrie. Our people there overstepped their mandate, no doubt to earn brownie points. They've been dealt with."

"And what is your mandate, Ms. Archer? You should know that we're not going down without a fight, and if we even get a sniff of you, or your people, near us, we'll destroy all information that might lead to the Emerald Tablet."

Gina looked at Jenna hard. She was reading her face, and intent. She saw resolve, determination, confidence, and great strength there. She smiled. There was no reason to hold back. Perhaps they could come to some arrangement. Everyone has a price. She was wrong.

"My employer is a very wealthy man. He's prepared to offer you a great deal of money for information leading to the recovery of the article in question."

"I'm not one of Carver's patsies who sells his soul for a few pieces of silver," Jenna spat out so forcefully, Gina took a step back. “You can tell Carver to keep his money, he’ll need it. Again, what is your mandate, Ms. Archer?”

Gina was taken aback by the forcefulness of Jenna’s reply. “I’m afraid I can’t tell you that, Ms. Carpenter.”

“Then, we both know where we stand. We must assume the worst scenario. As far as we’re concerned, you’ll be trying to abduct us for interrogation, and eventual elimination.” In a soft, sweet voice, she added, “I *assure* you, Ms. Archer, this will *not* happen. But I’m glad we had a chance to meet.”

“I don’t suppose you’re inclined to let me know where you’re headed to next.”

With a big, bright smile, Jenna replied, “Not a hope in hell!”

Robert was still staring down his opposite number. As he inched closer, Gina’s man retreated the same distance. Jenna took him by the arm. He broke his gaze to look at her. He too smiled. Jenna slipped her hand around his waist, and kissed him gently.

“Nothing more to do here. Shall we continue our little walk, my love?

“Nothing would please me more, sweetheart.”

As they walked away, Gina’s team converged on her. Both Robert and Jenna took notice of the two pairs making a bee line towards Gina, and smiled.

“Keep an eye on them. They won’t be hiding here in the airport. They might be cagey in regards to which flight they’re taking, but that won’t be difficult to figure out,” Gina ordered her team.

It was time to report in.

“Well?”

“We have them, sir.”

“Report!”

“It’s as I thought. They’re flying out of Cairo. Don’t know where yet. A watcher spotted a couple fitting their description, and reported in. She was made, and she knew it. Jackson and Carpenter never even flinched. They kept moseying on. When my team arrived, we surrounded the suspect couple. While I was trying to get a good view of her face, they turned, and walked straight for us...”

“What? Did you say they walked straight for you?”

“Yes, sir. Walked right up to us. While my associate and Jackson were staring each other down, Carpenter offered her hand. We shook hands, introduced ourselves, and had a little chat."

"You had a little chat!" croaked Carver.

"Yes, sir. She's not pleased about her treatment in Alberta. I extended apologies. Somehow, she knows it's you, sir, who's after the object in question. She was quite frank about it. It seems they are, in fact, chasing down clues to the whereabouts of the object. I suggested that my employer would be willing to pay a handsomely for information leading to the object."

"Which she flatly refused."

"Exactly, sir, and quite vehemently! Took me completely by surprise."

"Did you come to any sort of arrangement?"

"Not exactly, sir. Since I wouldn't elaborate on my mandate, she made it clear they would assume the worst: we would try to abduct, interrogate, and eventually eliminate them. She also assured me this would never happen. I must admit, these two are incredibly determined, and show absolutely no fear. I can only assume they'll make my job as difficult as possible."

"In your professional opinion, bruised ego aside, do you think I should replace you with another team?"

Gina dreaded the question. She had to be very careful how she answered. She also needed to forget her own feelings. Carver waited patiently.

"Professionally speaking, sir, I don't think it'll help the situation. They'll continue to assume the worst regardless of whether it's my team, or another. If we disappear, they'll be far more wary, looking for the next set of trackers, and we're more likely to lose them. These two are *not* afraid of us, or anyone else who's sent in. As Carpenter put it to me, they won't go down without a fight, and I think they can put up one hell of a fight, sir. If we stay on the case, even let them know we're there, but hanging back, they might become complacent. Knowing who the opposition is, can do that. They'll definitely try to give me the slip, but that won't happen either."

"What resources do you think you'll need, going forward?"

"Obviously, we won't be able to board the flight they booked, sir. We'll need ready air transportation. Is your jet still standing-by here in Cairo, sir?"

"Yes. I thought it prudent to keep it around. It's at your disposal."

"Thank you, sir."

"You've done well. Maybe your little face-to-face may prove useful. Stay on them. Let me know where you're headed, and I'll get watchers there to make sure there are no gaps in coverage. Do you have a new photo for me?"

"Coming now, sir."

As they sat waiting for their flight to be called, Robert pulled out his iPad. The WiFi in the airport wasn't great, so he switched to mobile data. Jenna watched to see what he was up to. He had that wry smile again. She waited patiently.

"We have a room booked in a hotel in Larnaca."

"Yes, I know."

"I want to see what they have in Paphos, since that's where we're headed anyway." In a few minutes, he settled on a hotel, and showed Jenna pictures of various suites."

"Oh, RJ, you spoil me so much!"

"I'm not just spoiling you, my dear. I'm enjoying these places too!"

He reassembled his smartphone, and called the number for the Elysium Hotel. After a short conversation, he announced they would be staying in the Royal Suite, with their own swimming pool. Jenna was almost in tears.

"It's about two hours from the airport at Larnaca to Paphos. We'll boot it out of the airport as quickly as we can. You're driving, remember?"

As expected, Jackson and Carpenter sat in the main departure area. They didn't commit to their gate until their flight was called. They had no way of knowing Gina had a private jet waiting to take off the moment they showed their hand. Gina nodded in admiration as they moved to one gate, as a flight was called, only to return to the main hall. She wouldn't know until they walked down the gangway to the plane. Finally, Flight MS741 to Larnaca, Cyprus.

"Larnaca, Cyprus, sir."

"Cyprus!" he spat out. "Who the hell goes to Cyprus? I'm afraid you're on your own, Gina. I have no contacts in Cyprus!"

The flight landed on time, at about 4:30 p.m. It took almost 30 minutes to clear customs and immigration. A representative from the rental car company was waiting when Robert and Jenna finally made it to the arrival hall. Robert booked a Range Rover from a company in town, and they were courteous enough to meet him at the airport. The paperwork was mostly filled in from the reservation information, so it only took a couple of minutes to complete the rental.

"Another Range Rover, darling?"

"Yes, but this one's grey. I wanted something with power and speed. The other offerings were all cheap SUVs."With a big grin on his face, he added, "With all our luggage, a Ferrari would've been impractical."

The rental was waiting for them at the exit. After loading their considerable luggage, Robert set the GPS coordinates to the Elysium Hotel in Paphos. At first, Jenna thought Robert was getting ready to drive again, as he entered the left-side door, and was a bit crestfallen.

Robert smiled, and asked, "Well, aren't you getting in? You're driving this time."

Jenna looked at him curiously. She opened the right-side door to find the steering wheel was on her side of the SUV.

"It's a right-hand drive, Jenna; you drive on the left side of the road here. Will that be a problem for you?" He was grinning from ear-to-ear.

Jenna entered the car; Robert handed her the keys; and they left. The airport is west of Larnaca, so they didn't have to go through town first.

Robert sat back in his comfortable seat, glad he didn't have to drive. It was obvious Jenna was a great driver, as she manipulated the big SUV through tight spots, and difficult corners, at speed—even on the "wrong" side of the road. She glanced at Robert with a look that said, *See, I told you I can drive!*

"Did you notice our friends at the airport?" she asked.

"No, did you?"

"No. Do you think they're here yet?"

"Hard to say. They know us now. They can stay in the shadows, and we won't notice them. They might've changed trackers too."

"I haven't noticed any watchers, RJ, not even in the shadows."

"Somehow, I don't think they waited for the next flight out. I'm sure they have a private jet at their disposal. Carver put his best team on the job, because he wants the Emerald Tablet badly. He won't be stingy with costs."

"I hope they leave the existing team in place, especially now that we know what they look like. I must admit it was pretty stupid of the whole team to converge on Archer like that. It exposed their whole squad."

"I agree with you there. Still, we need to keep our eyes and ears open for a second team. By the way, Jenna, that was really ballsy of you to walk right up to Archer, and call her out. It must've thrown her off her game a bit. You're just full of surprises!"

"You were magnificent yourself, RJ, the way you stared down that accomplice of hers. Did you notice he was stepping back as you stepped forward? No one has ever stood up for me like that. You've no idea how turned-on I was back there."

"Then we should spend most of the evening discussing that," sniggered Robert.

Jenna drove fast, watching the mirrors often. Robert pulled down the passenger side visor, and watched through the vanity mirror. So far, they hadn't seen anything suspicious. They arrived at the Elysium at about 7:30 p.m. A quick scan showed no obvious watchers in the lobby. They checked-in quickly, and were treated with deference, befitting anyone staying in a Royal Suite. Robert made the same request as in Alexandria—to register as Mr. and Mrs. Green. The desk clerk was very accommodating.

Jenna never ceased to be amazed at the beauty of the elegant suites they were staying in. The sun had sunk beneath the horizon, but its last rays filled the sky with deep colours that reflected on the sea. She turned to Robert, swallowing hard. She loved this man with all her being. He felt the same. Carver, Gina Archer, and the Emerald Tablet faded into an oblivion of love.

Gina and her team didn't deplane until nearly 6:30 p.m. because of a delay with customs and immigration when they landed at Larnaca. There were no officials to meet them, and they had to wait for over an hour before someone showed up. She knew her quarry's plane landed earlier, and they would be well ensconced in a hotel in Larnaca by now.

Gina was frustrated. What good was having all the resources in the world, when officialdom works against you? If Carver had contacts here, they would've been watching Jackson and Carpenter arrive. Now, they were gone again. Carver would be livid.

"We've landed in Larnaca, sir, but I regret to inform you that we've lost them again. We couldn't deplane until just now because there were no officials here to meet the plane. We've been sitting on our hands waiting. Jackson and Carpenter are long gone."

Carver was seething. He was only too aware of how officials could hold things up. That's why he had contacts where he felt the need. He calmed himself down.

"What are your plans to recover them?"

"Of course, we'll do a search of hotels in Larnaca. There aren't that many luxury hotels here. The biggest problem is that we don't know if Larnaca is their final destination or not. If our efforts in Larnaca yield nothing, I propose we camp out at the airport. There's no other way out, sir. There are no passenger ships going anywhere, except to Turkey. Just in case, we'll have a team of local watchers keeping an eye on the port where the ferries dock."

"Keep me informed the moment anything changes!"

"Yes, sir."

Gina turned to her team. "Damned if they haven't gotten away from us, *again*! Lady luck has definitely cast herself against us, so far."

It was becoming a custom for Robert and Jenna to wake early, and cuddle for a while, engaging in small talk. So, this was a typical day. A while later, they got up, showered, donned bathing suits, and headed for the pool. They both found swimming laps refreshing and invigorating. Today was no different. On their way down, they looked casually for any suspected watchers. To their surprise, there were none. Was it possible they gave them the slip again?

Back in their suite, they prepared for the clue hunt.

"Where do you think Ms. Archer has gotten to, darling?"

"Don't know, Jenna, and I hope they're somewhere we're not."

"We need to go to the Archaeological Park, don't we?"

"Yep. Doesn't open until 8:30, so we have plenty of time for a nice breakfast before we leave."

They headed down to the restaurant, and decided on the buffet, which they ate out on the terrace. It was a beautiful day, and the view was spectacular. They pushed the quest out of their minds. They simply enjoyed one another's company. They wondered what the folks back home were doing. It seemed ages ago. They both laughed when they calculated it had only been just over three weeks since they first met on a dusty road in Alberta. How far away that seemed to them now, sitting on a terrace in Cyprus. So much had happened. And yet, neither would trade an instant for all the gold in the world.

After breakfast, they went up to the suite to grab Robert's "tourist" camera. They still needed to keep up appearances for the locals, as well as for any watchers. The Paphos Archaeological Park was close to the hotel, so it was a quick drive there. Jenna drove, of course. Strangely, she found driving on the left side more natural.

Once in the park, they perused the fold-out map they received when they bought their admission tickets. There was lots to see before they would arrive at the amphitheatre called the Odeon. They casually made their way around the ruins. Jenna was in her glory. Anything archaeological. She loved to poke around here-and-there. Finally, they arrived at the Odeon. There was only one side of the Odeon that had the prerequisite 14 rows.

Robert sent Jenna up first, taking photos as she walked up the narrow aisle. Once at the 14th row, there were more shots. Robert then made his climb to meet Jenna. They dropped down a couple of rows so they could look under the seat stones without being too obvious. They split up, each going down one side of the row.

Jenna was the lucky one. She spotted a likely-looking gap under the 14th row seat which had some odd stones pressed in place. She sat on the seat below, and was able to dig out the stones with her finger tips—at the cost of a fingernail. When she retrieved the clue, she casually stuffed it in the pocket of her shorts. She called over to Robert, giving him a daring pose, which he shot with his camera. They both laughed. She extended her hand for him to join her. He did so, and they sat together, talking about how it would have been, back in ancient times, watching a Greek play. They wondered if there was a real Aphrodite living on the island. Robert was sure she would be just like Jenna.

In a spot where no one would see, Jenna removed the envelope from the zipper bag, and placed it in her pocket again. A note in a bag would attract attention. An envelope in her pocket would not. She disposed of the bag in a convenient trash can. The sun was high, and it was quite hot now. They made their way back to the exit, and their vehicle. Before leaving, Robert put some money in the donation slot.

Jenna drove quickly back to the hotel. They were both curious about where they would be heading next. In their suite, they got out the iPad and the nail file once again. It was Robert's turn to open the clue. He gently slit the envelope open. The small sheet of paper within was pressed flat on the table between them. It read:

> *En la urbo kie ŝi plantis olivarbo,*
> *Parko proksime de la palaco, de lageto por akvaj birdoj*
> *Ripozas malnovan riphava marmoro, kie pli estos trovitaj.*

After a few minutes of translating, they had the English version:

> *In the city where she planted an olive tree,*
> *A park near the palace, by a pool for aquatic fowl,*
> *Rests old ribbed marble, where more will be found.*

They both stared at the riddle, then at each other. Slowly, a broad smile began to appear on Jenna's face.

"Time for lunch, I think."

Robert burst out laughing. She was right, of course. After taking a photo of the note, and the translation, with his smartphone, he hid the note in his favourite place—the hotel amenities folder—and they made their way down to one of the terrace restaurants.

They were given a table with a perfect view of the entire restaurant. No one would be able to enter without being seen. They both gave the existing patrons a quick glace. They noticed none of Carver's team they met the previous afternoon, and no one else looked remotely suspicious.

They ordered a platter of seafood for two. While they waited for their meal to arrive, they spoke quietly about the riddle. Robert brought it up on his phone, sharing it with Jenna, sitting next to him.

Jenna smiled, biting her lower lip trying not to laugh. "I'll volunteer to decipher the last phrase. I think it means we'll find another clue there."

Now it was Robert's turn to laugh. "I'm very grateful for that insightful interpretation."

"Well, we're not in Egypt anymore, my love. I'm finding myself a bit out of my depth with this one. Besides, it's your turn to shine!"

"Thank you so much! Okay, maybe backwards is the best way to go with this one. It might help figure out the more difficult lines above."

"I never though of you as a backwards kind of guy, RJ," she sniggered. "But you're probably right."

"So, *old ribbed marble*. We've seen a lot of that today—marble column. I'm going to guess that if it's *resting*, it must be laying down on the ground, rather than standing."

"I'll go with that. Makes sense." She squeezed Robert's arm tenderly.

"Next, *a pool for aquatic fowl*. What would you say are the most common types of aquatic foul?"

"Hmmm. Ducks, swans, geese, loons, herons, flamingos. Maybe a lake. There are plenty of palaces with lakes near them."

"Scott knows he has to be specific enough for someone to zero-in on the location. The word *pool* is significant here. A pool is small-ish. What's another word for a pool of water?"

"Pond?"

Robert thought of the water fowl they'd enumerated. "Duck pond?"

"Of course! It's in a park. Parks often have duck ponds."

"So, we're looking for a fallen column by a duck pond in a park near a palace...somewhere."

"Somewhere...and we haven't a clue as to whom Dr. Scott was referring—only that she planted an olive tree."

Just then, the waitress brought out their food. She overheard what Jenna was musing about.

"That would be the goddess Athena, ma'am, and she planted the tree in Athens," the waitress informed her.

"How do you know that?"

"All Greek children are taught about the old gods and goddesses. Athena was the favourite daughter of Zeus. It was she who offered the olive tree to the Greek people. A very great gift. There is a mosaic of it on the second level of the lobby."

"Thank you very much, miss. You've just earned yourself a special tip," Robert told her.

"Oh, it is nothing, sir. If you want anything, please call me over."

Jenna looked at Robert in amazement. "Wow! I'll bet Dr. Scott never thought we'd get help solving his riddle from a lovely young waitress."

"So, next stop: Athens!"

When they finished their wonderful seafood meal, Robert was good to his word, leaving the waitress a substantial tip. Before returning to the suite, they wandered around the beautiful gardens and pools of the hotel, holding hands, like any two lovers. With the riddle solved, they could relax for the rest of their stay.

Back in the suite, Robert began checking for flights and accommodations for Athens. Jenna stood behind him, with her arms around his neck, looking over his shoulder. She was amazed at how quickly Robert moved around the Internet sites, scanning, saving, and discounting information. Without noticing, she was kissing his neck, and biting his ear. Suddenly, Robert stopped.

"You realize you're making this almost impossible."

"Oops; sorry; force of habit!"

Robert got back to work.

"Looks like we have a real choice of flights from here to Athens, beginning at 5:40 in the morning through to 9:30 at night. Any preferences?"

Jenna considered for a moment. "I'm sure Carver's people are watching the airport, seeing as they haven't found us yet. I know the 5:40 a.m. flight is really early, but maybe we can sneak past them while they're having a snooze."

"Just a minute...I didn't realize there's an airport here in Paphos. Hold on...Bingo! There's a RyanAir flight from here to Athens leaving at 11:35 a.m., arriving in Athens at 1:20 p.m., and they have business class seats available."

"Do you think they're watching the airport here, RJ?"

"It's possible, but my money's on them keeping the main airport at Larnaca under lockdown. It's the most logical, since they don't seem to know where we are. There aren't many flights out of here."

"It would certainly give us a nice sleep-in, instead of a very early start."

Robert booked two business-class seats on the next morning's flight. Now, he began his search for accommodations.

"Let me know if you see anything you like."

"RJ, what about this one? The Penthouse Suite looks so—unexpected—for a place like Athens!"

Robert took out his cell phone, and dialled the number on the web site for the NEW Hotel. Strange name, but it *was* billed as eclectic. When he got through to the reservation desk, he asked if the Penthouse Suite was available for tomorrow and the next day. To his surprise, they had a cancellation, and he could have it for a week. He confirmed the booking for two nights under the name Edward Green, and advised they would be arriving between 2 p.m. and 3 p.m.

Once that was done, Robert called the car rental agency in Larnaca. He asked if it would be possible for them to pick up the Range Rover in Paphos. He agreed to the high pick-up charge without argument. He told them they could get the vehicle at the Paphos airport, where they expected to be by 10:00 a.m.

This time, it was Robert who took the initiative. He stood up holding Jenna's hands, flipping them over his head. He pulled her against him, kissing her passionately, and squeezing her back. Before she could respond, Robert pulled her top off, complete with bra! Jenna was surprised, and instantly aroused. She tore the clothes off her man. With her arms around his neck, and her ankles locked behind him, he walked her to the bed, and gently tossed her on it. In a moment, her shorts were in the corner of the room. They made passionate love, totally lost in each other.

Chapter 20 - Guns & Knives

Gina woke-up at six on Saturday morning. She was used to short nights. Her team kept a 24-hour watch on the Larnaca airport—three pairs of watchers, including her. They rotated every two hours during the day and evening, with 4-hour shifts overnight. There was only one entrance into the airport, and it was well covered. Her local watchers at the Turkish ferry port reported no sightings. She expected none. All major airlines flew from Larnaca. She was certain Jackson and Carpenter would fly out of here, once they deciphered the latest clue, assuming they found it.

She showered, dressed, and ate a good breakfast. She and her companion, Kate, would be going on shift at seven. She felt the usual tingle through her body this morning. Something was happening. Her quarry was getting ready to move on to their next destination. She knew it. She was glad she would be on watch next. She wouldn't leave the airport until they had a sighting. They wouldn't get past them again—not on her watch! Gina shared her thoughts with her watch companion, who chuckled, and gave her some gentle ribbing. She'd worked with Gina for years, and knew Gina well enough to know how far she could go.

"Ten bucks says they'll sneak out," Kate said, with a smirk.

"A thousand says we'll bag them before sundown."

"Confident, are you?"

"My tracker sense tells me they're close, and getting ready to move."

"I trust your instinct, Gina, but these two always seem to find a way. They're different than any quarry I can remember tracking down"

"I know what you mean, Kate. When this is over, I'd like to sit down with this pair for a complete debriefing. I'd love to know what they did, and where we failed. I don't ever want another mission to go like this one."

"You're the best, Gina. If anyone bags them, it'll be us."

With that, they finished up, and headed to the airport. Once there, they waved off the current pair of watchers, and took their positions to cover the entire entry hall. They were familiar with each other's tactics, so it was easy to move around without leaving any gaps. All of Gina's instincts were screaming at her. Both women were alert and vigilant to the extreme.

Robert awoke to find Jenna propped-up on her elbow, head resting in her hand, gazing at him. He turned his head, smiling at her. He ran his eyes along the entire length of her body. Magnificent! She seemed to become more beautiful every day. She did the same to him, with a flick or two of her eyebrows as she did. Her lips were parted and moist, with her tongue passing across them. On the return trip, she paused. Her smile broadened when she achieved her goal. Robert could stand it no longer.

They exhausted one another, and lay in bed breathing hard. Jenna began to laugh. It was infectious, and Robert laughed with her. He turned to look at the clock. It was already after eight. They needed to get a move on if they were going to be at the airport by ten. They were both invigorated from their love-making. After a nice shower, they packed all but their chosen travel outfits, and headed down for breakfast.

They both decided to put aside the Emerald Tablet until they arrived in Athens. They would enjoy themselves while they could. If Carver's watchers were at the airport, so be it! They felt relatively safe, now. It was obvious from Jenna's conversation with Archer, the watchers would be content to follow them. The time to panic would be when they found the last clue. Hopefully, before then, they will have come up with a plan on what to do with the tablet to keep it, and themselves, safe.

They arrived at the Paphos airport just after ten. As they pulled in to the curb to unload their baggage, Robert recognized the car rental representative who met them in Larnaca. They exchanged courtesies, and he even helped get the luggage out of the vehicle. Robert made sure nothing was left behind. The paperwork was filled-in, and the keys were turned over.

When Robert and Jenna walked into the airport, they took a quick look around the entrance hall. If there were any watchers, they were a cut above the rest, because they spotted no one suspicious.

RyanAir offered a priority check-in for business-class passengers, so there was no waiting to get rid of their luggage. The attendant stared at their two carts of luggage. Robert explained they were on a whirlwind romantic trip they expected to last 4 to 6 weeks, which meant packing a lot of clothes. The attendant gave them an understanding smile. There would be a substantial extra cost to accommodate all their luggage. Robert smiled, pulled out his credit card, and paid without argument.

An hour later, they were ensconced in their comfortable seats in the RyanAir jet. They were happy, and completely unstressed. They saw no one at the airport.

"Where do you think our pets have gotten to, darling."

"I hate say it, but they're probably waiting for us in Larnaca."

With a sly smile on her face, Jenna sniggered. "I'd love to see her face when she finds out we've left without them."

"Let's count our blessings, Jenna! These guys mean business. Any of Archer's team could take us down without breaking a sweat."

"I know, RJ; I know. This whole quest is so surreal. Here we are, madly in love. We're, sitting on a plane to Athens, where we hope to find another clue. We've travelled tens of thousands of miles across the world, and lived in grand suites, in the best hotels. We have a crack team of Carver's agents trying to track us down. We have no idea where we're off to next, or even if we'll find the mythical Emerald Tablet at all! Did I mention we're madly in love?"

"Absolutely right, my angel!"

"RJ, I get shivers just thinking of what would've happened to me if you hadn't swept me up nearly a month ago. And that's another thing—it hasn't even been a month yet!"

"Jenna, it feels like I've known you forever. I never want to stop knowing you."

Robert swallowed hard, as he pressed Jenna's hand in his. He gave her a soft loving look. Jenna held her breath. She could tell he wanted to say something, but was thinking hard about it. He was obviously uncomfortable. Finally, looking rather guilty, he leaned in to kiss her. *That was close*, she thought.

In the Athens airport arrivals hall, they counted no fewer than four watchers—two separate men, and a couple. They knew they were made. Archer's team was nowhere in sight, so they assumed she was off the case, and they had new people waiting for them. Either Archer discovered their destination, or Carver was watching all the airports in Europe. Since they were obviously found, they decided to play a little game with the watchers—they gave each one a wave. They even made little charade actions to show they were going to the car rentals. The watchers didn't quite know how to respond.

This time, they rented something smaller—a Honda CRV. Robert couldn't imagine doing any high-speed chases though the streets of Athens. They arrived at the NEW Hotel with watchers in tow. When they checked-in, they saw no reason to use an alias, since Carver's watchers knew exactly where they were, so they registered as Mr. and Mrs. Jackson. Before going up to their suite, Robert went to the Concierge desk.

"Excuse me, do you happen to know of a park near a palace here in Athens?

The Concierge smiled genially. "That would be the National Gardens which is across from the old Royal Palace, about a 15-minute walk from the hotel, sir." He handed Robert a brochure, complete with map. Robert tipped him gratefully.

Jenna gave a little squeak when they entered the Penthouse Suite. "This is incredible, RJ! It's so different!" Her eyes sparkled brightly.

"I have to say, it's not your average hotel room."

"RJ, make sure the door is locked," she said quietly, with a coquettish smile.

By mid-afternoon, Gina's heart sank. Her instincts told her Jackson and Carpenter were long gone.

"Damn!" she said to Kate. "They've done it again!"

"Better call the boss before he finds out some other way."

Gina dialled.

"Yes, Gina. What news?" chuckled Carver.

This couldn't be good, she thought. "I'm pretty sure they've left Cyprus, sir. We had the airport locked-down—24-hour watch. No sightings, but I know they're gone, sir."

"I wondered when you'd report in. I haven't lost confidence in you, Gina, but this pair has the luck of the devil. I looked at a map to consider where they might go next, and had agents blanketing those airports. They were picked up in Athens, and we have them pinned down at the NEW Hotel. Get yourself there, and take over."

"Yes, sir. Thank you, sir."

"They spotted our watchers the moment they arrived, even waved to them. You'll have to think ten steps ahead of these two. And remember, keep them in sight, but no contact."

"Yes, sir." She never got to finish before the phone went dead.

Gina looked at Kate, and heaved a great sigh."Let's round up the team, we leave immediately for Athens. They're at the NEW Hotel. They know they're being watched, even waved at them."

"Good grief! The boss told you this?"

Gina nodded. She knew her team was on thin ice. They couldn't fail again.

Four o'clock in the afternoon found Robert and Jenna munching on some fruit from the beautiful basket in their suite. They were happy and content.

Robert looked at his watch. "We still have a few hours before sunset, feel like taking a walk to the National Gardens to check out that duck pond?"

"Will we take our little friends with us?"

Robert considered this question carefully. Sometimes, it's expedient to be completely honest. He gave Jenna a wry smile, picked up the room phone, and asked for the hotel manager.

"Yes, sir, Polemonos here."

"Good afternoon, Mr. Polemonos. I'm afraid we have a little problem that requires your experience, and authority."

Polemonos scrunched up his face. "Something serious, sir?"

"My lovely lady and I are being followed by a group of criminals who desire to steal something from us. They have followed us all over Egypt, Cyprus, and now here in Athens. If you take a quick look in your lobby, you will no doubt be able to spot watchers there. They will probably be watching the entrances and exits as well. For now, we believe they are content to observe, and we suspect they will eventually abduct us."

"This is very serious, then, sir. Give me a moment please to consider the situation."

Polemonos rose from his desk, and wandered out to the front desk area, where he casually scanned the lounge. Just as Robert told him, there were at least three obvious watchers in the lobby. He took a little walk outside pretending to look down the street, and then up at the side of the hotel. Yes, there was a couple sitting on the bench checking each time someone passed through the entrance. He had no doubt there were watchers at all exits. He returned to his office, and picked up the phone.

"Mr. Jackson, I have taken a few minutes to verify you're your claims. There are, indeed persons in the lobby, and the front entrance. I asked an employee to check the other exits."

"I'm sure they will not cause a disturbance in your hotel, so you need not worry on that account. However, we must find a way to leave the building, and return again, without being noticed. This is where your experience, and expertise are invaluable."

Polemonos was well aware that his guests were occupying the Penthouse Suite. This often meant special considerations. In the past, he had provided many different discreet services to penthouse guests. This was different, a new challenge. He decided to take it on—something in his guest's voice.

"There is somewhere specific you must go, sir?

"Yes, but within walking distance. We only need to be hidden for a short distance, as I believe they will be concentrated on the hotel,"

"We have trucks and vans delivering supplies here very often. It would be possible to hide you in one of the vehicles, which could then let you out wherever you need. When you are ready to return, I could have a different vendor pick you up. There will be some costs involved, as I am certain you understand."

"We need to go somewhere quickly. Would that be possible?"

"In fifteen minutes? I will make the arrangements, and meet you at your suite, if that is suitable?"

"That would be excellent. I'm afraid I don't have much cash on my person, but if the driver stops at the nearest bank, I could get some."

"Not a problem at all, Mr. Jackson. I am pleased to provide this service for you."

Jenna watched enthralled at what her man just arranged. He really was her own private Indiana Jones! She was filled with admiration for him. He always seemed to know what to do, and she had yet to see him flustered. Robert put down the phone.

"It's all arranged, we leave in fifteen minutes. Are you ready to go?"

"You bet!"

A few minutes later, the doorbell rang. It was Polemonos. He took them down the service elevator through the kitchen, and finally to the loading docks. There was a delivery van there. Polemonos spoke rapidly with the driver, and gave him some money. The driver laughed, turning to Robert and Jenna, he told them this was the first time he would take guests out of the hotel. With the van parked inside the building, there was no way anyone would notice them getting in. A few minutes later, they were dropped off at the entrance to the National Gardens.

With their trusty map in hand, they made their way towards the only three bodies of water on the property. There were two small ponds, and a much larger one. Jenna suggested they go to the smaller ones first. She didn't think Scott would place his clue at the larger one, which had more tourists milling about. At the first small pond, there were no columns, so they moved on to the next one.

Jenna was huffing and puffing from the fast pace of their walk. "Of course, it would have to be at the far end of the park!"

Robert just laughed. "We can both use the exercise."

When they arrived at the duck pond, they knew right away it was the place. There was a large marble column laying on the ground, with it's capstone laying beside it. There were a few people around, feeding the ducks.

Jenna scanned the area around the column. "I wonder where he would put it."

"The note said nothing about a capstone, so it must be tucked in somewhere along the column, or maybe in a crack in the column itself."

Jenna looked at the column carefully. "He would have to be sitting, or stooping over the column to stash his note. What spot would he pick? I think Dr. Scott would put the note in this section, where it's closest to the capstone."

"Do you want to go digging around, or would you like me to?"

Jenna sniggered. "I broke a fingernail last time, so it's your turn."

The duck feeders had moved on. They were alone now. Robert stooped down over the column, carefully running his hand along the column where marble met dirt. He dug deeply, to make sure he didn't miss anything.

"Got it!"

He shook the dirt off the bag. As in Paphos, he pulled the note out of the bag quickly, disposing of the bag in the convenient trash can. He slipped the envelope in his pocket. They casually made their way through the park. They were both starving, so they stopped at the Oasis Café on the edge of the park, where they devoured their meal. Across from the park, Robert spotted a bank, where he withdrew a sizeable amount of cash.

About twenty minutes after calling Polemonos, a truck pulled up where they were. The passenger quickly jumped out to open the side door of the cargo area. Robert jumped in, and pulled Jenna up. The door closed on them. It was pitch dark. Robert's cell phone flashlight, provided the only light. It was five or six minutes later that Polemonos stood there smiling at them through the open truck door. He accompanied them to their suite. Robert gave him the equivalent of a thousand dollars in cash to show his gratitude for this very special accommodation.

Gina's team arrived in Athens around five in the evening, and were settled in their rooms at the NEW Hotel by six. They saw no reason not to stay close to their prey. Gina asked the desk clerk if her friends, the Jacksons, had arrived yet. She was assured they had, and were in the Penthouse Suite. *Nothing but the best for these two!* she thought.

A quick check with the local watchers told her Jackson and Carpenter hadn't been seen since they arrived.

Back in her room, Gina considered for a moment. Jackson and Carpenter knew they were being watched. What would they do? They still had to get their next clue.

"What do you think, Kate, should we pay a visit to our slippery pair, maybe rattle them a bit?"

"The boss said no contact!"

"Yeah, I know. Just want to ruffle their feathers a bit. Besides, the boss meant no rough stuff. He wants us stuck to them like glue. Maybe we can put someone in the hall, you know, for protection."

"It's your call, Gina."

"Come on, let's go say hello!"

With their iPad and nail file, Robert and Jenna prepared to decipher their latest clue.

"It's your turn, sweetheart."

Jenna took a deep breath before she slit the envelope open. She pulled out the note, and laid it on the table. It read:

> *En Poggioreale sur la boto, ripozas nia kara amiko Giovanni Luciano Cabinoli kiu parolos sagxecon.*

"Oh, my! I have a feeling this one is going to be tough."

It didn't take long for Robert to get the translation:

In Poggioreale, on the boot, rests our dear friend Giovanni Luciano Cabinoli who will speak words of wisdom.

Robert murmured. "On the boot...on the boot. It's gotta be Italy! There are no other boots around here."

"Okay, let's assume Italy. Where is Poggioreale?"

Robert did a Google search for Poggioreale.

"It's a town in Sicily." He thought about this for a moment. "No, wait, Sicily isn't on the boot of Italy, it's getting kicked. Can't be this one. Let's look further down."

"There's a Poggioreale neighbourhood in Naples."

Robert reviewed the note again. "I don't think we can solve this one bit-by-bit. We need to consider the whole clue."

"If we consider a resting place, that would be a cemetery again. We should be looking for a cemetery either in Poggioreale or is named Poggioreale."

Robert scanned the web offerings. Finally, he looked hard at the neighbourhood in Naples that bore the name Poggioreale. Taking up a large chunk of the north side, was a huge cemetery, part of which was named Cimitero di Poggioreale.

Jenna stared at the iPad. "This might be it."

"Let's make sure. Let's keep checking the Internet."

After another twenty minutes, they exhausted all the possibilities.

"So, it's Naples, then," confirmed Jenna, cheerfully. "Never been to Naples."

They both laughed—until the doorbell rang.

They looked at one another. They weren't expecting anything or anyone. The door was locked. Robert told Jenna to stay by the room phone, ready to dial, and scream for help, in case it was trouble. Jenna did as he said. The bell sounded again. Robert went to the door, and peered through the peep hole. He couldn't believe his eyes.

"Call Polemonos. Ask him to come up with a couple of security guards. We may have some unwanted company," Robert whispered.

At the door, Robert called out, "Yes, who is it?"

"You know very well who it is, Mr. Jackson. You saw us through the peep hole," replied Gina. "We mean you no harm, just a friendly little visit."

Robert looked at Jenna, who nodded, and gave a thumbs-up. He unlocked the door, stepped back, and let them in.

"Well, how nice to see you again Ms. Archer, do come in," Jenna said, with a smile, and her sweetest voice.

Before Gina could reply, Robert added, "If you don't mind, would you please leave your weapons on the table in the entrance. I think it would make all of us feel more comfortable."

"In the interests of a friendly discussion, then." She took a gun out of the holster at her back, and a knife from the sheath strapped to her leg. She nodded to Kate to do the same. Kate put the weapons on the table by the door, and locked the door before entering the living room.

"I'm afraid I haven't had the pleasure, Ms..." Jenna said as she extended her hand to Kate.

"It's Kate, just Kate will do." Kate offered a firm handshake.

"I hope we can dispense with the staring contest, Mr. Jackson," Gina suggested.

Robert stood by Jenna, ready to defend her in a split second. His whole body was tense. This wasn't lost on Gina, or Kate, or Jenna, for that matter.

Jenna leaned over, whispering in Robert's ear, "I have a black belt in three martial arts disciplines, darling."

Robert looked at her, and laughed. "You're just full of surprises!"

With that, Robert loosened up, and became friendlier. Gina and Kate looked at one another. The doorbell rang. Robert rose to get it. Kate stood to block him.

"We called security when you first rang. Now that we're satisfied you mean us no harm, I'll send them away. And don't worry Kate. I won't touch your weapons—scout's honour."

Gina waved him through. Kate was still wary. Robert went to the door, and greeted Polemonos who had two strong guards at his sides. Robert thanked him for his prompt action, and assured him everything was fine. Polemonos examined Robert's face, and seeing no tension or fear, he retreated.

"Now, you see, we've both shown signs of good faith, so maybe we can all relax," suggested Jenna.

"That was a very smooth move on your part, leaving from Paphos. I admit, we never saw that coming," admitted Gina, to open the conversation.

"Robert's idea." Jenna gave him a look of admiration.

"Can't take full credit for that, I'm afraid. I didn't even know there *was* an airport in Paphos until I was checking for flights to Athens."

"Quite frankly, Ms. Archer, we expected to see you, or some of your people at the Paphos airport. We wondered what happened to you."

"Gina, please. I want you to know that our employer doesn't want you harmed in any way. He's interested in the object you're seeking, and nothing else."

"I suppose that's why you come armed to the teeth, then," responded Robert.

"In our line of work, we never know what, or whom we will be up against. You'd be very surprised to know how many docile-looking people carry weapons of their own."

"And what exactly will happen when we find the Emerald Tablet?" asked Robert. "Is that when you'll use your weapons to relieve us of the prize Carver is drooling over?"

"We'll have to cross that bridge when we get there. As I mentioned, my employer is willing to pay whatever you ask for the object in question."

"The Emerald Tablet is a priceless artifact that belongs to the world," asserted Jenna. "It's not meant to gather dust in some rich guy's private collection."

"Spoken like the true archaeologist you are, Ms. Carpenter. But it's not up to you or I to make that decision. We both have a job to do. At this moment, we both have a common goal—to recover the artifact. Where it goes beyond that, is really none of my concern.

"Exactly right. You have no concern, or at least, your concern is to be compensated for your efforts when you hand it over to Randolph Carver. Robert and I want the tablet to be available to the public. We're not being compensated in any way. In fact, Robert is spending a small fortune to make sure it happens."

"There are several others, besides my employer, who want the artifact as much as he does. We'd be pleased to provide you with some protection while you complete your mission."

"We're well aware of that," Robert assured her. "But my understanding is that Carver has the deepest pockets, and the most, and best, contacts. Dr. Scott knew that also. It's why he hid the tablet somewhere it was unlikely to be found again. It's why he's playing a hide-and-seek game of clues. It's why he's missing, and probably buried in the sand himself."

"As I mentioned before, we have no idea what happened to Dr. Scott. We only know he disappeared under suspicious circumstances the day he returned to his dig site. We can only assume he was taken by one of my employer's competitors."

"What do you make of all this, Kate?" asked Robert.

"It's not my job to decide who gets what. When I'm given an assignment, I complete it the best way I can. I have no desire for violence, and consider it a partial failure if I can't complete my assignment without violence. That said, when I'm forced to, I *will* use violence. I hope that when this mission is all over, we might be able to sit down together to discuss how you managed to slip through our net so often."

Robert and Jenna laughed. Jenna moved a little closer to her man. She squeezed his arm, with an unmistakable look of absolute love.

"We're both smart people, and Robert is my own private Indiana Jones. If it wasn't for him, I'd be laying dead in the ditch by some dirt road in Alberta." Then, turning to Gina, looking at her straight in the eyes, she said with confidence, "We're on a quest to find the Emerald Tablet. We'll succeed, and quite frankly, you don't count. You're nothing to us. Carver can watch all the airports he wants, but he'll never stop us, and if we want to disappear—we will!"

"Now, if you don't mind, Jenna and I have other things we'd prefer to do. So, please take your guns and knives, and leave us in peace."

Back in their room, Gina contacted the other members of her team. She ordered one man in the hall leading to the Penthouse Suite, 24-hour watch, 2-hour shifts. Jackson and Carpenter were not to be out of sight of the team at any time.

Gina and Kate discussed the meeting with their quarry. The two women were amazed at their composure, and their confidence. It was obvious they were truly in love. Both women felt a pang of emptiness in their own lives when they felt the love that passed between the couple. Neither said anything. There was more than a little envy from both.

Gina made a call.

"What's going on in Athens?"

"We've taken rooms in NEW Hotel, sir. They haven't moved from the Penthouse Suite since they arrived. They don't seem to be so willing to run around in the open anymore, now they know they're being watched closely. I have a man in the hall outside the Penthouse Suite door. Short of parachuting off the balcony, they're not going anywhere without a close escort."

"Do you know if they've found Scott's clue in Athens yet?"

"All watchers confirm they haven't left the hotel, sir."

"What is it you're not telling me, Gina?"

"When you said 'no contact,' I'm assuming you meant no physical contact, rough stuff, etc. Is that correct, sir?"

"You've had another little chat with our friends, haven't you?"

"Yes, sir. A colleague and I visited them in their suite. I wanted to assure them we meant no harm, and even offered protection from others who might be seeking the same object. I renewed your offer to compensate them handsomely for the return of the object."

"And?"

"The conversation was friendly. Both sides showed signs of good faith. We placed our weapons on the table in the suite's foyer, at Jackson's request, and they called off the security guards. I must admit, sir, this is no ordinary couple. They've only been together a few weeks, and already they move, and think as one. They show absolutely no fear, and exhibit extreme confidence. They confirmed they're looking for the clues left by Dr. Scott. They have no idea how many, or where they're going next."

"Stay on them. Do *not* let them slip through again!"

After Gina and Kate left, Robert and Jenna had a good laugh. It was obvious Carver's elite team was frustrated at being given the slip so often. They weren't used to this. Jenna reminded Robert of what they said at his home before they left. They would outwit Carver at every turn. He would have his hands full trying to bring them down, and he would *not* succeed.

Robert flipped on the iPad and began his search for flights, and accommodation. It would be the Aegean Airlines flight leaving Monday at 12:40 p.m. When it came to accommodations, Jenna was torn between two suites offered by the Romeo Hotel. They had a fabulous Wellness Suite with its own built-in spa, or the decadent Skyline Suite with magnificent views. In the end, the romantic in her took charge. It would be the Skyline Suite. After all, they wouldn't be hunting clues the whole time! Robert booked the flight, and made the reservations.

Chapter 21 - Passing Through

It was only six when Robert and Jenna awoke the next morning. The one thing the NEW Hotel didn't have was a pool, and they both missed their morning swim. Jenna cuddled tight. That night, they decided to use the outside bed, since it was a terrific evening. It was different sleeping under the stars in a cozy bed. It was also incredibly romantic.

Robert was curious, so he slipped out of bed, walked to the suite door, and looked through the peep hole. One of Gina's men was standing in the hall. Obviously, they weren't taking any chances of them getting away. With only a towel around his waist, Robert quietly opened the door. The watcher reacted instantly. Robert called him over. The man approached, but stopped a couple of metres away. To his surprise, Robert asked for Gina's phone number. The watcher pulled out his own phone, and called Gina for instructions. Gina, too, was surprised, but told him to give Robert the number. Robert thanked him, and closed the door.

He quickly returned to the bed and slipped in next to Jenna again. Jenna gave him a puzzled look.

"What was that all about, RJ?"

Robert had a sly grin on his face. "I wanted to get Gina's phone number."

"RJ, what are you planning? I know that look. You're up to something." She cuddled close again.

"I just think it's fair to let her know when we've left."

"We're going to sneak out again, aren't we?"

"At least we'll give it the old college try, my love."

She gave him a little pout. "You're not planning to leave today, are you? It's such a nice suite!"

Robert simply looked at her with his impish grin.

"Well, Mr. Jones, will you share your plan with me, or will I have to pry it out of you with sex?"

"Oh, by all means, pry away! *Please* pry away!"

And pry she did. Of course, she didn't care if he told her anything, she just kept prying!

Finally, they both got up, and took a long shower together. She loved how gentle he was as he washed her body.

Robert was very secretive, going to another room to check his iPad, make calls, and even wrote a note. Jenna was extremely curious, but obediently stayed away when he waved her off. He insisted that they completely finish packing their luggage. As they left for the restaurant, their watcher accompanied them. He stood closer to Jenna than Robert, thinking she was the lowest risk. If only he knew!

As they skirted the lobby, they spotted Mr. Polemonos at the front desk, and waved him over. Robert took his right hand out of his pocket, extending it to Polemonos. Cupped in his palm was a folded sheet of paper, which he pressed into Polemonos' hand. Robert greeted him cordially, and thanked him for keeping his hotel in such impeccable condition. Polemonos responded genially, and made no comment on the paper, which was now in his hand. Robert rejoined Jenna. They both waved to the lobby watchers.

Polemonos made his way back to the front desk, said a few things to the clerk, and retired to his office. There, he unfolded the note. He smiled, as he read it. He was well aware of the watchers hovering around the Jacksons. There appeared to be a truce of some sort. The truce, it seemed, was about to be broken. He began laughing out loud. *This couple has been so very entertaining, a nice change from the usual routine*, he thought.

Robert and Jenna enjoyed their last meal at the NEW Hotel. Seated only two tables away, were a pair of watchers. The lobby watchers were still in place. Gina always made sure the entire team was mobilized whenever they were on the move. The watchers had nothing to report except their quarry was as calm and amorous as usual. After coffee, Jenna excused herself to go to the powder room. One of the watchers was getting up to follow.

Robert looked at him, and rolled his eyes. "Relax, boys, she's just going for a pee." The man sat down again, figuring Jenna would never take-off without Robert. Robert sat there calmly looking out the window.

In his office, Polemonos picked up the phone to call the front desk. He asked for two specific porters to go immediately to the

Penthouse Suite, retrieve all the luggage found there, and bring it to the loading docks. He placed another call, this time to the restaurant, and asked for a specific waitress. When she was on the line, he told her Mrs. Jackson would go to the powder room at some point. She was to call him to let him know, then the waitress would discreetly go to the ladies' room to fetch Mrs. Jackson, and take her through the staff door to the loading docks. None of the people watching the Jacksons must see this happen.

A few minutes after the waitress notified him, Polemonos left his office, walking with officious purpose to the restaurant. He scanned the tables, and made his way to Robert's table, where he was now sitting alone.

"Mr. Jackson, I am terribly sorry to disturb you, but I am afraid there is a little problem with your credit card." He spoke softly, so other patrons wouldn't hear, but loud enough for the watchers to hear. "Would you please come to my office to discuss the matter?"

"I can assure you, sir, that my credit card should have no problem with the charges here."

"Please, sir. We can go discuss the matter privately."

Robert gathered up his things. "Ms. Carpenter is in the powder room. I need to leave her a note."

Polemonos asked a passing waiter for a piece of paper from his order pad, and retrieved a pen from his own jacket pocket. He handed both to Robert, who wrote a quick note to let her know where he was. One of the restaurant watchers notified the lobby watchers that Robert, and the manager, were headed their way. They would stay put until the woman returned from the powder room.

Back in his office, Polemonos shook Robert's hand warmly. "Mr. Jackson, I hate to see you go. You have provided the staff here some wonderful entertainment, an unusual diversion. Ah, yes, and you will need these." Polemonos handed him their passports.

Robert laughed. "It has been a fun game for us also. But make no mistake, these people mean business. When you so quickly responded to our call for help yesterday, there were two guns, and two combat knives, on the table next to the door. It was a gesture of good faith on their part."

"Are you serious? This is completely illegal in Greece. And they have been staying at my hotel, with weapons in their rooms!" Polemonos was almost apoplectic!

"Have no fear, Mr. Polemonos, they will be gone shortly after we leave, when they realize we are missing."

"Ah, yes. About that, Mrs. Jackson, and all your luggage have been moved to our handy loading docks. By now, the vehicle will be loaded, and making its way to the fire escape just next to the side door to my office. No one watches this side of the building, so you should be able to get out without being seen."

"Fire exits usually trigger an alarm when opened, do they not?"

"Yes, of course, but I had the alarm disabled for this little escapade. Ah, here comes the truck now. Quickly, we must hurry."

Polemonos led Robert to the side door of his office which gave out onto a short corridor. There was a porter loitering there to obscure anyone from seeing. The fire door was opened just as the vehicle pulled up. The cargo door was open. Robert could see Jenna inside with a big smile on her face. Robert quickly ran down the few stairs to ground level, pulled himself up into the truck, and the door swung shut. The dome light in the cargo area was left on as a courtesy.

A little under an hour later, the truck stopped, and the cargo doors were opened. The two men who were in the truck took out the luggage, and helped Robert and Jenna down. They were now standing in front of the airport hanger where the private jet Robert chartered was waiting. A man in coveralls came out with a dolly for their baggage. A flight attendant was waiting there to greet them. She looked rather perplexed at the entrance made by her two passengers.

"You're probably used to seeing your passengers arrive by limousine, and not in the back of a cargo truck," Jenna laughed.

"Yes, ma'am. That is the usual. I must admit I have never seen an arrival like this."

"I can assure you, there is a perfectly good explanation for this, and we are not fugitives of the law," Robert assured her.

"I am Madeleine, your host on the flight to Naples."

"I'm Jenna, and this wonderful man is Robert. We'll tell you all about our little deception when we're in the air."

They all boarded the plane, where the pilot and co-pilot welcomed them aboard. The pilot announced they would be taxiing to the runway in about 10 minutes. The baggage was stowed, and the door was closed. The flight attendant offered them refreshments, which were gratefully accepted.

"May I make a quick call before we leave?" Robert asked.

"Of course, sir, but you must not call once we begin taxiing."

"Do you have satellite phone available, and can I use it while in flight?"

"Yes, sir."

Robert dialled the number and put it on speaker.

"Yes," Gina answered.

"It's Robert Jackson. I just thought you should know we're on our way to our next destination. If you check-out of the hotel, and get yourself to the airport, I'll call again to let you know where."

"Not funny, Mr. Jackson. There's no way you could possibly leave the hotel, even if you gave us the slip temporarily.

"If you ask at the front desk, they'll tell you we checked-out an hour ago, which is plenty of time for us to get to the airport," added Jenna. "Oh, we have to go. No cell phones when the plane is moving. Bye, bye!"

Jenna had never been in a private jet before, let alone flying in one on the way to Italy. Robert was constantly blowing her mind, and he did again now. Her brain was reeling with today's adventure. She had no idea what he was up to. Robert said he wanted to surprise her, as well as Gina and her gang. All the time he was making the arrangements, he had an impish smile on his face. She could hardly contain herself, wanting to know what mayhem he was planning! The whole thing was so incredible, she thought she was a character in some spy thriller—*her own spy thriller*! She now found herself sitting next to her man, in a chartered private jet on the way to Naples. What else could Robert possibly do next?

Gina was livid! It was impossible! They couldn't have slipped away again! She called the front desk, where she was informed the Jacksons did indeed leave an hour earlier. Impossible! She and Kate went directly to the Penthouse Suite. They had all the tools necessary to unlock the door, but it never came to that. When they arrived, the door was wide open, and housekeeping was busy cleaning the suite.

She contacted her team. The lobby watchers saw Jackson going into the manager's office, and had not come out yet. The restaurant watchers previously reported that Carpenter had been in the powder room, and vanished. That Jackson disappeared also, was confirmed when the lobby watchers reported the manager was wandering about greeting guests.

Gina ordered her team to prepare for immediate departure

for the airport. She and Kate grabbed their luggage, and headed down to check-out. The manager greeted them cordially. It was obvious to Gina he was an accomplice in this whole mess.

Within ten minutes, Gina's team barrelled out of the hotel parking area on their way to Carver's private jet at the airport. They still had no idea where they were going. They sat idle in the plane. Gina's phone rang.

"Yes!"

"Think Neapolitan ice cream!"

"Naples," she told the captain.

What would Gina tell Carver? She wasn't sure at all. He would kill her, of that she was certain.

She dialled the number.

"Report!"

"We're on our way to Naples, their next destination, sir."

"They're on a flight to Naples, then?"

"Yes, sir."

"They got away from you again?"

"Yes, sir."

"No explanations, Gina?"

"No excuses, sir."

"Tell me what happened!"

"After our visit, we never lost sight of them, except in the privacy of their suite, sir. When they went out, the entire team watched them from very close quarters. They were having a great time. If they found a clue, we don't know where, or when. Today, they went for breakfast in the hotel restaurant. Carpenter excused herself to go to the powder room. We had no female there, so we waited. There are no exits from there. A few minutes later, the hotel manager approached Jackson about credit card issues. Jackson left a note for Carpenter, and went with the manager to his office. Carpenter, never returned from the toilet, Jackson disappeared from the manager's office. They called me about an hour later to let me know they were on their way to the next destination, but did not divulge the location. We waited at the airport until Jackson called with the destination—Naples. I assume they're already there or very close."

"What do you make of these two, Gina?"

"I approached the mission as though we were dealing with covert operatives. You mentioned they were just ordinary people. I don't think they're either of those. They're very shrewd, and intelligent people, who are just winging it. Thanks to their genial nature, and the obvious fact they're in love, they seem to be able to convince others to help them in their harebrained schemes."

"I think you have it right. It makes them the most difficult of prey—fearless, and empowered. Do the best you can. I doubt if you, or anyone else, will be able to stay on them. For some reason, you've established some sort of warped relationship with them. They generously gave you the next destination. Continue to exploit that."

"Yes, sir."

Carver hung up. He took a deep breath, and let it out slowly. He couldn't blame Gina for the chaos. She was the best. No, it was this crazy pair of lovers on a mission to save the Emerald Tablet. Scott, Carpenter, and Jackson, three persons with solid honesty. It was a long time since he dealt with such incorruptible integrity. Although he admired them to some degree, he would apply all his resources towards obtaining the tablet.

The company from which Robert chartered the private jet was certainly well organized. When the plane landed in Naples, there were customs and immigration officials waiting. The captain presented all the passports to the immigration officer, who checked them over. The charter employees were all European, and garnered hardly any scrutiny. Robert and Jenna, being Canadian, were asked the standard questions, and passed muster quickly. Their baggage was taken out of the hold. The customs officer questioned their declaration, as they had nothing to declare, but had a lot of luggage. Robert explained that whatever items they purchased abroad were sent on to Canada by courier because their bags were packed for a long trip. The officer looked at the four large suitcases, picked one, and asked them to open it on a nearby table. It was one of Jenna's. The officer looked carefully at the contents, all beautiful designer clothes, but her trained eye noticed it had all been worn. She smiled at Jenna, and said she could close the case now. As Jenna was doing this, she looked at Robert for any sign of nervousness, but there was none. Within 20 minutes of landing, they were on their way.

Robert arranged for a vehicle to meet them wherever they would be deplaning. They loaded their luggage into the vehicle. A few minutes later, after all the paperwork was completed at the car rental agency, they were on their way to the Romeo Hotel. It was just after noon, so traffic was terrible. Although the hotel wasn't that far away, it still took almost an hour to navigate the streets to get there.

When the desk clerk realized they were staying in the Skyline Suite, her demeanour changed somewhat. The manager Sr. Caldoni, was notified, and appeared to greet them. He personally showed them up to their suite, pointing out the many amenities offered by the hotel. If there was anything at all they needed, they should not hesitate to contact him directly.

Once Robert and Jenna were settled into their magnificent suite, they got down to business.

"Well, honey, now that we're here, we only have one small problem, which I didn't notice when we solved our last clue."

"What's that, RJ?"

"I'm just checking the opening hours for the cemetery, and it appears it's *only* open on Saturdays."

"Oh my, that would mean staying here all week. Somehow, I don't think Gina and her buddies will give us much peace after Athens."

Robert thought about it for a moment. Jenna could almost hear the gears whirling around in his head. Finally, he picked up the telephone, and asked for Sr. Caldoni.

"Sr. Jackson, I trust everything is to your satisfaction."

"Yes, the suite is excellent, Sr. Caldoni. It is about a different matter that I call you, and I'm hoping you can help us."

"But, of course! If it is within my power, I will be most happy to help you. Please tell to me what it is you require."

"When we told some good friends in Canada we would be visiting Naples, they were very excited. It seems they have a relative who rests in the Cemetery of Poggioreale, and they asked us if we could take a photo of their grave. On the Internet, I noticed that the cemetery is open only on Saturdays. I wonder if you know someone to contact who could allow us in to find the grave this afternoon. Of course, we would be willing to defray all costs."

"Ah, I see. That might be a bit difficult. I know the cemetery of which you speak. I have relatives resting there as well. I know the manager personally. I will call him to ask if this is possible. If it is, it may come at a high cost, Sr. Jackson."

"Unfortunately, we will only be here for a couple of nights, before we move on. I would hate to disappoint our friends, since we are so close, if you understand, Sr. Caldoni."

"I will see what I can do. Is there a specific time when you want to go signore?"

"Within the next two hours, if possible."

"I will contact you in a few minutes."

"Thank you very much, Sr. Caldoni. Of course, we would like to compensate you for your efforts as well. La signora and I will be having some lunch in the Il Comandante."

"*Molto benne, signore.*"

Jenna was amazed at how Robert was able to think through all the obstacles thrown in their way. After he hung up the phone, she put her arms around his neck, and gave him a long, loving kiss. They knew they had some time before Gina landed. They changed into something a bit dressier, and made their way to the restaurant. Caldoni saw the happy couple getting off the elevator, and made a bee line for them. He too, had a big smile.

"Sr. Jackson, I am glad to catch you. I had to do some begging and pleading, but the cemetery manager will have a caretaker meet you at the entrance at three this afternoon. He might be able to help you find your friends' grave."

Robert had some euros in his wallet, and handed Caldoni a one hundred euro note. Caldoni was very pleased.

Robert and Jenna enjoyed a wonderful, lunch. They tried, but failed, to push the quest out of their conversation. Jenna felt certain they were getting close to the final clue. They had already found six and were here for the seventh. Surely, Dr. Scott didn't leave more than ten. There could only be another two or three more. Robert agreed with her. Scott wasn't gone that long, and given transportation delays, and the fact he would probably be laying low, there were only so many destinations he could get to before returning to Jordan. Their biggest concern now, was finding the grave of "our dear friend Giovanni Luciano Cabinoli" in the chaotic jumble that was the Poggioreale Cemetery. They hoped the caretaker they would meet would be able to give them some rough idea of where to look.

After lunch, Robert filled his wallet with some additional cash from an ATM. They were finding it becoming more difficult with every new clue. Scott was certainly not making things easy for them. When he saw the manager at the front desk, he waved to him, and they walked over. Robert asked him if it would be possible to get a vehicle of some sort with a driver to take them to the cemetery, wait there, and bring them back to the hotel. Caldoni had the concierge arrange for a limousine immediately. Within minutes, they were on their way to the cemetery.

The driver explained, in broken English, they needed to make a long detour around the Poggioreale neighbourhood because of the one-way streets. When they finally arrived, the driver parked the limousine directly in front of the entrance. They all had a pleasant conversation while they waited for the cemetery caretaker to arrive. It was about 3:15 when the caretaker pulled up in his old car. The driver opened the door for Robert and Jenna to exit the limo.

Robert greeted the caretaker cordially. Using the driver as an interpreter, he introduced himself and Jenna, and explained why he was pulled away from his afternoon off. The appearance of two €100 notes made him much more amiable, and helpful. He explained where most of the Cabinoli tombs could be found, and offered to take them there.

It was a walk through a labyrinth of huge mausoleums, and small graves. Thankfully, the caretaker knew his way around. They couldn't believe how the mausoleums were built to look like houses, complete with bricked-in windows painted black. It took a good 20 minutes to get to the Cabinoli group of tombs. The three split up, looking for Giovanni Luciano Cabinoli. That took another 15 minutes. The caretaker called to them excitedly. And there it was.

Robert thanked the man, shaking his hand, and placing another €100 note in it. Then, in broken Italian, "*Momento privato, per favor.*"

The caretaker understood, and withdrew around a nearby corner. Jenna was already scanning the mausoleum for any sign of where Scott might have put his clue. Then, Robert spotted something. He looked towards where the caretaker had gone to make sure he wouldn't see. There was a small carving, that seemed to him to be a cross between a gargoyle and a zombie. It looked like it was moved recently, because of the change in the discolouration near the wall. He motioned to Jenna. They carefully pulled the relief away from the wall. It wasn't as heavy as they thought. Wedged at the back of the cavity was the telltale plastic bag with an envelope inside. Jenna plucked it out, and stuffed it in her purse. They quickly put the stone carving back in place. Robert took a photo, and they both stood back in a position of reverence. When the caretaker poked his head around the corner, Jenna nodded to him as a sign they were finished. For some unknown reason, the return journey to the entrance appeared shorter. Again, they thanked the caretaker—Robert with a handshake, and Jenna with a big hug, which had the man blushing.

Within 30 minutes, they were back in their suite at the Romeo. With iPad and nail file in hand, they prepared to open and decipher the clue. It was Jenna's turn. When she laid the note flat on the table, it read:

Urbo de Médicis iam tiom potenca,
444 en la loko de falintaj herooj.

Robert was quick to get the translation for this note:

City of Medici once so powerful,
444 in the place of fallen heroes.

"Oh, oh, RJ, I know this one! The Medicis ruled out of Florence, which was very powerful during their reign. And the place of fallen heroes must be another war cemetery."

Robert burst out laughing. "Well, darling, I'm glad you gave me all of a quarter of a second to work this one out!" He kissed Jenna hard on the lips, then looked down at his watch.

Jenna watched as he deftly searched for trains to Florence. He saw there were some seats left on the 18:00 departure.

Robert gave her a remorseful look. "Do you want to stay here tonight, darling, or shall we grab a train to Florence. We can be there by nine tonight."

"I'd really love to stay. It's such a nice suite, and we've made love in all the places we've been. But I know it would be better for us to stay ahead of that Archer woman, and Carver's watchers." It was a tough decision. "Let's go. We can make a night of it in Florence. I can pretend I'm a Medici girl, and you're my secret suitor."

Just as quickly, Robert checked hotels in Florence. There was a Four Seasons, and he decided to try for a reservation. He called the hotel, asking what suites they had available. When they said the Garden Suite was available, Robert smiled, and reserved it for two nights. He told the front desk clerk they would be arriving on the train at about 21:00. He was assured the suite would be ready for them when they arrived.

They took a quick shower, and changed again. Robert called for a porter. At the front desk, he asked for Sr. Cabinoli. He explained to the manager they would have to leave, immediately, but a friend would be arriving shortly, by the name of Gina Archer. She should be given the Skyline Suite for the two nights—at his expense. He also asked the manager if he could arrange for their vehicle to be returned to the car rental agency. They would also need limo service to the train station. He pressed a couple of €100 notes in his hand to cover expenses. Sr. Cabinoli was more than happy to accommodate them.

Within a half hour, they were at the Naples train station, with all their luggage, and first-class tickets in hand. They were on their way to Florence.

Once on the ground in Naples, Gina, and her team, began to canvass the luxury hotels to find Jackson and Carpenter. Gina was already furious at being a couple of hours behind them, not to mention their escape from Athens. It was about 5:30 p.m. when she arrived at the Romeo Hotel, and made her way to the front desk.

"Good afternoon, could you tell me if my friends the Jacksons have arrived yet?"

"Ah sì," replied the front desk clerk. "But you have just missed them. They left only a few minutes ago. What is your name, please, signora?

"Gina Archer."

"Sr. Jackson left a message for you," said the clerk, as she handed the message to Gina. "How many keys will you need for your suite?"

Gina opened the note:

Hello, Gina!

As you now realize, we have left Naples for our next destination. Please enjoy the comforts of the Skyline Suite with our compliments. It's booked for two nights. We prefer not being disturbed tonight. Call it a night off. You should do the same. We'll call you sometime tomorrow to let you know where we are. We're planning to stay at our destination for at least a couple of days.

See you soon,

Robert and Jenna

Gina took a deep breath. They were one step ahead, as usual. She contacted her team to order them all to meet at the Romeo Hotel. She dialled Carver's number.

"Report!"

"They didn't waste any time here, sir. It looks like they've found the Naples clue, and left immediately. They booked the Sklyline Suite at the Romeo for two nights, but left just before we arrived here. They also left a note offering us the suite, with their compliments, and would contact me tomorrow with their location. Their note said they planned to be at that location for at least a couple of days."

"As you say, they're not wasting any time. This is a departure from their norm. They've spent at least one night in each location, so far. This change is telling me they feel they're nearing the end of their mission."

"You may be right, sir. They're moving fast now. By the way, they didn't fly commercial to Naples—it was a charter jet. They could be boarding that same jet now."

"I don't think so, Gina. If that were the case, they wouldn't have booked a suite for two nights. They certainly didn't do it for your benefit. Now that they're on the continent, they could be travelling by road. It would be impossible to find them if they're driving. Play it out. I have a feeling they want us nearby."

"Sir, are you thinking they want to find the object first, then try to make a deal with you?"

"They consider this to be *their* quest, Gina. They've already incurred sizeable expenses travelling from place-to-place. At first, they wanted to keep you away from them. Now, they're inviting you to tag along, but at a distance. And they don't see any harm in the occasional face-to-face meeting."

"I see what you mean, sir. The closer they get to the end of their mission, the more they realize they need to come to some sort of accommodation, otherwise they know we'll continue to hunt them down."

"Precisely. Play it out, Gina. Enjoy your suite tonight. Give your team a night off. Tomorrow, you'll be fresh and ready to go again. When you see them next, you'll need to try to stay close. They have the advantage, and they know it. It won't be long now. I feel it in my bones."

Chapter 22 - Romantic Retreat

At the train station, Robert paid an unofficial porter to help get their baggage into the train. Each of their suitcases were stowed in a storage area at the end of the car. They took their carry-on pieces with them. Once seated in their comfy leather seats, Jenna held Robert's arm tight. She rested her head on his shoulder, sighing deeply. She'd never been on a real train before. This was a new experience for her. Robert and Christine travelled extensively in Europe, so this was nothing new for him.

As the train moved away from the station, Jenna looked out the windows. She was lost in a dream again. She looked up at Robert lovingly, and kissed him tenderly. Robert gazed into her eyes. All the stress built up during the day melted away. Jenna felt his muscles relax. She kissed him again. They were alone, away from their watchers. She kissed him again. He sat there smiling, accepting her kisses, and wondering if they should've stayed the night in Naples. At least, they knew they would have some private time together in Florence, before letting Gina know where they were. Tonight was theirs, and maybe most of tomorrow too.

When Gina's team arrived, they met for a few minutes in the Skyline Suite. They all whistled when they saw the opulence—a lot better than their usual digs.

"Okay, listen up, everyone! Jackson and Carpenter have flown the coop. They were already gone when Kate and I arrived. They kindly gave us the use of this suite with their compliments—for two nights if we want to. They left a note saying they would call us tomorrow with their location. They want a night off, it seems."

"Does that mean *we* get the night off too?" piped up one of the men.

"Yes, we all get the night off, since there's nothing we can do for now. You know the rules: all weapons are to be left in your room safes; stay out of trouble. I don't expect an early morning call from our two lovebirds, so we'll meet here for lunch, say 13:00."

"So, we're staying on the mission, then?" asked one of the others.

"Yes, the boss hasn't lost confidence in us—*yet*! I'm to try to exploit the strange relationship developing between me and our prey. He's of the opinion that no one will be able to hold on to these two, unless it's what they want. They showed their ability to slip out from under our very noses *twice* in *one* day. It's possible they're beginning to realize they need to come to some sort of amicable arrangement before they find the object in question. We're to stay close, but not interfere with their mission, at least until they find the object."

"Do we know how many more clues they'll need to find before they know the location of the target object?" asked the third female of the group.

"No. I don't think Jackson and Carpenter know either, but they sense it must be getting close to the end. They're moving fast now, and I don't think it's to escape us, as much as it's the excitement of knowing they're close.

"Ladies, and gentlemen, I don't need to remind you they've made us look like a bunch of agents in training—*total novices*. They have no covert training of any sort, yet they managed to slip by us *with ease*, and *impunity*. Despite seeing the weapons we all carry, they have no fear of us—none! They are completely confident they will succeed with their mission. In my last face-to-face meeting with them, they made a statement: *if we want to disappear, we will.* They've proven that capability on the Trans-Canada, in Suez, in Cyprus, in Athens, and again here, in Naples. As we all enjoy our time off, I strongly suggest we try to come up with some strategies to keep them in sight. We can't lose them again once we have them. Do I make myself clear?"

They all responded in unison, "Yes, ma'am!"

They arrived at the Santa Maria Novella Train Station in Florence on time. Robert quickly made his way to the platform, looking for an unofficial porter, since he was not able to schedule a regular porter before leaving. Porters must be scheduled in Italian train stations. Two men approached him, asking in Italian, if he wanted help with his baggage.

He replied in broken Italian, "*Non parlo italiano.*"

A little game of charades followed, where they made it clear they wanted to take his baggage. Robert rubbed his thumb to his fingers to ask how much. They asked for ten euros each. Robert agreed, with the proviso they would take the luggage to the limo stand. Immediately, both men went into the train. Robert pointed to their four suitcases, which they manhandled with ease. Robert and Jenna followed behind them almost at a run. Within a few minutes, they were waiting outside the train station, at the limo stand.

A gleaming white limousine pulled up in front of them—the next in line. The driver told them in broken English there was a flat rate to the hotel. Robert agreed, and the driver opened the door, then placed their luggage in the trunk. He obviously new the route well. He managed to get them to the Four Seasons Hotel in twenty minutes flat!

Robert identified himself to the desk clerk. He was informed that the suite was ready as requested. The porter led the way. Jenna was wondering where they were headed, as the porter was rolling the luggage rack outside. From one walkway to another, through another building, and out the other side. They crossed a park which seemed deserted. At the end, she could see a small building with lights blazing through the windows. The porter was heading straight for it. She looked at Robert, who had a broad smile on his face. Her eyes began to fill with tears. The porter swung open the big doors, unloading the luggage in the beautiful bedroom. He retreated quickly, accepting the tip Robert handed him as he walked by.

Jenna stood there in shock. The tears flooded down her face. She looked at Robert.

"Thought we might like some real privacy for a change. We have our own little piece of heaven, complete with a private park."

Jenna didn't know what to do. She was shaking. This was really over the top. She slowly made her way into the living room. On a table stood a large vase with two dozen red roses. There was a stand with a wine bucket, complete with a chilled bottle of champagne. *Oh, God, I love this man!* she thought.

Robert took her into his arms, held her very tight, and kissed her passionately.

"Won't everyone see us, with the doors open?"

"Private park. No one allowed but us. And if anyone wants to watch, I don't give a damn!"

With their clothes strewn about the room, they tore at each other with tremendous passion. They were lost in their love. Nothing else existed. Nothing else mattered.

It was late when they awoke. Jenna stretched out, then snuggled into her man. She was blissfully happy. Several times before, she thought it couldn't get any better, but Robert always found a way. Robert had his arm around her shoulders, sometimes drawing unknown figures with his fingers on her back. His joy with Jenna knew no bounds. Last night was incredible. Passion pulsated through them unabated until they finally fell asleep, exhausted, in each other's arms.

"Hungry?" asked Robert.

"Um hum."

"Room service?"

"Um hum."

"Nature's calling."

"Don't answer."

"It's a loud call!"

"Ignore it. It'll pass," Jenna chuckled.

"Oh, sweetie, don't jiggle!"

Jenna burst out laughing. Robert tore away from her, and ran to the bathroom with an audible sigh. Jenna laughed all the harder. She stretched out as far as she could.

Robert stood at the door. "That's one heck of a constitution you have there, my dear."

"My turn," she said, as she too moved quickly to the bathroom.

Robert walked to the desk, and pulled out the restaurant menus. He looked down the list, decided, and called room service. He was told it would be about thirty minutes. They took a long shower, then donned luxurious bathrobes.

When they first arrived, Jenna hadn't spotted the chocolates, wrapped in colourful, shiny paper, placed in little piles on the various tables in the living room. She was now examining the group forming a happy face on a side table.

"Twenty crunches for each one," Robert warned.

Jenna picked one, opened it, and took a bite. Her eyes rolled up in ecstasy!

"RJ, these are to *die* for!" She offered the other half to him.

Robert let the chocolate melt slowly in his mouth. "I think we've just found breakfast!"

A few minutes later, a waiter appeared at the open door.

"*Perdonatemi, signore, signora.* Do you wish to eat inside or outside, in the garden?"

"Outside, please." Jenna was trying not to let the chocolate dribble down as she spoke.

The waiter placed a clean white tablecloth on the table, set it with sparkling dishes and cutlery, and placed the food platters in the centre. He then withdrew. They had a feast waiting for them. Robert obviously ordered well. Jenna dug in. Both ate with gusto.

Jenna looked earnestly at Robert. "Carmen would die if she saw us enjoying anything but her food."

"We need to be sure to tell her, we missed her cooking."

After breakfast, they sat there, still in bathrobes, drinking some wonderful coffee.

"RJ, this has to be the best place we've stayed in so far. Even though we've had suites with magnificent views, or absolute opulence, this one is wonderfully private, and utterly romantic."

"I agree. We'll have to make a note to spend a week or two here, after the quest is complete."

Jenna moaned. "Ah, yes—the quest!"

"If you're agreeable, we should try to get the clue out of the way, and enjoy the rest of our time here."

She nodded. "I suppose so."

Robert went into the suite to fetch his iPad, and returned to the table. He looked up the Florence War Cemetery to get the hours of opening.

"Looks like the cemetery is open between 8 a.m. and 4 p.m., with an hour closed for lunch at noon. It's almost eleven now. We should try to get there shortly after one."

Jenna gave Robert a demure little smile. "That gives us a whole two hours, lover. What could we possibly do to pass the time?" She got up, took him by the hand, leading him to the bedroom. She dropped her robe as she walked through the door. Robert did the same. All thoughts of the Emerald Tablet evaporated.

Gina sat at the head of the table in the dining room of the Skyline Suite. Her team members were assembled around her. The waiters had just left after serving all the meals. Gina confirmed she hadn't heard from Jackson and Carpenter yet. She wasn't surprised. It was obvious from their note they wanted some time alone.

While eating, they discussed various strategies to make sure their quarry didn't get away from them again. The most popular was to use GPS tracking devices planted somehow in their clothes. This would work, as long as they didn't change—which they did often. Gina had Jackson's phone number from his calls to her, and they wondered if their boss had contacts who could provide them with his phone's GPS location. Gina would check this out. One member of the team bemoaned the fact they didn't have access to CCTV cameras like the major intelligence services did. Everyone agreed.

Gina couldn't help thinking that after this little escapade, her boss would be expanding his contact base to include more places, and resources. He wasn't used to this kind of situation. And yet, he almost seemed to be enjoying the challenge. In the past, it was always straightforward payoffs, quick recon and surveillance, some minor violence—but only when absolutely required. There were, however, a few occasions when death occurred—usually unnecessarily. She reported in.

"Yes, Gina, what news?"

"No contact yet, sir. The team is assembled, and ready to move a moment's notice."

"Do you still think they'll call?"

"Yes, sir. I have no reason to believe they won't. There's one thing I can say about this pair, sir, they're consistent, and straightforward in their dealings. Jackson said he'd call, and he will."

"I think it's safe to say they'll be getting the Florence clue before you arrive."

"I think so too, sir. They're a couple in love, who want some private time. I must admit, sir, I've never been up against a couple so much in love. It throws all normal convention out the window."

"Yes. Love can really throw things out of kilter—for everyone! It becomes almost impossible to predict behaviour with any degree of certainty."

"Have you decided on any strategies, going forward?"

"Other than GPS trackers, there's precious little we can do. By the way, sir, do you have contacts with anyone who has access to CCTV cameras at various locations?"

"Oh, I wish! Unfortunately, covert agencies with that kind of access don't do private jobs."

"What about access to Jackson's mobile phone GPS, sir?"

"That may be a little easier to obtain. Let me pursue that. Do you have his mobile number?"

"Yes, sir. 403-555-1100."

"I'll get back to you."

Carver dialled the number. The announcement said the customer was not available. He smiled. *This man is very clever*, he thought.

At two o'clock in the afternoon, Robert and Jenna found themselves at the entrance to the Florence War Cemetery courtesy of a hired limousine. They entered the cemetery with flowers to place on the grave, as they did in Suez. There was no one to be seen.

"The note said it was plot 444, but a quick look on the map of the cemetery showed a different numbering scheme. According the plan of the cemetery, the first 4 was Section IV; the second 4 would be Row D; and the third 4 was, in fact, grave number 4. As before, they wandered around for a few minutes, offered a moment of silence at the Cross of Sacrifice, and at the War Stone. With map in hand, they easily found the grave they were looking for.

As in Suez, there was a recently planted flower to the right of the gravestone. They followed the same procedure here, with Jenna on the left side and Robert on the right side, ready to dig out the plant. They did a quick scan around as though looking for someone. They could see no one peeking from anywhere, nor did they notice any security cameras. They both squatted down, Jenna placing flowers on the grave, while Robert carefully dug up the plant. Digging down a little further, after pulling the plant up, his fingers caught the zipper bag Scott used for all his notes. In a quick motion, he put the note in the inner breast pocket of his jacket. It took less than a minute to get the plant back in place.

"Thank you, old friend." Robert patted the top of the gravestone. They remained in that position for a minute or two, when the gardener appeared. They smiled at him. He was younger than they expected. Jenna extended Robert's 'tourist' camera to the gardener, asking by gesture if he could take a photo of them at the grave. The young man took the camera, took a picture while standing, then squatted down himself to take one at their level.

"*Grazie, signore*, for the work you do here," said Robert as he stood to take the camera back, and pointing around the cemetery.

"You are quite welcome, *signore*," the gardener replied in good English.

Jenna pressed his hand in hers, and followed with a formal cheek kiss—first right, then left. "You do magnificent work here."

"Thank you, *signora*. It is a matter of pride for me to work here, and make certain all is in order. You see, my grandfather's grave is over in that section there. Although I did not know him, I know he would scold me if I did not do a good job." He laughed, and they laughed with him.

"Will you do us the honour of showing us his grave," asked Robert.

The gardener, filled with pride, marched them to a section in the far corner of the cemetery. He stopped in front of his grandfather's grave, took off his hat, which he placed over his heart. The three stood there for a few minutes in silence. Tears trickled down the cheeks of the young gardener. Jenna moved to him, and gave him a big, long hug. He didn't blush. He simply wiped his tears away, and smiled at her. They parted company, leaving the man there by the grave. It was a quiet return drive to the hotel.

Back in their suite, they pulled out the iPad and nail file.

Jenna laughed. "You know, darling, we should just put our note deciphering apparatus on the table before we leave."

"I hope there aren't too many more of these notes laying around," admitted Robert.

"Oh, on the contrary, my sweet, precious, RJ. I hope there are dozens more!" announced Jenna brightly.

The note read:

Sur la blua marbordo en bela loko,

Sidas fortikajxon, sur la monteto de elemento 5;

Norde de norde, rigardas el la kabelo blua.

Robert murmured. "Hmm, this one is a bit longer. Let's see what you have to tell us, Dr. Scott."

With Jenna ensuring he typed in the words right, Robert quickly obtained the English translation for the note:

On the blue coast in a nice place,
Sits a stronghold of old, on the hill of element 5;
North by north, look down from the tile blue.

Robert chuckled. "Okay, miss know-it-all, you have five seconds to blurt out the interpretation for this one!"

"Well, RJ, this one is *so* simple, I'll let *you* have the first crack at it. I'm *sure*, you'll easily manage."

"You're so kind, my dear."

They both read the note out loud a few times, to see if anything popped up.

"I think it may be time to feed the little grey cells," Robert suggested, in a French accent, an obvious allusion to Agatha Christie's dandy little detective, Hercules Poirot.

Jenna burst out laughing. "I *knew* that was coming!"

They hid the note in the usual place, after taking a photo of the original, and saving the translation. They decided to lunch in the outdoor restaurant by the spa and pool. They had no reservation, but as they were guests in the Garden Suite, they were accommodated. The menu was magnificent. Their mouths watered as they read. They were quite hungry, and devoured their meal when it was served.

As they sat, feeling very mellow, they talked about the clue. They looked at it again on Roberts phone.

Robert's face became grave and thoughtful. "Scott had a limited amount of time. So far, all his clue locations have been fairly close in terms of the time it takes to get from one location to another. I think the next one will be no more than three or four hours away at the most."

"In Egypt, we were able to drive from place-to-place. There was no need for air travel, and trains are not a viable alternative. We flew to Cyprus—only a couple of hours from Cairo. Cyprus to Athens was under two hours. Athens to Naples was a couple of hours by air. Naples to here was three hours by train. So, I think you're right, RJ."

Back in their suite, they sat at the table with the iPad. They spent at least an hour searching for different variations of "blue coast," with nothing to show.

"Okay, *blue coast* must be the name of a place or area. The only thing we've found is in Provence, France, but it just doesn't seem to fit. What are other words for blue or coast?"

Jenna gave it some thought. "Sapphire, cobalt, azure, navy?"

Robert began the task of searching "sapphire coast," "cobalt coast," "azure coast," then he got a hit.

"Of course! Côte d'Azur—the French Riviera!"

"That's it! Look at the map. *A nice place*—Nice!"

"Damn that Scott! Had us on a merry chase this time!"

"We still have to solve the rest of the riddle, RJ."

"Let's see...the fifth element of the periodic table is...boron.

Let's look at the map."

Jenna pointed. "Can't be much simpler, it's a big green space—Mont Boron. Can you zoom in? Okay, there...Fort du Mont Alban. It's the only fortress on Mont Boron."

Robert zoomed in closer. The outline of the fort showed it had turrets on all four sides, with one more northerly than the others. "*North by north...north by north.* The north side of the north tower?" He brought up photos of the fort, particularly showing the multi-coloured roof tiles on the corner towers. He looked at Jenna with a smile. They had it—on the north side of the north tower, at ground level, below an overhanging blue roof tile, on Fort du Mont Alban, on Mont Boron, in Nice, France.

"RJ, this is the most difficult clue yet, and one that could easily mix you up. Something inside is telling me, Nice is the end of the line."

"You may be right, Jenna. If it is, we really need to come up with a plan on what to do with the Emerald Tablet when we find it."

They both sat quietly, considering the situation they were in. Then Robert began to smile, that broad, wry smile he had when a crazy idea was forming.

"I know that look, RJ! You've got a plan cooking in there."

"I think it's time to call our friends in Naples. I think we need to get Gina, and her boss, to help resolve this whole issue."

"Carver! You want to go directly to Carver? Are you crazy?"

Robert was chuckling now. "Yes, my ravishing Aphrodite. That's exactly right!"

She looked at him in amazement. So far, every scheme he planned went off without a hitch, and she had no reason to doubt him now. "Wanna share?"

"We'll talk about it in general terms while we're here, but we won't be able to make any firm plans until we know if Nice is, indeed, our final destination."

"How long will we stay here, darling? I just adore this place! Besides, my time of the month is due in two or three days."

"Then, we take a little break, our own personal retreat."

He went over to the phone, and called the front desk to ask if they could keep the Garden Suite for another two nights. They were assured it would be no problem. "Done! We don't leave until Thursday morning."

Jenna ran to him, throwing her arms around his neck, and kissing him passionately. Tears were streaming down her face.

He held her tight.

"One last detail, and I'm all yours."

It was after five in the afternoon. Gina and her team were waiting impatiently in the Skyline Suite in Naples. Each was casting surreptitious glances at Gina, who was pacing like a caged tiger. This was not a good sign. They all knew this mission had gone wrong from the start. No one spoke, except in hushed tones.

Finally, Kate spoke up. "Still think they'll call, Gina?" She asked the question on everyone's mind.

"Yes."

Her phone rang. She looked at the number. "Finally!"

"Yes."

"So sorry to keep you waiting. We're looking forward to seeing you again, now we've had a bit of time to ourselves. You'll find us at the Four Seasons Firenze, in Florence. The train, is faster than driving, but then, you have a jet at your disposal—even better."

"What can we expect when we get there?"

"We're planning on staying until Thursday. We like it here, so we're taking a time-out. You're welcome to watch us. We might do some sightseeing, but we plan to spend most of our time in our suite. Unfortunately, you won't be able to watch the suite."

"And why is that, Mr. Jackson?"

"The Garden Suite is in a building on its own, with a large private garden. Security will take a very dim view of Peeping Toms spying on their guests."

"I see. Will we have an opportunity to meet again?"

"We certainly hope so. Perhaps for lunch or dinner one day. Feel free to give us a ring when you arrive—hotel phone, not the cell."

"Very well. We'll be seeing you soon, then. And, thank you for calling."

Gina dialled Carver's number.

"Four Seasons Hotel, Florence, sir. They say they're staying until Thursday. We're leaving now."

At 6:45 p.m., their flight touched down in Florence. Forty minutes later they arrived at the Four Seasons Hotel. It was 7:45 when the phone rang in the Garden Suite. It took a while to answer.

"Hello," said Jenna, in a very mellow tone.

"We have arrived, and are at your disposal," announced Gina.
"That's nice. Goodnight."

For the next two days, and three nights, Robert and Jenna enjoyed the sights of Florence, and spent a lot of alone time in their suite. Jenna was over the moon, and Robert was in another world. Although they knew the watchers were never far away, they ignored them completely. From time-to-time, they talked about their next moves in Florence, and Nice, but mostly they talked about their love, the folks back home, the wonders they saw.

One evening, they were talking about home, with Jenna's head resting on Robert's lap.

"It seems like ages ago, since we left Canada, RJ."

"It has, hasn't it?"

"I wonder how everyone is doing."

"Good question."

"Do you think we should call Carmen, to let her know we're okay?"

"We could do. We could call from the hotel phone, since we're not hiding from anyone, at the moment."

Jenna smiled, and got up to get the hotel phone. She brought it over to the couch they were on. Robert dialled Carmen's cell phone number.

"*Hola!*"

"Hello, Carmen," said Jenna, brightly.

Carmen was ecstatic to hear from them! They had a great conversation. Carmen wanted to know how everything was going, where they'd been, if the criminals were still trying to catch them. She was brought up to date, and assured they were fine. They told her they had a truce, of sorts, with those following them. For the time being, they were safe. No, they weren't sure when they'd be home again—they were still following clues. Robert assured her they had lots of pictures to show her, when they returned.

Carmen was not at the house, of course, but she was in touch with her colleagues working in other homes in the neighbourhood. She gave them the scuttlebutt from the area—how the road workers suddenly disappeared, and everything was back to normal again. Robert and Jenna laughed. Carmen wanted to know if it was safe to return to the house yet. Robert thought about this, and suggested she stay put where she was for a bit longer.

"It was nice to hear Carmen's voice again. She was so excited at hearing from us."

"It was nice talking with her. A reminder that this will all end soon, and we have a real home to go back to—hopefully."

Did he mean, we both have a home to go to, or we have a together home to go to? she wondered.

"I wonder what my friends in Edmonton are thinking? It would be nice to call them too, just to let them know I'm still alive."

"For now, I think it's safer not to get them involved. At the rate we're going, I can't see this lasting for much more than a week."

She wanted, desperately, to ask what would become of them, when this was all over. She would have to wait. She knew they had to concentrate on the here-and-now, if they wanted to get out of this alive.

On Wednesday, Robert suggested they have lunch with Gina. He had that smile on his face again, so she knew he had something planned for their meeting. It was arranged, and they lunched at the outdoor restaurant again.

Gina arrived with Kate in tow. They were dressed much more normally than usual—like respectable ladies. Robert thought they cleaned-up nicely. Lunch was delicious, and cordial. No one was pressing anyone for information. There was some chit-chat about the fine weather, the beautiful sights they saw, courtesy of Robert and Jenna's travels. Jenna thought she detected a certain sadness in their eyes, despite the smiles on their faces. Finally, over coffee, they got down to business. It turned out to be the "Robert and Gina Show."

"I'm certain you want to know where we're off to next."

"It would be nice. It would save us a lot of trouble, and a certain amount of frustration."

"You have access to a private jet, I believe?"

"Yes, but you already know that."

"I have a proposition for you." (Jenna was all ears.)

"What might that be, Mr. Carpenter?"

"We tell you where the next clue is to be found, and you fly us there." (Jenna's jaw dropped, and so did Kate's.)

Gina and Robert sat there smiling, with eyes locked. *What a ballsy move*, she thought.

"You would place yourselves willingly in our hands—into the lion's den, as it were?"

Yes, with some stipulations, of course."

"Of course, and what would those be?"

"We no longer have any of the previous notes left behind by Dr. Scott, including the one found here, in Florence. We know the location of the next clue, and by now, you know neither of us will divulge anything under duress. You've already tried that with Jenna—and failed. So, it would avail you nothing to abduct us. It won't get you any closer to the treasure Carver so dearly desires."

"Go on."

"When we reach the destination, we will continue with our little truce. You can follow us as much as you want, except for when we retrieve the note. We'll take care of that alone. We're showing good faith, and we expect you to do likewise."

"So, we can all be friends?"

"Maybe not friends, so much as two parties with a similar mission."

Jenna and Kate sat silent, watching the game unfold. Robert and Gina had broad smiles on their faces. They were measuring each other up.

"The alternative?"

"We disappear, and you'll not hear from us again."

"I will only guarantee safe passage to your next destination. Our situation will be re-evaluated moving forward from there."

Gina extended her hand across the table. Robert reached out, and they shook hands. It was a deal. Jenna and Kate only had blank stares. Jenna trusted Robert implicitly, she slipped her hand through his arm, and squeezed it affectionately. Again, she noticed the sad eyes.

"May I now have the destination, so I can have the pilot set a flight plan?"

"One last thing, Jenna and I are not to be separated at any point, for any reason. That would be considered an act of aggression, which will be met with similar aggression, even at altitude."

"Agreed."

"Nice, France. We would be obliged if we could leave here tomorrow, around 11:00. We are booked in at the Boscolo Exedra."

"Nothing but the best."

"Exactly. For this lady, nothing but the best." It earned him another squeeze from Jenna.

Chapter 23 - Last Supper

"Correct me if I'm wrong, Gina, you did say your next destination is Nice, France, and Jackson and Carpenter are *flying with you?*"

"Yes, sir. According to them, they've disposed of all previous clues, including the one here in Florence, and they're the only ones who know the whereabouts of the Nice clue. We've agreed on a truce, of sorts, in the last couple of locations, and they're willing to continue that truce in Nice, with the exception of finding, and deciphering the Nice clue, which they want to do themselves."

Carver sat there silent for a few moments as he took all this in.

"What do your instincts tell you about all this?"

"When we had lunch, I watched Jackson carefully. He was leading the negotiations, and Carpenter was just as surprised as Kate and me. I believe he knows *exactly* what he's doing, and she's following along for now. I don't believe any amount of physical interrogation will yield anything. Carpenter's already shown her mettle, and Jackson is much stronger. They know we don't have much choice but to go along with their plans, for now. My instincts tell me they want an accommodation of some sort to ensure their own safety after they find the item."

"These two have been moving quickly since they smelled the end, with the exception of their stay in Florence, which appears to be primarily romantic. This is as much a honeymoon as it is a mission. Flying with you makes sense. They can get to Nice quickly, get the next clue, and find out if there is yet another clue. What did you promise them?"

"Safe passage to Nice, and a re-evaluation of our truce going forward, sir."

"They certainly have nerve. Carry on with their plans, for now.

Keep in touch, particularly when they want privacy to retrieve the next note."

"We'll try to follow them covertly when they want to go for the clue, sir."

"No! Don't do that! If they even get a whiff of your presence, or the presence of any other watchers, they'll disappear again! Play it close, but give them space when they ask for it.

"As you wish, sir."

"RJ, you could've blown me over with a feather when you said you wanted to fly with them in *their* plane! Kate's jaw dropped too!"

"I'm sorry for not letting you in on that little part of the plan, Jenna. It had to be a complete surprise. Gina was just as blown away, but tried to stare her way out of it. We need to throw them off, and make them think we're getting ready to make some kind of deal. They don't think we can win, but, my dearest Jenna, we know we can!"

Jenna put her arms around Robert, pressing herself against him. "I trust you absolutely, and completely, RJ."

"We wouldn't have made it this far if we hadn't worked as a team. We're in this together. And what's coming up in Nice will need both of us to be at the top of our game."

"I know. If this *is* the last place, we'll need to move fast, and get everything just right. We'll be leaving tomorrow morning, so let's just be lovers until then."

Robert held her tight. There was only love now. They remained in their suite until it was time to leave the next day.

As agreed, the watchers and the watched met in the lobby at 11:00 to check-out. Robert ordered a private limousine to take them to the airport, and invited Gina and Kate to ride with them. The remainder of Gina's team had the other vehicles. Robert and Jenna laughed, saying they felt like celebrities with guard vehicles in front, and in back, of their limo.

Gina and Kate were quiet. Gina was still trying to work out any down sides to their prey travelling with them. Kate watched as Robert and Jenna snuggled close, and chatted quietly together. Again, Jenna noticed the sadness in her eyes.

At the airport, the other vehicles boxed in the limousine. Robert and Jenna exited first, and were ushered up the steps into the private jet. The flight attendant was very friendly as she greeted them, telling them they could take their pick of the seats. They were quickly followed by Gina, and her team, who were all business. The luggage was quickly stowed. The co-pilot entered the cabin to introduce the flight crew. He also gathered all the passports, and other travel documents. The cabin door was closed, and the plane departed almost immediately. Two hours later, they were touching down at the Nice Côte d'Azur International Airport.

Before leaving, Robert noted the phone number for a limousine service in Nice. Once he knew their scheduled arrival time, he placed a quick call to the service to order a limousine to meet them once they cleared French customs and immigration. Being a gentleman, he offered Gina and Kate a ride to the hotel, which they accepted. The remaining members of the team would have to fend for themselves.

At the front desk, Robert identified himself. The desk clerk's eyebrows raised when she saw he reserved not only the Grand Suite Duplex, but also the Presidential Suite, and three Jr. Suites.

She was about to ask if his friends would be staying in any of the other suites, when she read the note on the reservation, telling her that Mr. and Mrs. Jackson would be staying in the Grand Suite, and not to mention the other suites to anyone who might be with them—only a simple confirmation that everything was as requested.

"Is there anything wrong?"

"*Non, monsieur*, everything is just as you requested."

Robert turned to Gina. "We'll be in the Grand Suite, on the 5th floor. I'm afraid you'll have to sort out your own rooms. Perhaps we can get together later."

"Thank you, Mr. Jackson. Were you planning to go on your private excursion today?"

"I'm sure we have plenty of time, darling. The flight out was short, and I'm game if you are."

"Yes, it's just after two. Plenty of time. I'll give you a call to confirm, one way or the other.

A porter was called to take their baggage to the Grand Suite, and they were ushered up without delay. Gina was left to make room arrangements for her team.

Once in their suite, Robert pulled out his iPad to do some more research on the Fort du Mont Alban. Time-wise, they had plenty of time. The question was how to get there without being followed by Gina's watchers, or any other watchers that might be around. Since they used a hired limo to get to the hotel, they had no vehicle they could use. After some discussion, they decided on a route. Robert dug the camera out of his carry-on. Again, they would have to play tourist.

They quickly made their way down to the lobby, and out the main doors. Robert called Gina to tell her they were headed out to get the next clue, reminding her this would be a private outing. She agreed, assuring him no one would follow. They got into a cab, and asked the driver to take them to the *Parc Castel des Deux Rois*, not that far away. When they exited the cab, they were able to make sure no one was following—no strange vehicles, no second cab stopping nearby.

Robert pulled out his phone to get some map bearings. They walked about 250 metres to a large store named *Bio Marché*. There, they took a cab to the Thomas Cook Travel Agency. They wandered up the street for a few minutes, then caught another cab to the Fort du Mont Alban. It would be more difficult for Gina to trace their movements using different cabs.

From then on, they fell into their role as tourist lovers. It's a role they both truly enjoyed. Once at the fort, they wandered around, taking pictures, exploring the structure—inside, and outside. There were quite a few people around, but they began to thin out after a while. Outside the north tower, Robert used the zoom lens on his camera to find a blue roof tile. He kept his eye on the roof, while Jenna guided him along the outside. He spotted a blue tile on the edge. They marked the spot, and kept moving around the turret. There was no other blue tile to be found on the edge of the roof.

They returned to the spot they marked a few minutes earlier. Now, both were scanning the outside of the tower wall. They doubted it would be higher than a person could reach, but could be accessible from a window. When that yielded nothing, Jenna, took off one of her earrings, and they began to search the ground at the base of the tower. A couple walked around the building. Seeing them searching, they asked if there was a problem. Jenna explained she lost an earring, and they were trying to find it. The couple wished them luck, and moved on. Robert and Jenna began to search the ground further away from the tower, wondering if they had the clue right. Nothing was jumping at them.

Robert pulled out his phone, and displayed the English text of the last clue. All the clues had been "disposed of" by encrypting them on his phone. *Look down from the tile blue*, he read. He looked up at the blue tile again.

"What is it, RJ?"

"*Look down from the tile blue*. There's something about that I can't put my finger on."

"We're below the blue tile, now." She thought about what she just said, *below the blue tile*. "RJ, we're *below* the blue tile, we're not really *looking down from* it."

"You're a genius, Jenna! If we look at the angle the tile is sitting, and draw a line on that same angle..." He stepped back a bit to better see the tile. "Darling, walk directly forward until I tell you to stop."

Jenna slowly walked forward until Robert shouted, "Stop!" Jenna stood still a moment, then took a tiny step back. Robert joined her, and they began scanning the area directly around where Jenna was standing. It didn't take long. They both spotted the fallen tree trunk just over to their left. They climbed down a short way to reach the trunk. On the far side, tucked in under the trunk, under some leaves, they found the zipper bag with the note intact. They quickly made their way back to the path, before being challenged by a guard why they were rummaging in the woods.

Robert took the note out of the bag. Jenna pulled the nail file out of her purse, and slit open the envelope. They opened the note:

> Reen, reen, reen al la komenco!
>
> 5298713, 84080008

Using his phone this time, he tapped in the first line. They almost died when they saw the English translation:

> *Back, back, back to the beginning!*
>
> *5298713, 84080008*

They looked at one another.

"Does this say what I think it says?"

"Full circle, sweetheart. I expected as much."

"And the numbers?"

"The hunt began in Taba. If I'm right, these numbers are GPS coordinates to where Scott buried the Emerald Tablet. Let's see what the coordinates are for Taba...Okay, Taba is at 29 degrees north by 34 degrees east. If I add those to the other numbers as GPS coordinates...bingo—a few kilometres from Taba, in the middle of nowhere."

Jenna burst out crying. "Oh, my gosh, RJ! We've found it!"

It took a few minutes for them both to calm down. They realized there was only one more stop, back in Taba, where Scott originally buried the Emerald Tablet before disappearing. There would be no searching for obscure cracks and crevices, books and trees, columns and cemeteries. They had the exact coordinates to within a few metres. Since Scott was alone, and constantly looking over his shoulder, it was unlikely he would dig a deep hole.

They walked around the fort to find a bench to sit on.

"Well, Jenna, it's time to set-up the rat trap."

"This is where it gets interesting."

Robert took out his cell phone, and dialled a number.

"Roland," answered Yves Roland, head of a private security firm Robert contacted while still in Florence, away from the prying eyes, and ears, of the watchers.

"M. Roland, this is Robert Jackson. We spoke a couple of days ago."

"Ah, oui! I recall. We spoke about a possible case for our firm, here in Nice."

"We are in Nice now, at the Fort du Mont Alban. Since we are not being watched, at the moment, it would be the best time for us to meet."

"You are being watched, monsieur?"

"Yes, my fiancée and I have been under surveillance by private watchers for weeks, that is why we need your help." Jenna almost fainted! *He called me his fiancée!* She struggled to remain calm and composed.

"Where are you at the Fort, M. Jackson?"

"We are sitting on a bench on the south side of the fort," replied Robert.

"I will be with you in about thirty minutes. I am tall, short greying hair, and will be wearing black slacks with a blue shirt," he told them.

"Thank you, M. Roland. We will remain here."

"Do you think this will work, RJ? It seems so crazy."

"You can say that again! When I left to get groceries a month ago, I never imagined I'd be sitting by a fort in Nice, France, with the love of my life, waiting to meet a security agent, to discuss a covert operation."

They looked at one another, and began to laugh. The whole

thing was absurd! They talked about what needed to happen, and wondered if the security firm would take on their case. M. Roland seemed interested, and his tone changed when Robert mentioned they were under surveillance. What they would be asking for was not exactly within the confines of the law.

Some twenty minutes later, they noticed a couple wandering around not far from them. They were looking at a brochure, as though trying to get their bearings. Were these Carver watchers, or were they Roland's people checking the meeting location? When Jenna looked over Robert's shoulder, she noticed a man making a rubbing of something against the side of the fort. He didn't seem to be interested in them, but was casting short glances about. They, too, watched, without watching. There were other tourists, but these three, in particular, weren't leaving their positions.

Along the path, they saw a man fitting Roland's description. He paid no attention to the couple with the brochure, or the rubbing man. He stopped, and stood directly in front of them.

"M. Roland, I presume."

With a little bow, he presented himself. "Yves Roland, at your service'."

"I hope the couple on your right, and the man on the left are your people, or we are now under surveillance again."

"You have a good eye, monsieur. Yes, these are my people, and they will watch to be sure we are not being observed."

Robert and Jenna moved over on the bench to make room for Roland to sit down.

Jenna smiled at Roland. "We are very used to picking out watchers lately."

"Your preliminary description intrigues me. Now that we are together, please tell me your situation, in detail, please."

Taking turns, Robert and Jenna unfolded their story to Roland. He sat quietly for a few minutes, considering what they said.

"To summarize, you are in the process of finding a precious artifact hidden by the archaeologist who found it. An unscrupulous private collector has sent a team of commandos to track you down. There is now a truce between you, because they are letting you find the artifact, and it seems the only way they can keep up with you. You are now ready to unearth the artifact, and need to come to some sort of arrangement with this collector, if you want to continue to live, and possibly also free the missing archaeologist."

Jenna nodded. "That would be an accurate summary."

"And how can we help you to accomplish this?"

For almost an hour, the three talked about what needed to be done. Several times, Roland's eyebrows would go up as he listened to the plan being proposed to him. He asked many questions, mostly regarding details. He was nodding his head as he mulled everything in his mind.

Roland smiled, and his eyes glinted. "I must admit, this is an unusual case you propose for us, far from the usual, rather boring, bodyguard and security functions. To be honest, I believe my team will find this case a wonderful diversion. It will call on us to be very sharp, and ready for whatever eventuality may present itself."

"So, you will take on the case?"

"Absolutely, madame! And now, there is much to do in preparation. You are certain these watchers are armed, and trained?"

"When they visited us in Athens, the women removed pistols, and combat knives from their person. Judging from the physique, movements, methods of surveillance, of the three men and three women watching us, they are fit, strong, and combat ready."

"You have several suites at the Exedra, you tell me, monsieur."

"Yes, we are in the Grand Suite. We also have the Presidential Suite, and three Jr. Suites. If you feel you need more, please let us know."

"You have the keys for all the suites?"

"Yes." Robert reached into his pocket. "Here are the keys to all the suites, except our own."

Roland put the keys in his pocket. "It will be necessary to do a thorough reconnaissance of each suite to decide how we will handle the watchers."

"Please understand, once we return, we will be under constant surveillance. Two of the women, Gina and Kate, will possibly approach us as soon as we arrive. They will place at least one person in the hall near the door to our suite."

"Would it be possible, M. Jackson, to have their entire team in your suite, say for dinner, since you are now on a truce?"

Jenna gave Roland a sly smile. "I think I can arrange that."

"Wonderful! Now, I will need a key to your suite as well. I will mobilize some agents there in preparation for your little party.

Do not worry, they will be unobtrusive. Please give us about an hour, if possible, to prepare."

"That will not be a problem. They don't know where we are, hopefully, and they don't know how long it will take to decipher the clue. One last item, a matter of business. Would you like a payment in advance? Since we are free for now, we can go to a bank to obtain funds."

"M. Jackson, if you can afford the Grand Suite, the Presidential Suite, and a handful of additional suites, at the Exedra, I have no concerns regarding payment. We can settle up after the operation is completed."

Jenna touched Roland's arm. "One last thing, M. Roland. No one must be harmed. I understand they may not be comfortable, but no one must be harmed."

Roland responded with a wry smile. "Madame, I assure you, my team is well trained in covert operations, and, shall we say, involuntary extractions."

For the next hour, Robert and Jenna explored Fort du Mont Alban. There were still a few tourists visiting, but it was getting dark. Robert called the hotel, identified himself, and asked for a limo to be sent to fetch them at the fort. He placed a second call—to Gina.

"Mr. Jackson, we thought you might've flown the coop. Nice of you to call."

"It took longer than expected to find the clue, and to figure it out."

Jenna extended the dinner invitation. "Gina, we would like to host your entire team for dinner this evening. We need to bring you up to speed, and discuss the next step in this little quest. We had a lovely flight over with all of you, and want to repay the hospitality. Since we'll be with you, we won't be disappearing."

They must have found the last clue, thought Gina. She did a thumbs-up to Kate, sitting across from her in their room. "We'd be delighted to attend. How would you like us to dress for this occasion?"

"I'm thinking since we're in the Grand Suite, we should go formal, if that's alright with you?"

"That would be fine. We haven't done formal in some time. It'll be a nice change. Are you back in the hotel?"

Robert spoke into the phone. "No, we've ordered a car to pick us up, we should be there in a few minutes. In the mean time, you might want to look over the menu, and ask for the meals to be served in the Grand Suite. We'll order as soon as we arrive."

"What time would you like us to be there?"

"We should be ready for you around 7:30. We can have drinks while we wait for the food."

"At 7:30 then."

The limo pulled up just as the conversation ended.

Meanwhile, Roland's team assembled with all the necessary paraphernalia they needed to quickly and effectively take down the Carver team. They reconnoitred the rooms, and knew exactly where they would position themselves. In the Presidential Suite, they placed many recording Internet cameras in carefully-chosen locations to make sure all areas of the suite were covered. Short of sweeping the room with a high-grade device, the cameras wouldn't be detected. Three speakers were also hidden in the suite. A laptop was placed unobtrusively on a desk on the second floor of the Grand Suite. This could be used to monitor all the cameras in the Presidential Suite. The built-in microphone on the laptop could be used to speak to its occupants.

On the way to the hotel, Robert placed a call to Roland, informing him of the dinner arrangements. If they were having drinks ahead of time, a full portable bar would be brought in. The bartender would be one of Roland's team—to keep an eye on things.

Roland explained the meal would be served by three more of Roland's team. With eight diners, this would be the norm, and wouldn't arouse any suspicion. The remaining members of the group would be waiting in the Presidential Suite down the hall.

Gina assembled her team in her room. They all cleaned-up nicely, and you would never suspect them to be hard-nosed covert agents. Gina told them it would be a friendly dinner, and there would be no need for the usual weapons—a small weapon if they absolutely felt it was necessary. Only Kate felt the need—a small derringer in a holster strapped to her thigh.

At the appointed time, they all made their way together to the Grand Suite.

When Robert and Jenna arrived, they found Roland sitting on the couch, waiting for them, and a lovely lady in her thirties standing at a rolling bar, getting it ready. It was rather disconcerting to have someone in their private space. They both greeted them with a smile. Roland introduced the bartender as Simone–the name on her hotel badge. He knew they had little time to get ready for dinner, so he went over the plan quickly, and introduced them to the laptop camera monitor. They could see Roland's team sitting comfortably in the Presidential Suite.

Roland spoke into the microphone. "*Mais non, alors! Pas de pieds sur les meubles, s'il vous plait.*" The man with his feet on the coffee table jumped, quickly removing them. Robert and Jenna burst out laughing.

"I hope we can make Carver jump like that too," she chuckled.

Roland excused himself, leaving them to prepare for dinner. They took a very quick shower, pulled out some formal apparel, and jewellery. They just finished dressing, when the doorbell rang downstairs. Jenna looked at Robert, moved in, and kissed him lightly on the lips.

"This is it, Mr. Jones. Game on!"

As they descended the stairs, the doorbell rang again. Robert nodded to Simone to let them in. At first, Gina was taken aback at the presence of an unknown person. She saw Robert and Jenna making their way unhurriedly down the stairs.

Robert caught her eye. "This is Simone. We thought it appropriate to have a full bar for the occasion. After all, this will be an important evening."

Gina and her five team members entered the suite, admiring its elegance.

"Nothing but the best," murmured Gina.

The Carver team ordered their drinks with half the usual alcohol; it was to be expected. Robert ordered a double Jameson neat, while Jenna opted for a highball. They both needed a good stiff drink. With Robert and Jenna betraying no stress, the Carver team slowly began to lower their guard. There was a lot of chit-chat, and poking fun at one another over the happenings of the previous few weeks.

When the meals arrived, it came with three servers—two men and a woman, each pushing a cart laden with food. There were two other men there, probably porters, who rolled in another table, and two chairs, on a dolly. The normal table that seats six, was moved away, and the larger table was set it its place. The servers set eight places, along with the myriad of cutlery and glasses needed for a formal, multi-course meal. They ushered the diners to their seats. The two porters retreated with their dolly, and the small table. Everything was done to perfection.

For the next ninety minutes, the servers dished out the various courses. When all the dirty dishes were gathered, the servers prepared for the coffee.

Gina's team never saw it coming! They didn't notice, or maybe didn't care, that the servers positioned themselves in such a way as to be between two team members. As they turned, in unison, to get the coffee cups, they had small injection devices in each hand. The others couldn't see because the servers' hands were behind the backs of others. With a quick movement, each of the Carver team was injected with a fast-acting tranquilizer. Within seconds, Roland and his remaining team entered the suite.

It happened so quickly, and with such precision, that even Robert and Jenna, who knew something would happen, were taken completely by surprise. This pleased Roland immensely.

"Don't worry madame. The drug is safe, and will wear out fast. They might have a small headache when they wake up, but they will be completely unharmed."

Roland's team quickly brought in three food carts slightly larger than the originals. On the shelf below, they placed one of the Carver team, beginning with the females. They would put the three females in one of the Jr. Suites, and the males in another. Robert picked up Gina's purse, before Roland could take it. He pulled out her cell phone. This he would need for part two of the plan.

It took no more than twenty minutes to clear everything from the Grand Suite. All of Gina's team was now incommunicado, and would remain so until Robert authorized their release. Robert told Roland he would keep him apprised of developments as they happened. Roland bid them goodnight.

With the door closed behind them, Robert and Jenna were finally alone. They held one another for several minutes, without saying a word. Jenna looked up at Robert, again admiring his foresight, and thankful for all the adventure movies he'd watched. She kissed him gently, sweetly, on the lips. With the evening's tensions releasing, Robert realized how stunning she looked.

"You know, I've been so stressed about this caper, I never even told you how marvellous you look."

"This must be the most stressful day we've had so far. But we got through it by working as a team, and letting love come first."

"There's only one more thing to do tonight. Then we can relax, maybe have a soak in that big tub."

"That sounds positively scrumptious!"

Chapter 24 - Rat Trap

"Bartholomew," Dr. Bart answered.

"Dr. Bart! Dr. Bart! We've found it! We've found the Emerald Tablet!" Jenna blurted into the phone.

"Carpenter, is that you?"

"Yes, it's me. I'm sorry. I didn't identify myself when you answered."

"Good heavens, Carpenter. You disappeared in such a hurry, and no one's been able to contact you, we thought the worst, and began calling hospitals and police."

"I'm sorry, sir. This quest has been such an incredible journey! I was abducted, beaten, lost, found, and travelled the world with an incredible man!"

"Slow down! Slow down, Jenna! What on earth are you talking about?"

"Dr. Bart, we've found the Emerald Tablet!"

"You've what? Found the Emerald Tablet? You'd better tell me all about it, young lady."

"Dr. Bart, you don't understand! Randolph Carver, and his goons, have been following us, trying to get a hold of us to tell them where the tablet is. They've been tracking us doggedly, sir, but we managed to elude them. We know they're close by now! We *found* the Emerald Tablet. They don't know yet, but it won't be long."

Dr. Bart suddenly became rather nervous. "What's all this about Randolph Carver?"

"Dr. Scott's map, sir. It wasn't really a map after all. It was a note he left telling us he found, and hid, the tablet. It said he was afraid that Carver would have him abducted and tortured to discover its whereabouts. The note said he would probably be killed if he didn't give the information. And as you know, Dr.

Scott disappeared, and hasn't been seen."

"You were able to decipher the note, then."

"Yes, sir. Would you believe it was written in Esperanto? That's why neither of us could make head nor tails of it when I showed you. I went to Airdrie, to consult an old university friend of mine who did a major in linguistics. If anyone could figure it out, it would be him."

"Esperanto! Of course! Cagey old Scott! Jenna, where are you now?"

Robert smiled. Dr. Bart took the bait—just as expected.

"I'm in Nice, France, sir. You've got to get here right away to safeguard the tablet. We don't want Carver to get his hands on it. Dr. Scott meant for this to be studied, and exhibited in a museum, not hoarded by a ruthless private collector. Come quickly, sir!"

"You keep saying 'we,' Jenna. Who are you referring to?"

"My knight in shinning armour who has pockets deep enough to afford this quest. His name is Robert Jackson. He rescued me after I escaped Carver's interrogation squad, just outside Airdrie. I'll tell you all about it when you get here, but you *must* come right away!"

"Very well, Jenna. I'll book a flight out as soon as possible."

"We'll book you a suite at the Boscolo Exedra, sir. Robert said he's happy to take care of the cost."

"Thank you very much. Your knight is very generous. You can expect me in the next day or so. Are you staying at the Exedra as well?"

"Yes, sir. Please call me at the number you have on your phone. It's a new mobile we bought here because mine was lost in Airdrie. Robert doesn't want to use his phone in case they have a way of tracking him."

"Very well. Stay put! Do you understand? Stay close to the hotel. We don't want anything to happen to the tablet, now do we?"

"Yes, Dr. Bart, we'll be waiting here."

Jenna disconnected. She smiled at Robert with her head cocked to the side.

"How'd I do, darling?"

"An award-winning performance, my dear. I think I can hear him dialling Carver now."

She put her arms around Robert's neck, and kissed him hard.

"Now, *we* play the part of the cat, and *they'll* be the mice!"

"Do you really think this will work, RJ?"

"If Carver thinks we have the tablet in our possession, he won't risk doing anything more to us. He'll come in person to claim his prize."

"And we'll be waiting for him, ready to spring the trap." She made a snapping motion with her hands. "RJ, you're a genius!"

"What is it, Bartholomew?" answered Carver gruffly.

"You won't believe this. I just got a call from Carpenter."

Carver jumped up. "What?"

"Carpenter just called to tell me they've found the Emerald Tablet. They want me to fly out to Nice, France to help safeguard the tablet before you can get at it."

"They found the tablet! They actually have it in their possession?"

"Apparently. They're staying at the Boscolo Exedra Hotel in Nice. They were kind enough to reserve me a suite."

"I'll have my people there box them in. They're not getting away from me again!"

"Carver, I don't want any violence. She said she was kidnapped, and beaten, in Airdrie. Was that you?"

"Watch your tongue, Bartholomew! Never mention my name. My people overstepped their authority, but I'd be very pleased to watch them get a good thrashing for what they've put me through!"

"No violence!"

"Very well. I'll tell my people to keep them on a tight leash, but no intervention unless absolutely necessary." He had many good leads from Dr. Bart in the past, and didn't want to lose this important connection in his network. "I'll meet you at the Edmonton International Airport in 4 hours. I'll call to tell you where to meet us. We'll fly out immediately for Nice."

"Very well, sir. I'll be at the airport when you call."

Carver wondered why Gina hadn't notified him that Jackson and Carpenter found the tablet. He knew they had gone out to find a clue in Nice, but there was no indication they actually had the tablet. He was concerned.

He dialled Gina's number again. It went straight to voicemail. *What the hell is going on out there?* he wondered. At the sound of the tone, he left a message.

"Keep an eye on the kids, but no spanking. They have the teddy bear. I will be home soon."

They heard Gina's phone ring, picked it up, and sent the call to voicemail. When the icon flashed, Robert pressed *1* to get the message. It was short. Robert put it on speaker. Carver took the bait. Robert was right. Carver wouldn't take anymore chances. He was coming for the Emerald Tablet himself.

"That didn't take very long."

"Didn't think it would. Bart called Carver as soon as you hung up, darling."

"I'll bet he's wondering why Gina's not picking up."

They both laughed. It was good to laugh. The tension was rising steadily since they turned the tables on Gina, and her team.

"Everything is ready for them in the Presidential Suite. The cameras and speakers are all in place. Once the trap is sprung, we'll have Carver and Bart over a barrel. They'll have no choice but to accept our demands."

Roland's team did a masterful job of placing the cameras. There was no corner where Carver could go to escape being seen. All the cameras could be remotely controlled from Roland's laptop in the Grand Suite with another in Roland's command suite.

Gina's team was now resting uncomfortably in two of the Jr. Suites, guarded by Roland's people. Roland opted for three agents in each room—one for each of Carver's team. This would dissuade any of them from attempting to become heroes. The agents were rotated on a regular basis, one at a time, to avoid the confusion of having six agents in the room at once.

To make sure the trap would remain sprung, Roland would take care of separating Carver and Bart from any bodyguards, and keep them in the Presidential Suite until a deal was reached.

"How long to you think we have before they get here?"

"A fast, private jet could fly from Edmonton to Nice in about 15 hours non-stop according to the Internet. But even the longest-range jet can't get here without making at least one stop to refuel, so add another two hours for that. If Carver is picking up Bart, say we add another two hours for that. So, we're looking at roughly 19 to 20 hours—almost a day."

Jenna looked flirtatiously at Robert. "So, we have some time to ourselves." She took his hands, and led him up the stairs.

In the morning, they thought they should go visit Gina. Jenna felt a pang of guilt, albeit a very small pang, for the dinner deception. They knocked at the first detention suite, which happened to be where the women on Gina's team were being held. Roland's guard looked through the peep hole, and let them in.

The ladies were laying on the king-size bed neatly trussed-up, and gagged. If looks could kill, they would both be dead.

Jenna couldn't stifle a giggle when she saw them. "Well, maybe now you know how I felt for those two days after I was kidnapped. The big difference here, is no one will be beating you."

Robert looked sternly at Gina. "Gina, if your gags are taken off, will you, and your mates, promise to stay quiet? After all, if you call out, you'll have a tough time explaining to the Police Judiciaire about all the weapons in your rooms."

Gina knew when she was beaten, and nodded her consent.

"*Veuillez enlever leurs bâillon*," Robert asked the guards.

One of the guards, called Roland for confirmation, telling him the captives promised to stay quiet. Roland considered this for a few moments, and gave his approval. The guards pulled the bed away from the wall, then one of them went from behind to remove the gags. These were professionals.

It was Jenna's turn to be serious. "We apologize for last evening's little deception, but you must agree, we had to do something with you, so you wouldn't spoil the rest of the plan."

"If you don't mind my asking, why is it necessary to have us trussed-up like this," asked Gina.

Robert softened his gaze. "You see, we needed to entice your boss, Carver, out here personally. To do that, we need you to be out-of-service, temporarily. We also needed your phone to contact Carver, and find out his orders for you."

Gina went white. "Carver is coming here in person!" They noticed her two companions where in shock also. "Oh, crap! We're dead!"

"We certainly hope not," responded Jenna brightly. "We need to make a deal with Carver, so we can have a life. For that, we need to catch him in the act, with his two hands in the cookie jar."

Robert continued. "Right now, he's flying out on the fastest jet he can get his hands on. When he arrives, he'll quickly find himself in a rat trap. If he's as intelligent as he appears to be, he'll know he has no choice but to acquiesce to our demands. You see, we have a couple of Interpol agents present as well,"

"Mr. Jackson, Ms. Carpenter, you are incredible!" admitted Gina. "You have earned my admiration, and that doesn't come easily. But, when Carver arrives, he won't deal with us gently, me in particular."

Jenna took Roberts arm, giving it a big squeeze. "Part of our demands will be that there be no reprisals against you. He knows, as well as you do, you guys never had a chance against us. Never underestimate the power of love!"

"Your captors have been given instructions to make you as comfortable as possible," advised Robert. "With a little luck, you'll be free to go sometime this evening."

With Carver's elite squad being held incommunicado, Robert and Jenna could enjoy a leisurely day taking the sights in and around Nice, without fear of being rudely interrupted. With all that happened to them, Jenna still felt she was in a beautiful dream. She travelled to places she could never think of going, without winning the lottery. Dr. Scott certainly took them on a magic carpet ride of enchanting places to find his clues. And now, on the arm of her wonderful Robert, she was basking in the sun on the French Riviera! They took hundreds of photographs. She couldn't wait to tell her friends about their quest. She couldn't wait to show off the man who stole her heart, literally saved her life, and made it possible for them to complete the quest.

Dream or no dream, Robert was diligently watching over the love of his life. Although they were having lots of fun, and a deep beautiful romance, he was still very much on the lookout for anyone who might spoil their pleasure. Until everything was sorted out with Carver and Bart, they would be in danger. It was obvious from conversations with Gina, that Carver was in a terrible state because of what he and Jenna put him through. She made it clear that Carver was not a man to cross, and would seek revenge, as well as his prize.

After their day in the sun, Robert and Jenna decided to order dinner from room service. When it arrived, they half expected to see Roland's agents serving it. They enjoyed some wonderful seafood, fresh from the Mediterranean. As always, it was an enchanting time, lost in love. There was no need to hurry, as Carver and Bart wouldn't be arriving until about seven or eight. They both realized their whole plan might blow up in their faces, and were making the most of the quiet time before their trap would spring shut, hopefully, on their prey.

When they were done, Robert fired up the computer for one last check of the cameras and speakers. Everything was in working order. There was one last call to Roland. They quickly went over what they could expect. Roland assured him they were ready. He had a couple of men at the airport to watch for the arrival of Carver's jet. A friendly chat with their airport contact revealed the jet was expected to touch down at around seven.

It was a waiting game now. About an hour to go before all hell would break loose. This was make or break for Robert and Jenna, and possibly Dr. Scott as well. They had no idea where Scott was being held, or if he was being held at all. Perhaps he was already dead, and buried in the sand somewhere in Jordan, or Egypt, or goodness knows where.

Robert sat next to Jenna on the sofa. They turned to face one another, and he took her hands in his. The strain was beginning to show on her face.

"Scared?"

"More nervous than scared. You?"

"My gut's been churning for a while now. Never done anything like this before."

"RJ, remember at the very beginning, seems ages ago now, I told you I was completely confident that we'd succeed in this quest?" (Robert nodded.) "Well, I haven't lost confidence in you, or in us as a phenomenal team. We've been all over the place. We've found and deciphered all the clues. We've been followed, and we gave them the slip every time. We have Carver's watchers safely put away. Now, we know where the Emerald Tablet is. The quest is almost at an end. We've frustrated Carver, and his motley crew, at every turn. I *know* we'll succeed. Tonight, we'll have the insurance policy we need to be free of them all."

Robert reflected carefully on what Jenna just said. He gazed into her eyes. There might be stress showing on her face, but there was no fear whatever in her eyes. Tension in Robert's body slowly released. He smiled a sweet, knowing smile. Jenna could see the strain falling from his countenance. She felt it in his hands. She too began to smile. Both were letting go of the tensions. This was a time to be in total control. They leaned in towards one another, and kissed deeply.

"Jenna, this is probably the worst time to bring this up."

"Bring what up?" She noticing he had a strange look on his face.

Robert shifted around nervously, looking down, around, and away. Jenna saw him swallow hard. *Oh, my gosh,* she thought, *Is he going to do what I think he's going to do?* She wasn't sure if she would shout for joy, or just faint.

Robert stammered. "Jenna Carpenter, will you marry me? You know, when this is all over. When..."

"Yes! Yes! Yes! Oh, my sweet, wonderful RJ, of course I will!"

The floodgates opened. Jenna threw herself at Robert, and with her arms almost breaking his neck began to weep in great sobs. Robert was nonplussed. He held Jenna tight. Her tears triggered tears of his own, and he felt a bit embarrassed. They sat there for several minutes with tears streaming down.

Finally, Jenna admonished him. "Leave it to a man to pick the very worst moment to pop the question to a completely unsuspecting girl!"

Wiping the tears from her face, she pulled away, laughing gently. Robert tried to find something to say, but couldn't. Jenna kissed him tenderly.

Robert felt he should say *something,* so he offered, rather sheepishly, "I think Carmen will be thrilled."

Jenna bit her lip. *Oh, this sweet, wonderful man!* she thought. For the next few minutes, they talked about the future, with little concern for what was about to happen.

Then, the phone rang. It was Roland. "The plane has arrived. They've cleared customs and immigration, and on their way by limousine to the hotel. Surprisingly, there are only two bodyguards. We have not seen any other security at the airport, or at the hotel."

"Besides the team in Nice, which you so ably captured, I don't believe there is anyone else here," Robert advised him.

"Then it will be easy work for us to separate your two men from the bodyguards."

They looked intently at one another. There was only resolve on their faces now. They knew their life ahead depended on the success of this little caper. They leaned in, and kissed gently. They left the sofa to make their way to the computer to watch the monitor. There were no less than 10 cameras, complete with sensitive audio pickup, distributed around the Presidential Suite, and one pointing into the corridor. They would be able to see them arrive, and enter the suite. It would be interesting to watch how Roland's agents would deal with the two bodyguards.

Carver's limousine pulled up outside the Exedra. Within moments, a porter was out to get the luggage from the trunk. The bodyguards, sitting in the front, got out first to do a sweep of the area. One of the men brusquely pushed away the doorman who was about to open the back door. They were a bit anxious, since Gina's team was nowhere to be seen. All calls to her cell went directly to voicemail. Finally, they decided it was safe for their boss to exit the vehicle. The men stood on either side of the door, and the doorman was permitted to open it.

Carver stepped out. He was tall, slender, with short grey hair, and a very hard look on his face. Dr. Bart got out after him. He was somewhat shorter than Carver. Where Carver had the air of an aristocrat, Dr. Bart was definitely an academic. As befits a pet on a leash, Dr. Bart walked slightly behind his master. One bodyguard was ahead of them, and the other bringing up the rear. They made their way to the front desk. There was no one ahead of them.

"I need a room, your best suite," Carver commanded haughtily.

"Your name, monsieur."

"Carver, Randolph Carver.

"*Ah, mais certainement,* M. Carver. The Presidential Suite has been reserved for you, and awaits your pleasure.

"Reserved for me?"

"*Oui, monsieur*, a very lovely woman came yesterday to make the reservation."

"Do you remember her name?"

"The name of the person who made the reservation is simply Gina, monsieur."

So, she's been receiving my messages, after all, thought Carver. *Good old Gina, I can always count on her*. Carver felt much more at ease now.

He turned to Bartholomew. "Do you see her anywhere in the lobby?"

"No, I thought she might be here waiting, but I don't see her. She gave me a phone number to call when we arrived."

"Then, come to my suite as soon as your luggage is dropped off in your room." He abruptly turned, and walked away to his suite.

"Will you be staying in the same suite, monsieur?"

"No, I believe there's a room reserved for me, Dr. Terrence Bartholomew."

"*Ah, oui, Monsieur le Docteur*. A Jr. Suite has been reserved for you. We can accommodate you on the same floor as M. Carver, if you wish?"

"Yes, that would be excellent, thank you."

Carver and his bodyguards quickly made their way down the corridor from the elevator to the Presidential Suite. When they reached the door, the porter opened it, as expected. What was not expected were the four men who came out of nowhere to disable the bodyguards. The porter, stifled Carver's call, and pushed him into the room, locking the door behind him. The bodyguards, sleeping like babies, were taken to the Jr. Suite being used to detain Gina's male agents.

Roland called Robert. "The first rat is in the trap. The bodyguards are having a little nap. The second man is on his way up."

Robert and Jenna watched the whole thing unfold. Roland's team worked like a well-oiled machine. There was no sound, no shouts for help. They watched as Carver was pounding on the locked door. The porter told him to be quiet, or he would be put to sleep. Although Carver was in a rage, he knew he was no longer in control. He walked to the living room, surveying the suite. It was well chosen, he thought. He pulled out his cell phone to call Dr. Bart, to warn him. He jumped when he heard a voice coming from nowhere.

"You'll find that your cell phone is useless. There are jamming devices hidden around the room. Please make yourself comfortable until Dr. Bartholomew arrives," advised the friendly voice, which, nevertheless, carried a very serious undertone.

Carver looked at his phone. It showed the "no service" icon. He knew that rage would avail him nothing. He would have to rely on his wits, now.

Dr. Bart's porter placed his luggage on the wide bench at the foot of his bed, and retired from the room. When he left, he gave a thumbs-up to Roland's watcher down the hall. Dr. Bart splashed some water on his face to refresh himself. He would prefer to take a shower, but knew Carver's invitation was immediate. He quickly left his suite, turning towards the far end of the hall, where he could see the doors to the Presidential Suite. He saw a porter waiting there, and made nothing of it.

"Monsieur is waiting impatiently for you," advised the porter. He was given the all clear to open the door, and pushed Dr. Bart in. With the same admonition, Dr. Bart was told not to bang on the door, or make a fuss. The porter made his way to the security room, and was replaced by two of Roland's plainclothesmen on either side of the door to stand guard.

Roland called Robert again. "The rats are in the trap. *Bonne chance monsieur!*"

"Oh, *shut up*, Bartholomew! They have us at their mercy."

"Who has us at their mercy? Carpenter and her man?"

"If it is, that fellow is damned good. He's got a whole team, and all the whiz-bang toys in place. I'd like to know what happened to Gina, and her people."

"Should I call Carpenter?"

"They have jamming devices around the suite. You won't get a signal. We might as well sit down, and see what plays out."

Jenna spoke quietly into the microphone. "That's a very good idea, Mr. Carver. Well, hello, Dr. Bart. Nice to see you again. We were wondering if the two of you would travel together. Igor and his master."

Bartholomew was flustered. "What's going on here Carpenter? You can't get away with this!"

"No, Dr. Bart, it's you who won't be getting away with this."

"I assume you have a proposal for us, young lady. Let's get on with it then, shall we? I don't like negotiating with invisible people. Will we have the pleasure of your company?"

Robert's tone was gruff. "Yes, of course, but in a moment. There are a few formalities to dispense with first. Each of you will strip down to your underwear, and will put your clothes in a pile at the door to your suite. You'll find bathrobes in the bathroom. Please don't try to slip anything out of your pockets."

Carver smiled a wry smile. This man was good. He was taking no chances. He would soon get to meet his antagonist. He stood up and began to remove his clothes. Dr. Bart was blustering in protest.

"Be quiet, Bartholomew! Just do what he says, and get the robes."

Robert and Jenna wanted to laugh deliriously at the scene unfolding before them, but knew they needed to remain calm, and well disciplined. They watched Dr. Bart take the clothes to the door. As he made his way back to the living room, the door opened, and the clothes were taken away.

Robert looked at Jenna. "I guess it's our turn to make an appearance."

"I'm ready if you are, darling. In fact, I've never felt calmer.

Strange!"

"Roland here."

"We are heading to the Presidential Suite."

"We'll be watching out for you, monsieur."

Robert and Jenna walked casually out of their suite, and down the corridor to the Presidential Suite. One of Roland's men opened the door for them.

When they walked into the living area, Carver and Bartholomew were sitting on different sofas. They both caught their breath when they saw Jenna.

"It's no wonder my teams kept telling me it was impossible for you to be the woman abducted and beaten in Alberta. There's a resemblance, but you look calm, radiant, and full of confidence, Ms. Carpenter."

"Look here, Carpenter..." Dr. Bart was cut short by a frosty stare from Jenna.

"Dr. Bart, you're a disgrace to your profession, a disgrace to academia, a disgrace to archaeology and all it stands for. I'm sure Mr. Carver, here, is paying you handsomely, but you really ought to be ashamed of yourself," Jenna told him in a scathing tone. Bartholomew physically shrank deeper into the sofa.

"As for you, Carver, you're nothing but a petty thief and a thug, when it comes right down to it. You stop at nothing to get what you want—even having innocent people, including Ms. Carpenter, kidnapped and beaten. I'm sure there are a few bodies lying about on your orders too."

"Mr. Jackson, I presume. I would be very interested to know what training you've had. You managed to elude even my best teams—and quite deftly, I might add. I'd like to offer you a very lucrative position within my organization. By the way, what happened to Gina, and the team that was watching you?"

Robert and Jenna looked incredulously at one another, shaking their heads.

"You're a rather pompous ass, aren't you, Carver? We're not interested in your illegal schemes. And as for your team, who've been hounding us for the last few weeks, they're currently being questioned by the Police Judiciaire."

Carver responded in a very surly tone. "You would do well not to cross me Mr. Jackson. Others have died for less."

Robert and Carver were staring each other down. By the look of things, Robert was winning.

Jenna broke the standoff. "Then, let's get down to business, shall we? Dr. Bart, I wasn't lying to you about the Emerald Tablet."

Carver was visibly moved and excited. "Where? Where's the tablet? I'll give you one million dollars for its delivery."

"All in good time. First, you must agree to our terms..."

Carver jumped up. "What terms?"

Robert took a step forward. "Shut up! Sit down! And let the lady finish. You take one step from that sofa, and I'll flatten you," Robert threatened seriously, as he took a step forward.

Carver was trembling with rage, but he knew he was no match for the man who confronted him. This was the first time he'd ever been challenged to his face. He backed down, and sat again on the sofa.

Robert returned to Jenna's side. Jenna gently placed her hand on Robert's arm, feeling the tightness of his muscles. She knew he was good for it. *What a man!* she thought.

"As I was saying...before you get the Emerald Tablet, you must agree to our terms. Both of you just nod your agreement as we describe each term."

"What are your terms, then?"

Jenna began.

"Before we proceed, rest assured that we know the *exact* location of the Emerald Tablet, where Dr. Scott hid it.

"As you're probably aware, this entire conversation is being recorded in video and audio. You've both admitted to your complicity in the illegal acquiring of a valuable artifact, including my abduction and physical interrogation. I'm sure Interpol will be very interested. (Carver bristled at this, while Dr. Bart trembled in fear.)

"Mr. Carver, we are willing to make the tablet available to you under these conditions.

"First, Robert and I will retrieve the Emerald Tablet from its hiding place *on our own*, and without interference from either of you, or any of your *elite* teams. In fact, if we even get a hint of suspicion we're being followed, or watched, all bets are off, and the video will find its way to Interpol in several countries." (Carver and Dr. Bart nodded.)

Robert picked up where Jenna left off.

"Carver, you will have two weeks to examine the Emerald Tablet minutely, but not destructively in any way, and under strict supervision. That will give you enough time to extract its contents, and look for any kind of key hidden in the stone itself. (Carver nodded.)

"After examining the Emerald Tablet, you will generously loan the tablet to the museum of your choice, for a period of at least 15 years, to be put on public display. After that time, you may have it for your private collection. (Carver swallowed hard, but he nodded his ascent.)

"We've grown quite fond of your tracking team, Gina, Kate, and the others. They had no idea who they were up against. You will ensure there will be no reprisals of any sort against them. (Carver nodded with a wry smile.)

"Many copies of the video of this conversation will be stored in the possession of different people around the world. If *anything* strange happens to either Jenna or me, even a weird accident, the video will find its way to Interpol. This is a form of life insurance policy to make sure you don't seek revenge on us after you get the tablet. So, you've got to leave us alone to enjoy our lives. This also applies to Dr. Scott. If you have him, you must release him immediately."

Carver nodded. "I don't have Scott, and have no idea where he is. I've had people looking for him, but he seems to have vanished off the face of the earth."

Jenna now continued. "Dr. Bart, I would like to see you in prison for what you had done to me, but here's the deal. You can keep your job if you completely sever your relationship with Carver, and *never, ever*, again conspire with *anyone* to obtain rare and valuable artifacts. *Never*! Do you understand?"

Dr. Bart cowered. "Yes, I swear to you, I'll never do this kind of thing again. I will behave as befits a man of my position and education. I swear to you Ms. Carpenter."

Robert now had a wry smile of his own. "There's one more thing, Carver, I've incurred significant expenses in traipsing around looking for Dr. Scott's clues to find your precious Emerald Tablet. I expect a full reimbursement of those expenses when we hand over the tablet."

"Given the circumstances, I would be pleased to defray all those expenses. Somehow, I think yours will be somewhat less than mine." Carver had the slightest hint of a smile.

"So, we are agreed?" asked Jenna.

"Yes," was Dr. Bart's simple reply.

"I am impressed with your terms, and agree fully to what you've proposed. It would seem to be a win-win situation all around. I get possession of the Emerald Tablet, Dr. Scott, wherever he his, will have his wish that the tablet be displayed publicly, Bartholomew gets to keep his job, Gina's team is given a reprieve, and you two will have your freedom, and safety, as well as getting your expenses refunded. Quite admirable!

"I know you think very lowly of me, but I would like to get together with you sometime to talk about the strategies you used to elude my best people. You were incredibly frustrating, and incredibly adept. Which brings us to my elite team, headed up by the lovely Gina. You said they are being interrogated by the French Police Judiciaire. Would there be a possibility of intervening on their behalf? I promise you they will not be seeking revenge on you."

Robert and Jenna looked at one another and laughed heartily.

Robert walked to the door of the suite, and spoke to one of the guards. He contacted Roland to inform him that all the agents should be released as soon as the audio and video recordings were secured and copies made.

"I'm afraid your bodyguards are still having a nap, but Gina's team will be returned to you shortly to take over security detail."

"Of course! Your agents must have taken them down, and you're holding them in the hotel. You would never want the police to be involved with this whole affair."

"Your clothes will be returned now. Carver, you can stay here, if you wish, while my agents remove all the electronic devices used for this little meeting. Of course, they may ask you to wait somewhere else, so as not to give away their techniques. In the meantime, we have some travel plans to make. You may want to obtain Egyptian tourist visas."

"We'll contact you when we have the Emerald Tablet in hand. I'm sure, Mr. Carver, that you have all the necessary contacts to move the tablet to wherever you wish. You may also want to consider which museum will be the beneficiary of the tablet," added Jenna.

"Mr. Jackson, Ms Carpenter, whatever you may think of me, I keep my bargains. I place at your full disposal the private jet being used by Gina's team. I will inform the pilot he is to fly you wherever you need to go." He moved to the desk, took out a piece of paper, and wrote down the names, and phone numbers, of the flight crew, which he handed to Robert.

Over the next hour, some of Roland's agents meticulously removed all the electronics in the Presidential Suite, while others made copies of the camera video and audio. They kept one copy for their files, as agreed, and gave Robert ten additional copies on SD cards.

"M. Roland, there is one more task I would like to ask of you."

"And what would that be?"

"I think it would be prudent to have one or two of your people accompany us to our final destination, to provide some of that boring security detail, you mentioned yesterday."

Roland laughed out loud. "Somehow, monsieur, I doubt if any work for you will be boring. I'd be delighted to accompany you, along with my best female agent, Simone. May I know the destination?"

"Egypt. How long will it take you to arrange travel documents?"

"Ah, the Egyptians can be a bit slow with tourist visas. Today is Friday. The consulates will be closed until Monday. If we press gently, we might be able to have visas by mid-day on Tuesday, if that is agreeable?"

Jenna gently touched Robert's arm. "That would give us a nice long weekend in Nice, darling. Is it true, M. Roland, that women can go topless on the beaches here?"

"*Ah, oui, madame.* It is *de rigueur*—very common on most beaches in France. On some public beaches, there are even sections designated for naturists, where you can go nude."

"We will release all of the detained agents, now, if you give the authorization."

Robert nodded. "I think it is safe to do so."

In the two Jr. Suites, Roland's agents informed their captives they were to be released immediately, and told their boss was in the Presidential Suite on the 5th floor.

Simone was responsible for the female detainees. She approached Gina.

"I understand you are the leader of this team?"

"That is correct."

"Your patron is wanting to meet with you in the Presidential Suite." She saw the blood drain from Gina's face. She understood only too well that Gina would be taken to task by her employer for her team's failed mission.

Chapter 25 - Surprises

Robert and Jenna walked into the Grand Suite, locked the door, and fell onto the sofa, exhausted. The intensity of the last hour was crushing. With all their strength, and courage, they played a harmonious duet, with every note to perfection. They sat there now, side-by-side, holding hands, breathing heavily. It wasn't over yet, and they both knew it. They still had to recover the Emerald Tablet, but that seemed the easiest task on earth. All they had to do, was go to Taba, grab a couple of shovels, and dig a hole. What could be easier? Right?

They looked at one another, smiling. Neither was sure what to say. They had four nights, and three full days to enjoy one another. No watchers, no rush, no danger, no nothing! It was just the two of them.

"Is it possible, RJ? Are we done?"

"Actually getting the tablet seems so anticlimactic."

"It seems ages ago since we started on this quest, yet like it was only yesterday."

"It's been exactly one month today, Jenna, since I picked you up of that dirt road."

Jenna began to laugh, as she remembered, that day, helped along by the easing of all the tension.

"Do you remember when we arrived at your place? I was in your arms, the door was locked, and you didn't know what to do..."

"And you stuck out your arm to ring the doorbell." Then in a mock-Bogart voice, We've come a long way, baby!"

"Do you remember what you asked me just before our meeting tonight?" Her eyes were soft, her face filled with love.

"My neck is still sore from your answer! How could I possibly forget?"

Now it was Jenna's turn to swallow hard, not quite knowing

what to say. “Any thoughts on when, darling?”

Robert’s smile grew wide, and a bit cheeky. “I’m sure Carmen will be able to tell us.”

“Carmen! We’ve got to tell her!”

Robert pulled her to him, and kissed her with increasing passion. His heart pounded, his hands began to tremble. Jenna looked at him with concern. His eyes filled with tears. “Oh, God! I love you, Jenna Carpenter!” he finally shouted. She held him tight. She realized it was the very first time he spoke the words! She completely disintegrated in his arms, in a veritable sea of tears. The most beautiful words a woman can hear, and *he meant it*! She heard them before from others, but *he really meant it!* They came from deep, deep within him.

Gina waited for her team out in the corridor. One by one, they came out, stiff and sore, from being immobilized for so long. She told them to go to their rooms, and clean themselves up. They were to post two guards at the door of the Presidential Suite as soon as possible. Inside, Roland’s team was cleaning up the suites. They untied, and tucked-in the two Carver bodyguards for the night. It would be hours before they awoke.

Gina sent Kate back to their room. Kate was concerned. Gina would have to face Carver alone. It would not be a warm reception. Gina nodded to her to go. Then she took a deep breath, fixing herself up as best she could. She slowly made her way to the Presidential Suite. At the door, she took another deep breath, stood tall, and confident. She rang the bell.

Carver opened the door, and stepped aside to let her pass. After closing the door, he ushered her into the living room.

“Sit down, Gina,” He had his back to her.

“I prefer to stand, sir.” She stood tall, in the military at-ease position.

“Sit down, Gina, please.” There was no anger or malice in his voice, only a quiet softness.

Gina hadn’t heard this tone from him in a long time. She softened, moved to a sofa, and sat.

“Looking a bit dishevelled in that formal gown, my dear.” He stood there, with his back to her, looking out the window.

Gina sat quietly. She didn’t know what to say. She would let him lead; it was best that way.

“Gina, I think it’s time to take you off active duty as a tracker, and interrogator.”

No matter how hard she tried, Gina couldn't keep her eyes from filling with tears. "Does that mean you've lost confidence in me, sir?"

It took Carver what seemed an eternity before he responded. He slowly turned around. Tears were trickling down his cheeks. Gina hadn't seen tears on his face since her mother died, many years before.

"No, Gina, I've come to my senses."

He sat close beside her. Both were crying. He put his arms around her.

"I've become a hard-hearted old fool, since your mother slipped away. I forced you to become as hard as me, so you wouldn't feel the pain I felt. I was wrong," he croaked through his anguish.

"Oh, father!" She held him tight.

They held each other for several minutes. A myriad of thoughts, and memories, flowed through their minds.

"Gina, I want you to come home. Take over one of my companies. I know you're good for it."

"Father, I'd love to. I've missed you so much. I miss mother terribly."

"Thanks to me, I don't think either of us properly grieved her death."

"We can do it together, now. What made you change your mind?"

"That damned Jackson and Carpenter, with all their love, passion, and unshakable integrity! We didn't stand a chance against them!"

"No, we didn't. We couldn't figure them out at all. Whenever Kate and I were with them, we both felt more than a twinge of jealousy."

"Gina, the Emerald Tablet is the last artifact I pursue. I will be glad to get it, so I can examine it, but I think I already know its greatest secret—love conquers everything—eventually!."

"Does that mean you'll be disbanding our team?"

"I'll be discontinuing all illegal activity, and all the associated connections. I'll continue to exploit existing contacts for the sake of the greater good. All this collecting was meant to take my mind off your mother. In the end, it hasn't worked."

"Kate and I are close, father. I would like to continue that relationship in whatever capacity possible in the legitimate world."

"Of course, Gina. It's your call."

Thank you, father. I truly appreciate it."

Gina, you're not a stupid girl. You have a good head on your shoulders, and I think you already have some ideas you want to toss at me."

"Yes, sir. I sure do."

After all the stress of the past few weeks, it was nice to just lay in bed snuggling with no reason to rush. Robert and Jenna lay in each other's arms, smiling, happy. It was already eight in the morning. They knew they were just being lazy, but who cared? Jenna began to feel a touch of tension in Robert's body.

"What's going on inside there, darling?

"Could really use a good swim."

"Um, is that all?"

"It's been so crazy, I can't believe we can just relax. Seems odd, somehow, like we should be getting ready to do something, go somewhere, or planning some mayhem."

Jenna began to giggle. "You're right! Let's get up, and sneak away without having to!"

That got Robert going. He began laughing so hard the bed shook. The whole idea seemed absurd, but Jenna hit it right on. *They didn't have to sneak around anymore!*

"Jenna, whatever shall we do when we get back home? Maybe I'll have to hire someone to sneak around trying to follow us, so we can go covert again."

"Maybe I'll go to the salon to change my hair colour again, just to throw someone off. By the way, lover, which was your preference—blond, black, or red?" She expected her man to hem and haw about this, feeling it was a trick question.

His answer came without hesitation. "Forgive me, sweetheart, but you drove me to absolute distraction with that long raven hair you had in Egypt!"

"That was quick! I expected at least a moment of reflection. I'm glad you chose black, though, because it happens to be the one I enjoyed being the most. So, I'll be your raven-haired, Egyptian queen." She cuddled tighter, and he wasn't complaining.

The doorbell rang. They both froze. *What now?* she thought.

"Breakfast," chuckled Robert. Remember, I ordered last night. He quickly jumped out of bed, donned a bathrobe, and padded barefoot out of the bedroom, closing the door behind him, and down the stairs. At the front door, he peeped through the hole to find a man in waiter's livery. Robert couldn't help himself.

"*Quel est le mot de passe?*" he demanded, still observing through the peep hole.

"*Le mot de passe, monsieur?*" blurted the startled waiter.

The guard at Carver's door heard this, and began to chuckle, thinking, *Now, he's having fun!*

Robert opened the door, with a big smile on his face. He apologized for his rudeness. The waiter entered, quickly set the table, and laid out the meal. He left with a smile of his own when Robert gave him a big tip. When he was gone, Jenna came out of the bedroom, still nude, and laughing.

"RJ, that was terrible!"

"Jenna Carpenter, you look absolutely delicious!" Without another word, he dropped his bathrobe, climbed the stairs by threes, and swept her into his arms on the way back to the bedroom.

An hour later found them microwaving breakfast, which was now stone cold. They were dressed, lest they never eat again.

As they sat back enjoying a fresh cup of coffee from the Nespresso machine, the doorbell rang again. This time, they both wondered who it could be.

"Maybe it's Roland, with my bill for our little caper." He went to the door, and peeped. It was Gina. He opened the door for her. She looked different, somehow.

"Good morning, Mr. Jackson."

"Good morning, Gina, please come in, we're just having a coffee before we decide how we'll spend the day. Would you like to join us?"

"Thank you, that would be very nice."

As she entered the living room, Jenna smiled sweetly at her. "I promise you there won't be any unexpected sleep drugs, this time."

Gina chuckled. "Good morning, Ms. Carpenter, and thank you. I think I'll remember that last little jab, for a long time."

"I think it's time we were all on first name basis. Please, RJ and Jenna."

"Thank you, I'd like that." Jenna too, was noticing the change in Gina. Something must've happened.

Gina sat down on the couch, across from Jenna. Robert brought in the coffee, and handed it to her, before sitting down next to Jenna.

"I wanted to come by to thank you for all you've done." Before they could reply, Gina held up her hand to stop them. She had tears forming in her eyes. “Please let me explain. The two of you were impossible to figure out. You threw us off at every turn—with impunity. You were able to do so because of your deep love for one another.”

Gina composed herself to continue. “Last night, I expected the worst for my total failure to bring you in, or even keep you in sight. Instead, my father, Randolph Carver, reclaimed me as his daughter, and we made our amends.” She was shaking so much she had to put the coffee cup on the table. She was weeping tears of joy.

Robert and Jenna looked at one another with understanding. Jenna moved to the other sofa, sat beside Gina, and held her in her arms. Gina, didn’t resist. They stayed that way for several minutes, until Gina composed herself again. She smiled at Jenna. They held hands.

“My father and I would be pleased if you would join us for lunch today in his suite, say one o’clock?”

Jenna looked at Robert, who nodded almost imperceptibly. “We’ll be there.”

“Thank you. Kate will be joining us as well. I must go now, dad and I have a lot of catching-up to do. I’ll see myself out.” Gina, stood, gave Jenna a parting hug, and left.

“Wow! Now, *that*, I didn’t see coming!”

Jenna smiled. She reached for his hand. “Do you think there’s time to get my hair changed before lunch?”

At the appointed time, Robert and Jenna presented themselves at the door of the Presidential Suite. The guard on duty knocked, and opened the door.

“You’re to go right in, please.”

They entered the suite, and walked directly to the living room. There was a slight gasp from Carver as he saw Jenna enter the room. She was wearing a casual designer dress, and sporting her luxurious straight black hair. Carver rose to greet them, as did Gina, and Kate.

Carver extended his hand. “Ms. Carpenter, you look stunning! Another disguise?”

Jenna chuckled. “Thank you, Mr. Carver, and no, this is actually close to my natural look. It’s been quite a while since I’ve worn my hair black. My ex-husband wanted a blond, so I accommodated him, and never bothered changing back again.

You can imagine how pleased I am that RJ likes me like this."

"Mr. Jackson, very pleased to see you again."

"Maybe we could dispense with all the Mr. and Ms. stuff, and just go with first names."

"Agreed! Please call me Carver. I can't stand Randolph, which only my parents called me, or Randy, which my late wife called me. You've already met Kate Hunter, I understand."

Kate smiled, extending her hand, first to Jenna, and then a firm handshake with Robert. "I thought it might be too much giving you my last name when we first met. What with a Carver, and an Archer, a Hunter seemed a bit much."

They all laughed. It was obvious the mood was much lighter than before. Everyone was at ease. No one was on their guard.

"I must admit, Carver, RJ and I were both blown away to find out Gina is your daughter."

"Yes, that was a well-kept secret amongst my contacts, and various covert teams." He went on to explain that after the sudden death of his wife some fifteen years prior, he changed, became a hard and bitter man, and hard on his daughter as well. He pointed to a small framed picture on the side table. It was the spitting image of Gina. "You can see where Gina gets her good looks. Her mother was a stunner, to be sure."

"I understand exactly what you mean, Carver. I lost my precious wife just over five years ago. In my case, I simply withdrew from business, society, everything. The pain and the loss get to you."

"Yes, RJ, it does. And then, in comes a marvellous woman named Jenna Carpenter to completely turn all our lives inside-out."

Jenna blushed deeply. Not knowing what to say, she reached out, taking Robert's arm, and squeezing it. Everyone burst out laughing.

"And, I think, we're all very glad you did, especially that man you're holding onto so tightly, young lady! If not for you, none of us would be here, and none of us would be feeling the joy we now have in our hearts."

"Well, someone had to do it!"

Everyone laughed, as they gathered around her. She certainly was the catalyst that changed so many lives.

"By the way, since all eyes are on Jenna, I have the pleasure of announcing that Jenna has consented to be my wife."

"Well, this requires champagne!"

Gina looked in mock seriousness around the room. "I wonder where Simone has gotten to, I'm sure she'll have some."

They all laughed hard at this, except Carver, who didn't understand the joke. Gina took his arm, and explained that Simone was one of RJ's agents, acting as bartender at their fateful take-down dinner.

Lunch arrived, and was served. They all sat at table, trading jokes, and inside stories. Quiet Kate finally spoke up, asking for details of how Robert and Jenna managed to elude, and escape them so handily. There was a great deal of mirth as they explained, in glowing detail, how they played their game. In the end, Carver reiterated his offer of the night before, that he wanted them both in his organization. Jenna thanked him, but made it clear, Robert would be a member of only one organization—hers!

"I don't think I've had quite as much fun as this in a very long time. What do you think Gina, dear?"

"No, dad, not in a terribly long time!"

"Gina, and I have a lot to talk about. I've had a tremendous change of heart about a lot of things. There are new ideas, and possibilities, milling around in my mind, that I want to discuss with her, and her very able friend, Kate."

"I think even you will be surprised," said Kate.

"RJ, Jenna, I offered you the use of my private jet last night. Today, I want to offer you the services of my very capable daughter and Kate. They could be of great use to you in case anyone else is trying to get at the Emerald Tablet. You see, I'm concerned about the disappearance of Dr. Scott. That was not of my doing. I fear a competitor has taken him, and if that's correct, you'll be in danger when you retrieve the tablet."

"We've already taken precautions against that very situation, Carver."

"The agents you hired for your little escapade of the last couple of days?"

"Yes, we're waiting for them to obtain Egyptian visas before we make a move. Our visas are still good for another week or so after we leave here."

"They're good agents, dad. They took us down quickly, and effectively. Of course, we were lulled into a false sense of security by our genial hosts here." Gina smiled teasingly at Robert and Jenna.

"Don't remind me! That was positively embarrassing!"

exclaimed Kate, resulting in more laughter from around the table.

"Still, if you will allow it, I would like Gina and Kate to watch over you when you go in."

Robert smiled as he looked at Jenna. "Maybe, we're the ones being lulled into a false sense of security, now, darling."

Gina glanced at Kate, and her father. "They're good! They don't miss anything. Always thinking."

"Yes, Gina. They are *very* good. But I assure you there's no malice, or covert intent in making this offer. You've gotten this far, but this is the last step, and take if from someone who knows, this is usually when the earth falls away from under your feet."

Jenna squeezed Robert's hand under the table. They looked at one another, and smiled. Robert squeezed back.

"RJ and I would be delighted to have Gina and Kate accompany us. Two of our hired agents will also be acting as bodyguards—including Simone, I understand."

"We're planning a mid-Tuesday departure. I'll inform M. Roland, the team lead, of the change. I would still prefer Roland to be the lead on this little junket as well. I was very impressed with his abilities. No offence meant, Gina."

"No offence taken, I assure you. His team was very slick. Kate and I would be happy to serve under his supervision."

Robert took out his phone, and immediately placed a call to Roland. Roland listened to what Robert was telling him. He asked Robert if he was 100% certain of the loyalty of the two women they had detained only last night. Robert indicated there were massive changes since then, and he would be confident placing his life, and Jenna's, in their hands. Roland agreed to the change.

"Your confidence in us is not misplaced, RJ," Kate assured him.

"May we know the final destination," asked Gina.

"Back, back, back, to the beginning!" said Jenna. "Taba, Egypt. That was the last clue."

Everyone groaned. It was to be expected.

"Your plans? If you care to share." asked Kate.

"We'll probably have to clear customs and immigration in Cairo, so that will be the first stop. If possible, we'd like to fly directly to the Taba International Airport. The Internet says it's only charters that use this airport—no commercial airlines. Hopefully, we'll be able to rent a couple of vehicles there. We'll stay at the Swiss Inn, where we stayed before. My only concern is raising suspicion showing up with four bodyguards."

"Our original watchers were at the Mövenpick, weren't they, dad?"

"Yes, that's right."

"I would suggest that RJ and Jenna return to the Swiss Inn alone. They're known there and won't raise any suspicion. The rest of us could book in at the Mövenpick, and take turns watching. When it's time to retrieve the tablet, RJ and Jenna can go directly to the location, while Kate and I take one vehicle, and Roland and Simone take a second vehicle to protect their flanks, hopefully without attracting attention."

"It might be hard not to attract attention, Gina. The location is out in the middle of nowhere. The only thing we're likely to spot out there are scorpions. It might not attract attention for one vehicle to go off-roading, but three, I don't know."

"We need to get Roland in here to go over the details. He might have some good ideas."

Robert pulled out his phone, and contacted Roland again. Roland agreed that everyone should be on the same page. They settled on a meeting in the Grand Suite at 16:00.

"Carver, are you in on this?"

"Well now, that would be a first! "Count me in!"

Back in their suite, Robert and Jenna prepared for the meeting. They asked the hotel for an assortment of juices and water, along with some snacks. He also requested a free-standing whiteboard with markers. Robert had what he needed to hook his tablet into the large TV in their suite. They understood it was important for detailed plans to be made sooner than later, to allow the team to arrange what they needed here, and at the destination.

When everyone arrived, they all took seats around the dining table which was repositioned to have a good view of the whiteboard and TV. Introductions were made all around by Robert and Jenna.

At first there was some tension between the parties, but after a while of back-and-forth shuttling of ideas, they were all on-side, with respect building for each other. In the end, a very detailed plan, along with several fallback contingencies was agreed upon.

Even Carver was in the thick of things, it was up to him to gather together all the authorities needed to safeguard the tablet, and ensure it would make its way to the selected museum. The biggest problem would be the Egyptian and Jordanian antiquities people, but Carver felt he already had them well under his control. They didn't need to know of his change of heart, only that an artifact needed to be moved without undue bureaucratic red tape.

It was a gruelling three-hour meeting, and everyone was exhausted, but they were all on the same page. All the necessary information was recorded, sketched, saved, and everyone had their to-do list.

After the others left, Robert and Jenna looked at one another. Compared to their previous movements, this was proving to be a monumental task. They began to wonder if they should've simply slipped away, gone to Taba on their own, dug up the tablet, and *then*, call everyone.

They decided the best way to de-stress was a nice soak in the big tub, so this is exactly what they did. After a long, romantic soak, they dressed formal, and made their way to the main dining room, where a table was always reserved for the Grand Suite. They ordered some wonderful seafood dishes, and feasted.

It was ten when they returned to their suite, realizing they forgot to do one thing.

"Hola!"

"Hola, Carmen!"

Carmen spoke excitedly. "Señor Robert! It is so nice to hear from you again! Are you well? Are you coming home soon? Can I return home again?"

They both laughed to hear her.

"Carmen, slow down!" Jenna told her.

"*Sí, señora. ¡Perdon!*"

"Carmen, before we answer your questions, there's something you need to know. Señora Jenna and I will be married when we return."

"*¡Ay! ¡Qué susto! ¡Ay!*" Carmen shouted so loud, they jumped.

Then she started crying. They knew these were tears of joy, of course. They waited a moment.

"Carmen, calm down!" said Robert, gently. "It's okay."

Slowly the crying abated. They could hear Carmen blowing her nose.

"Señor, señora, I am so happy for you!"

"Thank you, Carmen," said Jenna.

"Carmen, you can return home again, and you can tell Andrea, and Jake they can return as well. I will notify the security service you are returning."

"Sí, señor. I will leave shortly. I will have everything ready for you." She was still sobbing quietly.

"Carmen, I would like you to take all of the clothes out of the boxes and hang them up in the room, ready for Jenna when she returns with me."

"Sí, señor. All the clothes will be pressed, ready to wear."

"All is well with us, Carmen," Jenna assured her. "I expect we will be home in about a week. We only have one more thing to do here. When we get back, we'll have about a million pictures to show you. Then, you can cry."

"Perdon, for my crying. I love you both so much. I am filled with joy you are getting married. It will be a happy house again."

"Carmen, I have sent many parcels to Señora Matheson's home because there was no one to receive them at our home. When you're ready, you can perhaps get them from her?"

"Sí, señor, I will get the parcels."

"Now, Carmen, you need to sit down for a few minutes, and have a nice cup of tea, and maybe some soup. You've had such a big shock," suggested Jenna.

Carmen finally began to laugh. "Sí, señora, a nice cup of tea of camomile will calm me down."

"We'll call you before we leave for home, to let you know we're coming."

"Sí, señor. We will all be waiting with excitement."

When they rang off, they both looked at one another, and burst out laughing.

"Poor Carmen! She completely fell apart!"

"Carmen is a tough old bird, but soft as mush on the inside. She's been needling me for at least a couple of years to get off my backside, and become a human being again. It took you to do that!"

Jenna chuckled. "And when you return to society, it will be as anything you choose: travel, adventure, covert operations, finding lost artifacts, reuniting families, and making one particular lady the happiest woman on the planet."

With the two full days they had left, Robert and Jenna enjoyed themselves. They were no longer looking out for trackers, so it was easy for Roland to secretly have agents always watching their backs. They were very discreet. Although they expected nothing to happen, they made sure it stayed that way.

On the Sunday, Jenna wanted to go to the beach. She knew there would probably be a mass of people there, which suited her, since it would be her first topless outing, and the crowd afforded greater anonymity. Robert was fine with that, although he was a tad concerned about his own reaction.

When Roland's watchers realized they were heading to the beach, they called in a male-female pair of agents to take over. Even on the beach, the agents blended in, with the female going topless, and definitely not looking out of place with all the other 'beautiful' people.

Monday was a shopping day. Robert and Jenna visited many shops in Nice, and made lots of purchases. Most of the things Jenna bought were for her friends, but there were other items for RJ's staff, and for herself. She insisted on paying for these things with her own credit card.

As they passed a jewellery store, Jenna saw something in one of the display windows. It was a magnificent watch. There were other items there she admired, but it was the watch she was really looking at. They walked on, sitting down at a quiet little café. They ordered coffee, and would share a pastry. Jenna quietly excused herself, telling Robert to wait right there, and vanished down the street. Needless to say, Robert was surprised, and very curious. But he obediently followed instructions, sitting, patiently sipping his coffee.

Some twenty minutes later, Jenna returned—all smiles, and hardly able to contain herself. She sat next to him, took a sip of her lukewarm coffee, reached into her purse, and pulled out a gift box. She placed the box on the table before him. He opened the box to find a beautiful Seiko Antron solar-powered, GPS-controlled watch. He was speechless. He knew this was an expensive watch, and probably sent her credit card over the limit. It was her first major gift to him. He leaned in, and kissed her tenderly. The new watch was on the right time, so he took off his old watch, and slipped on the new one. Jenna spent the next few minutes excitedly explaining how it would need to be kept in the light for a couple of days to be fully charged, and how the time would automatically change when he moved from one time zone to another. A perfect watch for her very own adventure hero.

On their last morning, they snuggled together, in blissful happiness. They all but forgot about the Emerald Tablet, and their last sortie. They had breakfast in their suite. They wanted to take their time to prepare to leave for Cairo. They lounged around in their robes. Robert was feeling very amorous, and paid Jenna a lot of affectionate attention.

When the suite phone rang, they both groaned. Robert picked it up.

"Bonjour, M. Jackson."

"Bonjour, Roland."

"Everything is ready for departure, monsieur. We leave at your command."

"Very well. We will leave for the airport in an hour. Let's all meet in the lobby."

"Very good, monsieur. I will notify the others immediately."

"Thank you, Roland. As always, the master of efficiency."

"Well, Jenna, it's time to get our game hats back on."

"With luck, we'll be in Taba this evening, and checked-in at the hotel, in time for a nice spa treatment," Jenna replied with a broad grin. "You know, to keep up our cover!" As she spoke, she loosed the sash of her robe, taking on a very sultry attitude.

"You sexy vixen, don't you dare. It's tough enough as it is!" But there was nothing for it. Jenna was tugging gently at her lower lip with her teeth.

An hour later, the phone rang again. Robert picked up, explaining they were running a little bit late. They heard the others laughing in the background.

Carver's private jet touched-down in Cairo at 17:45 local time. Egyptian customs and immigration were there to meet the jet as soon as it landed, as was the fuel truck. The jet was in the air, en-route to Taba, in an hour. It was obvious Carver used his many contacts in Egypt for such a quick turnaround. At 19:45 local time, everyone was deplaning at the Taba International Airport. As Robert previously reported, it was an airport used for charter flights into the area. Here again, Carver's contacts came through. There were three SUVs standing by.

Robert and Jenna's luggage was placed in the back of one of the SUVs. The GPS was set to the Swiss Inn Dream Resort Hotel, where they were staying. They were glad to have the GPS as it was already dark. Carver, Gina, and Kate, took the second vehicle, while Roland and Simone took the third. It was decided in the planning meeting that the Carver vehicle would take point, Robert and Jenna in the middle, and Roland's vehicle would take the rear.

It was normally a 45-minute drive from the airport to the hotel, but Gina, who was driving the lead vehicle, drove fast, getting them there in 32 minutes flat. Robert had no trouble keeping up with her, but Jenna was hanging on for dear life. As they approached the Swiss Inn, the convoy slowed down, with Robert peeling away down the roadway into the hotel. The other two vehicles continued on to the Mövenpick Hotel, just a few minutes away.

Robert and Jenna were recognized immediately by the desk clerk, who welcomed them warmly. They were given their old suite, which suited them fine. When asked if they would want dinner, they declined, explaining they ate in the plane on their way in. It took a moment for the clerk to realize they had flown into the Taba airport. Suddenly, their presence took on a heightened importance.

"Perhaps you are part of the various delegations gathering at the Mövenpick Hotel, not far from here."

"What sort of gathering?"

"There are important antiquities officials, museum representatives, and even Interpol has agents there," he replied. "In a small place like Taba, you find out about these things quickly."

"I'm afraid we don't know any of those people. We loved the diving at Pharaoh's Island, and decided to come back for another dive, and perhaps a little cruise on the Gulf of Aqaba, before we return to Canada."

Once they were alone in their suite, Robert made a quick call to Roland.

"Just thought you should know, Roland, everyone seems to think there's some kind of special gathering going on at the Mövenpick—antiquities and museum reps, even Interpol."

"Ah, this will make it more interesting when you go for the item, monsieur. All these people were expected, of course, but they were not supposed to arrive for at least another day or two. M. Carver must have put the wind up with them."

"I think Jenna and I will go to our fallback cover of being two people in love, out for one last kick at Taba before heading home. It has worked for us before, and we want some of the dust to settle before we tear out into the wilderness to fetch the item."

"Your plans, then, M. Jackson?"

"Diving tomorrow at Pharaoh's Island, and perhaps a little boat cruise on the Gulf on Thursday. Since Friday is a religious day, that would make Saturday, retrieval day. Maybe you can talk to Carver about having a meeting with the authorities tomorrow, to keep them occupied."

"Very well, I will inform the team. Someone will be watching your back the whole time."

They rang off. Robert and Jenna burst out laughing.

"It was so much easier when it was just us, darling," Jenna admitted.

"Yes, this is getting a bit ridiculous. If I had my druthers, we'd be out there digging right now."

"Too bad it's dark already. Maybe we can sneak out early tomorrow, go to the site, and dig the tablet out."

"Good idea, sweetheart, but the locals' curiosity is piqued, and we arrived by jet, not a long, hot trip from Cairo, like last time. They'll be keeping an eye on us to see if we're part of *the gathering*."

"You're right—as always! For some reason, I'm beat! The pool looked so inviting. What do you say, my love? Time for a little dip before we turn in?"

"Absolutely! Let's go!"

Scott had his arms around Zahra, as she was making breakfast. She complained, in a teasing way, that she was going to end up making a mess. They both laughed. She turned around in his arms, putting hers around his neck. They kissed gently, tenderly. As they were doing so, Zahra's phone rang. It was early for a social call. They both looked at it with some misgivings. This could not be good.

Zahra answered it, and put it on speaker, so her husband could hear.

"Zahra, it is Ahmed, there is much happening here in Taba."

"What is happening, Ahmed?"

Ahmed took a deep breath. "Many strangers have arrived. Most are staying at the Mövenpick—authorities from antiquities department and museums, Interpol, others who look like security. Lots of big shots. The Canadian couple has returned also, and they are staying again at the Swiss Inn."

"It sounds like there is a group here to dig up the artifact I buried months ago. Can you contact the Canadian woman, Jenna Carpenter?"

"There are no watchers on them yet that I can see, so maybe I can get close to them."

"Go buy a new mobile phone, with a prepaid card. Call Zahra to give her the number, then give the phone to the Canadian lady, and tell her it is important, someone will call her. Let us know when you give her the phone."

"And please continue to let us know what is happening," added Zahra.

"Very good. I will do what you say, goodbye."

Scott and Zahra looked at one another with some concern.

"What are your thoughts, my husband?"

"I'm not sure what to think. If Jenna and her man are here to dig up the artifact, who are all the others? Why are they here? That's why I want to speak to her."

"Are you worried for her?"

"Yes, Zahra, my love, I am worried for her. It is strange that they are at the Swiss Inn while all the others are at the Mövenpick. Does that mean they are not aware of the others? Perhaps Carver knows they're here, and will take the tablet from them when they dig it up."

"Is it usual for this man, Carver, to bring the authorities with him, and the international police?"

"Ah, that is another puzzle. The security people could be from Carver to get the tablet, but I have no idea why authorities are here, particularly Interpol. He would want to stay away from Interpol at all cost."

Zahra sighed. "I feel much stress in your body. I think it will be better for us when this artifact is found. Then you will not stress over it anymore."

"Soon, I think, all will change—for the good. Besides, there is nothing I can do about it, and there is nothing I will do to spoil our life together!"

It was seven in the morning, on what promised to be another glorious clear day. Robert and Jenna lay snuggling as usual. There was a calm, and yet it was an edgy calm. They both felt it, talked about it. They just wanted to get it over with, so they could move on to their wonderful life together. Finally, Robert groaned, as he pulled himself away from his gorgeous bride-to-be. He donned his trunks, and extended his hand to Jenna. She too groaned, as he pulled her up, and into his arms. She dug out her one-piece swimsuit. She knew this would be a gruelling session in the pool—and she was right.

An hour or so later, they were sitting in the dining room

waiting for their meal to be served. They sat there quietly, gazing into each other's eyes, holding hands. Certainly, their love hadn't diminished. It was deep and steady. They took their time with breakfast, sitting back, sipping their coffee. They wondered if the watchers were at their post, or if they slept in; there was no sign of them.

They decided to take a little walk around the hotel, like they did the first time, looking at the flower beds, and surreptitiously glancing around for any sign of the watchers. There was no one. They walked, hand-in-hand, towards the beach. They noticed a boat coming down near the shore. A man in the boat was waving, and calling to them. As the boat approached, they noticed there was no one else nearby, and wondered why.

"You want nice little ride in boat?" the man shouted at them. He was dressed neatly in the local style. The boat approached as close as it dared, so as not to hit bottom. There were two other men in the boat, dressed similarly. One of the other men jumped into the water, and held the boat in place. The first man jumped in, wading to the shore. Jenna found it funny they didn't seem to mind getting wet.

"I am Ahmed." As he drew nearer, his face was easier to see. It was well-weathered, as though he worked outside most of the time. The third man in the boat jump out, and was headed for them from the other side.

Robert was concerned. "Looks like they're trying to divide our attention. Take off your shoes, and get ready to run directly away from the farthest man. I'll take down the closest one."

Jenna kicked off her shoes, and picked them up. "Remember, darling, I'm well trained in martial arts, and I'm not running anywhere!"

Neither was smiling anymore, and both were wondering where the watchers were hiding. The second man on the beach walked slightly past them, but made no indication that he would approach any closer.

"We have a nice little boat." Ahmed's eyes were moving across the beach, and beyond. He was scanning the area for trouble. A quick glance at the other man suggested he was doing the same.

Ahmed moved in closer, focusing on Jenna. Robert moved to block his path. Ahmed held his hand up, as a warning to stop.

He spoke very softly. "Lady, are you Jenna Carpenter?"

Robert touched her arm, as if telling her not to say anything. Jenna looked closely at Ahmed, trying to detect any sign of deceit, or threat. When she was satisfied, she replied, "Yes, I am Jenna Carpenter."

He spoke very softly. "You know a man named Scott?"

"Yes, I used to work with him in Canada."

Ahmed's face lit up. He reached into the folds of his tunic, and pulled out a mobile phone. "You must take this. He will call." He switched to a loud voice. "I am sure you will like our little boat, very clean, nice trip, you see."

They both realized he was saying this for the benefit of a small group of tourists walking by behind them.

"Maybe tomorrow, we will make a trip in your boat. Today we go diving at Pharaoh's Island."

"Ah good, mister. What is the time tomorrow? Better before sun too strong."

"At ten o'clock tomorrow morning. Where shall we meet you?"

"At dock, near Hilton; ask for Ahmed, yes?"

"Until tomorrow then, Ahmed." Robert extended his hand. Ahmed shook his hand furiously.

The two men returned quickly to the boat, and with a wave, they set off down the coast.

Jenna looked at the phone in her hand. She was rather puzzled. "Looks like I have a new phone, RJ."

"That has to be the weirdest part of this quest!"

"Do you really think Dr. Scott will call me on this phone?"

They sat down in the sand, discussing what just happened. It was obvious that Ahmed was happy he found the right person, judging by his big toothy grin. As they sat there baffled, the phone rang. Jenna was so surprised, she dropped it in the sand. She quickly picked it up again.

"Hello!"

"Jenna, how the heck are you?" thundered the voice at the other end.

"Dr. Scott? You're alive?

Scott chuckled. "Yes, it's me alright, and if I were dead, I wouldn't be talking to you. I'm sure you have a hundred questions, but they'll have to wait. Scuttlebutt has it you've got yourself a man. Is he there with you?"

"Um, yes, sir. Robert Jackson and I are engaged. He's sitting beside me now."

"Oh, just call me Scotty, forget this Dr. and sir business. Are you alone and able to talk?"

"Yes sir, um Scotty. We're sitting on the beach, rather

bewildered."

"Are you in Taba again to dig up the tablet? Did you find the last clue?"

"Yes, Scotty, in Nice," replied Robert, more to let his presence be known.

"Excellent! Are you aware of a gathering of vultures at the nearby Mövenpick Hotel?"

"Yes, we've been made aware. Some of those people are with us, but we don't want anyone to know they're with us, if that makes any sense."

"You might be surprised by this, Scotty, but Randolph Carver, and two of his agents, along with two of our own agents, accompanied us here," added Robert.

"Carver! Jenna, have you thrown in with that scum?

"Not in the way you're thinking, Scotty. We needed to come to some sort of arrangement about the tablet, or he would've been chasing us all over the world. His trackers have been dogging us since we left Alberta. In Athens, we started getting friendly with the trackers. We were still able to give them the slip, and we're still the only ones who know the exact coordinates where the tablet is buried. In Nice, we sprung a trap on Carver and Dr. Bart..."

"Bart! Are you telling me *Bartholomew* is in on this too?"

"Yes, sir. Dr. Bart was a Carver informant. He called Carver after I showed him your note. Carver's goons kidnapped, drugged, and beat me. That's when RJ, Robert, came to my rescue. As I was saying, in Nice, we got them into a trap where they were compromised, which is all on video. When Carver saw he had no choice, he agreed to our terms."

"Whatever you do, *don't trust Carver*!"

"Scotty, a lot of things have changed in the last weeks. Carver is actually on our side now. The antiquities, and museum, people are here at his behest to take charge of the tablet," advised Robert.

"What?"

"That's right, sir. Everything has turned around. The only concern we have is why they're here so soon. Even Carver was surprised. There's also word that some Interpol agents are here as well. They were *not* invited to this little party."

"So, you haven't unearthed the tablet yet?"

"No, sir...Scotty...We were going to do that today, but the 'gathering of vultures,' as you call them, caused us to change our plans. We're playing the role of tourists for now, until we know what's happening at the Mövenpick. When we feel everything is good-to-go, we'll go to the location. We'll have a security detail on both sides, on the lookout for trouble."

"We're hoping things will be sorted out by Saturday," said Robert. "They're all meeting today to decide things. Our lead agent will let us know if we can move or not."

"You have agents?"

"We hired a private security firm to help us set the trap for Carver and Bart. They took down all the Carver watchers, then his private bodyguard. They also did all the video work. They're efficient, and very effective. M. Roland is chef d'équipe, but we call the shots."

"Good grief! This is right out of the pages of a spy thriller!"

"You're absolutely right, Scotty. We thought digging up the Emerald Tablet would be the easiest part, but it's turning out to be the most complicated. We even had a phone handed to us by a grinning boatman."

"Maybe a bit of overkill, Jenna, but I thought it prudent. Oh, congrats on your engagement. I'm married now, myself."

"How wonderful!"

"More on that later. Right now, we need to figure out what to do about that damned tablet. You can trust those fellows who gave you the phone. They're close associates of my wife, Zahra. It's thanks to them I'm still alive. I'll call you this evening, if that's convenient, and you can bring us up-to-speed on the Mövenpick meetings."

"Okay, Scotty. In the meantime, we're going diving at Pharaoh's Island again."

"It's best if you don't mention you spoke to me, or that you know I'm alive and well—for now, anyway."

Scott disconnected. Robert and Jenna were a bit startled. Out of the blue emerged Dr. Ambrose Scott, author of this little intrigue. Not only was he in good health, he was married, too! What else could possibly happen?

Carver had truly outdone himself in terms of gathering authorities of importance regarding the recovery of the Emerald Tablet. Although he told the participants not to arrive until Saturday, or Sunday, they all arrived the previous day—the same day as Robert and Jenna's entourage.

He sat at the head of the large boardroom table. Gina and Kate sat on his right, Roland and Simone on the left. There was some concern about leaving Jackson and Carpenter unprotected, but they all felt they could probably handle anything odd that came their way. Further down the table were the group of officials who were already arguing amongst themselves.

There were two senior representatives from the Egyptian Ministry of State for Antiquities. They were invited because the Emerald Tablet was now on Egyptian soil. It was important to get their approval to relocate the tablet to any other country.

Across from them, sat Dr. Shareef El-Amin of the Department of Antiquities of Jordan, who was initially responsible for the dig at Tel Al Hajiwa.

There were deputy-curators representing three museums Carver contacted to offer the Emerald Tablet for display. These included The Royal Ontario Museum, in Toronto, The British Museum, in London, and the Louvre, in Paris.

Besides arguing noisily, the officials all wondered who the people at the head of the table might be. They all felt one of their own should be conducting the meeting.

The two Interpol agents, who were known to be on the property, did not approach anyone regarding the Emerald Tablet, or the meeting about to begin. No one knew exactly why they were on the scene in the first place. Carver could only speculate they wanted to be on hand to apprehend anyone trying to steal the tablet—like Carver himself.

Carver sat quietly, observing the chaos before him. He turned to look at Gina, and rolled his eyes. Gina had to use all her discipline to keep from bursting out laughing. Finally, he stood. Without saying a word, everyone stopped talking, and took their seats. Gina was in awe of her father. His haughtiness exuded power, and commanded authority.

When Carver introduced himself, there was an audible gasp from the officials. They all knew of him, and they all feared him. He then introduced his daughter, Kate, Roland, and Simone as security advisors.

Carver explained they should be having the meeting *after* the Emerald Tablet was recovered, and sitting before them. He told them harshly, that because they descended, *en-masse*, the persons who so diligently, and expertly followed Dr. Scott's clues to the tablet's final resting place, had been spooked, and backed away from getting the tablet, because they were now unsure of its disposition. When they began protesting, he simply held up his hand, and the room fell silent again.

"Ladies, and gentlemen, we cannot leave this room without having agreed on the final disposition of the Emerald Tablet.

"We need to assure these persons about the safety of the tablet, and where it will be displayed, and studied. We also need to assure these persons of their own personal safety. After all, they did not seek out the tablet for their own gain. They sought out the tablet so it could be available to humanity, which is exactly why Dr. Scott hid the tablet, the moment he found it.

"As I am sure you all know, I have been a collector of antiquities for many years. Dr. Scott was rightly concerned I, and other private collectors, would want it for ourselves. In fact, I mounted an all-out effort to recover the tablet for myself. He wanted to keep that from happening, so he hid the tablet here in Egypt. We now know he prepared riddles written in an obscure language, and hid them across Egypt, and many foreign countries while he was on his unofficial vacation.

"The courageous persons who found Dr. Scott's original note and first clue, then followed each link to the next. They did so despite my considerable efforts to pursue and take them. They consistently eluded my best trackers. Whenever they wanted to disappear, they did. And please note, they are not trained agents. We're talking about an archaeological research assistant, and a real estate mogul.

"I called you all here because you are all involved in what happens to the Emerald Tablet. It was found in a dig in Jordan, and buried again in Egypt. I chose what I consider to be the three most respected and honoured museums I know of, and they are represented here as possible resting places of the tablet.

"So, let us all discuss this situation honourably, and reach a firm consensus. As I said, we will not leave here until this consensus is reached. There are toilet facilities adjacent, and if necessary, I will have food brought in. Are there any questions?"

"Are you telling us you don't want the Emerald Tablet for yourself?" asked one of the antiquities officials.

"That is correct. After a discussion with the tablet seekers, I had a complete change of heart on the matter. Like them, and Dr. Scott, I agree this artifact is of great importance, and should be studied, and offered to the world at large."

The next ten hours were fraught with disagreements. Attendees were surprised that a security advisor accompanied them to the toilet, and made sure they didn't wander off. Allegiances were made, and subsequently broken. Carver moved about, speaking to each of the guests, individually, and then in pairs. There is no doubt his subtle, and not so subtle, diplomacy won the day.

"It is agreed, then, that the Emerald Tablet, will rotate, on a five-year basis, between the Royal Ontario Museum, the Jordan Museum, the British Museum, the Egyptian Museum, and the Louvre, in that order," summarized Carver.

When everyone ratified the proposal, Carver asked Gina to draft up an agreement which would be signed by all before anyone left the room. It took her about thirty minutes to come up with wording acceptable to all participants, and still be strong enough to resist challenges. When everyone signed all copies of the agreement, the room was opened, and some very exhausted attendees left.

Carver, and his security advisors, returned to his suite. Roland called Robert a few times to make sure all was well with them. They seemed to be taking it well, playing their role as tourists.

Robert and Jenna were having a great time at Pharaoh's Island. They weren't looking for clues anymore, so they could truly enjoy the underwater spectacle. They wandered about, just being in love. They both knew it would soon be over, and they'd be on their way home. From time-to-time, they wondered what was happening at the Mövenpick. Roland called to check on their status, but reported only that the meeting was chaos.

Although their official security detail was not in place, they never felt in danger. Their boatmen were standing off, never too far from the shore, keeping an eye on them. They knew it was Scott who sent them to make sure they weren't harmed. Jenna thought it was very sweet of him.

They had a wonderful, leisurely day, with a lot of discussion about the wedding. Jenna couldn't believe the total change in her life since she found the note in early June. She kept pinching herself to make sure it was all real. Robert was in heaven. A man could consider himself exceedingly fortunate to find one woman devoted to him, but to find two—that was nothing short of a miracle!

It was about ten o'clock in the evening when Scott called again. They told him there was nothing to report yet from the gathering of vultures. He simply laughed, offering his insight on the workings of archaeology, and the length of meetings. They were still speaking to him when Robert's phone rang. It was

Carver. He explained the agreement the group nailed down the whole of that day. With everything in place, they could retrieve the tablet at their leisure. Robert had the phone on speaker so Jenna could hear, but Scott could hear as well. He was amazed that Carver brokered such a deal. After Carver rang off, Scott asked what their plans were. Robert and Jenna agreed they would discuss their options.

"RJ, this is so unreal, and I can't get rid of a feeling of pending doom."

"Yes, I'm feeling it too. There's something wrong in this whole mix-up here. What are your thoughts, darling?"

"I'm thinking we should've disappeared, as we always did, and come here alone."

"We had to get an agreement in place with Carver, before we could go dig up the tablet. And the Carver-Gina father-daughter thing blew everything to bits. I think Carver is genuinely on our side."

"Same with Gina and Kate, and I don't get any bad feelings about Roland and Simone either. So, what is it?"

They looked at one another, and the light bulb came on simultaneously. "Scott!" they both blurted out at the same time.

"RJ, Scott has been the dark horse in this entire quest. We really only have his word the Emerald Tablet exists at all. There were no pictures, and the description was vague, to say the least."

"But why would Scott go to the trouble, and expense, of creating a bunch of riddles in Esperanto, and hiding them in so many places? It doesn't make sense."

"Maybe he's been out in the sun too long, and he's gone gaga!"

Robert laughed. "You may be right! But, in the meantime, what do we do?"

Jenna snuggled up next to him, slipped her hand through his arm, and gave it a squeeze, with a sly little smile on her face. Robert couldn't figure her out.

"What would my action hero do, in this case, my love?"

Robert broke into a grin of his own. "Go for a walk, of course!"

They decided to go for a walk around the pool area. There was no one about, so they could let the stress fade into love. They both breathed the cool night air, as they watched, in fascination, the splashing fountains with their rotating colours. Neither spoke much. They walked to the pool. Jenna had shorts on, so she sat down on the edge with her feet paddling in the water. She was surprised to see Robert pull up his pant legs, and slip off his shoes and socks, to join her. She leaned against him, staring into the illuminated pool.

"Maybe we take the day off tomorrow," she suggested.

"Ah, I think I know what you're up to; hold back and see who twitches."

"No, darling. I just want to go on a little cruise on the Gulf of Aqaba–honest!" With a little giggle, she squeezed his arm at the same time.

In the morning, everyone thought they would hear from Robert and Jenna to know their plans for unearthing the tablet. They gave them plenty of time, remembering they were deeply in love. By ten o'clock, Carver was pacing in his suite. His security advisors were there too, and getting a bit antsy. Finally, Carver could take it no longer. He called, putting them on speaker.

"We're all sitting here wondering what your plans are for today."

"We're going on a little boat ride down the Gulf," replied Jenna. They all had the same shocked look on their faces.

"You realize we have a solid agreement with the authorities."

"Oh, yes, we know, but these three crazy guys want to take us out for a boat ride. We decided to go. They promised to show us some really cool things only the locals know about."

"Perhaps one of the teams should go with you," offered Roland. "After all, you're the only ones who know where this tablet is located, and we wouldn't want anything to happen to you."

"I think we'll be fine. We have some company coming along—a couple of Interpol agents. Ta-ta, for now. We'll call you when we get back. If you're so inclined, you really have to dive the reef off Pharaoh's Island." With that, Jenna rang off. They spoke to Scott earlier, and gave him the same story.

"What, in hell, are they up to now?"

Gina laughed. "They're just being RJ and Jenna, dad. They're not in a hurry. This quest has been pure romance for them."

Carver sighed. "Never a dull moment, with those two!" At this, everyone in the room laughed heartily.

"I'm just concerned about those two Interpol agents. Why are they here, and why are they joining Robert and Jenna on their cruise?" wondered Roland.

Robert and Jenna had a marvellous cruise with Zahra's

fishermen friends. They visited some beautiful coastline on the Egyptian side of the Gulf. The Interpol agents told many stories from cases past.

When Robert asked if they ever heard of a guy named Randolph Carver, the agents both laughed. They certainly had, many times over. They described him as a ruthless collector of precious items, who would stop at nothing to get what he wanted—and he always seemed to manage it, without getting his hands dirty. His agents were sometimes captured, but never talked about their boss except as a voice on the other end of a telephone. Robert looked at Jenna, and chuckled. She knew exactly what he was thinking. It was obvious they didn't realize the infamous Carver was under their very noses.

The group stopped at a grubby restaurant on the coast for lunch. The food was to die for! It was a great day, with few thoughts of the Emerald Tablet. No one bothered them for the rest of the day.

On Friday morning, Robert and Jenna awoke early. After the ritual snuggling, they got up and did laps in the pool. They ordered breakfast from room service, so they could discuss their plans regarding the tablet.

"No one has twitched yet, have they, RJ?"

"Not a twitch in Taba, sweetheart, even Scott hasn't called since yesterday morning."

"Today is a religious day here, isn't it?"

"Yes, I believe so."

"If we go digging around today, we might offend the locals, not to mention the authorities gathered at the Mövenpick."

"Might do, indeed. Are we going to try to force a twitch?"

"I still can't shake this feeling that something's wrong."

"If I had my druthers, we'd be going home, and Scott can come take charge of the tablet!"

Jenna reached over to hold his hand. "The sooner we get home, the sooner we can get married, and live a normal life."

Robert burst out laughing. "What on earth is *normal* for us, Jenna?"

"I think maybe we spend some time with the others today. No digging, though."

"Agreed!"

They called Carver to see what they were up to. They explained they wanted to spend some time with the team to discuss the details of the recovery, and to just have fun, seeing it was a religious day. Carver heartily agreed.

Later, they all met in Carver's suite. Jenna suggested a day trip to Mount Sinai. To her surprise, everyone thought it was a great idea. They would use two vehicles. Jenna, Robert, and Carver could travel together, while the security team brought up the rear. Needless to say, the entire group had a ripping time. If anyone was stressing out because of the delays, they weren't showing it.

When Robert and Jenna recapped the day later, they both agreed there *was* a twitch–they hadn't heard from Scott the entire day!

Robert and Jenna went through their early morning ritual of snuggling and swimming. They both enjoyed it, and they both felt they needed it after all the stress, and rich food. The previous day, the group decided today would be the day to dig up the Emerald Tablet. They would leave early in the day to avoid the hot sun.

Robert and Jenna wore some comfortable working clothes—shorts and T-shirts. Even in this basic attire, Robert thought Jenna looked stunning, and the dig was almost postponed. Jenna appreciated Robert's attention, and never turned him away.

"I think I'll make you do the digging, so I can watch that tantalizing tush of yours swinging back and forth."

"If that's what turns you on, lover, I'd be glad to," she teased, with her head cocked to one side. She did some mock digging motions to show him what it would look like.

He rolled his eyes, groaned, heaved a heavy sigh, took her by the hand, and dragged her away. "If we don't go now, we're not going anywhere for the next few hours!"

Jenna laughed, and willingly followed her man out to the vehicle.

They decided to use all three vehicles, convoy style, for the main party. The authorities would bring up the rear in two other vehicles. This was no longer a simple dig-it-up recovery, it became a veritable event with no fewer than 13 in attendance, an unlucky number, and that didn't include Zahra's friends who were keeping an eye on things from a distance.

Because it was flat open space, the security vehicles drove next to Robert's. They all had communications devices, so they could speak to one another while they drove. Jenna was keeping track on the GPS, notifying Robert when they approached the coordinates given by Dr. Scott. Robert notified the others he was slowing down, and would soon come to a stop.

They were about 7 kilometres in the wilderness. There was nothing around. Robert came to a stop. According to the GPS, they were about 30 metres from Scott's coordinates. Robert asked the security team to keep everyone back until he and Jenna called them forward. Robert exited the vehicle, walked around, to open the door for Jenna. They both grabbed one of the shovels in the back of their vehicle. Using the portable GPS, they targeted the final location. Roland was not happy. He wanted to make sure their back and flanks were protected. In the end, he and Simone had to resort to high-power binoculars to scan the area.

Robert insisted that only he and Jenna, would move to the Scott coordinates. Carver asked if he could accompany them, and they gave him the nod. Robert explained he was looking for any signs the ground had been disturbed recently. As they walked slowly, scanning the earth for footprints, or signs of digging, Jenna kept an eye on the GPS. At the given place, she told them to stop. Robert planted the shovel in the sand. He and Carver kept moving forward, scanning the ground before them. After a few more minutes, Robert returned to where Jenna was standing.

"There are no visible footprints, but you can tell the ground here was disturbed. It's impossible to know when, though. After all, it's only been a few months since Dr. Scott buried the tablet."

"Do we begin digging, then, RJ?"

Robert contacted Roland and told him they could all move forward carefully, and form a large circle around the dig point. Roland and the team had a difficult time keeping everyone disciplined, but made it obvious, they weren't kidding.

When everyone formed a circle, Robert spoke.

"Ladies, and gentlemen, Dr. Scott's last clue was simply that we needed to return to Taba, and gave exact coordinates for the location of the Emerald Tablet. According to my GPS, this is the spot. I want the security team to keep a very watchful eye for any activity around us. I also authorize the security team to use weapons, if necessary, to keep anyone other than us at bay. Ms. Carpenter and I will dig, you will watch."

"May I help with the digging?" offered Carver.

Robert nodded his approval, and all three began to dig carefully. They dug a pit about 1.5 metres deep, and about 10 metres in diameter. It was back-breaking work. They found nothing. Several times, Robert checked the GPS, asking others to verify their coordinates were the same. He returned again to Scott's last clue. There was no doubt.

"We've dug a pretty big pit here. Scott's last clue showed only the last part of the coordinates: 5298713 and 8408008. We added the first part of the coordinates from those for Taba: 29 degrees north by 34 degrees east, assuming he would want to bury the tablet quickly. It's possible that we need to switch the degrees to the other fractions, which would put the alternate location of 29.8408008 by 34.5298713, some 46 kilometres northwest of here.

"I assume all vehicles are fully fuelled and we have plenty of water. We can either expand the pit here, to make allowance for the limitation of GPS precision, or we can move right now to the other location."

The general consensus was to drive to the new coordinates immediately. So, the convoy headed off across country to the alternate location. It took over an hour to get to their new location. As before, Robert, Jenna, and Carver walked forward looking for any sign of recent disturbance. Again, they found nothing.

Following the same pattern, the three began to dig a pit about the same size as the first. After only a few minutes of digging, Robert called a stop to the work. This ground had not been disturbed for a very long time. This could not be the location of the tablet.

"What are you thinking, RJ?"

Robert leaned on his shovel, looking quietly into the distance. Carver was about to say something, but Jenna cut him short. Robert was running things through his mind. Then, as Jenna suspected, a wry smile began to appear on Robert's face.

She smiled at him. "You've got it figured out, don't you?"

Robert's smile broadened. "This place has never been dug up. In the last place, the sand was far less packed, showing it was dug up. The first place is where Scott buried the tablet. Of that, I'm quite sure. We dug a big hole, and found nothing. We dug down until we found hard-packed dirt, so if the tablet is buried there, we've dug deep enough. We can expand the hole, but I don't think we'll find anything there."

"Are you telling us someone else got to it first?" Carver asked the question everyone had on their lips.

"Yes."

"So, the entire mission has failed?"

Gina looked at her father. "No, dad, there's more to this. Robert, when you spent the last three days effectively delaying the final recovery, you were trying to figure out if someone in the group was having a change of heart again, is that right?"

"RJ and I both have a feeling there's something wrong about all this, but couldn't put our finger on it. We wanted to see if anyone twitched, and someone did."

"I've noticed no 'twitching' from within our group."

With a broad smile on his face, Robert replied, "Dr. Scott twitched."

"Scott!" Carver and Dr. El-Amin looked stunned.

"Yes, Dr. Scott contacted us through his wife's friends who gave me a telephone he used to call us. That's right Dr. Scott is alive, well, and *married*. We heard from him shortly after we arrived. He was notified of all the activity in Taba, and wanted to know what was going on. We haven't heard from Dr. Scott for a couple of days."

"I think Scott, himself, dug up the tablet while no one was looking. After all, he knew where he buried it," added Robert.

"What does he plan to do with it?"

"If only we could be mind readers! The best thing we can do now, is for all of us to return to our hotels, and wait for Dr. Scott to make his move."

The others weren't convinced. There was a lot of talk about a country-wide police search for Scott, before he could take the tablet out of the country. When Robert and Jenna began walking back to their vehicle, everyone stopped shouting.

Jenna, turned to look at them all. "Dr. Scott is an honourable man. He did not hide the tablet so he could keep it for himself. He was quite serious in his initial note when he spoke about the possibility to being kidnapped, tortured, and even killed. If he recovered the tablet, it could simply be to take one last look at it before turning it over. He is fully aware of the agreement regarding the safekeeping of the tablet. If we hear from him, we'll let you all know through Mr. Carver."

With that, Robert and Jenna entered their vehicle, and began driving away, in the direction of the hotel. Carver and the security team, quickly ran to their vehicles, and fell in on either side of them. The authorities, too, scrambled into their vehicles, and dutifully followed.

Robert and Jenna were famished by the time they arrived at their hotel mid-afternoon. They were also feeling sweaty and grubby from all their digging. The first order of business was to clean up. A long warm shower not only cleansed their bodies, it helped relieve the tension built up over the missing Emerald Tablet.

They made their way to the dining room, and ordered a huge meal. As they were waiting, Robert noticed a couple walking towards them, behind Jenna. He was Caucasian, and the she was obviously of Arabic descent. They were both smiling, looking directly at him and Jenna. Jenna was watching Robert's face with curiosity, as his expression was changing quickly. He was looking over her shoulder, not at her. She began to turn around, but Robert told her to wait. The couple walked over to their table, stopping behind Jenna.

Robert stood, holding out his hand out, "Dr. Scott, I presume."

Jenna turned quickly. Her eyes opened wide when she saw Dr. Ambrose Scott standing directly behind her. "Dr. Scott!"

"Hello, Jenna. Sorry to put you through all this drama today." Scott had a big grin on his face. "May I introduce you to Zahra, my wife."

Jenna was still in shock, and speechless. Robert extended his hand to Zahra, who offered a firm handshake. *She's certainly a looker*, thought Robert.

"May we join you?"

"Of course, please."

"I'm sorry. I'm so stunned to see you again. We all thought the worst—that you were dead."

"I would've been if it wasn't for Zahra, and her friends."

Zahra stuck out her chin. "I was not going to allow anything to happen to my Scotty!"

"You led us on a merry chase, Scotty! All over hell's half acre, only to find no pot of gold at the end of the rainbow."

"Yes, *Scotty*, that was very rude of you!"

"When I saw my chance, I returned to the hiding place, and retrieved the tablet myself. I wanted to get it all cleaned up. You see, it was covered in casting plaster. That's how I got it out of Jordan, and into Egypt. Once I had it, I was loath to put it back, just in case it was swiped by some lucky grave robber."

"So, you have the tablet?"

With a broad smile, Scott answered, "Yes, Jenna. I have it.

And I'll give it to the two of you shortly. But, first, you must be famished, after all that work."

"You were watching us!"

"My friends were keeping an eye on you, and reporting back to us," admitted Zahra.

Scott and Zahra ordered as well. The foursome feasted, and traded tales of the Emerald Tablet. Zahra said she didn't really understand what the big deal was about this artifact, but she was happy it brought her and her Scotty together, and was very happy for Jenna and Robert as well. Scott was wondering if the Interpol people were looking for him, for what could be considered stealing the tablet in the first place, or were they here to try to nab Carver. They all laughed to hear they were just two agents on vacation who had no idea of all the drama going on around them.

After lunch, they all went to Robert and Jenna's suite.

"When were you planning to give us the tablet," asked Robert.

A wide grin appeared on Scott's face. "You already have it."

Robert and Jenna looked at one another, rather puzzled. Scott pointed to a shelf above the desk. There were some books there, laying down. In the midst of them, there was a book that looked pushed in further than the others. There was just the slightest glint of green from the light coming through the window.

Jenna laughed. "It's like RJ always says—the best place to hide something is in plain sight. It's how we made it through this quest."

They sat chatting for some time before they decided the authorities should get a peek, and the tablet placed in safekeeping.

"Any news yet, RJ?" asked Carver politely.

"I think you and the gang should come by for a visit. We do indeed have some news, and it would best be told to you all face-to-face."

"I'll gather the clan, and we'll be there shortly. Should I bring champagne or whiskey?"

"If it's Jameson Irish, the whiskey will be fine for me, but the others might prefer champagne. Of course, you'll need something a bit softer for our Arab friends."

It didn't take long—only some twenty minutes. The poor hotel staff didn't know what to make of several vehicles packed with people suddenly appearing on their doorstep, with everyone heading towards the Jacksons' suite. In fact, the clerk called to warn them of an invasion, and did they need anything? Robert assured the man they were all expected, and would they send some suitable refreshments for the Arab guests, a bottle of Jameson Irish whiskey, and a couple of bottles of champagne? They would also need additional chairs for all the guests. The desk clerk assured him it would all be sent immediately.

The invasion arrived first, almost at a run. Robert already had the door open. They marched in, finding themselves milling around, until the extra chairs arrived, and then the refreshments. Once the staff left, the impromptu meeting got underway.

Robert stood in a prominent position, with Jenna standing close beside him.

He began. "Before we discuss matters further, I would like to introduce you to Dr. Ambrose Scott, and Mrs. Zahra Scott."

There was an audible gasp from those who were aware of his disappearance. Dr. El-Amin wasn't sure whether to go over, and shake his hand vigorously, or to have him arrested. His confusion showed on his face, which elicited a few chuckles.

"Dr. Scott did indeed recover the Emerald Tablet just before we went looking for it. It seems it was covered with plaster, and he just wanted to clean it up for us. Of course, he could have saved Jenna, Carver, and me all that arduous digging."

"But where's the fun in that," sniggered Scott. Zahra, too, laughed at this.

Robert touched Jenna's arm gently, as a cue for her to take over. "I always knew Dr. Scott as an honest man with unquestionable integrity, unlike others I know of (with a scowl on her face). I for one, am very happy he is alive and well. He took it upon himself to safeguard an artifact that may prove to be the most significant discovery since King Tut's tomb. That it is here today, is due to his foresight."

Robert slipped quietly towards the shelf, moved the books on top of the tablet. No one noticed what he was doing. All eyes and ears were still on Jenna. He pulled the tablet from its hiding place, and walked over to where Scott and Zahra were sitting.

When Jenna finished, Robert handed the tablet to Scott. "I believe the honour should be yours, to hand over the tablet to these authorities for safekeeping, according to the agreement they made."

Scott took the tablet from Robert. He stood. You could hear a pin drop in the room. All eyes were on the tablet. Scott walked over to Carver.

"I never thought in a million years I would ever be doing this, Carver, but here I am! I am grateful that you brought your powers of persuasion to bear in brokering a very fair and effective deal with all the authorities represented here. It's my pleasure to offer you the Emerald Tablet. Please take good care of it."

Randolph Carver stood there, holding the Emerald Tablet, the prize he'd sought so diligently for the last several weeks. He was speechless. He felt proud to be part of the quest for this priceless, and immensely important artifact. Gina moved to stand by his side. She could see the tears welling up in his eyes. This was certainly a different man than she'd known for the last 15 years.

Gina spoke with dignity. "On behalf of my father, who is overcome at the moment, I want to express our gratitude to Robert Jackson and Jenna Carpenter for their relentless determination in finding the Emerald Tablet no matter how much they were detracted, watched, followed, tracked, and threatened. Without them, we would not be standing here today, with the Emerald Tablet in our midst. We trust the agreement signed by all, will be carried out to the letter, and the museums involved will make the tablet available for public viewing, while protecting it from the hands of the many thieves who would take it for their own possession. My father, along with many others will be wanting to study the inscriptions carefully with the hope of being able to decipher them for the benefit of all humankind."

Everyone applauded. The refreshments were poured out, and many toasts made. Everyone had a chance to look at, touch, hold, and admire the tablet. There was much discussion, jovial banter, and interest on what happened to Scott.

Robert and Jenna, surreptitiously moved outside of the circles of conversation, until they were able to slip out of the suite, making their way to the beach, where they sat quietly on the sand, the love flowing between them. Jenna leaned her head against his shoulder, holding onto his arm.

"Ready to go home, darling?"

"More than ready, RJ."

Robert pulled the phone from his pocket, and dialled.

"Hello, Jackson residence."

"We'll be home in two days."

CPSIA information can be obtained
at www.ICGtesting.com
Printed in the USA
LVOW10s0353311017
554377LV00003B/9/P

9 780973 748055